Light Minded arts

The Gearlock Series
BOOK ONE

HARD BOILED CABBAGE
BRENT LINDSTROM

Blue House Publishing

This book is a work of fiction. This book is derived from the imagination of the author. If any parallels to actual people, places, businesses, or institutions are present, it is used fictitiously and or is purely coincidental.

BLUE HOUSE
PUBLISHING
an imprint of
LightMinded arts

791 N. 100 E.
Lehi, UT 84043

© 2026 by Brent Lindstrom

All rights reserved. Unless written consent is given by the author or publisher, any reproduction of this book, partial or full, whether in print, electronic, or other form, is not permitted, with the exception of small quotes for reviews and comments.

Artwork is by Ash Amos - Penrose Artist Co., all rights reserved.

For information regarding bulk purchases, send a request to Blue House Publishing via Storyteller@LightMindedArts.com

ISBN-13: 978-1-943239-17-7
Library of Congress Control Number: 2025920968

Special Thanks To:

Any reader who gives this book a chance and leaves a review on any of the many online places of purchase or forum.

Contents

If Only A Fortune Teller Could Predict The Future.......... 4
Surface-Dwellers Have No Manners................................... 24
The Worst Type Of Trouble..35
Tea and One Too Many Witnesses.......................................47
A Sour Aftertaste..58
A Simple Case of Theft Turned Deadly.............................. 82
Suspect Number One... 91
Shady Company.. 111
The TomFather.. 121
No Job For Sissies... 135
The Way to His Woman's Heart... 142
One Slick Armpit.. 154
Little Things, Dangerous Things... 168
No Dainty Punches Here... 173
Dog Breath... 182
Not Easy Being An Outlaw.. 196
Politics As Usual... 208
Lot of Pain For Blessed Little Gains................................... 222
Broomsticks and Beefcakes.. 227
Bad Poetry, Disturbing Prophesy....................................... 238
To Be A Killer.. 249
Midnight Stroll... 254
What Game Am I Playing?.. 261
The Bells of War... 268
Too Late.. 286
The End of a Partnership... 295
Partners.. 303
Who's Fooling Who.. 306
The Tomb Of Ascension.. 315
Falling... 319
Hanging On The Edge... 325
Two Dogs with One Stone... 330
Running Away Or Fighting On.. 335
Ashes Ashes, They All Fall Down....................................... 338
Courting ka'Nairie.. 345
Afterward... 354

Hard Boiled Cabbage

Big Trouble In Spur Central

The GearLock Series

Book 1

Chapter 1

If Only A Fortune Teller Could Predict The Future

With a splash, Dick hu'Mar lifted the squirming mess of cat from his wooden wash basin. Vinegar dripped from his hands as hu'Mar held the tangled mop of fur tighter. Unlike other cats hu'Mar had bonded over the years, Vinegar was mangy to the extreme. Nothing could've looked sadder, except for maybe hu'Mar's dinner of boiled cabbage, which grew colder by the minute. He hated boiled cabbage, but such was his life, miserable and pathetic, forced from his home all for doing the right thing.

Some days, he missed home, but being top dog in a stuffy kingdom had a way of wilting even the best of men. Only the strong-willed people ruled those places while everyone else contented themselves to subjugation. Though, by that account, strong-willed as he was, hu'Mar should've been running Nebylon rather than hiding out here in Spur Central.

What else was a fortune teller to do?

As hard as finding work had been here, at least, the Toughs were civilized people. Nobody discriminated against you for something as silly as telling the truth, like informing the king of Nebylon that his princely son was secretly courting an Albino, or Bule as most people tended to call them. That should've earned hu'Mar a commission, but the king had his pride to worry about. To him, hu'Mar either knew too much about the prince's disgraceful romance or he was lying through his teeth to damage their royal reputation.

At least here, the rules made sense. All anyone of Spur Central cared about, was how well you could roll with the punches . . . and the kicks and the headbutts.

The flexible floorboards creaked as hu'Mar crossed the room and splashed Vinegar onto the wobbly table, and Vinegar's extra long fur, as long as a man's hand, pooled in a puddle of wet tangled fuzz, etching the cheap varnish with his claws. Hu'Mar didn't have to be a palsy to understand Vinegar's apprehension. Likewise, Vinegar could sense hu'Mar's unspoken angst over the scratches in his most expensive piece of furniture, especially when it served so many purposes, but that didn't stop him from clawing at it anyway.

The short wooden table, which doubled as his office desk, had a wobbly log standing on one side, like a sawed-off tree trunk for him to sit on, and his square chest of clothes on the other side for guests to sit. The table was small, with only room for a single drawer underneath, facing the log side. On top, it was only big enough to fit his crystal ball, "was" being the key word. He'd sold it to some kids who wanted it for a game of throwing. Money was tight, which led to the third thing he liked to use his table for: a kitchen table, whenever he could afford it, which was not this month. In fact, if he didn't get a good case soon, one that Vinegar couldn't botch, he might not have this apartment much longer either.

Anyway, losing the crystal ball didn't matter. It didn't do anything. Why would it? This was a volcanic area. Crystal could be found all over the place here. Most people didn't keep them as a centerpiece, which is why he liked it, because the oddity of it would distract his clients long enough from his hands as he sorted through their pockets. Now he'd have to find another way to con his visitors out of the little money they offered. After all, he was no prophet. Usually people didn't expect him to be either, but he had a knack for solving mysteries, and so what if some called it magic? If people were dumb enough to believe in magic, then they deserved to lose a little salt for his services. This wasn't the best way to make a living, but he was good at it, and nobody had threatened to run him out of town. They'd threatened to kill him, but that was everyday life in Spur Central.

As for these Toughs, those who dominated Spur Central, they were stronger than the average human, and they loved fighting more than anything. These were the zealots of the Beadledom. If Dick hu'Mar couldn't make it here, he'd never get a chance anywhere else because he'd be dead. That could be a good thing, he'd be reborn into some pathetic family again and hopefully have a better run at life than he'd had this time around, but that wouldn't be him, not for a long time, he was Dick hu'Mar, the best fortune teller around. All he needed was one good case, a pocket full of money, and he'd be back on top again, but first thing's first. He had to take care of Vinegar.

Vinegar howled, or rather, meowed as loud as ever.

"Don't you dare. These floors and walls are thin enough as it is." Hu'Mar pinned his palsy partner against the table with a thick callused hand.

"I thought you were supposed to get rid of that critter," a voice called from below the cracks of the drafty floorboards that separated his apartment from the lower floor. Rain hu'Grooshy, the dentist, lived and practiced below hu'Mar. Even Toughs had cavities.

"Yee-ah," Thelma ka'Skrut added from the apartment next door as if she were in the same room. All his neighbors might as well have lived in his apartment. "You know we isn't allowed pets in here, especially cats."

Her trademark high-heeled boots clicked on the other side of the wooden wall. She was hu'Mar's age—mid-forties, nosy, and nasally with enough interest in him to make him nauseous.

"You tell anyone I got a cat up here, maybe I'll start telling people what you're putting in that hair jelly you sell," he warned.

"Aghy!" Ka'Skrut gasped as if hu'Mar had slapped her

in the face.

Many would consider a cat living here as disgraceful, and hu'Mar could live with being called disgraceful. After all, since he and Vinegar were bonded palsies, they were stuck with each other. But if Toughs knew about his palsy bond, well, it'd be bad for business.

"You won't hear me complaining to anyone," Rain hu'Grooshy said through the floorboards.

"Ye-ah, me neithers. In fact, I never even said a thing." Ka'Skrut's voice faded, so she must have gone into one of her farther rooms. No doubt she found something shiny, like a polished shield, and lost herself in her own reflection. That woman.

Vinegar tried squirming away, but hu'Mar held firm with his left hand as he reached for his boot dagger with the right. "I don't know how many times I've warned you. We mess up here, and we get killed." He actually tolerated Vinegar, most of the time.

The cat was good at sneaking around, hiding, and spying. The only problem—well, the biggest problem—was that Vinegar's level of self-importance was a little too big to fit into his hairy body. The cat's cocky attitude made him miss critical details, like how he never remembered his tail. It had given them away on more than one occasion. At least this time, it only cost him a paying client. But a single paying client, when you were limping by on boiled cabbage, was a big deal. Plus, a mistake like that, here among Toughs, could easily cost more than a meal—it could cost them their lives.

Vinegar's eyes widened at the sight of hu'Mar's boot dagger, and his claws spread wider.

"This is your own fault," hu'Mar said, tightening his grip. "And if you put one claw into my skin, I'll send you down to hu'Grooshy. He'll take his teeth puller to each and every one of your claws."

Vinegar retracted his claws, a little. From within his throat or chest or wherever cats grumble from, came Vinegar's anti-purr. You didn't need to be a palsy to understand Vinegar was unhappy. Well, what did Vinegar expect? Hu'Mar was nothing if not a man of his word.

He gave Vinegar one more cold stare.

"I hate you, Dick hu'Heartless," Vinegar communicated through a combination of noise and body language that only a cat palsy or another cat could understand. "I wish I never met you as a kitten."

Hu'Mar was not one to trifle with empty threats, and Vinegar understood this more than most. Whatever ka'Skrut put in her hair products, it was nothing compared to how hu'Grooshy performed dentistry, so Vinegar wisely sheathed his claws even farther.

"Better," hu'Mar said. Then without further warning, he slammed the dagger down, severing Vinegar's tail. It was half a finger width closer to the cat's rump than he'd intended.

Vinegar screamed in a "Yeaooww—yeaooww" sort of way.

Everyone here was pretty used to the sound. In fact, hu'Grooshy's current client also screamed in a similar, "Oooww—yeooww—I'm going ta kill you" sort of way.

Hu'Mar should've seen it coming since he'd only warned Vinegar not to scratch. The ball of fur squirmed around and sunk his teeth deep into hu'Mar's hand, the dark hair on the back of his palm began to channel rivulets of blood across his darkly tanned skin. Hu'Mar lifted the cat by the soft flesh of his punctured palm. With his free hand, he tried to pry the fangs off when the door to his apartment office opened.

Hu'Mar stood still and let his hands fall to his sides with Vinegar still attached to one of them. Hu'Mar's thick barrel chest proudly protruded, and the extra barrel in his belly sucked in as tight as he could pull it. Business time. Blood dripped from Vinegar's tail just as often as it dripped from hu'Mar's hand, but he couldn't do anything about that at this moment.

In the doorway stood a silhouette against the light from the setting sun as it angled up the stairs and filled the hallway. Thin wrists, nearly hidden by brown leather gloves, closed the door, suggesting that this potential client was a woman. With the sunlight now gone, the shadows before her found contrast, though not much. From her ankles to her face, she was all but hidden under a dark brown coat. She took two cautious steps closer.

"I thought cloaks went out of fashion at the last shifting of the Gears." hu'Mar said, relaxing his posture, even bringing his free hand up to stroke the thick stubble that had grown around his strong sun-reddened face for the day.

"Odd behavior," she said without missing a beat, "from te man who wears a fedora indoors?"

Hu'Mar moved his hand adjust the brim of his hat. "It's going to rain soon. I like to keep my head dry."

If the robe-like cloak and the disturbing red eyes didn't give her away, that distinct foreign accent would do the trick. Most Albinos, or Bules as they were loath to be known, had that sharp, but slightly melodic clip to their voice. Despite such pale skin, her attitude had plenty of pigment, and that could get her in trouble around here. He liked her already.

"Some fortune teller. Tere's not even a rain cloud outside."

Just then, water dripped from the ceiling and splashed all around for about thirty seconds, then stopped.

"Time for a rinse, open your mouth. I hope you like the soapy wooden flavor," came the soft reassuring voice of Rain hu'Grooshy as the water fell another floor onto the dentist's client.

The stranger examined the gaps in the ceiling, then the floor, then hu'Mar again. Hu'Mar tapped the side of his full-brimmed hat once, his brown leather vest stretched over his thick frame as he gestured.

"Did anyone see you come in?" He wished he didn't have to care, but business was slow. Gossiping neighbors could quickly create a famine of fortune seekers and anyone else looking for someone, other than the law, to dig their nose where it otherwise wouldn't be welcome.

"Relax, I'm not going to spoil your business." She pulled her hood down, revealing a pair of smoked goggles on her forehead as she evaluated the room.

There wasn't much to judge other than the stone stack where his cook fire had died out and his evening meal grew even soggier. He really needed a curtain to hide his sparce living quarters.

She sniffed and crinkled her nose. "Tat is to say, I can't see how anyone could spoil it any furter. Are you te real deal?"

Finally, she rested those unnatural red eyes on him, eerie, like they had evil fire burning within. Hu'Mar didn't consider himself racist. He'd seen plenty of Albino's in the past, but of all human races, they were the most distinctive and uncommon around here.

"He's the real deal, hon" came the whiny voice of Thelma ka'Skrut from the wallboards which creaked as she pressed against them to eavesdrop. Hu'Mar could almost imagine her leaning into the wall, like a lover with one foot lifted to the air. "Speakin of deals, he's running a promo too, ain't ya, hon? Buy two fortunes and get three chips off a month supply of my deluxe hair care package. Stop on by when you're done."

"Mind your own business," hu'Mar said, impatient as always with his next-door neighbor. "She's just a Bule."

He flapped a dismissive hand, the one without the cat, toward the wall to assure the Albino that ka'Skrut was nothing more than a pest. Besides, the last thing this girl needed was ka'Skrut's hair jelly. This girl's smooth transparent hair was pulled tight into a bun, the typical style for her people. Most Albinos kept their hair up or cut short, probably because of the heat. Those underground cities where they lived, deep beneath the desert planes, were intolerably hot.

"Ohhh—sorry dear," ka'Skrut added. "I didn't know. I don't have nothing against your sort, but you know how it is, with atheists running around and all. I'd have to charge you full price, and for the record, I was minding *my own business*."

Hu'Mar doubted that atheists had anything to do with ka'Skrut's price change, but it was a convenient excuse. While most of the world's population believed in the Greater Gear, the atheists, though they didn't outright deny the existence of great cosmic gears, were thoroughly against ascending.

Hard Boiled Cabbage: Big Trouble In Spur Central

While nearly every species in the realm competed for the Tomb of Ascension, atheists consisted of small gangs of people and animals who believed the Tomb of Ascension was a doomsday device that targeted a certain species. When one species got trapped in it, rather than send them off to a higher gear or realm after death, they believed it killed the entire species' souls. Not only would there be no shifting to a higher world, but there would also be no rebirthing on any world, ever again. Often, Bules made up at least half of the roaming atheist gangs that were found, even though most Bules were believers. This girl probably wasn't atheist. Plenty of Albinos lived in the city, most peaceably trying to get by in a culture where the deck was stacked against them.

"I tink I've come to te wrong place," this Albino said.

"Relax. Money from an Albino is just as good as money from a Tough, as far as I'm concerned."

The Albino tilted her head and pursed her lips as if to say, "you'll take my money, but will you really help me?"

"Hey, Thelma ka'Skrut will still sell to you, too. She's here for when the fighting breaks out. Our local dentist downstairs is another case all together," hu'Mar whispered. "Try visiting him, and he might pull a few of the wrong teeth, just for fun." It was true too.

She rubbed her jaw, then shook some water from her cloak. "How did you know it would rain?"

"Uh, fortune teller."

She folded her arms and lowered her head.

"Hey, you came to me," hu'Mar said, jabbing his chest with his thumb

The cat still dangled from his other hand, teeth locked onto the meat of his palm. If he didn't dislodge Vinegar soon, the cat might develop a taste for human flesh.

He adjusted the brim of his hat. "Not all rain comes from the sky. Around here, it also comes from the neighbor's laundry."

"Tis place is disgusting." She was clearly avoiding eye contact.

What was there to be disgusted about? The apartment got

a soapy rinse multiple times each day. Plus, it was mostly barren, so it couldn't be called dirty, just antique. The only thing anyone might frown over was the rotting floorboards and wallboards, which were little different than the other homes around Spur Central. She was probably used to sturdier surroundings, like the stone from her people's caves. Even the dripping blood from his hand and Vinegar's tail wasn't wholly out of place. Lots of Toughs decorated with blood around here. After all, to be a Tough was to be a warrior.

"Don't dog my dig. I'd rather live here than whatever damp hole you dug yourself out of. Speaking of holes, what brings you topside?"

Most Albinos in the city worked nights at jobs no respectable Tough would want to tackle and received poor compensation for it. The fact that she dared appear during daylight hours suggested that she was either gutsy, desperate, or new to town. Probably a mix of all three. He hoped she wasn't in danger.

"Why do you have a cat attached to your hand?"

"I can tell you're not a frivolous girl. Don't waste my time and yours with pointless questions." Hu'Mar shook his right hand roughly.

Vinegar detached and smacked onto the floor. Without his tail to balance properly, the cat landed squarely on his head and complained with a long drown out, "Reaow-reow-rooouugghh."

Hu'Mar ignored him. He could well understand what Vinegar had actually said, and it wasn't worth repeating to a client, hopefully a paying one. Besides, the less people that knew he was a palsy to a cat, the better.

Hu'Mar advanced toward the girl, whipped out a brown handkerchief from his vest pocket and wrapped it around his palm to stem the bleeding. "Can I take your cloak?"

The girl leaned away from hu'Mar's bleeding hand and into his free hand. As soon as she realized he had his arm around her, she quickly sprang away.

"Grease me, you're flighty." What was she hiding? "Fine. Come." Hu'Mar led her to his bloody desk.

Hard Boiled Cabbage: Big Trouble In Spur Central

"You want tis ting dead or alive?" The girl stared at the overweight hairball. She was on edge and on trial. He wouldn't let her squirm out of the candlelight this easy.

"Does it matter? Death is only temporary." He stuffed his left hand into his pocket.

"Memories are life," the Albino countered. "We might all be reborn after we die, but if we can't take our memories with us into te new life, we might as well have died permanently."

"Sometimes you need a good reset. Life can be hard, and the memories difficult to erase," hu'Mar suggested.

"But wisdom is stifled if we never learn to pick up te pieces after our lives get shattered."

Great, a philosopher. No wonder Toughs didn't like these people. "Cut to the chase, girly. Why's an Albino come sneaking around the Tough slums of Spur Central?"

She ignored him and leaned over to examine Vinegar's tail. "Such butchery. I'd expect no less from a stupid Tough."

"Hey, I cleaned it first." Was there any point in arguing that he wasn't a Tough? He flicked the tail off the table. It landed next to Vinegar who sniffed it.

Those red eyes accused him of being too stupid to even know what he'd done wrong. Albinos were like that. Always the smart ones. True, they were intelligent. A lot of the persecution they faced was from unfounded fears that they were a bunch of hooded witches. Hu'Mar knew better. Witchcraft was nothing but hokey superstition. The ignorant always imagined magic if they couldn't explain something. Even these thready cloaks they wore above ground were only little more than sunrobes, meant to keep their pale complexions from attracting stares and sunburns. Their supposed magic was nothing more than advanced technology that they refused to share with the stupid surface-dwellers.

As she bent to pick up Vinegar, a necklace with a wooden pendant slipped from her cloak. It was the classic gear within a gear. Hu'Mar had seen many Albinos beaten and killed for wearing such pendants, so she couldn't have been topside very long. She set Vinegar on the table, then tucked the symbol back into hiding. She hummed as she carefully worked her sorcery.

First she stroked the cat, flinching back as a sharp cocklebur poked her from inside Vinegar's fur.

Vinegar flinched at her touch, his stare directed right at hu'Mar. It was the sort of stare that said, "Is this gopher going to hurt me any more than you did?"

Hu'Mar shrugged, not sure what to think either, but said, "It's ok." Just as his palsy bond helped him understand cats, Vinegar's human bond helped him understand what people were saying. That didn't mean Vinegar always trusted what he heard though.

As soon as the Albino pulled a razor and a balm from her cloak, Vinegar's claws came out. Hu'Mar was glad that she hadn't allowed his hands near her for more than a second when he'd offered to take her cloak. Otherwise the razor and balm would now be in his left pocket also. While she tended to Vinegar's stump, hu'Mar faced away from her and withdrew the other items he'd picked from her pocket while she had been distracted by his bloody hand.

You could tell a lot about a person from the things in their pockets. In his line of work, the less guesswork, the better. This girl had a small leather wallet lined with fine tools, like only a master Beadledom gear smith might own. So she did more than merely reverence the Gears of Accension: she used the sacred symbols to tinker with worldly affairs. That gear within a gear pendant had already suggested as much, but this confirmed it.

Black market tools for black market gears led to dangerous hobbies. If the Ministry found out about whatever she was tinkering with, she'd be arrested for such blasphemies. A Tough might pay a fine, go to jail, or just endure a simple beating. An Albino on the other hand, well… Blasphemy was one thing, but this would be like a pig getting into the Holy Grease. At least the pig would meet a quick savory end.

He'd clipped one other thing from her pocket. A blackish pellet, the size of a saline. It wasn't salt, so it was of little value. Was she trying to pass this off as currency? Even the underground currency was purer than this. He decided to hold onto

Hard Boiled Cabbage: Big Trouble In Spur Central

it for now. It was the only thing he couldn't understand, so he wanted to do a little more research.

Hu' Mar edged closer, leaned over her to watch and discreetly returned the other items to her pockets. She shivered with his presence but tried to ignore him. He rubbed his fingers together, then brought them near his face, smelling for anything he recognized. The pellet was as foreign as this girl.

He knelt down next to her. "What's that?"

"We call it antiseptic. It's like an alcoholic balm. It'll keep te wound from infection." When she finished, the stump was shaved, cleaned, and no longer bleeding.

Vinegar leapt up and ran to the opposite end of the room.

The girl smelled her hands, clearly disgusted. Well, hu'Mar hadn't made her touch the cat, so she got what she deserved.

"What do you charge?" she asked.

"Depends what you're seeking."

"Te future of tis city."

"For a saline, that's easy. For two more, I'll tell you who'll turn you over to the Beadledom for playing with gears."

Her red eyes went wide. "What do you know?"

Hu'Mar rubbed his fingers together. "If only I had a saline."

She pulled a white pellet from her pocket and tossed it.

Hu'Mar caught it. Pure white. He didn't even have to lick it to know it was real. So she wasn't passing those black pellets off as dirty counterfeits. He closed his eyes and rubbed his temple, humming slightly, all part of the show.

"Cut te act." She wasn't buying it. He should've known. She was too smart for that.

"Some people like to imagine that their fortune teller can tap into the Cosmic Gears of the universe," hu'Mar explained. "They like the idea of magic since they don't understand common sense."

She folded her arms. "I'm not impressed."

"You want it straight? Fine." Hu'Mar sat on his log and stretched. "First thing is you're going to walk out of my shop."

"I'm guessing for te second saline, you're going to tell me

tat you're te one to turn me in. You are a fraud."

"Maybe. I've been hanging around cats too long. I like to play with my meal." He tossed the saline up and caught it again. Then he opened the single drawer on his desk and dropped it in. It landed with a hollow click beside the blow dart tube in the otherwise barren drawer. He shut the drawer. He would've like to place the saline directly into his money pouch, but she might see how hungry his moneybag was. No sense in giving her any clues to his temporary poverty. People didn't trust poor businessmen. Either they're bad at business, or they didn't know what they were doing. Hu'Mar might admit that he wasn't a top businessman, but when it came to his real skillset, he was the very best.

"You want your future read, sit down."

She stayed standing. He usually got two types of clients. The first understood that fortune tellers were really private investigators. Technically, this was frowned on because the Beadledom employed ministers who kept the peace and investigated crime, leaving fortune tellers to those who didn't want the local government involved. The second sort of customer assumed that fortune tellers were like prophets and could actually divine the unknown. Hu'Mar had a sneaky suspicion that this girl was that sort. With a little luck, he could often satisfy this ignorant sort enough to get a meal or two paid for.

Hu'Mar leaned in, his turned-up logs rocked forward with his weight. He rested his forearms on the table, careful to avoid Vinegar's blood. He watched her face closely. The art of being a private fortune teller involved noticing every minor twitch or contracting of the pupils. Being unable to divine the future wasn't a hinderance. Most people didn't ask for the future, and if they did, the context was usually vague. Most of his clients wanted a mystery solved, and that was something that he could do.

"Within the Tomb of Ascension, the Great Clutch is about to lift." He parroted the preaching of the Ministry.

Every seven hundred and seventy-seventh years, give or take, the most clever or dominant species of a given world competed for the chance to move up in the Cosmic Cog works. Most species sought to ascend from one gear, or world, to the next, till eventually they inhabit the Final Gear, or realm. Many believed it to be the Controlling Gear, where ultimate authority over the Cosmic Cog work was controlled or some unimaginably spectacular thing like that. Nobody really knew for sure.

"Tell me someting tat I don't know."

Not good enough? Time to mine her. He stood and paced a too tight circle around her. There were two ways of making a person spill extra info. Make them very comfortable or make them very uncomfortable.

"You're out of your element girly. This city is going to be a warzone pretty soon." Hu'Mar started with the obvious, all the while, studying her reaction. "Any animal that thinks, is going to make a final push to control Mount Exclusion."

Already, signs of these intrusions had been popping up for a few years. Toughs had conquered Spur Central over four hundred years ago, and their dominance had gone relatively unchallenged till this year. Other animal armies were rumored to be converging on the city, and why not? Any animal wanting a chance at the Tomb of Ascension needed to go through this city.

"I know all about your people. You're smart, you're clever, but you're not Toughs. When war breaks out, you'll want to hide deep in those caves you call home."

She remained as rigid as a pole. No slipping, bending, or breaking, but she was hiding something. Did it have to do with the black pellet?

"I didn't ask for advice."

Hu'Mar returned to his stump and studied her face. No, she hadn't. She wasn't afraid for her safety either. What was she after? Did she want to know the outcome?

He ventured more carefully this time. "The Toughs control Spur Central, and thus they control the easiest route to Mount Exclusion. It would take overwhelming odds to keep them from the Great Clutch this time around."

If the Toughs placed just one human inside the Great Clutch, a massive rock tomb that opened and closed at predictive intervals within the volcanic mountain, all races of humanity would ascend, including the Albinos. They wouldn't have to lift a finger. So why was she worried about the city? Then again, even if humans achieved ascension, the whole race would continue living on this world until all their dead had been reborn out of this world's limbo, so they could die and move on to the next. Some species for whatever reason, never managed to deplete this world's limbo in time for the next shifting, and thus a few stragglers sometimes get stranded forever, being constantly reborn here instead of ascending.

"Yes, but what will happen to te city before tat?"

"War can be hard on any city, even one run by Toughs, but I imagine that it'll survive in some state of functionality until every last human has ascended. After that, it might crumble."

"You've been a waste of my money. You speak too generally to know anyting of te future."

"Do I look senile to you? I'm a fortune teller, not a prophet." Prophets weren't all senile, but they got there eventually. Any good prophet tried to depress his or her ability. The more one looked into the future, the more one lost their past. Dick hu'Mar was no prophet, nor did he ever hope to develop that attunation. He preferred the tried and tested method of investigation, extrapolation, and a bit of cunning.

"Goodbye." The girl stood. Her cloak flapped as she spun toward the door.

Hu'Mar sighed. She came for a prophesy, and she had gotten a sounding board. What did she expect? The least he could do was give her some advice. Gears knew she needed it. "Don't go peddling or buying near the outer city slums. Those areas are full of crime, so the Beadledom ministers focus down there. If you're tinkering with or selling working gears, do it on the outer fringes of the city where the rich live. They won't like doing business with a Bule, but they don't want trouble either. They won't turn you in to the Ministry."

"I'm not paying you for tat."

"Don't sweat it, girly. That one's on me."

"Maybe you're not so bad." She tossed him another saline anyway.

Hu'Mar tossed it back. "I might be a fraud, but I'm no cheat."

"Hey hon," Thelma ka'Skrut called out. "For a saline, I can—"

"Take your ear off my wall," hu'Mar scolded. When he turned back to the Albino, she was in the doorway.

Vinegar meowed from across the room. Not a bad idea, hu'Mar interpreted, then passed it along as if it had been his own idea. "Maybe you should take a trip to Crazy Ish, er, I mean Ish hu'Narmin. He's not the easiest to get a foretelling from these days, but he's a real prophet. Maybe you'll get lucky."

"Right," was all she said before entering the hall.

Hu'Mar closed the door behind her. He walked over to his desk and opened the drawer to look at his income. One lonely saline. He should've kept the tip. Why didn't he? It wasn't like he'd get repeat work from her. He shut the drawer.

She wasn't a bad girl, and he'd hate to see the Ministry get their hands on her. They'd be unforgiving. Ministers enforced the Beadledom's law and preached the doctrine of ascensionism, which was that every seven hundred and seventy-seventh year, give or take several months, the Great Clutch opened to allow a new species the opportunity to shift gears. Whatever species could place a sacrificial member into that chamber, would have the chance to shift to a higher cosmic gear. If you didn't shift gears, then you were stuck here or this world's limbo, being reborn over and over again as this gear ground around and around.

Vinegar leapt onto his lap. The cat must have gone out into the sun to dry off. He was still damp and stinky, but his shaggy fur was drying and looked more normal. That was to say, it looked like a fluffy black tangle of hair poking through lint with gray speckles. Mangy, yes. Made worse by incongruent patches as if some kids had thrown red clay clods at the thing and the stains had stuck. Without a tail, Vinegar was the ugliest animal hu'Mar had ever seen. He'd thought that before, but now it was doubly true.

"What do you think of her?"

"Typical human," Vinegar hissed. "You all look alike to me."

"How long have you been able to understand humans? Seven years? And you still don't see the differences?"

"Please." Vinegar shrugged. "I don't get why you all discriminate against some colors and not others. You pink and brown humans get along just fine, but you can't stand the white, red, and orange ones? You'd never see me turn away a bone-white female, whether she had short or long fur."

"I'd imagine you, of all cats, would settle with whatever you could get," hu'Mar laughed.

"No thanks to you, Dick hu'Harsh."

"Hey, don't hold it against me! How many times have I told you? Business means money, money means food."

Vinegar just glowered back.

"It's not my fault your tail was bigger than your oversized head."

"You're talking to me about having a big head?" Vinegar guffawed.

Hu'Mar ignored the snarky rebuttal. They both knew that Last month, of their few contracted jobs, mostly solving petty crimes of fidelity from suspicious spouses, it had been Vinegar who botched them. None of these jobs were paid because his investigations required snooping and anonymity. These were things Vinegar could do well, except when it came to hiding his tail. In every case, Vinegar got discovered, then hu'Mar had to save him and was forced to forfeit his commission. It wasn't easy being a palsy with a cat, but last month had strained their relationship. At least that tail wouldn't ruin any more jobs.

Vinegar jumped off his lap and landed on his head. He must have bumped his tail on the ground as he rolled back to his feet, because he released a pained, "Reaw!" before running off to a corner as if that would put distance between him and the pain. Stupid cat.

Hu'Mar massaged his thick forehead. He dwarfed the small table as the stumpy log wobbled under his weight. He was a strong man, two hundred and twenty pounds, give or take ten more in his belly though he could usually hide that when he needed to. Another month of this though, and he might not have to hide it. He peeked at his pot of dinner across the room, the steam having long since died away. In some of the outer regions, even several of the inner kingdoms like the one he'd come from, he'd be considered mighty, but here in Tough country, he was average, maybe less than.

He had half a mind to find work some place quieter, but he kind of liked the grind. Plus, in this part of town, it was distracting and comforting, in a sense, to be surrounded by others who were just as bad off as himself.

From the apartment below, hu'Grooshy's proud voice drifted up, "One tooth out. That'll be two salines."

Hu'Mar knew what was coming. Hu'Grooshy was not a gentle tooth puller. There it was: the familiar slap of fist on face from another unsatisfied customer. Bad idea. Hu'Mar counted silently. One, two, thr—

Another slap sounded. This time from hu'Grooshy hitting back. "Make that three teeth, and you now owe me a bromine."

Hu'Mar smiled. Yeah, there was no way he could leave the city. It always had room for a slum digger like him around here. He pulled a rag from his pocket and soaked up the soapy water on his desk from the impromptu rainstorm the widow above had provided. While wiping Vinegar's blood up, he thought of his upstairs neighbor.

She was a quiet and decent sort. Deaf as a cat acted and smoky as a forest fire, Gracie ka'Muunel didn't always empty her laundry water straight down like this. She was an old Tough, and with as much as she washed, she was bound to spill a few times a day. Hu'Mar didn't mind. She was a nice hag, and she always made it up to him by doing his laundry for free. Of course, his clothes always smelled of smoke because of that thick cloud of tobacco that followed her around like her own personal weather system. Most people would've died from the amount of smoke she inhaled, but she'd probably been smoking so long, she'd die quicker if she ever inhaled fresh air.

Wet rag still in hand, he cleaned his dagger. He didn't have to oil the steel since his boot sheath was oily enough. So he dried the knife on his pants, then slid it back into his boot.

Hu'Mar nearly tossed the rag when one more spot of blood on the floor caught his eye. A blood beetle swooped from the ceiling and sucked at the stain. Better that than hu'Mar's arm. Blood beetle bites hurt, but they didn't bite humans much anymore since they were busy filling in for flies, which in a roundabout way, was the reason Spur Central even existed.

That was the way it worked around here. One species moved on, and another filled the gaps. It all came back to the Gears of Eternity and that ever-present Clutch within the Tomb of Ascension on Mount Exclusion. Every realm had a staple of insects and plants specific to that realm, so they weren't meant to shift. Only sentient animals shifted which includes just about all animals from humans down to fish. But last time, the fighting created a stale mate, and when the Great Clutch fell, it had trapped only a common house fly between its stones.

So as each fly died, they were reborn into the next higher realm. Considering the short lifespan of a fly, it only took a couple of years before they had emptied both this world's limbo and the physical world itself of their kind. Obviously, hu'Mar wasn't around to experience that, at least, not in an incarnation that he could remember. Everyone forgot their past life after rebirth. Except rabbits for some weird reason. They remember each of their lives, deaths and the limbo in between, which is part of how everyone knows so much about it.

Stories still lingered about the flies and how a few short years created decades of hardships. The insect world eventually balanced, but not till after a huge mess in the ecological food chain.

The Ministry intended that the fly incident would never happen again, so they continually preached to humans about how important it was to be the dominant species. That way humans had the best chance of shifting this next time around.

Hu'Mar smashed the blood beetle with his rag, then wiped the rest of the blood off the floor when Vinegar me-

Hard Boiled Cabbage: Big Trouble In Spur Central

owed. What now?

Vinegar gazed at a shadow blocking the hall light through the gap below his door.

He pulled open his drawer and took out his blowgun. He kept it out of sight, but if necessary, he could fire a poisoned dart just as quick as someone could release the bolt on a crossbow. He could probably shoot more accurately too. It was funny what you could learn after telling a few too many girls that their husbands were cheating on them, especially in Tough country.

Someone pushed the door open. Hu'Mar swallowed. The silhouette in the doorway told volumes. Unlike his last visitor, this one owned her silhouette, even turning sideways to give a jaw dropping visage of every curve in her body. Very obviously a woman, she was confident and cool, not another angry or suspicious spouse. He could've stared at that outline for hours. He gripped his blowgun tighter. Play it cool, Dick hu'Mar.

Chapter 2

Surface-Dwellers Have No Manners

Juniper ka'Shino stopped outside the closed door to Dick hu'Mar's... office? The evening light still glowed orange in the hallway. What a dump. He hadn't even tried to hide that moldy bedroll in the corner. Did he actually live here too?

She should've known better. Finding any prophet was difficult, and finding one with enough sanity leftover was nearly impossible. This guy advertised fortunes over prophesies. Apparently, there was a difference. From what she surmised, hu'Mar made a study of people so he could trick you into thinking he knew the future.

A real prophet was another attunation, like palsying animals. She'd thought that this Dick hu'Mar had palsied time, but few willingly palsied time since it ate at past memories to help them see future, unmade memories.

But hu'Mar was too young to be a real prophet. Most people willing to palsy time waited until they were old so that they'd have more memories to exchange, and they were closer to not needing those memories anyway. Some of them realized that their memories were on the way out, so they might as well profit from the loss. The only hint that he could've been a prophet was that cat, for who in their right mind would let a cat like that live with them? Maybe some of the aristocracy nations would, but those cats would be the short-haired, diva-bred variety. Hu'Mar's cat seemed more likely to carry all sorts of diseases, and she'd pricked her finger on some garbage tangled in its hair. Anyhow, hu'Mar was too sharp to have dabbled as a time palsy. He and that cat were nothing more than con artists.

Ka'Shino pulled her hood over her head. Still, he'd treated her better than she would've expected from a Tough, but that was probably the only good thing about him. She hadn't seen that sort of respect in a while. He still called her a Bule, short-speak for *Blistering Mule*. She wasn't sure if the blistering originated from Albinos' sun sensitive skin or the fact that their employers enjoyed blistering their hide if they didn't act like the subservient mule that the topsiders treated them like. Hu'Mar had been rude, but his demeanor seemed a ruse. Maybe he was down on his luck and willing to treat anybody almost like an equal to get paid. Maybe he didn't even know himself how degrading the B-word was.

Before she walked away, hu'Mar talked quietly to someone in his room. Probably the cat. She smiled, self-satisfied, so he was a cat palsy. He still had a lot of humanity left in him, so he must've bonded the thing. Ew. She didn't have anything against cats, but that cat looked like a hairball that a larger mountain cat might've puked up. Those two probably ran their pathetic scam together.

Well, he'd gotten her money. She placed a hand on her side where her salt purse rested, grateful that he'd returned one of her salines. Skilled as she was, finding work that didn't risk bringing down worm tunnels on her head was a welcomed relief. This could even be her big break, since for the first time, someone with real influence had noticed her abilities. This might even be an in-road to make some real money and even do something worthwhile.

She shook her head at what sounded to her like hu'Mar's one-sided conversation with the cat as she left for the stairs. Animal palsies were one of the least risky of the four attunations, though it was one thing she would never do. Relics use was less risky by far, in her opinion. Messing with relics was one thing, with its own consequences, but they were usually temporary. Being an animal palsy, or worse yet, a time palsy or prophet or whatever they liked to call themselves, came with permanent side effects. She shuddered to even think about the fourth attunation.

Another woman came up the stairs, and ka'Shino pressed against the stairwell wall to make room. In the caverns, you always made yourself small. As the well-toned six-foot tall Tough glided closer, six inches taller than ka'Shino and a good fifty pounds more of lean athletic grace, this lady made ka'Shino feel small, but not just in size. Something about the lady's style shouted, "You're inferior to me." She was dark skinned, unlike hu'Mar's peachy pink. Those two races dominated the surface-dweller nations, and while they looked different enough, they got along well with each other, unlike the way they treated her people. Those two even tolerated the Pissers more than Albinos.

The woman flattened ka'Shino painfully to the wall. Oh, gross, that smell now stuck to her too. It was like a mixture of urine, mold, and flowers all put together. They called it something like per-fum, por-fum, or maybe it was pur-fume. Since it stunk like a cat, both parts, "pur" and "fume," seemed a fitting description.

Even if ka'Shino could afford those stinky scents, she wouldn't want one. Though a nice outfit would be welcome. One day, she'd join the Tuberlow University, and a nice outfit would come in handy. Then she too could hold her head high, even around a Tough like that.

Ka'Shino's cloak snagged on the wallboard and pulled a thread. She tried to dislodge it, and a large sliver of wood stuck her finger. Biting her lip to suppress a scream in anger, she calmly plucked the sliver and stuck the bloody tip of her finger in her mouth. Her only consolation was seeing the lady open hu'Mar's door. That woman probably spent hours each day working out to look as perfectly fit as she was, but despite her irritatingly perfect body, she was clearly a sucker.

All the way down the squeaky stairs, ka'Shino kicked herself. In the caverns, she'd never have let herself be pushed around; however, you learn a thing or two when you spend that much time in the wild systems. One of the most important lessons was not just how to fight, but when to fight. A lot of people died in the wild caverns, but the ones who lived had learned patience and respect. In some ways the city was similar, only more crowded. After only a week, she already longed to be back underground. And while people here were intimidating, they were still just people. Ka'Shino couldn't afford to lose her confidence now.

Hu'Mar was alright, for a Tough. Clever too. He'd mentioned buying black market gears from the wealthy neighborhoods. She wouldn't have suspected that, but it made sense. It would stretch her already tight budget, but maybe she could get an advance from her employer.

Surface-dwellers reverenced gears differently than Albinos. Like the shape of the land, the whole cosmos was patterned after a series of gears. The gears kept turning and meeting with each other in an eternal machine. Every time the gears turned, they connected with another gear, and a species had a chance to jump to the next gear.

She hesitated at the doorway leading out. There was no actual door. If ever there was, it had long since fallen off. A shaft of uninvited light from the setting sun threatened to burn any exposed skin.

Where she came from, people reverenced the whole set of gears as part of a grand, eternal machine. Thus, they valued technology and learning. A gear might be used to create a simple, or even complex, machine.

Above ground, people only viewed the gear as a singular objective. Their goal was to advance from one world to the next, like it was a race. To do more with a gear than wear it as jewelry, a religious token to remind them of the Gears of Eternity, was weird, and in some cases, blasphemous.

Ka'Shino placed her hand over her own pendant before

cinching her hood around her face to shade her eyes from the unforgiving sun. Her gear within a gear was unique to her beliefs. The big gear, like that worn by surface-dwellers, symbolized the Gears of Life. The inner gear symbolized ingenuity within their realm.

Sure, the Beadledom knew gears could be more than a means of understanding the universe. They might even sanction a few simple cog machines such as those used to draw water from a well, but for the most part, surface-dwellers didn't use gears as practical things.

Technology above ground was limited to making better swords, impractical clothing, and stinking hair and body products. Selling the reverenced gears for any practical purpose was discouraged. Selling to an Albino who put the gear to some productive use was even worse.

And somehow, hu'Mar had figured out that she was tinkering with gears. How much more might he have learned? Was it that obvious to others? Hopefully she wouldn't have to kill him, at least, not directly. She'd have to keep her eyes open. Falling into the trap of suspecting that others were stupid, or more ignorant than she, was dangerously easy.

She stepped out of the rotting building, and with her cloak effectively giving her tunnel-vision, she had to turn her whole body to inspect the street.

Her finger still ached from the cat's cocklebur. Considering the source of the prick, it probably would get infected. She sucked on it as she checked both sides of the street, or spokes as they called them here. The narrow road extended a long way, lined on each side with those weather-rotted apartment buildings, hitching rails, and merchant shops, all as dilapidated as hu'Mar's. She hated this part of town. Several streets like this circled each other, and the same sort of drab people filled them. All thought they were better than her, but none of them had enough pride to fix up their homes.

She'd wanted to find a hungry blacksmith, someone who would make and sell her a few small gears while keeping his mouth shut. Then she'd seen hu'Mar's advertisement burned into the side of his apartment building, probably with a hot stick or metal poker. The worry that lived in the back of her conscience was dragged into the forefront of her mind, and she had to know. So she'd detoured to see if that sign meant answers. After all, it did read: "Fortune Teller–Problems Solved Privately."

The whim had been a waste of time. Hu'Mar reminded her of a minister, clever, soul-searching scoundrels. Aside from enforcing the law, their whole objective was to help you become a more dominant species so that when the Great Gears shifted, the human race could take the Holy Clutch. Hu'Mar, on the other hand, might've been half decent at dissecting your mind, but he didn't seem the sort to take the law at face value.

She turned away from his apartment building. Passing chariots left thick clouds of dirt in the air. A blacksmith might still be open somewhere, but as hu'Mar had stated, this wasn't the place to buy a gear. Where to now?

After two steps, she stopped by a nearby stable and watering trough. Yeah, better put these goggles on. The sun would fully set soon, but till then, the goggles would come in handy. She tried to reach into her hood and slip the smoked glass goggles from her forehead to her eyes, but they caught on the cloth of her tightly drawn hood.

Crossing the street to put them on in the shade would be the smart thing to do. Grease that. She unfastened her hood and pulled it back. The sun felt too hot on her skin. How did these surface-dwellers handle walking around in full view of the sun and not writhe in discomfort?

Ish hu'Narmin, or Crazy Ish as everyone called him, would her best source to learn the future. Granted, she was a single player in the larger whole, but her part of the plan scared her. People could get hurt, and as much as she hated their prejudice, they were people too. If anyone could help her see the consequences of her future actions, it would be Crazy Ish.

He'd palsied the Gears of Time themselves and had already sold his whole mind to the future. He could barely be counted on to speak in plain words because the prophesies he gave now were seldom comprehensible, but when he did tell the future, it could be relied upon.

Ka'Shino finished fastening her goggles on. Toughs walked along the busy streets, and peddlers pulled their carts while war chariots recklessly weaved between them all. There was an occasional horse, and in the distance, even a coach cruised by.

"Phhhbbbffhhtt," the lips of a horse flapped near her ear.

Ka'Shino jumped, wishing she'd pulled her hood back on already. She wiped the horse slobber from the back of her neck with the sleeve of her cloak. A bucktoothed stableboy led the largest tan horse she'd ever seen back from a clay watering trough. Instead of tying the horse to the hitching rail, he threw the reins over the horse's neck, careful not to bump off the large brimmed hat the horse was wearing.

"Like I needs to hear it from you too," the boy said as he leaned against the rail and eyed ka'Shino.

The horse dug at the ground and shook its head before it too stood on its hind legs and mimicked the boy by leaning against the building like a loafer, watching the crowd go by.

"Oh, that's real smooth, comin from you." The stableboy elbowed the horse. "What make you so much better? You ain't bonded nobody neither."

The horse flapped its lips and grunted.

The stableboy shifted his weight to his other foot, eyed ka'Shino, then winked back at the horse. "She's a Bule. You might just have a chance," he snickered.

She dipped her clean sleeve into a nearby barrel of water and wiped at the horse slobber on the back of her neck.

The horse rubbed at his side as if he had an uncomfortable itch, then aimed that long face at ka'Shino and said, "Neigh-he-he-heh."

The bucktooth boy offered the horse a bite of a very large carrot. It had to bend over quite a bit as it chomped half of it in one bite. The boy examined his much-diminished root, shrugged, then kept chewing at it himself.

With half a cheekful, he said, "My dear girl, you look radiant today. Could I interest you in a leisurely gallop?" Little carrot flakes flew from his mouth as he talked.

"Pardon?" Ka'Shino wrung out her sleeve. Maybe a sliver from that cat's cocklebur was still stuck in her finger. She wiped her hand dry and tried biting at the sore spot.

"Pffftt. You deaf? Beauford wants to know if you likes kissin big lips." The boy stepped close and puckered his large adolescent lips in exaggerated kissing mockery. He needed to be taught a lesson in manners, and luckily, he wasn't so old that she couldn't take him.

She pulled her finger out of her mouth and slapped him hard across the face, her fingernail accidentally scraped his cheek "I'd kiss him over you any day." She wiped her finger on the side of her cloak as he stumbled backward. "And I tink you're bōt palsies tat have gone unbonded far too long. Maybe it's you two who are made for each oter." She pulled her hood over her head.

"Snort," the horse said with a shake or two of his head.

"This Bule's got'er gears in a bind, I'm half tempted to give her a lesson she'll never forget," he said to the horse as he examined the blood slowly dribbling from his face. Then he mumbled "Oh, and Beauford sez, 'Good heavens ma'am, I'd was merely commenting on your positively luminous skin tone.'"

She turned her back to them.

"Yeah, an what's up with them things you wearin over yer eyes? Somethin wrong with'em?" the stableboy laughed, his confidence obviously returning.

Ka'Shino fingered her goggles. That was the problem with being a palsy: go too long without a bonded partner, and you'd turn into whatever animal you became familiar with. Whether it was a horse acting like a human, or a human acting like a horse, or rather, a horse's—

Another Tough came riding on what looked like a normal horse. He hopped off his mount. "You must be the stableboy."

"Ptbbb," the boy said, imitating the horse's flapping lip, as if he was indifferent to this man and his questions. "What's it to ya?"

The man slugged the boy in the face, but Juniper wasn't

surprised. Playful shoves and uppercuts took the place of handshakes around here. She had to be weary of Tough greetings. She intentionally made herself look small so the man wouldn't come and say hello to her also. Being a *Bule* helped in that regard since no self-respecting Tough would be caught pleasantly socializing with one of her *kind*.

The stableboy gave the man a weak shove, then took his horse.

The man strutted toward the door, pausing to stare at the tan stallion leaning against the building.

"Ptttbb," Beauford said, more jovial than the stable boy had, then it slammed its front hoof square into the man's face. It nodded its long head as if to say, "Yeah, I'm the Tough one here."

The tall beefy man lay on the ground, a large horseshoe-shaped bruise on his forehead. He stumbled back to his feet, then to Beauford and shook his head once, as if to clear it. The horse was still nodding when the man swung his own fist like a charging chariot. His knuckles connected with the horse's head on a downward nod. The horse toppled in a heap on the ground.

They both laughed at each other, the man with a "Ha, ha, ha!" and the horse with a "Snort," nod, "snort," nod. Then the man entered the building, and the horse returned to his hind feet.

Ka'Shino crossed the street and followed the walking path, thankful that she dodged getting involved in that little greeting. The walks weren't terribly crowded right now, but she still got bumped out of the way twice. Toughs wouldn't yield for a small nobody like her. Eventually she ducked down an alley and took a small clock from her cloak. She'd made it herself despite it being illegal topside. The Beadledom insisted that anyone who tinkered with gears, especially gears as intricate as a clock's, be licensed. Most surface-dwellers would call a pocket clock heresy, using religious symbols to perform complex tasks that the average person couldn't begin to comprehend. Little things like this supported surface-dweller rumors that Albinos were involved in some form of dark magic. Bah! There was no such thing as magic.

Too bad these rumors hadn't caused a respectful sort of fear. Instead, it enforced the discriminatory sort of fear. If ka'Shino was a Tough, or any other race of surface human, knowing what she knew, she too would be afraid of the Albino community. While the rest of the world reverenced the symbol of the gear, the Albinos didn't limit themselves to tinkering with gears. For all their ignorance, the surface-dwellers might as easily have reverenced something more primitive, like a wheel. After all, a wheel turned as easily as a gear. They could call it the Wheel of Time. Ha! That did have a nice ring to it. Perhaps she'd heard or read it someplace before.

Ka'Shino scratched at her neck and stumbled through a fresh horse biscuit on the road. She should've paid more attention. She examined her smelly foot. Disgusting. This would've never happened underground. Surface-dwellers were such hypocrites. They didn't trust other animals, yet they still lived side by side with them, bonding them even. Of course, horses weren't really after the Holy Clutch as far as she knew.

They were dumb creatures, enslaved by humans, bought and sold as property, and they still served their masters with love and admiration. But that was the way of it. Be the dominant species or be dominated. She scraped her shoe on the corner of another apartment. Like anyone would even care. This whole primitive city was a mess. Another quick glance at her pocket clock told her that there wasn't much time. She couldn't be late for her rendezvous. Maybe though, she could still squeeze in enough time to visit Crazy Ish. She hid the round, palm-sized clock in her cloak, then hurried out of the alley. If anyone caught her with it, she'd be in real trouble. Even if the Beadledom didn't execute her, her own people would, if just to keep her from talking about other things.

Since the whole universe was patterned after gears, that ought to be a sign that everyone had the right to understand and work with the mechanics. Not in the Beadledom's way of thinking. Gears were too holy for the average man or woman to fiddle with.

The Beadledom might be the prevailing government in Spur Central. They might even have a lot of influence on the neighboring kingdoms, but ka'Shino was pretty sure that none of the Beadledom's ministers had penetrated the Albino strongholds. They'd be in for a surprise if they had.

A mile down the road, she found the small hovel of Ish hu'Narmin and entered.

Chapter 3

The Worst Type Of Trouble

Dick hu'Mar stood. "We're closed for the night."

Silhouetted by the dusky hall, the living portrait remained in place framed by the weathered wood of the door jams. She was the sort of sight that could inspire artists to paint and connoisseurs to praise. Then the visitor took a single jaw-dropping step forward and out of silhouette. She could enchant any man with that dark brown face and lips that pouted, "Kiss me, hon, before I change my mind."

This woman was nothing but trouble. The kind you wanted to wrap your arms around while hoping your teeth and breath were clean.

"Ohhh," she moaned like a goodnight kiss. Her hips swayed as she advanced, dragging hu'Mar's eyes with them. "It's only late afternoon. I wouldn't even call it early evening yet."

The politician's tan vest seemed ready to split the zippable gear-strip seams from around her busty frame. Toughs were so weird like that. They loved to fight, anything to prove their dominance, but a vest like that looked like it would never hold up in a brawl. Maybe that's why they liked it so much. Completely impractical for a real battle, but perfect for stealing a man's attention, and Dick hu'Mar's attention was stolen.

He managed to sit on his log stool before his knees melted. He knew who she was. He had no idea that she knew of him. Since she could've accessed the Beadledom's prophets, her being here meant she had something to hide from the public, or more likely, from the Beadledom itself. He replaced the blowgun in the drawer as she glided around his desk. He wouldn't need it, he hoped.

Her brown leather side-split hiking skirt was hiked high so that a hand width of scandalous, milk-chocolate skin was exposed above and below her knees before diving into a rough pair of leather boots. If you wore boots, why go through all the trouble to wear a pair so impractical? They raised her heels up so high, that her butt had to pucker just for balance. It looked exhausting.

As if sensing his thoughts, she rested her posterior on his lap. Her smooth dark fingers tickled his pink ear.

"Please, sit down," he offered too late.

"I have a problem," she cooed.

Hu'Mar forced his eyes up to meet hers. "You have a problem?"

She was only toying with him. For one, Tough's didn't flirt this way. Even if she'd fallen madly in love with him at first sight, a big—big unlikelihood, this sort of behavior would only be considered hardcore courtship back in Nebylon. No, impossible. She had to be messing with him even if he would've liked it otherwise. Here in Spur Central, this might have made a man drool and caused him to fight for her hand, but hu'Mar wouldn't dare court this woman. She wanted to throw him off balance, and she was doing a bang-up job of it.

Her lips were so close. Her breath smelled hot and inviting as she leaned in. The stool gave way, and they both toppled to the floor.

She gasped.

He groaned. Her knees dug into his hip as she pulled her muscular body from the floor. He climbed slowly to his feet. He half sat on the desk and tried his hardest to maintain eye contact. Jodeign ka'Nairie's political campaign mirrored that of most who found their way into the Beadledom. She was a Tough, obviously, with plenty of opportunity to prove her strength. She was devoted to obtaining the Great Clutch for humanity. Most of all, she was smart, something in short supply around most of these meatheads, so she only had a few rivals left before the vacancy in the government was hers. That had to be why she was here.

"Have a seat there, please." He pointed to the trunk across the table from him. "And before you ask, I'm no political dirt digger."

Like the Albino before her, she didn't sit. Why did everyone have to make things so hard for him?

Her eyes slid around the room as if seeing it for the first time, but still having a good time.

Hu'Mar followed her attention for a moment, wishing all the more that his place was more presentable. Vinegar, who normally stayed hidden for a visit like this, casually walked to the only window, jumped onto the sill, and stared at the street. Hu'Mar would clearly get no help from him. He'd have to do this solo till Vinegar bled off some anger.

Returning his attention to the woman, hu'Mar found that he could easily read her. She was a work of art, all right, but her manner was predictable. She was a Tough, a very attractive Tough, but still the same. This sort of women would never take no for an answer. Jodeign ka'Nairie might be a little more on her game than others, but that was the way it was around here. Forget survival of the fittest. It was dominance by the dominant. Whatever advantage you had, you played it hard.

"I've heard good things about you, hu'Mar." Her eyes painted the opposite side of the room as she bent over. Was she still trying to manipulate him or convince him to help? He forced his gaze away from her distracting features. She was just scratching a small rash on the inside of her leg. Maybe it was just an excuse to bend over in front of him, but he took note of the rash anyway. It was the only anomaly to this otherwise prime specimen of Tough breeding.

"You've heard wrong." Hu'Mar glanced at the items he'd nicked from the small leather bag tied at her waist when they'd fallen. Old habits or professional necessity. Still, he had to be careful about focusing too much on the items since she hadn't sat down and might easily notice.

One item especially caught his attention, a ring made of bone. A relic, dangerous indeed.

"Relax, fortune teller. I don't need you to tell me about my competition's weaknesses."

Yeah, she probably had better sources than him for that. He had to connect the dots. This lady tapped into the abilities of other species by way of the third attunation. The bone ring relic made that clear. But he hadn't found its companion piece, at least, not in her purse. Only money was left in it. He knew the texture of that well, even if he didn't feel that salty grit as often as he liked.

The smell of the meat market wafted up from the streets. In his mind, he saw a cleaver chopping a slab of meat. His own neck had once been close to such a chopping block. Of course, when offered the choice, he'd chosen the noose instead of the axe. He stood, rubbing his neck at the memory. Last time, he'd helped politically powerful people, they had greatly underappreciated his services.

Hu'Mar might be a lot of things, and while he didn't consider himself racist, he did try to do what he thought was right, even if that meant saving a spoiled prince from a relationship with that Albino. A lot of thanks the king of Nebylon had given him for that. The King had been saved from a potentially disreputable daughter-in-law, one that he would've likely had assassinated if the prince pursued that little love affair, yet it was hu'Mar who had to be silenced. He'd been discredited, humiliated, and if not for an owed favor from the carpenter of the gallows, he'd be dead. So if he felt mildly hesitant to helping a politician like Jodeign ka'Nairie, it was because he didn't want to run away from another city. It was hard to make a living when you burned bridges at every place you settled, even if you were as good as he was.

Hard Boiled Cabbage: Big Trouble In Spur Central

However, that wafting scent of freshly butchered meat reminded him of one other important fact. You couldn't live without food, and you couldn't buy food without salt, and one pot of boiled cabbage aside, he had very little of both. His stomach chose that moment to growl its confirmation. He sighed. *This better end well.*

Hu'Mar replaced the items into her bag, then tucked them in his palm as he stood again, rounded the desk, and wrapped his arm around Jodeign ka'Nairie, guiding her to her seat. He might not be a Tough, but he was still strong enough to fake it. She sat, and he palmed her money bag back onto her belt. As he did, he examined her thoroughly. Aside from being obscenely attractive, she had no other bone jewelry or deformities on her.

"Such a strong man, Dick hu'Mar. I'm guessing by now you already know my name." There was something about that smooth flowing voice, especially when she said his name, which made focusing a challenge.

"Why's a dame like you crossing over to the rat flats of the city?" He sat next to the desk and leaned back, trying to look casual without tipping his log again.

"You're the fortune teller. How about you tell me." She stared into him like the Tough she was. It was the daring glare of a bully. Vinegar had taught him to never look away from a stare like that.

"A man's got to make a living." He crossed his arms, keeping his eyes steadfast. "You want parlor tricks, you pay the parlor."

Her eyes sparkled with a hint of suppressed moisture. At last, she blinked, then flipped three chips on the table.

Hu'Mar grunted and lowered his chin in disapproval. "Is a saline too much to ask for a fortune?"

"Sounds to me like you just want my fortune?"

"I'll take it if you're offering, but a dame like you ain't no doll. You might fool most, but you're more business than play. And remember," hu'Mar added, "you came to me."

Jodeign ka'Nairie eyed him carefully, then dropped three more chips on the table to make it a full saline. He opened his drawer and slid them in. If the ceiling produced another rainstorm, it would be better for the salt to stay dry. He'd hate to lose all his money in the laundry.

"You've lost something important to you," hu'Mar ventured.

"So you're perceptive," she said. "Are you a prophet?"

"What do you think?"

"No. But can you tell me what I've lost?"

"You testing me?" he asked.

"These are the rat flats, as you so willingly pointed out. You have a reputation for being—good. I like that, but that could be little more than marketing on your part. I also like thorough and discreet. Besides, I paid you, and if I like what I hear, you can expect more where that came from."

Hu'Mar studied her for a long moment before answering. It helped to increase the tension. Tension was good. He also had to admit, looking at her felt good too. She was out of his league, but if she was going to toy with him—

"You dabble with bone relics."

Being a relic palsy wasn't at all like being an animal palsy. Nothing about this third attunation was permanent. For one, it didn't prevent you from using multiple relics. Whereas everything about being an animal palsy was permanent and limited to one animal. Sure, you could still channel one of the other attunations, like relics, but you could only bond one animal.

"Don't ask me what your relic does for you. I don't know. But you've lost your companion piece. You've come to see if I can help you find it." That was the other thing about using relics: they worked best in pairs.

Ka'Nairie leaned over the table. Her eyes pinned hu'Mar's in place. "You lied to me."

Hu'Mar slapped her across the face, hard. It didn't even leave a mark.

She grabbed his hair, yanked him over the table, and planted a firm throat collapsing kiss on his lips. Then she bit his lip on the way out, drawing blood. She smiled. Hu'Mar slipped back onto his stool.

Hard Boiled Cabbage: Big Trouble In Spur Central

He touched his lip and smiled back. "I didn't lie."

"You said everything I heard about you was wrong, but it would seem that you're just the kind of man I'm looking for. How much?"

Back onto his feet, hu'Mar stretched as he crossed to the other side of his flat, his stomach slightly unsettled. Within a small cubby behind his stone cook-station, he retrieved a skin of watered-down wheat mash. It wasn't enough to get drunk on, just alcoholic enough not to get sick on. Nobody drank straight water in this city. In his old life, he'd preferred tea, but tea meant boiling water. Boiling water meant starting a fire, and that would take time.

He filled two cups and handed one to ka'Nairie.

She sniffed it, then pushed it aside. "Well?"

"Well, what?" hu'Mar asked. "You don't want the Beadledom to know about your relics because your relics aren't registered and are therefore black market. You could get me into some big trouble."

He didn't know a ton about relics, other than they were the bones of past sacrificed species who were pulled from the Great Clutch. Unlike normal bones, these ones had the ability to grant limited characteristics of that particular species to whoever was in possession of them. They were very rare, and if you couldn't trace your relic's history, they could easily be confiscated. The Ministry was always on the lookout for someone with poor records and a relic or two. Often it amounted to legal thievery, but that was the Beadledom for you. And Jodeign ka'Nairie was campaigning for a seat in that organization.

Hu'Mar savored the taste of blood on his lip from her kiss. Then it reminded him of the smashed blood beetle, and his stomach churned a little. What about the smashed remains of the fly that was currently trapped in the Great Clutch? When the clutch lifts, would someone collect and grind up the fly's remains to save it for a relic too? What kind of a power might that insect's dust bestow? It would likely become a gag relic. Hold this and you'll gain an appetite for eating poo.

"Mine are perfectly legal," ka'Nairie said, her voice as seductive as when she first walked into the door. "Can't a gal keep a few secrets for herself? It's a competitive city. Word spreads easily. How else do you think I found out about you?"

"I don't do this sort of thing anymore. My sleuthing days are behind me," he lied, testing her purse.

"How much?"

Hu'Mar sighed. "Five salines per day, plus expenses." It was high, but only by a saline or two. There used to be a time when he could've gotten double that, back when people knew the value he brought to the table. With the right set of cases, word might get around. He could be back on top again. For now though, if he were honest, he couldn't afford to lose this job.

"What kind of expenses?" She leaned forward.

Hu'Mar leaned in to meet her. "People get nervous around nosy strangers. Sometimes it's good to grease a few mouths. You suspect theft?"

"Would I be here if I didn't?" Her breath reminded him of that last kiss. He wanted more but knew she wouldn't give it. She'd been playing him, hooking him, and setting him off balance. It had worked. He even suspected that this might be one of those cases that could re-establish his reputation.

Now it was his turn to close the deal.

"You wouldn't believe the sorts I get coming through my doors," hu'Mar lied. The Albino had been the first person to visit in over a week that he'd been able to collect any salt from.

She reached into her bag and counted out one bromine and four salines. "Two-days advance pay." She placed them on his desk. "Find it within that time, and I'll cover expenses, plus pay an additional two days' worth to show my appreciation."

Hu'Mar slid them into his desk drawer. They clattered loudly next to his blow darts. He shut the drawer quickly and lifted his cup of wheat mash. Two days to find a relic. Shouldn't be too hard.

For formality's sake, she stood, crinkled her nose, and raised the cup to her lips. She took as little of a sip as she could.

Hu'Mar couldn't wait to get started, so he downed his cup in under a second. It was time to be serious. "So tell me about your relics. What do they do?"

Ka'Nairie lowered herself like she was melting into a slow dance, though no longer was her movement meant to encourage hu'Mar. The grace in her movement now was pure, natural, and in its own way, even more beautiful.

Her elbows rested on the desk as she leaned forward. "How much do you need to know?"

Hu'Mar suppressed the urge to gulp and tried hard to keep his face calm, unphased, and level with hers. "We drank to it, didn't we? If you can't trust professional confidentiality, what can you trust?"

"Well," she hesitated, poised and practiced, like he was now little more than a child, "It—"

"Wait a minute." He needed to break her stride. She was trying to control the conversation with this new attitude. It was too practiced, too political. Not that he blamed her. For her, it was habit, a tool she used to get where she was politically, but a tool that was counterproductive to their arrangement.

Luckily, he had a good excuse to throw her off balance. He stood, paced quietly to the side of the room, then slammed his palm against the wall.

"Yipe!" Thelma ka'Skrut fell to the floor in the other room.

"Take a hike, you old gossip, and I promise to send this lady your way when I'm done with her." Hu'Mar wasn't really afraid of ka'Skrut blabbing. Even if she did, most people didn't care to listen to her. Nobody liked listening to salespeople, especially pushy ones. Especially pushy ones that sold hair products that'd catch fire faster than the driest kindling if you got close to a candle.

"You gon'ta make me deaf, Dick hu'Mar." The thin wall didn't dampen her voice even a little.

"Not my fault you had your ear plastered to my wall. Give us ten minutes." He waited for thirty seconds, then slammed his fist into the wall again.

There was another, "Yipe." Then her heels clicked away from the wall. "Fine, but you listen, dearie, when hu'Mar's finished with you, come over and see me. I got the best hair stiffeners in the city. Style your hair and make it healthier at the same time. All my customers swear by it."

Hu'Mar waited until ka'Skrut's door opened and slammed shut. Then for good measure, he tilted his only wall furnishing on its nail. He hadn't rearranged the calendar since moving in, and it still reflected the month of the wolf, four months behind now.

Behind the calendar, a knot in the wood had fallen out. The hole was the entire reason hu'Mar had placed the calendar there in the first place, and this time, it was his turn to be nosy. He put his eye up to the hole.

He let the calendar swing back down. "She's gone. Here, I'll give you a chip or two back. Just promise me you'll stop by her shop on the way out. If I were you though, I'd get rid of anything she sells you."

There was still the dentist downstairs, but hu'Grooshy would keep his mouth shut. Above them, hu'Mar could hear the faint sloshing of laundry being scrubbed. Mount Exclusion could erupt or the war for the Great Clutch could begin, and that lady wouldn't even notice.

"Well," ka'Nairie said, more cautious, as if by dismissing one neighbor, hu'Mar had gained three more. "I have a certain relic, a, um—"

"A ring?" hu'Mar offered.

"Yes, how'd you—never mind. Okay, so they were paired, obviously. My ring was from six shiftings ago."

"And the one missing?"

"It's a pin needle, from three shifts ago. It takes away toxins in the body."

"Okay, good enough. What's the downside?" There was always a downside to any relic, but the right pairing would counteract the side effect.

Ka'Nairie stood from her stool and paced. With her back to hu'Mar, she said, "It makes you poisonous."

"Huh, not that bad. I know a lot of poisonous people who don't even have relics and others who wished they were."

"No," she said. "Your sweat, your saliva, any fluid of yours that touches another person, will make them sick, possibly even kill them. It has great healing powers, but if it kills everyone around you…"

"And your ring?"

"I'd rather not talk about that one."

Hu'Mar nodded his head. So he was looking for a Pin of Poison. "Who else knows about this?"

"Very few people know about my relics. I can't imagine who would've stolen the pin."

"Any enemies?" hu'Mar asked.

She puckered her lush lips and looked at him the way a woodpecker looks at a bore-infested tree. Then the ceiling rained, mostly on ka'Nairie. Suds and dirty water dripped from her disappointed lips, making her flat, black hair glisten, and her brown skin shine. So beautiful, as long as he ignored the suds. His brief nausea left almost instantly. Humor was such a tonic. This could be more fun than he'd anticipated. As for her, she could've been dipped in mud, and hu'Mar's heart would've only pumped more furiously.

"Stupid question," hu'Mar conceded, trying so hard to conceal a smile. "Instead, let's start with the people who know about your relics. That's probably a shorter list. Tell me their names and when you last saw each of them."

Hu'Mar tried to commit each name to memory. Lost and found cases weren't usually too hard. The stakes were higher only because the missing relic was worth a lot of salt. All relics were expensive. There were two possible outcomes: One, she'd misplaced it; or two, someone stole it.

Hu'Mar would investigate based on the assumption that it had been stolen. Besides, the trail there would grow coldest, fast. Whoever stole it would want to either keep it or sell it. Either way, hu'Mar would find it. He had a knack for this sort of thing. It might take a few days, all the while he'd be paid, with the slim upshot of knowing the famous Jodeign ka'Nairie better. She was politically minded, but he liked dangerous women. When your life had become anything but interesting, a good jolt of danger was perfect for breaking the monotony, and more especially, for proving your ability.

He suspected something dangerous about that Albino that had visited him earlier too, but he liked this danger better. It had the potential to pay better. That Albino could have given him some trouble, but he doubted that she had the salt to pay him for whatever mischief she was up to.

Chapter 4

Tea and One Too Many Witnesses

Crazy Ish poured her a cup of tea. "May I take your cloak, dear—uh—um?" He set the tea kettle on a small decorative stand next to the front door.

"Juniper ka'Shino, and no tanks," she said. "Te light hurts my skin." Besides, she wouldn't be here long, and if anyone happened to glance through the glassless window of the formerly great Beadledom prophet, she'd rather they not identify her. She only needed answers to calm her anxiety since the job she planned to do had the potential to kill thousands. Crazy Ish hopefully would forget everything she divulged in minutes anyway.

"Very well. Make yourself comfortable." His voice was high and as thin as the loose paper he called skin. He smelled like he hadn't bathed in a year, and he'd probably forgotten he needed to. Of course, his frail body would likely dissolve if he sat in a tub for more than thirty seconds, so it was just as well.

His wicker sofa was flimsy and barely able to support her weight. Only a surface-dweller would make furniture from weeds. She sipped at the tea. It almost tasted good. She wasn't a fan of bitter tea, especially this variety. More than likely, he'd steeped it too long and neglected to add any honey.

As Crazy Ish walked to his wooden rocker, ka'Shino dumped the tea into the fishbowl nearby. The goldfish swam in circles. Most people couldn't afford such luxuries as crystal fishbowls. Crazy Ish, despite his failed memory, was a man of means. Prophets in their prime were paid handsomely until they'd spent all their memories and were left the bumbling buffoons that hu'Narmin had become. But if they were wise with their money and trusted it to someone honest, they could live out their retirement in comfort. She wouldn't want to end her days as an imbecile, nor would many others. That was probably why the Beadledom paid so well for anyone selfless enough to offer their services as a real future forecaster.

Much of the Beadledom's success came from prophets. Ka'Shino wasn't sure if hu'Narmin had been in the Beadledom's service long before he lost his mind or if he was the short-burn sort. Given how many people knew and respected him, she guessed that he'd lasted several years.

"Well dear, what can I do for—" hu'Narmin paused. "Oh my, how rude of me. It seems that I didn't get you any tea." He looked around, then shuffled his way back to the kitchen.

"No, no. It's okay," ka'Shino protested, but hu'Narmin simply flapped his knuckled hand as if to say that it was no trouble.

She slumped in her chair. Maybe he'd put sugar in it this time. Ka'Shino's sleeve was still damp from where she'd dipped it in water to wash her neck off earlier, so she rolled it up her arm. The other sleeve with the horse slobber, had dried into a crust already, and she was about to roll that sleeve up as well so it would match the rolled up side, but she paused. The horse's drool had caused her neck to itch even though she'd wiped most of it off.

She pulled her hood down and rubbed her neck. It actually stung a bit. She looked for a mirror, but the only reflective objects in the room were hu'Narmin's forgotten copper tea kettles. She'd seen very few mirrors above ground. Of course, nobody here even had glass in their windows. Someday soon, surface-dwellers would look underground and appreciate that little thing Albinos called a brain.

She picked up two shiny kettles and tried to catch a reflection of her neck. The rounded reflections were impossible to discern. She clanked the two pots together as she eased them to the floor.

This sort of thing would've never happened underground. Stupid surface-dwellers were so uncivilized. Why would anyone park a rude slave like that horse, so close to the front door where people had to walk? Ka'Shino had nothing against enslaving other species since it kept them from obtaining the Tomb of Ascension, but horses become so intolerably dumb, docile, and dependent that no human worried about guarding Mount Exclusion from them.

The only thing humans had to worry about from a horse, apparently, was occasional bad manners. She couldn't really blame the horse itself. Take away something's freedom and self-respect, what should she expect? She scratched her neck again. She must be allergic.

She dug in her pocket till she found and applied the same balm she'd used on hu'Mar's cat. It instantly felt better. With her hood down, she stood and paced Crazy Ish's home.

This was the nicest surface-dweller home she'd ever been in. It was so large, especially for one man. This room alone could've slept at least twenty Toughs, but it was only used for sitting. Hu'Narmin had a spare room for sleeping and a kitchen. Space underground was a luxury. Here it was wasted, not to mention primitive.

It all made her miss the upper caves more. She loved being a frontiersman and exploring the unmapped caves that led to great city-sized caverns, completely uninhabited, that would serve as great places for the future growth of her people.

She returned her attention to the sitting room. Four additional kettles of tea sat around the room, including the one hu'Narmin had just set by the door. Either he hadn't noticed them, or he'd forgotten them as quick as he'd seen them. Not a good sign for her. She brushed her fingers across a small bookshelf, the only thing here that seemed half civilized. Not many up here knew how to read and write. These books would be filled with hu'Narmin's prophesies, dictated by him, written down by others. She'd be surprised if he could even read them.

He came back a few minutes later and poured another cup of tea for both of them. Then he walked over to his goldfish and poured a little in its bowl. "A spot of tea for you too, Jerry?"

The fish swam in a figure eight.

"Ah don't be silly. You'll love it." He swirled his finger in the bowl.

The goldfish got caught in the whirlpool before Crazy Ish took his finger out and licked it. "I do like a good cup of tea." He stared at the fish, then laughed.

"Hu'Narmin, I was hoping tat you could help me know some tings. I can pay."

"Absolutely. What can I do for such a fine young lady? By the way, are you sick? You look very pale. Please, try your tea. It'll help you feel better."

The steam hinted at mint and spice. It actually smelled very good this time. She took a sip, and it—was good. "I've got some tings coming to me, and tere's tings I need to do, but I'm a little worried about side effects."

"Oh, big plans, eh, sweetheart? Who's the lucky man?"

"No man." She shook her head. "I'm going to use a bomb near te city, and I'd rater not say what for. It's just, I don't want anyone to get hurt. So I was wondering if you could tell me anyting of say, two days from now, what condition te city will be in if I go trough wit tis?"

Crazy Ish put his cup of tea down on the floor next to him. "What's a bomb, dearie?"

Of course, stupid, stupid. Why would he know what a bomb was? Her people had kept that secret from the surface-dwellers for some time now.

"Let's just say, I'll be excavating a lot of rock on Mount Exclusion, and I'm worried about te volcano's instability."

He closed his eyes and let out a fart, then a sigh. "The future is like a cup of cold tea. All you can do is drink it, drain it, or ask it why the weather is so ridiculously cold these days."

"I... uh..." Juniper ka'Shino hesitated.

"Rickety tickety clock, the mouse consumed the hawk. Lickety split and splittery goo, the world will wa, wa, why, hello dear." He opened his eyes. "Do I know you?"

"Yes," Juniper ka'Shino sighed. Was there even any use in asking? "What were you just saying?"

Crazy Ish thought for a moment. "Hello, dear. Do I know you?"

"No, I mean, before tat, were you prophesying someting or just rambling?"

"Oh, my dear, I don't really know what you're talking about. You kids are always so eager for, for—pardon me, where are my manners. I didn't get your name?"

This was going nowhere. She'd been here for fifteen minutes. This was why she'd risked visiting that hu'Mar fellow. True, she should've come here first, but it hadn't crossed her mind until hu'Mar had suggested it, or was it his cat that suggested it and he translated? It didn't matter. Crazy Ish didn't have enough memories to trade for a proper two-days of foretelling. She'd have to kidnap him and keep him from looking into the future for a couple of days if she were to get any foretellings from him. Even then, she had no way of preventing him from accidentally wasting a look into the future for something stupid, like teatime, and it would be too late by then to change anything.

For the moment, her goggles were on her forehead. She put her teacup down, bowed her head and rubbed her eyes as she tried to interpret what he'd started. But that was the problem, he'd only started a prophesy. He hadn't completed the prediction or even hinted at where it was going.

A splash drew her attention. The goldfish swam in excited circles.

"Oh yes, yes, I see. We've already been introduced." Crazy Ish nodded to the fish before smiling at ka'Shino.

Juniper ka'Shino gasped. "You and your fish are palsies?"

"Huh? Oh—yes." He said looking around the room like he forgot that she was even here. "Yes, Jerry and I are bonded." Then in a whisper he confided, "He doesn't have the best memory He keeps telling me his name is not Jerry." Then returning to his normal cheerful volume, he continued, "But he seems to remember more than me. I-I'm sorry, but have we met before, dear?"

Juniper ka'Shino was about to give up when Crazy Ish opened his mouth again. In a more monotone voice, he said, "You shrimpy seaweed for brains. She's come here to find out what will come of her actions?"

Her chest tightened. Crazy Ish was looking at not-Jerry. These weren't Crazy Ish's words. The fish was acting as a spare memory bank for him, and Ish hu'Narmin was just interpreting it.

It only made sense. If you knew you were losing your mind, the only logical thing to do was bond yourself with another animal. She'd assumed that since hu'Narmin had palsied time, that he wouldn't palsy an animal, but they were separate types of attunations, so it was possible. And why wouldn't he? Of course, it was pretty sad when a goldfish had a better memory than you.

"You walk a dangerous road, Juniper ka'Shino," Crazy Ish interpreted.

Ah, it remembered her name. This was dangerous. It should've kept its thoughts to itself, but an animal that mistakes a metal hook for food wasn't usually smart enough to know when to hold its tongue.

"Sir," she interrupted. "Might I boter you for a cup of tea?"

"Oh, yes, yes, sure. How rude of me. Look, Jerry, we have a guest, and I didn't even get her a cup of tea." Crazy Ish searched around and didn't notice the five kettles littering the room, so he walked back to his kitchen.

Ka'Shino picked up her teacup and walked over to the fishbowl. "Sorry Jerry. I can't have you telling anyone about me." She dumped the rest of her hot tea into his bowl.

Not-Jerry swam behind a leaf of lettuce. Ka'Shino dipped the cup into the bowl and chased the fish around for a few seconds. She cursed as the sleeves of her cloak fell into the bowl. Now both sleeves were wet again.

Unfortunately, she couldn't fish the fish out. It was too fast. Crazy Ish was coming back, so she withdrew the cup and wrung her sleeves out in the tan water.

The goldfish swam in excited patterns as Crazy Ish walked by. He didn't notice, but it was only a matter of time. She had to get out of here. She could just empty the fishbowl onto the floor. Crazy Ish would forget within moments anyway, so why not? Instead, she got another idea.

"Are tose your prophesies?" She pointed to his books.

"Oh, yes, I believe they are." He smiled. "Do you read."

"I do. Do you mind if I have a look?"

"My pleasure." He set his tea kettle down and escorted her to the small bookshelf. "Is there anything in particular you're interested in?"

"Someting tat references our day right now or at least te near future." Why hadn't she thought of this before? Chances were good that Crazy Ish had seen these days. Even if he hadn't done so during his service at the Beadledom, he might have done so on his own and them written down here.

He brushed un-gentle fingers across the spines of the leather bindings, like he was caressing them with a clumsy arm-length pole, made of arm. Most of the books had the official emblem of a gear with the capital letter "B" inside, clearly from his time with the Beadledom. She was surprised to see three other books with no such emblems. He pulled the first book from the shelf.

"I wrote this one myself, I think. It details my entire life: past, present, and future. If I ever wonder who I used to be I, I…" He cradled it to his chest. Was he sad? Or could he even remember having read it? "If there's anything relevant to this day, it will be in this book."

"I didn't know you could read, let alone write," ka'Shino said softly.

"I can't anymore. I've forgotten how. My memory is like shattered clay. I know certain things, such as the fact that I used to be able to read. Maybe someday I'll forget how to talk, but the worst part will be knowing that I once knew how." He sighed.

"I can't expect you to understand."

"Do you mind?" Ka'Shino reached for the book.

"Do I mind what?" He smiled, completely oblivious to why they were kneeling at this bookshelf.

She tapped the book in his hand.

"Oh, this." His voice went higher, surprised to find himself holding it. "You want to read this? I've never shared this with anyone, not even the Beadledom, at least, not that I remember. I'd hate to forget that you borrowed it. Did I tell you that it's my only solid link to who I really am, but you may read it on one condition." Hu'Narmin handed over the book. "Read it out loud, so I can hear it again."

The pages were worn well. Ka'Shino flipped from page to ink-spotted page. Hu'Narmin had beautiful handwriting, so the book was easy to read. She flipped to the back where predictions of his death might be. If her exploits were to harm anyone, they might be responsible for hu'Narmin's demise too.

They weren't there.

She tried the middle. Nothing again.

Okay, so obviously, the first foretelling he cared to divine was his own end. Fair enough. She flipped to the front of the book and leafed through a few pages. These passages were as cryptic as bad riddles from someone trying to sound too clever for their abilities. Clearly not everyone was meant to be a poet. She stopped on one page, "Destiny." This prophesy held promise.

> Someday I die though better yet,
> The mystery will unfold;
> I'll be so dim that I'll forget,
> This is my destiny.
> But I'll profess:
> Death is best
> When memories go away,
> And others face their own uncertain destiny.
> With not a thought of what I've seen,
> I'll be glad that I am dead,

For times come soon when change must be,
Rebirth is my soon destiny.
Fear not this tree,
My death she'll morn
But not for plans she's made,
Her visit sets the stage of Mankind's destiny.
For one who follows unafraid,
For some he will presage;
Her plans, not hers, will be fulfilled,
Great Gears of Destiny!
Through darkened paths comes Dick hu'Mar,
Who's chasing the wrong thing;
Men's fate he holds both near and far,
And death's true destiny.
One man—one Bule,
hu'Mar—ka'Shino,
And me no more a tool,
You and me they'll kill—tis their destiny.
We'll war in vain;
The ground will crack and tremble.
No blood run cold will offer gain;
We're but slaves to destiny.
Death will come in splendid glory,
For when the world will shake,
The next few lines she read silently.
The Tomb in lava's crematory,
Will change our destiny.

Ka'Shino shoved the book into hu'Narmin's hands. So, was Dick hu'Mar, of all people, responsible for hu'Narmin's future death? Or was she? Whether intentionally or not, hu'Narmin had left out some crucial details. It did mention lava, but only in respect to the Great Clutch. There were incriminating things in here though, and not at all conceivable. For one, she never planned on seeing hu'Mar again. Also, she had no intention of killing hu'Narmin, though, maybe this meant that his and other's deaths would be the result of her upcoming actions. This wasn't what she hoped to see. It even called her out. The tree was no doubt a play on her name, but it also mentioned her actual name.

She could very well be one of the last people to visit hu'Narmin. Someone would read that book and possibly be put onto Dick hu'Mar, and if they saw her here now, herself and her people too. She briefly considered ripping out those last few pages and running, but hu'Narmin had taken it back and was cradling the thing like an infant, she didn't dare. He could raise an alarm, and it'd be like robbing from a small child. Sure, she could pry the thing from his hands, but he would make a terribly loud fuss over it. Maybe later, when he was asleep.

She'd also have to silence that fish. She'd do it when she came back for the book. The fish had hidden itself under a small rocky arch at the bottom of the bowl. She glared at the thing, unsure if it noticed. If it did see her, then as a palsy to humans, it might understand the threat she posed and keep silent. But she planned to kill it later, whether it tattled or not. What choice did she have? She couldn't risk it interfering.

She adjusted her goggles as Crazy Ish filled her teacup from a sixth kettle. How many kettles could one man have?

"I hope I haven't kept you waiting, dear, but my mind isn't as good as it used to be. I all but forgot that I had company," he said sincerely, the book still tucked under one arm.

He hadn't had much time to heat this pot of tea, so he drained it quickly. He poured himself another cup. "I apologize. I feel so thirsty all of a sudden. Could I pour you another cup also?"

Ka'Shino shook her head and raised her hand. "Goodbye, Ish hu'Narmin." She hadn't gotten the answer she wanted, but she'd gotten the answer she needed, which was more a sense of urgency and distraction than relief. It was enough. She'd do what was required of her. As the prophesy affirmed, she "Will change our destiny."

Chapter 5
A Sour Aftertaste

Vinegar raised his rump high into the air, like a blood beetle about to bite, and sprayed the wall. Dick hu'Mar closed his eyes and slowly exhaled through pursed lips. He would not let the gesture of disapproval goad him. Hu'Mar finally had a break: Jodeign ka'Nairie, a client with money and style. Most of all, she was single. He didn't want to imagine the possibilities, but when your only companion in a new city was a cat, possibilities imagined themselves for you.

He'd arrived four months ago. Admittedly, not much had happened since arriving. He liked to think that most of this time was spent catching up to the culture and struggling to make a chip. It wasn't a matter of ambition or hard work: of that—he had plenty to spare. So why did he feel—

"Hey, Dick hu' Distracted," Vinegar said with minimal sound. Cats often meowed or did some other annoying noises when they wanted to communicate, but most of their language was in body motion.

"I'm never distracted," hu'Mar replied.

He knew that to Vinegar, his speech sounded little more than a bunch of "wala-shula-wala blah blahs." But when combined with the little body language he unconsciously expressed, the cat understood him and all other humans. Being a palsy was all about the ability to understand a different species fluently, even when their form of communication was foreign to how your mind was wired.

"What was up with that first girl? She seemed very nice," Vinegar asked as he curled around to sniff the stub where his tail had been.

"You're only saying that because she called me a stupid Tough."

"Well." Vinegar uncurled and tossed his head up and to the side like an arrogant aristocrat. "She at least got the first half right. As for the second half, we both know you're a washout."

"You're just mad at losing your tell tail." Hu'Mar buttoned a vest and slid the desk drawer open. He deposited the salines into his money bag that he kept tied to his side.

"You're so prejudice," Vinegar added.

Okay, since Vinegar's last insult failed to produce a response, where was he going with this one? Vinegar held grudges better than any human, male or female, hu'Mar had ever met. Like a comedian added humor bits to his routines, Vinegar had a whole collection of insults and was always delighted to add more to his list.

"Remember, I have a better nose than you," Vinegar said. "I could smell your desire for Jodeign ka'Nairie. That other girl was as good-looking as any human I've ever seen, but because she's the wrong color, you wouldn't even take her money."

"And those red eyes?" hu'Mar asked.

Vinegar shuddered. "Okay, those were a little disturbing, but on the whole, she's a human, you're a human?"

"I don't tell you which felines to chase, so don't lecture me on humans." Hu'Mar paused as three small battle chariots raced past the streets below, their owners shouting and goading each other.

Aside from horseback or simply walking, these chariots were the most common form of transportation around Spur Central. Each had only one or two occupants who stood in the wheeled basket and was pulled by two strong horses. Back where he came from, there were very few Toughs. Most folks were farmers, laborers, merchants, and aristocrats. They preferred to travel sitting down, in carriages, which made a lot more sense. They often used the same number of horses as a Tough chariot, but carried a lot more people.

When hu'Mar heard a fssss sound, he side-glanced Vinegar, who was spraying the door of the apartment. "What are you doing, you stinking skunk?"

Vinegar stretched out, pretending not to hear.

"Real mature of you."

Vinegar wasn't always in a pissy mood. When he wasn't, hu'Mar actually enjoyed the cat's company. But on days like this, he wanted to kick the animal through the window. Thinking of windows, this place needed airing out. Few things smelled worse than cat urine, and this place would need to air out for weeks to get rid of Vinegar's protest.

Vinegar then lifted his head high, back to hu'Mar, utterly indifferent. He was making a point of how little he cared. Vinegar skittered sideways, then over-corrected and landed on his back.

Hu'Mar folded his arms and nodded. Vinegar couldn't act too snobby when he couldn't even keep his balance yet.

In three strides, hu'Mar was at the single window.

"First you take my tail, now you take my sunning spot?" Vinegar said, hurrying back to reclaim his windowsill.

Hu'Mar ignored him. He wasn't taking away light, he was adding it. Only one shutter was open, so hu'Mar swung the second one out. Then he leaned out the window to latch the wooden panel to the exterior wall so that no wind could bang the thing around while he was out. The fresh sulfuric air was a relief to the musty cat urine that clouded his apartment.

Some days, hu'Mar wished he'd never palsied a cat. Any other animal would've done. If he'd been smart, he would've known that cats were easy enough to understand without palsying them. All they ever seemed to say was, "I don't care one bit about you; feed me; and leave me alone!"

Hard Boiled Cabbage: Big Trouble In Spur Central

Hu'Mar rested his thick forearms on the windowsill and suffered another breath. Now Nebylon had nice air, but he could never go back. His head would be on a chopping block if he showed his face again. They wouldn't risk a faulty hangman's gallows a second time.

Below, he had a great view of Jodeign ka'Nairie as she mounted her large tan horse. Her purse was in one hand, a gourd full of hair stiffener in the other. After she'd left, she'd dutifully stopped by Thelma ka'Skrut's place where the two gabbed over hair care for longer than necessary.

Apparently, they both shared a passion for perfectly manicured hair. Stupid. That was why he owned a hat. Of the little conversation he'd overheard while choking down his cold soggy cabbage, ka'Skrut relied solely on her own hair styling products and abilities, while ka'Nairie had a hair stylist that frequently touched up hers.

Ka'Nairie snapped at the stableboy. He removed the horse's five-gallon hat from his own head while he slid the reins over the horse's head. The hat, something that would look like an oversized human pigpuncher's hat, had the relative dimensions and style of a fedora when the stableboy replaced it on the horse's larger head. Two slits had been cut for the horse's ears, and it wore it like a gentleman. Clearly, the horse had palsied humans, so it could easily understand them, but for whatever reason, was currently unbonded.

"That's the only reason I stick around. Can you imagine me, wearing such a ridiculous thing on my head?" Vinegar said.

"If you wore anything, you'd need a helmet."

Vinegar ignored the jab or maybe tried to turn his disgust in a direction that couldn't come back to bite him. "Can you believe, I actually saw those two sharing carrots? I'd never put anything in my mouth that a human had already slobbered on."

Hu'Mar adjusted his own hat and left Vinegar at the windowsill. There was a real temptation to push the cat out. See how it liked the three-story drop then. Hu'Mar controlled his anger. "What do you think of her, really?"

"Well, I saw her hit the stableboy." Vinegar yawned. "So

she can't be half bad."

"What, just now? I didn't see that?" Hu'Mar leaned out the window.

"No, I didn't mean your dream lust," Vinegar said with obvious annoyance. "I meant that pale female."

"Why do I even bother asking you?" Hu'Mar slumped and admired ka'Nairie as she mounted her ride.

Vinegar yawned again.

"Oh, so now it's the silent treatment?"

Vinegar stared at him. "It's not dignified for me to address the lower life forms so casually."

"Oh, please," hu'Mar guffawed. "If it's undignified, it's only because cats talk far too much. Why else would there be so many books about talking cats that never get read?"

"If humans were more literate, they might get read." Vinegar prepared to jump off the windowsill.

Hu'Mar watched, ready to laugh. The pressure was on.

Vinegar hesitated only a moment, then to both their astonishment, Vinegar landed on his feet.

"Wow," Vinegar said aloud. "That felt so—right. Anyhow, Dick hu'Disgraced, even if humans were more on a cat's level, you personally would still be the bottom buffoon." Then haughty as ever, Vinegar took two steps before he lost his balance, cantered, and smashed the side of his head into the wall.

Hu'Mar laughed. He couldn't help it. He almost teared up. "Ho, oh. Why didn't I cut your tail off years ago?"

Vinegar hissed.

"What do you say we go for a walk?" Hu'Mar wiped his eye.

"If it's all the same to you, I'd rather take a nap, forget today ever happened."

"Come on, I'll treat you to dinner on the way. I won't even make you catch it yourself."

Vinegar lay on the floor, too annoyed to stand. "Don't tell me you're bringing your leftover boiled leaves with us. You know I wouldn't dare touch that stuff."

"You must think I'm really stupid."

"I'm glad we agree on your stupidity," Vinegar said.

Since Vinegar wasn't used to walking tailless, a long walk would be difficult. Hu'Mar needed him though. If not for his small sneaking size, then for the fact that being close by, meant that hu'Mar wouldn't act too strange, like ka'Nairie's horse. People who palsied needed their bonds near, or they'd adopt the other's mannerisms.

"Fine," Vinegar said at last. "But don't assume this makes everything right between us."

"This is why I never got married." Hu'Mar stepped out of his apartment as he pulled an overcoat on his broad sleeveless shirt and vest. "Why would I ever need a wife when I have a talking cat?"

"The reason you didn't get married, is that females of your species are too clever to get involved with you," Vinegar said as he followed hu'Mar down the stairway.

"How is it that you can track a mouse through a thistle field, but you struggle on any decently smooth surface," hu'Mar ribbed, not needing to watch Vinegar to know he was avoiding the splinters in the fraying wooden floor as carefully as an old-timer who was one fall away from never getting up again.

"How is it that on a perfectly hot evening like this, you humans still prefer to wear all that extra fluff?" Vinegar countered. "You're one of the few species in the entire animal kingdom that feels some illogical need to wear more than you were born with. On top of that, most of your clothing is impractical and restrictive. Explain that to me."

Hu'Mar didn't have a good comeback. Cross species cultural differences were always hard to bridge and took supreme patience and understanding to cope with. Vinegar was never willing, and hu'Mar wasn't in the mood for it right now. The street was busy as hu'Mar settled on a direction.

"Hey, Dick hu'Hairless, when's dinner?" Vinegar asked, veering as he ran along the packed earth to catch up, but hu'Mar wasn't cutting the cat any breaks. If anything, he quickened his pace.

"Just one fast visit first," hu'Mar said, annoyed with the

hairless comment. "Besides, it's still early." In fact, he had a very nice thick set of dark brown hair, and a healthy shadow on his face that he kept close shaven, not to mention the very manly hair that covered his chest and arms. It was about as close to fur as a human could get, not that he wanted fur.

The smell of sulfur from Mount Exclusion was strong tonight. The volcanic activity had slowly accelerated the whole time hu'Mar had been here. No doubt, the next shifting would come soon. Hu'Mar wasn't sure that he wanted to be around when that happened.

He paused only once, and that was when Vinegar screeched, "Ouch!" Vinegar had probably run into a street sign. There was hardly anything else for him to walk into except a Tough's boot. There were plenty of those, and they had a funny way of finding contact with smaller animals like Vinegar whenever they could. He suppressed a chuckle. Sometimes, the cat deserved a dose of humility.

Vinegar trailed at an ever-expanding distance. Hu'Mar wanted to glance back every now and then to make sure that he hadn't veered under a chariot, but that would be showing more compassion than he cared to show. Besides, Vinegar, nor any cat for that matter, would want to be seen following a human like a chick following a hen. Eagerness to follow a human could really ruin a cat's reputation, something Vinegar cared very much about. As he allowed for more distance between them, hu'Mar barely noticed his bond to Vinegar weaken.

In this hub, eight alleyways met. If Vinegar got lost, he could home in on their bond. There were several such hubs around. All of Spur Central was patterned after giant gears, the hubs being the center of each little gear. This one was far from the biggest hub, but it was full this hour. Several ministers with large, polished canes prodded three sorry prisoners into the middle where a sunken platform gave a full view to every morbid passerby. If it was a crier, it might be different. News was always welcomed, but a minister's trial—hu'Mar didn't have the stomach for it.

The whole purpose of developing a city of Toughs at the

edge of Mount Exclusion was to create a pocket of fanatical ascensionists, and they were fanatical all right. Back in Nebylon, hu'Mar considered himself a good ascensionist. Moving here took most of that out of him. That apathy alone could get him into serious trouble if it was known. It would be even worse if he were arrested.

For some reason, working for a politician gave him the feeling that the ministers would eventually get involved in his case, and then things would go badly. Why else would ka'Nairie come to him instead of them for a simple case of theft? There had to be more to this than she'd told him. If he were smart, he would've given her money back and walked away from this case.

He'd made up his mind.

But had he? His mind shifted almost imperceptibly. He scratched his ear. Maybe he could keep the money and tell ka'Nairie that he hadn't found any useful info for her. That might work.

Then his mind grew steady again. No! He couldn't back down on a case he'd accepted. He was Dick hu'Mar, his reputation was at stake. He saw every commitment through to the end, no matter how hard or dangerous. Even if it bit him in the heel. But this one shouldn't be like that at all.

He growled. "Vinegar, get over here."

Vinegar finally caught up to him. "Someone sounds grumpy."

"I had to talk myself out of being lazy because you trailed too far behind and weakened our bond."

"How do you think I felt," Vinegar retorted. "I was struck by this unnerving sense of duty, drive, and self-importance, which made me want to catch up to you, against all my better judgements."

Hu'Mar ignored the slight. It wasn't his fault how palsy bonds worked.

At the intersection of the hub, the ministers hushed the crowd. Hu'Mar tried to ignore the proceedings. Today's display of ignorant fervor earned a disgusted sneer from him. Vinegar trotted closer. Neither felt comfortable with the human barbarianism that might claim either of them on a bad day.

"Think those ones are guilty?" Vinegar asked, failing to sound indifferent.

Hu'Mar touched his neck. Scars from his own execution in Nebylon still bothered him. He remembered how the rope made his neck itch, how each fiber ripped and shredded his flesh when they dropped the floor out from under him. He'd been lucky then. If the Beadledom ministers had tried to execute him, hu'Mar would've surely died that day.

Sure, the Beadledom sent ministers into Nebylon too. It sent traveling ministers abroad to all kingdoms and townships, regardless of who governed those lands. They preached the gospel of ascensionism and enforced much of the law. Who better to keep tabs on the other kingdoms, than a government run by the biggest and best fighters? Since they dug their fingers into the other governments' business, they had to be strong and intimidating. The ministers were annoying, but those who ran the Beadledom relied upon more than mere arrogance. They had to hold a high degree of cunning, compared to their peers. Jodeign ka'Nairie was just the type to contend for such an office.

As far as trials and executions went, the Ministry took too much pleasure in them. Sure, they might do a hanging every now and then, but only if they wanted to watch you squirm. No quick drops from them, just slow strangulations. Usually they opted for more sporting methods. Hu'Mar had lucked out. Not many men could claim to have dangled on the end of a rope, only to have the lynching tower collapse.

In Nebylon's defense, most executions were conducted by ministers, so those Nebylon guards had little experience, especially when hu'Mar knew the carpenter who had built the gallows. He'd saved the man's daughter once, and so the workmanship that went into the wooden structure somehow was less than able to support hu'Mar's weight.

There would be no such luck for the prisoners in the middle of this hub, surrounded by blind ministers who were more than happy to dole out their brand of perceived justice. Hu'Mar preferred to be anywhere but here.

Hard Boiled Cabbage: Big Trouble In Spur Central

One of the ministers called out, "Billy hu'Wier, suspected of blasphemy, caught transporting brass ingots for what could only be the fabrication of black-market gears, how do you plead?"

Hu'Mar cringed. They're executing a man on a hunch of blasphemy? He kept walking but couldn't help peeking at the buffoonery.

Billy hu'Wier, a lanky man with arms like knotted oaks, pleaded, "I swear, I'm just a weapons maker. I've never built a gear I wasn't authorized to make!"

"Few weapons are made from brass anymore," the minister argued. "Steel has taken the market over completely."

"I'm only selling my weapons to kids! You think they can afford nice steel?" hu'Wier defended.

"If you're so good at making weapons, then I assume you're good at using them too. To be fair, and in traditional Spur fashion, your trial will end with a final test. If you win, then you will be freed. If you lose, then may you be stronger in your next life!"

The minister tossed hu'Wier a wooden cane and three large ministers stepped forward with canes of their own. Vinegar was lucky. Tall muscular men and women blocked his view, but hu'Mar's gaze was drawn to the absurd odds. This trial would end the same as always, in execution.

Cheers, shouts, and fleshy wooden thumps echoed loudly as hu'Wier was beaten to death. The display prodded hu'Mar onward, faster. What sick impulse insisted that he notice the injustice of it all? He argued with his conscience as he tried to ignore it. Finally, another larger street. A little more distance, and the injustice was behind him. The fading voice of the minister could still be distinguished as he called, "Our next suspect—"

Hu'Mar could've been a minister at one point. It paid terribly because most ministers were zealous enough that they didn't demand much money. He'd even had the religious zeal when he had first moved here, but their style of law quickly drained his fervor.

Four hubs later, hu'Mar passed a city crier. "Men on trial—four hubs to the East. Political debate, tomorrow afternoon at the Spur Central Amphitheater. Today's news, brought to you by Brink hu'Statin and Sons, Spur Central's leading manufacture of spear tassels: Distract your enemy with a flourish of color, personalized with any embroidered logo of your choice. Buy two, get one half off, this week only."

Hu'Mar refocused on the case at hand. Vinegar was at least able to walk in a straight line now, if he really concentrated on it.

They passed one alley with a furry street gang.

"Despicable," Vinegar said. He'd often complained that to be feral was to suggest that cats were inferior to all other species.

The street cats in this ragged gang would hide from all humans, rather than use them for their own comfort. They were wiry little kitties, but they all eyed Vinegar with reverenced awe. Any cat that could lose his tail and still hold his head high while walking among the humans would have to be a tough customer, or at least, that was what hu'Mar read in their expressions. One scrawny feline even cast wanting glances at Vinegar. Hu'Mar's bond allowed him to discern the meanings behind the slight fragrance of desire that rippled like heat from her.

Yeah, whatever Vinegar's body language said. Losing his tail wasn't the end of the world. He could use this, if he really wanted to.

After thirty minutes, and surprisingly no complaints, Vinegar returned to his predictable nature. "My paws are aching. I thought you said we were going for a little walk. Do I look like a horse? Next thing you know, you'll be nailing metal shoes to my paws."

"I never said it would be little," hu'Mar said. "But relax. We're there, sort of."

"And where is there?"

The place was pre-suburb, on the edge of town, next to Lake Tallow. On this side of the natural moat that ringed Mount Exclusion, the tall unforgiving cliffs of that holy mountain loomed over the city. Guards were rare here. No animal in their right mind would attempt swimming across, only to face the challenge of those cliffs to gain access to the Tomb of Ascension. There were flying animals, but the guards had probably thought of ways to deal with them, like the nets stretched in certain places in the waterways to block the marine life. So with relatively low probability of being attacked from this part of town, the population was less sparce. The homes weren't the crammed apartment style that Vinegar lived in with hu'Mar. They weren't the nicest either, but they at least afforded more privacy. Plus, Vinegar wouldn't have to worry about freak indoor rainstorms, unless it actually rained since only half these homes looked like they'd keep out the water.

Hu'Mar evaded Vinegar's question. Instead he asked a few questions of his own to every passing person. They walked for another block before they found it. Stacked logs surrounded the small yard, and the only flowers that grew within were on wild slab berry bushes.

Slab berries were only good for attracting paper wasps and people with death wishes. The rancid-meat smell of the blossoms turned hu'Mar's stomach. Even worse was the smell of the distillery around back. He couldn't see it, but that smell could be from nothing else. He'd tried the alcoholic drink once, and that was enough to last a lifetime. Slab arrack was only for the most serious of drinkers.

Careful not to alarm the wasps that swarmed around the slab berries and the house, hu'Mar crept closer to the door. Vinegar didn't mind. He had a lot less skin exposed to the annoying bugs, so he sat on the porch while hu'Mar knocked a sleeve-covered fist on the door. The last thing he needed was to smash a half living wasp against the heavy wooden planks. Each knock rattled the whole house and sent up a cloud of wasps buzzing around the bushes next to him, their countless humming wings practically vibrated the inside of his skull. Much more of this could drive a man crazy.

"Absurd humans," Vinegar said, then curled under himself and licked his butt, pausing only a moment to add, "You'd never see a cat smacking his paw that hard against a huge slab of wood."

Hu'Mar wanted to say something, but words were completely inadequate as Vinegar's gritty tongue scraped at his own anus. In mid-lick, a wasp landed on the tip of his nose. Vinegar froze just as the door to the cottage cracked open. As much as hu'Mar wanted to watch Vinegar's little drama play out, he had work to do.

"Who is it?" The voice sounded old and gnarled, like a scrub oak that had drunk too much slab arrack.

Right before hu'Mar averted his attention, a second wasp landed on Vinegar's frozen nose. He couldn't help but smile as he faced the woman at the door. Even the slow drifting stench of her breath, which completely overpowered the sulfur and threatened to wilt the hair under his hat, couldn't dampen his humor.

"Renu ka'Feebal?" he asked.

Vinegar, careful not to disturb the passengers on his nose, sidled up to hu'Mar and squeaked so softly it could've been from a mouse he'd swallowed earlier. Hu'Mar refused to be baited. One glance into Vinegar's pleading eyes would be too much, and hu'Mar had work to do. Vinegar could deal with his own problem.

The sour old hag could've been forty years hu'Mar's senior, or she could've been less than five years older. Her weathered face, most likely from hard living, made it difficult to tell. If hu'Mar was a betting man, and he was, he'd say she was a lot younger than she looked. He understood that himself. He was in his mid-forties, but most people mistook him for being mid-fifties.

She shifted a toothpick in her mouth, then spit, as if to ask, "what's it to you?" Yep, this had to be Renu ka'Feebal alright. She wasn't your average Tough though. Instead of a tight muscular frame, she had a loose layer of flab, covered by an even looser layer of skin. Somehow, though, she looked ready and willing to wallop any muscle-bound Tough that pushed her too far. He didn't know yet what to think of her. Vinegar should be happy though. Her loogie had landed on his nose and scared away his two wasps.

Vinegar hissed at the retreating insects then at ka'Feebal

Hard Boiled Cabbage: Big Trouble In Spur Central

for her method. Wetting his paw, he tried to lick himself clean, but the slime smeared into his forehead. When he licked his paw a second time, his eyes went wide, and then he got acrobatic. Ka'Feebal's saliva probably had a nasty punch to it from the slab arrack. Not many people could handle the drink, and she made her own.

"I'm interested in relics," hu'Mar said. It was hard to hear himself think with the cat making such a racket.

Vinegar kept hacking, gagging, and meowing as he writhed around and tried shoveling his face into the ground. Hu'Mar nudged the cat with his foot, reminding Vinegar to show some manners. Instead, the cat ran down the dirt path. It dragged its head in the dirt, then its tongue.

Hu'Mar returned his attention to the dealer. "Can I come in?"

"Who told youz I worked with relics, boy?" she slurred. "I hain't got nothin' to tell no minister. Git outa here fore I get annoyed."

He was no minister, but she'd never buy that defense. No, there were only two ways to get to a woman like this. He didn't have enough money to buy her a drink, so instead, "When I said I'm interested in relics, ka'Feebal, what I meant was I have a thing for sour old ladies. Call me crazy, but I think I'm in love."

Ka'Feebal's lips parted in a half sideways smile, revealing two incomplete rows of perfectly yellow teeth. She stroked her gnarled gray hair but got her fingers stuck in it. She nearly lost her balance getting her hand out. It was funny how much she reminded him of Vinegar. Then, faster than hu'Mar could respond to, she slugged him in the face.

Hu'Mar blinked away the stars that floated in circles around ka'Feebal's pudgy wrinkled face. He crawled to his feet, stood tall. She'd played her hand, surprisingly strong. That punch was a traditional Tough greeting, and maybe even a "fight me for my heart, if you dare." He didn't dare, but he had to get her to let him in. If he slugged her back, then according to Tough tradition, she'd assume they were courting. Instead, he'd have to take a page from ka'Nairie's book and play this like no minister would dare. One quick glance at his retreating partner caused him to hesitate, but determination won out. He shot both hands toward ka'Feebal's head. She didn't flinch. He didn't punch.

Instead, he grabbed her tangled mess of hair in both hands and said, "What a woman!" Then he slammed his lips into hers and nearly got drunk on her saliva.

She pulled back, stared at him through hazy eyes, then smiled. "Ha!" she practically squealed, "Come on in, boy. You hain't no lawman. They's not abalo-abbblla-hmmm, they's not can see true beauty when it's standin' before'em."

Ka'Feebal fell backward. Hu'Mar stumbled in after her, wheezing from the sour aftertaste. He hoped he never had to kiss her ever again. In comparison, even Vinegar's butt licking might've been less disgusting. If there was anyone else that could help him, he would've rather gone there, but given how rare relics were, and how closely they were regulated by the Beadledom, there weren't many experts he could trust. Plus, ka'Feebal was on ka'Nairie's list of people who knew about her relic. Careful not to look too closely at her loose-fitting, stretched nightgown, which probably hadn't been changed in days, he helped her to her feet. It was hard to imagine that she would be an expert at anything other than irritating her neighbors.

"Let's go sit down," he said

The house was dark and dusty. The smell of her urine was stronger here than even the cat urine in hu'Mar's apartment. The smell aside, how could anyone live like this? Sure, his own apartment was depressing in a barren sort of way, but this place took depressing to excess. A sea of empty wine skins flooded the room, and wicker furniture jutted around its shoreline, deformed from too many nights or days of being slept on. The only other things of interest were some fairly well-kept maps. They displayed not only Spur central but most of the known world. They were very detailed, and maybe she'd drawn them all herself from travels she'd had in her younger days. It was amazing how the world looked so much like a gear with the major lakes shaped like moats around each continent, dissected only by a few rivers, and Mount Exclusion at the very center of it all.

Hard Boiled Cabbage: Big Trouble In Spur Central

The rest of the house, though messy, was typical of these nicer neighborhoods. She had a kitchen and a sleeping room. Plenty big for one person or even a few people. She did have a heavy wooden time peace in one corner, but it didn't even have any hands. Around the face of it, it read: Too Sober.

"Did ya bring me some booze?"

"I never bring my own booze on a first date," hu'Mar said as he led her into the main room. "I'd hate to be taken advantage of."

Ka'Feebal tried slapping him in the face. She missed, then plopped down in her chair. It groaned under her weight. Hu'Mar walked to her kitchen. It wasn't hard to find the liquor since it was where all her food should've been.

Every dish was dirty, so he wiped down two metal cups and debated cleaning them with soap. He unstopped the skin of homemade slab arrack and took a whiff. He coughed through teary eyes. Nope. This would sterilize anything. He poured the alcohol into the cups.

A splash of setting sunlight lit the wall, and hu'Mar left the cups alone for a moment while he leaned against the wall hoping for some radiating warmth, kicking wine skins away as he stretched.

He blinked, then shook his head. "Stupid cat." The thing had walked out of range.

With any luck, Vinegar would realize that he was acting more human, and a cat wants to be human like a human wants to be a cat. Vinegar would find his way back.

Hu'Mar took the cups to ka'Feebal's room.

"You'a brought me a drink, sucha good boy." Ka'Feebal knocked hu'Mar's hat off and ran a hand through his thick dark hair.

Hu'Mar leaned forward and rubbed his forehead into hers. He blinked and shook his head again. "Vinegar!" he cursed through clenched teeth, then picked up his hat. He'd have to be extra careful to act like a normal man.

Ka'Feebal laughed. "A-right mister. What's yer busnis'ere?"

"You sold a relic to a woman some time ago." This was a

guess, but he suspected a safe guess. Ka'Feebal was on ka'Nairie's short list of possible enemies, and in some circles, she had a reputation for dealing with relics. "I need information about it."

She looked through his eyes, literally. Was she staring at the wall behind him? She swayed, brought the cup to her lips, and downed half the cup in one gulp. Her eyes brightened for a moment. "Naturilly, I don't know nothin'bout relics. That's illi-ah-illegoo-illah, hmmm, not lawful, and I'm a very upstanding respeca-respectacle citizen. But you'ere not with'a Beadledom, I can tell. They's too sober. So jusss between you an'me, I-uh, what'er we talkin'bout?"

"Jodeign ka'Nairie. I believe you sold her a couple of black-market relics."

"Never heard of 'er," she said, downed the last of her cup, then looked at it like it had betrayed her by going empty.

Hu'Mar sipped his and nearly choked. His taste buds were on fire, and his skin almost got rich from sweating big salty droplets. "Here." He wheezed as he handed over his cup.

"Oh, sucha sweetheart," she said as she gulped half the cup again. "I don't know this Jodeign ka'Hoochie. But I don' know mosta the people who visit me."

"She bought a bone needle from you. It heals your body but makes you poisonous. Does this sound familiar?"

Ka'Feebal nodded her head as she listened. Only, when hu'Mar had finished talking, she was still nodding her head.

Then he smelled it: the familiar scent of fresh ammonia competed for stale aromatic space in the hovel. It dripped from her chair.

"Um," he said, but her eyes were closed, that head still, nodding, albeit slower. "Ka'Feebal?"

She snored as the last few drops of urine splashed onto the floor.

"Just great." But as long as she was asleep, he could do a little snooping. She was lying. She knew ka'Nairie because ka'Nairie had already said as much. Plus, given ka'Feebal's reputation for dealing in black market bones, there could very easily be a link to ka'Nairie's relic and this lady.

Hard Boiled Cabbage: Big Trouble In Spur Central

He found a strong box with a lock, half buried in the packed earthen floor. He picked it open. It was heaped full of expensive clay wine bottles. This lady, whatever her appearances, obviously had some salt to her name. The bottles, each easily worth as much as hu'Mar made in a month, were half buried in their own thick layer of dirt. This would help keep them cool and keep the box from being stolen.

Hu'Mar locked the box again. There had to be something around here. He looked around for anything else. He was about to give up when he saw the obvious. On the table in front of ka'Feebal, next to a half completed wooden puzzle, was a book titled Obituaries Almanac: Collector's Edition. It was the sort of book that you added a new leaflet to each year.

From the looks of it, it got used a lot. This wasn't unusual in old people's homes. For some reason, they always wanted to reminisce over everyone who was dead. Young people liked the books too, but mostly for the comic relief. Ka'Feebal, though old in appearance, couldn't be much older than himself, hu'Mar decided, and she didn't seem the sort to read for sport. He reached for the book.

The thing usually reported who died, when they'd likely get reborn, and when you too would most likely die. They claimed to use star patterns, cosmic weather theories, and even a secret proprietary clock that was meant to mimic the Gears of Eternity. After years of observing others stake their fortunes on its predictions, hu'Mar was pretty sure the only patterns they really followed came from their marketing studies.

Maybe ka'Feebal cared for such things, but he doubted it. He opened the cover. She snorted and kicked him in the back. He scooted out of her reach while she snored. The first leaflet was as expected: obituaries, jokes, and wooden teeth adhesive ads. Most of the leaflets contained exaggerations of reality, pictures drawn for the purpose of conveying meaning, rather than relying on words.

The Bules invented reading actual words which was one of the many reasons people disliked them and their "progressive" way of thinking. Words, bacterial salves they thought should be shoved into wounds for healing, and mathematics—yikes, that was even worse than words! It was all an assault on traditional ways of living, and people around here liked their traditions.

So the obituaries were broken into several panels, each showing some cartoonish depiction of the person's life. Even if you didn't understand the accompanying words, you could still get the meanings and jokes when you saw a rendition of a dead grandpa in comic form. It was a great way to remember and even laugh your way through the mourning.

Hu'Mar had tried to learn reading once, but he still had to strain. The next several leaflets were sales transactions and notes. Ka'Feebal snorted again.

Hu'Mar studied the woman. She slept on.

"I could really use Vinegar here to read this," hu'Mar said softly to test if ka'Feebal was really out as cold as she appeared.

In truth, it would be easier if Vinegar was here. Years of transactions were recorded here, and it would take forever to fully decipher.

He wished ka'Nairie had told him when she'd acquired the relics. Six years ago? More recently? Best to start with recent transactions and work his way back. He flipped through the pages until he found the right timeframe. Whatever else ka'Feebal was, she was clever. Nobody would ever suspect her of being literate, let alone thorough. It was rare for a non-Bule to be so familiar with the written language.

On a whim, hu'Mar picked one transaction. It wasn't ka'Nairie's, but after carefully sounding out the words, he found references to earlier transactions. He tried it again with another transaction. The painstaking work made his head ache, but these ledgers looked like they could trace every black-market relic back several owners. In fact, many of these relics appeared to have been traded up to four times each. Hu'Mar was no expert on relics, but that seemed like a lot of transactions for something that usually stayed in one's family for generations.

Now for the really hard part. He focused on the approximate timeframe and sounded out each name. "Da-re-z-n-a-a-are-da—Dreznard; Ma-ah-ta-ta—Mat't—Matt . . . no." A

Hard Boiled Cabbage: Big Trouble In Spur Central

few minutes later, "Here, I-s-h—Ish hu' N-ah-r-m-ah-na—Ish hu'Narmin, Ma-ay-z-y hu'Di-i-l-l-i-e—Maizy hu'Dillie," then, "Ja-oh-d-ee-I-ga-na—Jode-igna, no that can't be right . . . what's the rest of it, ka, Na-ah-ir-ie-ee—Nairie, ka'Nairie. Jodeign ka'Nairie. That's got to be it."

Wait, Maizy hu'Dillie and Ish hu'Narmin? Could that really be Crazy Ish, the prophet? He used to own ka'Nairie's relic? And hu'Dillie? Ka'Nairie said that it was a Maizy ka'Dillie that knew about her relic, along with Jef hu'Rino, Duke, and obviously ka'Feebal. So was Maizy a man or a woman? Hu'Rino shouldn't be too hard to track down since hu'Mar recognized the name. Duke might be more challenging. Hu'Mar didn't usually get involved in non-human affairs. From what he'd seen in this book, ka'Feebal might have stolen the relic back, so she could turn around and sell it again for more profit. He'd need to investigate further. Ish hu'Narmin would be a harder visit: the guy's memory was worse than holding water in a wire basket, but as long as he was on this rim of the city, why not stop in?

He needed more info on the relic itself. He had an idea of what it could do, but Jodeign ka'Nairie hadn't been too free with information about the relic she paired it with. Each transaction referenced the pin, but given how thorough ka'Feebal was with this record, she probably had a separate book somewhere that detailed every relics' attributes.

She stirred. Even as drunk as she was, there was no way he'd get through any book in a timely manner, not without Vinegar here to help him. He didn't even know where that book might be. In the meantime, maybe he could learn more from Ish hu'Narmin.

"I'll be back." He patted ka'Feebal's arm.

She didn't even flinch. If a fat woman could be called crusty, that was her. Drunk and irreverent, but under better conditions, she might be cooperative. He resolved to catch her when she was sober, or at least, not so drunk that sleep was preferable to conversation. He needed to know more about her relics and her customers, and especially what she thought about ka'Nairie. Considering how often she resold many of her relics, there was a high probability that she, in fact, was the culprit. But hu'Mar would hold judgement until he gathered a little more info.

Before leaving, he draped a blanket over the sour hag. He liked crusty old women. They didn't play games with you, or at least, the games they did play were a lot more fun. You always knew where you stood, and if you had an extra bottle of hooch, you could always be on their good side.

"We'll talk again soon," hu'Mar promised. "In the meantime, sober up a little, won't you?"

He stepped through the front door, and the hum of hundreds of wasps filled the air. He passed through them without incident, through the weed-infested yard, and finally through the rotten gate where Vinegar stood, shaking. The slab arrack saliva on top of his head had been replaced by a part.

"Nice hairdo," hu'Mar laughed.

"What hair—" Then Vinegar realized what he'd done. While hu'Mar's separation from him had caused him to act like a cat, Vinegar had started acting like a human. At some point, while the cat had been wiping ka'Feebal's loogie, he'd parted the fur on his head like a human might.

Vinegar quickly rubbed his head against a fence post. The neatly combed strands returned to a nest of tangles.

"Don't look so annoyed." Hu'Mar laughed. "You look good with your hair styled."

"You promised dinner," Vinegar's stare said. "Yesterday's mouse feels like it's gnawing a hole in my stomach."

It never failed to surprise hu'Mar how much language the body of an animal could convey. Humans relied too much on words. In hu'Mar's opinion, the world would be a much quieter place if they took that lesson from the wider animal kingdom.

"I'll get your dinner." Of course, humans did have body language too. A really astute man might read it, but they rarely took the effort. That's one thing nobody ever talked about: humans being a palsy to a human. It happened more than most people thought, and some didn't even recognize when it was happening.

Usually it occurred between a man and a woman. Since a

married couple spent so much time together, it often just happened. They were the ones who needed the greatest amount of understanding anyway. Hu'Mar would never understand a woman or any human on that level, mainly because he was already bonded to a stupid cat. Even if his cat died, he could only ever bond another cat.

Jodeign ka'Nairie might be one such palsy. She wasn't married, so she was likely unbonded, but she had a way with people. She was, after all, a politician. She played off people, and most successful politicians were suspected of being human palsies. How else could they manipulate everyone so skillfully?

Vinegar followed close behind as hu'Mar rounded the street corner and headed west, skirting the outer ring of this cog. "You know," Vinegar said, "some humans actually treat cats like the royalty we deserve."

"Funny," hu'Mar said. "But even in those kingdoms, humans hold the throne."

"They might hold the throne in public," Vinegar countered, "but the cats sit on it more than the monarchs of those nations."

"What are you complaining about?" hu'Mar asked. "You know as well as I do that if I hadn't bonded you when I did, you could've easily ended up feral." It was true, too. Vinegar couldn't argue with that though he'd probably try.

"Yeah, cats might have a couple early months that shape the rest of our lives, but at least we're not like humans. You guys have a whole decade of adolescence. And where a wild cat might only live for five years, feral humans can last as long as eighty!"

Well, the cat had a point there.

After two more cogs and spokes, hu'Mar felt that familiar tug of a palsy too far from its bond. He turned around.

Vinegar had stopped a block away. He'd gotten distracted by some distant, feral cats. Hu'Mar was about to call after him, but instead he watched and read Vinegar. Vinegar was apparently reminiscing about his youth. It was no secret that Vinegar regretted his childhood stupidity of deciding to bond with a human. Despite how badly he talked about feral cats, Vinegar might've even preferred going feral as opposed to living in hu'Mar's shadow. Feral cats lived shorter, harder lives, but they were their own cat. Pride in oneself was a thing hu'Mar could respect. Besides, what was a shorter life when you could simply be reborn again?

Still, they did make a good partnership most times. Hu'Mar would work the clients, and Vinegar would snoop around or play cat-burglar, digging up clues during hu'Mar's investigations. They never had much money, but they got by. What more could a couple of honest scoundrels ask for?

"You about done feeling sorry for yourself?" hu'Mar hollered.

Vinegar snapped his head up. "I was thinking about dinner, and how there are no food joints on the outer teeth of this cog," he meowed.

"Sure, you were," hu'Mar said. "But yeah, we're going to get dinner. It's just that if we don't stop at Crazy Ish's place while we're in the neighborhood, then we'll have to backtrack later."

"Why bother?" Vinegar asked.

"Crazy Ish." Hu'Mar paused to study a street sign. "His name was in ka'Feebal's list of past clients, and it's the only name I actually know. Since ka'Feebal's worthless till she sobers up, that leaves hu'Narmin or his fish to help me understand more about this relic, and maybe why ka'Feebal sold the same thing multiple times."

He didn't have high expectations for this meeting. The last time hu'Mar had met the prophet, he'd gotten a bellyache of tea and a lot of nonsense.

Hu'Mar would be lucky if Crazy Ish could remember his breakfast, let alone a relic he'd owned a few years ago. But that fish of his had a decent memory. Hopefully, the fish knew something. Relics were treasured things, so people didn't just own them for a few months to a few years at a time. They kept them for life, even generations, passing them down, but never getting rid of outright. So why was ka'Feebal reselling them over and over again?

This case was looking like it would be pretty cut and dry.

Hard Boiled Cabbage: Big Trouble In Spur Central

The dealer sells a relic, steals it back, then hocks it to the next unsuspecting customer. Hu'Narmin had obviously dealt with her before, and if hu'Mar's suspicions panned out, he could pocket his pay, go home, and waste another few weeks wondering where his next payday would come from. It was almost depressing. He was too good at this sort of thing to be living like a bum. If only there were a better market for people with his skills. Money might not bring happiness, but it could fix a lot of problems.

The sun left only a red horizon to light the exterior of Ish hu'Narmin's cottage.

"Hey, you said this guy has a fish?" Vinegar asked.

Hu'Mar shrugged. "Yeah, but it's bonded to hu'Narmin."

Since time and animals were different attunations, one could bond both. Most prophets did so to preserve some memory, though a fish was a funny thing to bond. Maybe some fish lived as long as a man, but they had very small brains. Then again, if brain size was any determinant factor in intelligence or memory, a lot of humans weren't using nearly enough of theirs. So maybe size wasn't all that important.

"Maybe I won't starve after all." Vinegar ran ahead to the front door.

Chapter 6

A Simple Case of Theft Turned Deadly

Dick hu'Mar stopped short of knocking on the door. The noises inside weren't frail and gentle like the way he remembered Ish hu'Narmin's voice. Ministers were here, along with some ranting lady whom they were trying to calm. The only thing worse than a pissy cat was a hysterical woman. The smart thing to do, would be to walk away, come back another time. So hu'Mar let himself in.

In cases such as this, he often ran across the Ministry in some capacity or another. It was a hazard of the job.

Vinegar poked his head around hu'Mar, looked from one side to the other, then rudely squeezed into the house. Hu'Mar followed, latching the door behind him.

The whole house was dark. The illumination inside, came from two oil lamps. One rested on the table in the main room while the other danced behind shadow figures in the kitchen where the ministers were talking. Hu'Mar lifted the unattended oil lamp and examined the room. Vinegar didn't seem to mind the dark. That was one thing hu'Mar couldn't do, even if Vinegar left him too far. He might take on the personality of a cat, but physically, he'd never see in the dark like a cat.

Hard Boiled Cabbage: Big Trouble In Spur Central

As his eyes adjusted, light from the lamp reflected from the shiny brass surfaces of several tea kettles strewn about. He brushed his fingers across one as he passed it.

Cold.

Ish hu'Narmin was dead. He'd gathered as much from what little he'd overheard. That put a bind in his gears. He'd hoped to learn something about ka'Feebal or the relic from the old prophet. It was a long shot before, and now it was likely impossible. He should leave, yet something about this whole thing felt wrong. It smelled even worse. Was there a connection between ka'Nairie's missing relic and its former owner? Was his investigation about to turn dangerous? Was hu'Narmin's death natural, an accident, or murder, and if murder, why would anyone bother to kill a previous owner of the relic?

Then the lamp light caught the crystal bowl. Crazy Ish's palsy partner floated sideways in the brown water.

"Bolt me down," he whispered. Murder. It had to be. Why else would both hu'Narmin and his fish be dead?

Vinegar leapt onto a couch near the fish. "So much for picking Goldie's brain." Vinegar pawed the floating fish. "Looks like it's been dead only an hour or two." Then, as if to sample the marinade, Vinegar licked up three splashes of water before jumping back. "Uggh," he meowed. "That water tastes like boiled plants."

"Hu'Narmin always had a thing for tea," hu'Mar agreed as he crept slowly to the kitchen, stopped, then clenched his fists. Who would want to do this to a senile old man?

"Evening, boys!" hu'Mar boomed as he entered the kitchen.

Two ministers, a man and a dog, and the hysterical lady all stood around Crazy Ish's body which lay on the floor beside a tea kettle.

"Say, mister," the human minister said. "Whose you think yous is?"

"He's got a flat nose," Vinegar commented. "A good sign that he's taken a few strong knuckles to the face."

True, this guy could likely take a punch alright and return

the favor, but with a thin writing pen or a mini dagger poking through his knuckles to level the field. He might have smarts, but with no brawn in a place like Spur Central, his only chance at surviving as a minister would be to play dirty.

"Right," the dog barked, shifting the bone dangling from his jaws like a man chewing on a large toothpick. "Rish ish argh ach'ive criiime scene." Clearly an unbonded human palsy, as it was so rare for one to even attempt speaking human. The fact that the dog stood on his hind legs was further evidence of this. He had with the same red fur as the man's red hair.

"A fresh minister and a talking dog. How long have you been without a palsy bond, poochie?"

The dog growled softly.

The dog couldn't be the minister's palsy because ministers weren't allowed to bond other animals since it was almost akin to treason in some circles. The only exception were special agents, spies commissioned to keep tabs on certain other species. In most cases, ministers merely kept a list of palsies that they could use as interpreters. It was funny how some people forgot that all animals had eyes and brains and, for a price, were usually willing to rat someone out, except coincidentally for rats who were a very tight knit sort.

"The names is Banner hu'Tanner," the man said, "and this'us my partner, Bacon."

"Hu'Mar, Dick hu'Mar, fortune teller." He stuck out his hand to shake.

The minister ignored the hand and spit on the floor. He clearly didn't think much of private investigators.

Then the lady, a tall skinny brunette, shrieked. "Dick hu'Mar! He did it! He did it!" Her knobby knuckled finger pointed with conviction straight at hu'Mar's face.

He wanted to swat the thing away, not so much because of the false accusation, but because her finger looked as if it belonged on a skeleton. She inspired images of old woody asparagus wearing a long, black tube dress. It was kind of creepy. "And who are you?" he asked her.

When she only crossed her arms, hu'Tanner said, "This'us

Yolick ka'Kilden. She doos the cleanin arounds here."

"Any idea what she's talking about, boys?" hu'Mar asked.

"It was you, you and that Bule I saw here earlier!" she shrieked. "I know it was! Arrest him!"

"Banner hu'Tanner, that's your name, right? What happened here?" hu'Mar asked, ignoring the cleaner. She was obviously too distraught to think clearly.

"You means, aside from the perp, returning toos the crime scene?" hu'Tanner folded his arm.

"Sure, if that makes you feel better," hu'Mar played along. "What's this about a Bule?"

He had to play this careful. The Ministry would suspect him on little more than a false accusation. Spur Central was a rough place, true, but the men here were fighters and there was hardly a woman here who couldn't best any of those men. Killings happened all the time. They were never investigated if they looked like they'd come from a fair fight. Murder by poison, or in this case, possible drowning, was less respectable, and thereby criminal. A killing like this wouldn't come from a Tough, and though he could fake it most times, hu'Mar wasn't born here. He was no Tough.

"Turns out, she's seen a Bule, hurrying away from her-es. She'us comin over to doos some cleanin. When she walks in, she finds—"

"Even the fish is dead!" ka'Kilden said. "If it was just that, I wouldn't have suspected anything and cleaned away. But then I found the prophet..." She glanced at hu'Narmin's corpse, then glared accusingly at hu'Mar. "He was just a crazy old man! What did he do—"

"Yeah, yeah," hu'Tanner interrupted. "She runs out and snags us from our beat."

"And a lot of good you've done!" she shrieked again. "I'm telling you, it was him!"

"Geez, would yous lets us work, lady?" Hu'Tanner turned to hu'Mar. "Now you tells us, whats a pretend minister doin around heres?"

"I gots—" hu'Mar paused. "Grease me," he mumbled, this

guy's stupid accent was contagious. "I have an investigation of my own. Tell me more about this Bule."

"Only that she'us a real determined lookin sort in a brown cloak." hu'Tanner added.

"Hrey arll wear brauwwwn croaks," Bacon added. Dogs had a hard time making certain sounds, and hu'Mar had to think for a second before realizing that Bacon had said, "They all wear brown cloaks."

"I said, she'us real determined looking, not likes all thems other Bules 'round heres, that just puts down their heads and does their business," hu'Tanner corrected.

Bacon grunted, accepting the clarification.

"Lady," hu'Tanner asked, "did yous see this man too?"

"I didn't have to see him to know he did it!" ka'Kilden squelched.

Hu'Mar had enough with the accusations already. "Any idea as to a motive yet?" he asked.

"Listen, bub." Hu'Tanner puffed a cloud from his extra thin cigar, one of those new kinds that were shredded and rolled in paper. "You's ain't spose'd to be here."

Well, hu'Mar had gotten more info from this minister than he'd expected. It was probably on account of his youth. Hu'Tanner still had that baby smooth skin, marred only by his scraggly attempts at facial hair. If he'd been smoking a normal-sized cigar, he would've looked like a peach-colored worm with a tree trunk stuffed in his face.

"Listen, lad, you're new to this, so I'll tell you straight," hu'Mar started. "It's like this: I'm following up on a private case, and I'm bound by professional obligations to keep that case private. However, it has led me here to an active murder scene. Now granted, there's a good chance it's not related at all, but if it does turn out to be related, then if I unearth anything useful to you that you wouldn't have found otherwise, since I'm pursuing an entirely different angle, I'll turn over the relevant facts so that you can look good to your superiors and prosecute whoever's responsible."

"Orrr," Bacon growled, "yrou share youarrr angle now,

an' we deshide if we arrresht yrou now."

"Just arrest him!"

Did the lady ever stop? "Hey poochy," hu'Mar frowned, ignoring the cleaner. "It appears you have a bone to pick. I said I'd share any relevant info I gather with you, didn't I? When the time is right, and right now, it's completely irrelevant, I'll find you. But to threaten me with arrest." He tsked at the dog and waved his hands dismissively, pressuring hu'Tanner to take his side. "Right now, I'm your best ally. Consider me a volunteer minister who works for you."

Hu'Tanner chewed his thin cigar and shifted it in his mouth, thinking. Bacon did likewise, but with the fibula he had dangling from his mouth. The fact that they were even considering hu'Mar's proposal, suggested that they were fresh to the Ministry and would chomp at any advantage hu'Mar could afford their career.

"Are you people crazy?" the cleaner shouted. "Dick hu'Mar is responsible for this!" She pointed at hu'Narmin's corpse.

Crazy Ish looked about as comfortable as a dead guy on the floor could look. His neck and head didn't lean at any awkward angles, though his wet wispy hair was drying at an unusual point, like he'd been dunked in a water basin and his long gray hair had been the last thing out. Hu'Mar wanted to make a closer inspection, but he wanted to be on the ministers' good side first.

"Ah, pipe down, yous shriveled broom pole," hu'Tanner sneered. "Yous said it you'self. You only seen a Bule leaves this place."

"It's true though… I read it… somewhere. Hu'Narmin prophesied about it." Ka'Kilden crossed her arms as if she'd made her point as clear as it needed to be.

"Is that so?" Hu'Tanner eyed her, then turned his attention to hu'Mar. "What yous say about such a thing?"

"I say, show me," hu'Mar challenged.

The cleaner pointed her arm like a charging general and marched into the main room. Before hu'Mar followed the ministers after her, he leaned over Crazy Ish's body for a closer look. No apparent broken bones or bruises. Some water still clung to the front half of his thin hair and face with only a few small drips around the water basin next to him. The only sign of splashing was from the tea kettle at his side.

He pressed his fingers to the man's neck, and of course, no pulse. The kettle though was still warm, so hu'Narmin couldn't have drowned more than an hour ago. He hurried to join the others. The cleaner leaned over a small bookshelf, fingering through leatherbound spines, but not finding whatever she was looking for.

Bacon barked a booming, "Raw-oufff!"

All eyes followed Bacon's pointing snout to the end desk where an empty fishbowl sat.

Hu'Mar slapped his forehead, then stretched his cheeks as he ran his hand down his face. This wasn't good.

"Ummm," hu'Tanner muttered, not understanding why Bacon and hu'Mar were getting so worked up. Then, like an old wick in a cheap candle slowly flickering to life, realization dawned in the minister's eyes. "Wait, the fish is gone. Someone's stolen evidence!"

Hu'Tanner ran to the window and searched the streets. "Theres is folks out there, but none in no hurry to gets away, and no Bules neither."

Bacon sniffed the ground, almost gagged, then announced, "I shmell a pusshy.

Hu'Mar did a quick search of the house, but Vinegar was nowhere inside. Then he felt the tug of his bond. He let out a sigh of relief. Vinegar must've known that a dog was here, so he was at least a block away, maybe farther now. Keep on going, Vinegar.

"I think I needs some help with this case," hu'Tanner said, pacing the room. He might have appeared contemplative, but when he tripped over a tea kettle, he lost any semblance of dignity. He had no idea what he was doing. Hu'Tanner was still a beat minister, not an investigator.

He was probably lured into this job because of the dream each and every Tough shares. History stated that humans failed to shift last time because of basic human contention. Too many people did or didn't want to be the sacrificial body for the Great Clutch. That in-fighting, next to the greater fight against the other contending species, led to the ecological disaster of the flies advancing. It was like the gears of eternity were punishing the sentient beings for their weakness. The Ministry was here to prevent that from happening again.

"Lady," hu'Tanner made up his mind, "yous go home. I knows where to find you if I needs you."

"Don't you dare!" She wrinkled her nose and sidestepped along the wall.

Hu'Mar followed, getting too close for her comfort.

She took another sideways step away from him. "What're you doing?"

"I was thinking of going home and getting smashed. What do you say? Want a drink?"

"I never!" she gasped. "Young man, you are the most brash murderer I ever knew! Here, you stick around, just to harass anyone who thought to check up on him. You disgust me."

"I take it you've known hu'Narmin for some time?"

"I've been checking in on him ever since the Beadledom dumped him here." She said, bumping into a wall and losing her composure. "His landlord has me clean for him."

"Did he ever have any relics that you know of? A needle or a ring by chance?"

"What's this about relics?" hu'Tanner asked.

"Is that what this is about?" Ka'Kilden stood erect, like a stretched and starched scarecrow, brushing off her black gown. She was old fashioned. Dresses had gone out of style fifty years ago. "You come here to burgle the place, kill the simple man, then have the audacity to ask me, his cleaner, where you can find his loot to steal?"

"There you go again," hu'Mar said as he tried to stand between her and the door. "I know he doesn't have these relics, but I'm looking for someone else who's interested in them. They might be involved in his killing.

"So wait a second," hu'Tanner asked, "you think this has to do with a relic hu'Narmin owned?

"I'm tracking a stolen relic," hu'Mar admitted, trying to decide how much he dared tell. He needed to satisfy the ministers and remove their suspicion from him while protecting the confidentiality of Jodeign ka'Nairie.

"Hu'Narmin once owned a relic," he continued. "Good old Crazy Ish, or his fish, might've known something about whoever the thief was. I think that the murderer tried to get it from hu'Narmin before, or he was looking for a different relic that could pair with one he or she had."

But this cottage hadn't been ransacked. Either the killer had found the relic without much trouble, or they'd searched more carefully than most would have. If that was the case, they were clever. The dead body would be hard to hide, but the motive could still be concealed. No, the most logical answer was that the killer was looking for information only, but hu'Tanner looked satisfied for now.

"Thanks for the tip, hu'Mar, but yous better be moving," hu'Tanner said. "I'll lose any respect the Ministry has for me if they knows a fortune teller is helping me. And that goes for yous too, lady. Run on home. We'll stop by with more questions for yous later."

"You better stop on by." The cleaner hurumphed, then sniffed at hu'Mar. "I wasn't born yesterday, you know. You kids are always guilty of something. If you didn't kill hu'Narmin, I'm sure you've done something, sometime, to deserve a good execution."

As she stormed out, she declared. "I want to see justice!"

The door slammed.

"Some broads." Hu'Tanner shook his head as if sour old women were all he ever dealt with. "Now you'll still lets me know if you find anything, right?"

"You'll be the first one I come to," hu'Mar promised.

"Good, now yous git outa here."

Outside, hu'Mar casually meandered, homing in to where he felt Vinegar the strongest. A few blocks away, he found the cat, hacking on the streetside.

Chapter 7

Suspect Number One

Vinegar arched his back like it was held from the sky by an invisible string. Each time he hacked, the grating cough got more desperate.

"How in cognation am I going to deal with you?" hu'Mar complained. "You have a real talent for jamming the gears of our operations."

"What?" Vinegar asked. "You promised dinner."

"You ate evidence!"

"No, I ate a fish. Not a very good one either," Vinegar said weakly.

Hu'Mar removed his hat, ran his hands through his thick brown hair, then rubbed his eyes.

Killings happened all the time. Murder, on the other hand, was different, especially when it was such a well-known, helpless figure as Ish hu'Narmin. Given the justice style of the Tough's, hu'Mar was best off dropping this whole case. The last thing he needed was to go on trial for being in the wrong place at the wrong time with an evidence-eating cat.

And what about that cleaner's accusation? Hu'Narmin's prophesy?

Hard Boiled Cabbage: Big Trouble In Spur Central

With any luck, it was nothing. Like he had any luck these days. Hu'Mar scratched his whiskers.

He had to make a decision. Follow through on the case, please the most beautiful politician who'd ever graced his office, get paid, restore his reputation, and possibly lose favor with the Ministry. Or take a walk on safe street and forget this ever happened. Maybe he could take a long vacation until this whole mess worked itself out?

Who was he kidding? This sort of work was what he did.

"Vinegar, lets go." He started walking, but Vinegar didn't follow. He heard another series of hacks. "Vinegar! Now's not the time for hairballs."

Hu'Mar relented and picked Vinegar up. "Come on, why are you just standing there?"

Vinegar's stomach twisted, and hu'Mar could feel the churnings through his fur. It didn't seem good. It was a known fact among humans that cats couldn't physically burp. Vinegar failed at keeping up this guise; he burped.

"Wow-ho," hu'Mar said. "That's some nasty cat breath. You feeling okay?"

Vinegar jumped from his hands. All he had to do was ask to be let down. Instead, the ground came before Vinegar was ready. He walked a few unsteady strides, then it came.

The cat stopped, swayed, eyes nearly bulging. Hairballs were always annoying, but watching a goldfish come back up was pure torture. All those prickly little pin bones, broken into sharpened shards, catching on the cat's throat. Even after the steaming remains of the fish were laying in a goopy pile before him, Vinegar couldn't stop hacking at the slivers in his throat.

Hu'Mar felt his own stomach flip. "You about done yet?"

Vinegar glared at hu'Mar, tears of strain and anger dotted the corners of his eyes, and he hacked again. "How about you swallow a box full of broken toothpicks, then try vomiting those up. My throat feels like I could weave a basket with all the shrapnel left in there." A chunk of regurgitated goldfish dangled from his mouth.

Hu'Mar happily gave Vinegar a little distance. When most

of the hacking had died, hu'Mar tested Vinegar by moving to the end of the street.

With some degree of reluctance, and a large degree of audible discomfort, Vinegar followed. "I think it was all that tea in the fish's water," he called. "Hey, wait up."

Hu'Mar stopped at an intersection while Vinegar trotted closer. His hacking was now reduced to once every ten seconds.

Nearly out of breath, Vinegar complained, because that's what cats do. "I think I'd have been better off without a human."

"Jef hu'Rino, Maizy hu-ka'Dillie, and Duke."

"Who are they?" Vinegar asked.

"Huh? Oh, Maizy hu-ka'Dillie owned the relic sometime before hu'Narmin and ka'Nairie, and he or she, along with hu'Rino and Duke knew that ka'Nairie currently had the Pin of Poison," hu'Mar said. "I need to visit with each of them."

"Humans make as much sense as the moon. Interesting to look at, but utterly pointless," Vinegar continued his complaint. "Don't you see, we should drop this case? It can only bring trouble and pain."

After two strong brown horses pulling a chariot passed, hu'Mar crossed the street. Vinegar weaved through hu'Mar's moving legs. Hu'Mar had little time to prepare when Vinegar's claws emerged, aimed right where hu'Mar's pant legs lifted, and swiped at what Vinegar must have thought was his wooly ankle.

"What the—" hu'Mar said with a kick.

"Socks!" Vinegar hollered in pain. He had forgotten that humans wore socks. Vinegar lay on his back, his paw dripping blood. Two of his claws were stuck in hu'Mar's socks.

"What's the big idea?" hu'Mar accused, plucking the pointed nails from his stockings.

"Oh, you're asking me?" Vinegar rolled back to his feet and limped over. "First you chop off my tail, then you drag me all around the city looking for a stupid bone when you had promised me dinner, then you poison me. Then right when you appear to have a little sense in that oversized cranium of yours, you decide to keep pursuing that stupid relic. You expect me to be overjoyed with this little quest of yours? She's not worth it."

Hard Boiled Cabbage: Big Trouble In Spur Central

Hu'Mar stared at Vinegar.

Vinegar stared at hu'Mar.

"Well?" Vinegar asked.

"Well what?" hu'Mar asked back. "You want me to apologize? Scratch behind your ear and agree with your every pressing demand?"

"However you prefer to do it, I will humbly accept." Vinegar closed his eyes and leaned against hu'Mar's leg.

Hu'Mar sidestepped, causing Vinegar to stumble. "Do you know what it means to be big-headed?"

"How daft are you?" Vinegar threw the insult back. "I've been stuck with you and that cranium of yours for most of my life!"

"And so you should know that we both need this case. We have to see it through." hu'Mar argued, but the cat was moving slow and awkward. It really was sick. Maybe he was pushing a bit hard today. "Fine, we can rest for a minute." They found a few stairs to sit on while Vinegar waited for his stomach and nerves to settle.

Spur Central was always a crowded city. During the day, war chariots raced up and down every street. People were always exchanging hello punches. Weirdest of all, was how everyone went about their jobs armed. They didn't all put on their full armor, but most of them carried some form of weapon with them. Hu'Mar was among the few exceptions. All he ever carried was his sheath knife, and occasionally on more dangerous jobs, his blowgun. Most people though, carried their weapons as a fashion accessory except that they probably all knew how to use them.

Tonight, like most nights, the formality of the workwear was shed, and the trendy attire of unmarried Toughs were emerging. Hu'Mar hugged closer to the stair railing while a group of men passed arrogantly by with puffed out, bare muscular chests. Their only upper body adornments were a sash with metal gear-studded knuckles for serious punching and the occasional arsenal of smaller throwing knives.

They paid hu'Mar little attention. While he was single,

his chest wouldn't have looked nearly as good without his shirt. Huge, hairless, and perfectly sculpted was theirs; plain and hairy was his. Despite the warm night, he cinched his overcoat tighter around his torso. He might not be able to compete in a topless display with this crowd, but that wasn't his style anyway. He wasn't sure what his style was, but he had other problems right now.

Contrary to the men and their bare-chested puffery, single women donned more clothing and more armor.

It was all part of the courting procedure here in Spur Central, something he was loath to try at this time. Unlike the kingdom hu'Mar came from, where women dressed in more revealing outfits and the men suited up in fancy cloth, taking the women to rich dances or poor dances, as their economic situation allowed, the people here fought for their mates like many do in the other animal kingdoms. However, Toughs didn't hold sparring matches with others of their same gender, but with the ones whose hearts they wished to win. Never to the death, obviously, but it wasn't hard to tell if you'd been bested.

Before the single men passed hu'Mar by, a smaller woman dressed fashionably in brass and steel plate approached them.

Hu'Mar placed a hand on Vinegar to protect him. The cat was shivering and glared at him. Not good, but Vinegar still had the energy to bite him. Fine, the cat could have it his way. He withdrew his aid, though Vinegar might change his mind once this got started.

Instead of picking on one of the smaller guys like hu'Mar had expected, the woman blocked the alpha male, a particularly tall, muscular, not to mention handsome man with two iron batons at his side.

"Move aside, I'm not interested in any woman under two hundred pounds," his voice was condescending.

She punched hard in his stomach, followed by a sweeping kick that tripped the bolt-head to the ground. Despite her heavy armor, she moved quick and efficiently.

"I'm not little," she said. "I'm condensed!"

And feisty. She smashed a gauntleted fist into the ground,

Hard Boiled Cabbage: Big Trouble In Spur Central

missing his face by mere hairs as he rolled away. He was back on his feet now, his sneer replaced by a grin of excitement.

He removed his clubs and charged, swinging. If he defeated her, it was his option to drag her home, and no ceremony necessary, she'd be his wife if he didn't mind her petite size. But even if he did win, if she hadn't put up a good enough fight, there was no way he'd want her. He had his pride to worry about after all. If she won, then they would go their separate ways.

His first two swings missed her completely, but he was no amateur. He followed up with a good roundhouse that would've put hu'Mar in bed for a week.

She shrugged it off like one might brush off a blood beetle and returned the attack with some impressive martial agility.

The fight was brief, and despite hu'Mar's predictions, the little lady left the man in a heap. She spit on him, taunting, "What good are all those muscles if you can't even fight!" She strutted away.

The pack of men that had originally been following him now followed a short distance behind her. There would be another fight tonight; she'd piqued their interest enough for that, but hu'Mar doubted that any of them would win the option of taking her home. This was the reason Tough breeding produced such tough people.

If hu'Mar ever wanted to settle with a woman, this would be a difficult city to find one in. This was the same reason he knew that ka'Nairie had only been messing with him earlier at his apartment. Had she really been interested in him, then hu'Mar might be nursing some critical wounds, and she'd be looking for another fortune-teller.

Hu'Mar could only end up with ka'Nairie if she willingly threw the fight, which was very unlikely. He'd have to work really hard to get her to lower her standards. But if he could get her to throw a fight, he'd take her in a heartbeat, who cared if she lost her honor by doing so. Of course, that wasn't going to happen, but he didn't care, too much.

As the winner strutted past hu'Mar, she gave him a curious once-over but didn't seem interested. Hu'Mar wasn't dressed, or rather, undressed for the occasion, which was really the point of wearing his overcoat. He knew he'd be out after dark and didn't want any confusion.

The men, though larger and stronger, lost more of these dates than they won, probably on account of not wearing any armor and partly because the women here never went easy on any man. The entire five years before a woman was of wedding age, was spent in finishing school. Unlike hu'Mar's kingdom culture where this meant learning manners, housekeeping, and job skills, here, it was full-time battle training.

In a culture where war was revered, looks and love were always secondary to strength, cunning, and pure-bred fighting ability. Granted, a pretty face might suggest that you didn't often lose a fight, so looks might start a friendly fight, but nobody ever threw a fight. That would only lead to weak offspring, and what would the neighbors think?

"Hey, Vinegar, how you doing?" hu'Mar asked, trying to take his attention off the dating scene. Watching those people only made him feel inadequate. He shouldn't compare himself to them, but seriously, how could anyone completely avoid comparisons?

Usually, Vinegar only acted drunk if he'd fallen too hard on his head, but this fish had really done a number on him. Vinegar burped and moaned again. Despite puking up that fish, Vinegar only got worse. Hu'Mar scooped his cat up and cradled him all the way back to the apartment.

As they rounded the last block, he paused. Vinegar was squirming in his arms, but was too weak to do much more.

"You okay? You're not going to puke again or crap all over me, are you?"

Vinegar's hackles rose, and he released a labored meow, "Dog."

Hu'Mar's followed Vinegar's gaze to his apartment. The weathered, four-story building was being inspected by two of the Beadledom's least finest. This couldn't be good.

"Ick hu'Mar," the gruff red dog in his ridiculous blue uniform barked.

"Bacon," hu'Mar acknowledged. "You boys do get around."

"I shou'ha figurrred." Bacon half growled.

"Hey pooch, whose bone you chewing on now?" hu'Mar said with a little more salt than he could afford.

Bacon growled and rolled what was now, half a fibula from one side of his mouth to another. "Shame bone."

"I was afraid of that," hu'Mar muttered quietly to Vinegar.

"You can take them," Vinegar urged.

Hu'Mar saw the doubt in Vinegar's expression. No. He wouldn't even try. Sure, he was strong, but he was no dummy. This might turn into nothing. Besides, Vinegar was in no condition to help.

Since Banner hu'Tanner would be a dirty fighter and Bacon had as much in common with a dog as a wolf had to a schnauzer, they'd both be too unpredictable to risk a fight with at this time.

"You live here," hu'Tanner spit, his loogie forming a muddy lump in the dirt street.

Hu'Mar spoke, "We all get by. This place might be a heap, but it's no worse than what half the other people in this city live in."

"Listen sonny, yous—"

"Don't sonny me." Hu'Mar jabbed the minister with a couple fingers. "I've got at least a decade on you, and the Ministry owes me."

"Hey, Bacon, hear this joker? He thinks he's so much better than us," hu'Tanner laughed. "Yous almost mades me think as much back there at Crazy Ish's place, but I gots eyes, you know."

"Wisten Ick hu'Mar," Bacon said. "You gots'a stiff'ere. Wha you know?"

"Dead guy? You mean hu'Narmin? We already went over this." Where were they going with this? He tried to sound calm as Vinegar tensed in his arms.

"Come'ere," hu'Tanner said in that whiny tattle-tale voice of his. He led them around to the stable.

Hu'Mar followed, Vinegar still in his arms. He'd rather leave the cat by the apartment, and Vinegar would normally prefer that too. Something about large heavy hooves kept Vinegar from the stables most times, but hu'Mar needed every bit of wit he had available to him. These ministers seemed fickle, so he carried Vinegar in, along with all the lip that went with him.

"I don't know why I kept away from here so long," Vinegar said as they entered the stable with the same rotten walls as his apartment and musky straw-strewn floor. "In fact, I might have to give this place a visit on those nights when you snore like a hog under a thunderstorm. Hey, was that a mouse?"

Hu'Mar dropped Vinegar on a small pile of straw so that his head wouldn't get smashed again. If Vinegar was thinking about mice, then he was feeling good enough to get around on his own.

"Augh, ooh, yeow," Vinegar meowed as he stumbled onto solid ground.

"What are you complaining about now?" hu'Mar asked.

"You know," Vinegar said as he curled into a bean shape and licked straw from his scabby tail "My tail is still tender. All this horse, ouch, fodder, ooh, is painful. You humans have no sense of decency." Then while at it, he gave his butt another few licks.

Why did the licking always coincide with a verbal berating of human decency? Hu'Mar stretched his lip in disgust. Vinegar was right about one thing. The stable didn't appear too bad. In a pinch, he wouldn't mind sleeping somewhere like this as long as he avoided the hooves of the horses and the dead boy lying in the middle of everything.

"Word has it that yous and only two others was around 'im before he died. A couples of dames. Ones, a fancy socialite, the others, a dirty Bule."

Hu'Mar didn't need to hear hu'Tanner's emphasis on "dirty Bule" to connect the accusation from the cleaner to himself and these deaths. "I don't know Jack," hu'Mar said.

"Hu'Tanner."

"Huh?"

"Banner hu'Tanner, not Jack. What you think I am, some dirty animal?" hu'Tanner said. "No offense, Bacon."

"None taken," Bacon said.

"See here," hu'Tanner said. "The boy's been poisoned. You's one of the last to see 'im. That makes you either a suspect or a possible witness. What can you tells me."

"Us," barked Bacon.

"Yeah, what can you tells us," hu'Tanner corrected.

Hu'Mar could see that hu'Tanner wanted to give Bacon a quick kick to the ribs. He'd been there plenty of times with Vinegar, but Bacon was a big dog. Big dogs, especially ones that think they're human and live among Toughs and carry a badge, aren't usually afraid to fight back. Hu'Tanner wisely held his foot.

"What kind of poison we talking here?" hu'Mar asked.

"Wouldn't you likes to know?"

"We oun't know," Bacon said. "But rook at da scrape on hish face."

"Bacon!" hu'Tanner scolded.

"Ick hu'Mar's as rude as a cat, but he's no murdur-rur-rur."

"Bacon tells me you used to be a minister?" hu'Tanner said. "Washed up? Couldn't handle it? Or did it not sit right with you? But I heard yous a palsy, and the Ministry don't like that sort of thing. It's kinda like colluding with the enemy."

"Colluding. Big word for such a small man, but no, I was never a minister." Hu'Mar knelt in the straw to inspect the wound. "Though I have helped the Ministry solve a case from time to time when it was convenient for my clients."

The dead boy's face had some post-mortem bruising along with a puffy spot that surrounded that thin scrape on his cheek. The bruises made little sense, but chances were good that Bacon was right on the cause of death. Hu'Mar's own blow darts used a poison similar to this. A little prick from that stuff could kill most humans though the delivery method here wasn't from a dart.

Hu'Mar's face heated with anger. He tried to calm himself. If he'd learned anything from Vinegar, it was that several animals, dogs especially, could smell anger.

Hu'Tanner stared hard at hu'Mar.

Hu'Mar stared back.

Bacon wagged his tail as if any moment someone would give him some attention too.

As per usual, Vinegar simply yawned.

Hu'Tanner broke first, of course, because hu'Mar had learned the art of staring from a pro, though he'd never thanked Vinegar for it. Besides, he'd added his own flare to the stare. It was one thing to hold eye contact, another entirely to intimidate at the same time.

"Fro me a bone," Bacon said to break the tension. "Eiber tell us you know shomehing or you 'on't."

"What's there to know. I've been out for the last couple hours."

"Yeah, where you been?"

"Working. None of your business."

"Maybe I'm mistaken," Vinegar meowed. "But haven't you been doing their business?"

Hu'Tanner shot Vinegar an accusing finger. "Hey, this your palsy pal? What's he saying?"

"Says he's hungry and tired of jabbering about nothing to do with us. Cats can be sort of selfish even when it comes to murder."

"Get outa here," hu'Tanner said. "If you thinks of somethin' helpful, you come talks to me."

Hu'Mar shoved past the little minister. Hu'Tanner might carry authority from the Beadledom in his back pocket, but this was a Tough city, and Toughs were, by definition, tough. Hu'Mar hadn't done a thing wrong or unexpected. Nothing that was, except lie.

This death was one more clue that implicated the Albino that had visited him. He remembered Vinegar's off-handed remark about how she'd struck the stableboy when she'd left, and he wouldn't doubt it if the Bule which the cleaner lady had seen at hu'Narmin's was the same Albino. Perhaps Crazy Ish's fish had been poisoned too? That would explain how badly Vinegar felt after eating it. So there was a poisoned fish, a poisoned stableboy, and each had come in contact with that girl, all while he was looking for a relic that caused a person to become poisonous.

Hard Boiled Cabbage: Big Trouble In Spur Central

But who was she? And how could she possibly be connected?

Rain hu'Grooshy was cleaning his tooth-pulling tools as hu'Mar passed his door.

"Hu'Mar, you hear about that stableboy?" Hu'Grooshy dropped his tools in a sink right along with a skinned chicken that would soon be his supper.

"That minister interrogate you too?"

Hu'Grooshy pointed to his dinner. "Would've had this bird cooked by now if not."

"Too bad, the stable boy was pretty young. Didn't you give him a couple of gold teeth? Seems like I remember you working on him," hu'Mar said.

"Huh? What? No, not me." hu'Grooshy said with a wry smile. "That boy didn't own no gold teeth. Go see for yourself if you want. He got no gold teeth in his mouth."

Obviously the boy must've owed hu'Grooshy, so before hu'Tanner showed up, hu'Grooshy had collected the debt. That explained the post-mortem bruising. Of all the metals in the world, gold was soft and nearly worthless for anything practical beyond teeth, but hu'Grooshy was cheap and not beyond scavenging from the dead to save a few chips of salt.

"I take it you saw the boy before anyone else," hu'Mar said. "Notice anything odd about his death?"

"Nah. The kid was a prick, but a place like this, I'm guessing there were plenty who might want 'im dead."

"Yeah, who?"

"Good night, hu'Mar."

"Right." Hu'Mar shrugged. "Good night to you too." He retrieved one of the many palm-length cinder sticks that poked out of the hallway oil sconces, its slow-burning ember barely illuminated the dark stairs that led to his own floor. In the dark, the long hallway stretched down the length of the complex and seemed to go on forever. The hundred unit building actually housed a hundred and one flats because allegedly, the architect counted wrong when the place was designed. Thelma ka'Skrut's place was down the hall, next to his place. Her door was shut, which meant that she was out fighting shirtless men or some such. Whenever she was home, she made a point of leaving the door open.

Hu'Mar fumbled with his key and opened his door. Nobody had been here. He was sure of it. There wasn't much to ransack if they had. He removed his overcoat, tossing it onto the trunk, then plopped down onto the stump at his desk.

"Hey, you owe me dinner!"

Hu'Mar's concentration broke. Vinegar leapt onto his desk and stared at him. Hu'Mar was in no mood to stare back, so he brushed the cat off and lit a cheap candle with his cinder stick.

Vinegar leapt back up and hissed, "You promised me dinner."

"Yeah," hu'Mar said as he stretched his tired back. What he'd give for a seat with a backrest. "And you got your dinner. Not my fault you couldn't keep it down."

"It was the water. Something was wrong with that water."

"Yeah, it was full of tea. People drink the stuff all the time. Besides, I'd have a lot more sympathy if it hadn't been incriminating evidence you'd swallowed."

"You always have to complicate everything." Vinegar said. "You know, I see what you're doing."

"What do you know?" hu'Mar asked as he counted his salt then shoved it into his pocket purse. He also retrieved his blowgun and every poisoned dart that went with it. The Ministry was sure to search his apartment. With two deaths by poisoning, he couldn't risk them finding this here. Then again, if they nabbed him with the darts, that wouldn't go over well either. He set them on the table for now. Still, if they found it prudent to arrest him, it wouldn't really matter what he had with him. Chances were, they would've already made up their minds.

"Please," Vinegar whined. "I can read you like a dog. You're not giving up on this case. Take it from me, we have instincts for a reason. You're about to ignore yours. There's way more hair here than you bargained for, so let this case go. And for the record, it wasn't the tea in that fishbowl that made me sick. That water was bad."

"You do know," hu'Mar lifted his hat and scratched his

matted hair, "it's only a matter of time before the Ministry arrests us in connection with these killings. Hu'Tanner and his dog are easy enough to bully around, but there's a reason why they were here tonight, instead of still combing hu'Narmin's place. They reported the murder, and the Ministry sent real seasoned ministers to investigate. They would've been told to bug off, and then, while they were sitting at the station, feeling stupid, someone reports this stableboy's death here. Pretty soon, the whole Ministry will be asking us questions. We'll be on trial just like that blacksmith we saw a few hours ago."

"That's too bad," Vinegar said as he rubbed his head against hu'Mar's arm. "Can I have your kidney after they execute you?"

"Hey, do you really want them to separate us? Given how much they hate palsies, you can also bet they won't have much sympathy for you."

"Maybe I'd be better off away from you." Vinegar stretched and dug his claws into hu'Mar's table. "It might be inconvenient at first, but once you're dead, I can always find some little boy or girl to trick into a bond. I could then raise them how I want them to be."

"Remember," hu'Mar pointed out, "you ate the goldfish. They'll probably consider you an accomplice. Don't be surprised if they just feed you to Bacon."

Vinegar rolled a growl in his throat. "You know as well as I do, that humans have a blind spot to non-humans. They hate us all equally, and rarely waste effort tracking us down for prosecution." He weaved away from hu'Mar, nearly smacking his head into a wall as he did so.

"Hey, don't go peeing on my walls again!"

"They're just as much mine as they are yours," Vinegar hissed.

"Watch it," hu'Mar threatened. "Your tail isn't the only appendage my knife can cut off."

Ish hu'Narmin, died by drowning. His fish, by Vinegar's reaction, could be from poisoning. This stableboy by poisoning, definitely. These were all non-Tough crimes. The fact that he owned a blowgun with poisoned tips and had been near each crime, same as that Albino with that cleaner lady's accusation would be all the evidence they cared to collect before executing him.

He slammed the drawer to his desk shut, and it sounded like another saline rolled in the desk. Had he missed some salt? He opened the drawer again and at the back of the cubby, he found the Albino's black pellet.

"What are you?" He grabbed it and stood, pacing the dark apartment as he tried to examine it. No good. He grabbed the candle from his desk and crossed the room. It was never a good idea to sit in the middle of his room where the laundry lady was likely to rinse out his candle. Since Vinegar had already hogged the softer bedroll, he settled for slumping under the outdated calendar, his back against ka'Skrut's wall. This side of the room always smelled a little better.

Unlike the normal rotten wood stench, years of his neighbor's hair jellies, mixed with essential oils, essential only because her hair jelly would smell terrible without them, had stained even his floor. One spill looked as if she'd knocked it over as recently as this morning probably in her excitement to do something stereotypically Tough, like fighting someone or something. The trail of fruity-scented slime that had seeped under the common wall and into his apartment was crusty by now.

He sighed, careful not to get the flame too near the flammable hair care remnants, and tipped a pool of melted tallow from the candle to anchor it to the floor. Once set, he rested his tired back against the wall. "Vinegar, do you have to eat your food on my bed?"

Vinegar had a mouse tail hanging from his lips. The panicked tail whipped back and forth.

Vinegar ignored him.

"At least you must be feeling better," hu'Mar said.

As clumsy as he was, Vinegar never had a hard time finding a mouse around here. This place was infested with vermin.

"Yeah, but you promised I wouldn't have to catch my meal tonight," Vinegar mumbled.

Hard Boiled Cabbage: Big Trouble In Spur Central

The mouse was probably saying something too, but hu'Mar could only guess what it was. "How about you quit torturing that critter and finish it off?"

"We all suffer in our own way," Vinegar mimed. "Besides, its fate could be worse. It could be a palsy, bonded to you."

At least he got his meal. That would be one less complaint hu'Mar would have to deal with tonight. "When you're done playing with your food, come over here and tell me what you think of this." He held up the black pellet.

There was a crunch. Hu'Mar slipped Vinegar a sideways glance. The mouse's tail had stopped moving. Vinegar was still taking his sweet time, but at least hu'Mar didn't have to watch the mouse struggle anymore.

Not entirely sure he wanted to stand, hu'Mar did anyway. He hated waiting. Instead, he paced, first to one side of his flat where he was tempted by a round of cheese, but he opted instead for a small swig of wheat mash. After a couple swallows, he re-corked the skin, then paced to the other side where he rested his elbows on the windowsill. Two deaths by poison, a missing relic called the Pin of Poison, and him, stuck in the middle without a clue. There had to be a connection to it all. Outside, in the dim starlight, steam and smoke rose from the rocky, pitted faces of Mount Exclusion. Deep rivers ran through cave systems there, supposedly, right into the chamber of the Great Clutch itself. That way, even the water dwelling creatures would have a chance at shifting.

Four months he'd lived here, and he was losing reverence for that mountain with every passing week. He shouldn't have. After all, it was more than a smoldering mound of volcanic rock. It was the center of the world. The axel of existence on this realm. The temple of the Great Gears of Creation. So powerful and awe-inspiring, but all hu'Mar wanted was for Vinegar to finish eating.

Also, how had that cleaning lady at Crazy Ish's house known his name? Had hu'Mar truly been in a real prophesy, one that involved Ish hu'Narmin's death? What was the prophesy, and what could it mean?

"Done yet?" he asked Vinegar.

Vinegar stretched and ripped at hu'Mar's bedroll. hu'Mar clenched his jaw, trying not to say a word. Besides Vinegar could probably read his annoyance. Back at the wall with the candle, hu'Mar slumped back to the floor to examine the black pellet closer to the candle.

Vinegar trotted over. "What you got?"

"Something from that Albino who visited us earlier." Hu'Mar held it to the flames light for Vinegar to see better. "Ever see anything like it?"

Vinegar sniffed it, then jerked backward. "I don't know what it is, but I'd get rid of it if I were you."

Hu'Mar tapped it on the ground and broke a small chunck off, setting half of it next to the candle while examining the other half. He rubbed it between his fingers. With a little effort, it turned to powder, like loosely formed salt. He dabbed a bit on his tongue, and it was unlike anything he'd tasted before.

"Not salty. Sort of metallic." It actually made him think of a blacksmith for some reason. He wiped his tongue clean on his vest.

"Like I said, worthless," Vinegar walked toward the other side of the room. "By the way, I think I'm going out tonight."

"Suit yourself," hu'Mar said, only half interested. Since being apart from each other caused their bond to weaken, they usually only separated at night when one was sleeping, inconveniencing only one of them. Vinegar was leaving earlier than usual, but hu'Mar didn't care. Without Vinegar around, he'd sleep a little better. That was one cat attribute that hu'Mar would welcome tonight.

Vinegar was halfway across the room when Gracie ka'Muunel's laundry water poured through the ceiling again. Sometimes she washed till the late hours of the night.

Reflexively, Vinegar dodged toward hu'Mar, but he stumbled and rolled, bumping the candle.

Hu'Mar whipped his hand out to catch it, but was too slow.

The flame bounced on the crumbs of the black powder

from the Albino's pellet. Bounced was the best way to describe the fire as it bounced in a lightning flash of fire, expanding and blinding him with its light.

Acrid smoke choked him, smelling much like it had tasted, only more threatening. He scrambled back, trying to get a grip on himself. Every bit of hair from the backs of his hands to his face was singed to stinking curled nubs. He rubbed at the stinging pores and then at his watering eyes. When he blinked the tears away, the room felt too hot. He jumped back—ka'Skrut's hair jelly!

The fresh stains of hair product had ignited and sent flames up the aged timbers of the apartment. He balled his vest into a bat and slapped at the flames to smother them before they spread any further, but his vest caught on fire along with the rest of the wall.

The fire licked up the thin dry planks like Renu ka'Feebal lapping up liquor just as quickly. Funny, the things your brain thought about in times like this.

Hu'Mar ran to his trunk, brushed off his overcoat, and retrieved a new vest. He filled the inner pockets with his blowgun and spare darts. At the bottom of the trunk, he took a leather satchel.

He grabbed only the essentials: the round of cheese, some bread, and his half-a-skin of wheat mash. He stuffed these into the leather satchel, then slung it over his shoulder.

"Come'on Vinegar," he called to nobody because Vinegar was already out.

Hu'Mar ran for the door, a new batch of soapy water rained from the ceiling, drenching him as he passed.

He yelled, "Fire!" as he bounded toward the stairs and to the street. The flames were literally hot on his heels.

He burst out of the building, only then realizing that if he hadn't been thinking so selfishly like a cat, he might've tried to save the lady upstairs. He cursed himself. It was too late now. The whole building was ablaze. Everyone from this section of the apartment complex was standing in the street, except for the laundry lady and Thelma ka'Skrut. Ka'Skrut hadn't been home, so hu'Mar wasn't worried about her, but Gracie ka'Muunel was another matter.

The apartment burned like a paper house. As it spread, more people poured out of the adjacent units. The planks melted away quickly, and soon all that was left were several charred stilts and a single untouched platform, too wet to burn, resting at the very top like a wooden hammock.

As the smoke cleared, a single figure squatted on the platform, a shriveled old lady, no less dried out from the flames as she was by age. She scrubbed linens in large pans of bubbly water.

She paused for a moment as if she just now realized something was off. Ka'Muunel patted around her damp laundry pad like a blind person who knew something was wrong but couldn't understand what it was.

At last, her hand returned with a big fat cigar. She lit the end with the embers of an old stub that was still stuck between her teeth. Puffing away, she plunged her head back into a cloud of her own smoke and her hands back into the soapy water.

Hu'Mar drew in a deep breath, then let it out. At least he knew what the black pellet did now. He didn't even bother searching the crowd for Vinegar. Vinegar was nowhere near. He knew it as instinctively as his freshly adopted indifference to his burnt home. Normally, hu'Mar would've felt bad about having displaced so many people. Instead, he only thought about the rent he wouldn't have to pay, so he casually turned his back to the ashes and walked.

He didn't know where to go, but that didn't matter much. In the back of his mind, he was cognizant that this fire would be another strike against him to the Ministry. Hu'Tanner and Bacon would receive reinforcements to investigate the murdered stableboy, and since the attached stable burned down too, there wouldn't be much body to investigate. That might work in his favor, unless they discover that the fire started at his apartment. Then it'd be the last tidy spear of suspicion they'd need to pin this all on him.

If he were smart, he'd leave Spur Central right now, but

he'd only gotten here four months ago. He wasn't ready to leave yet. Not even the executions they'd passed earlier worried him. Not tonight. It wasn't a pretty situation, but without Vinegar here, he found it difficult to worry too much. Tomorrow would be different.

Tomorrow, he'd have to think more about his good name. Finding that Pin of Poison was more than bread money now, and more than the admiration of the smooth-talking Jodeign ka'Nairie. Finding it was the only thing that could connect all these crimes and save his hide at the same time.

Chapter 8

Shady Company

Juniper ka'Shino sucked in a deep breath though pursed lips, then snapped her pocket clock shut. She tucked the timepiece away as she knocked on the thick wooden door. She didn't like meeting all these people, so the quicker she completed her business with them, the better. This job was well within her expertise, which was why they'd picked her, but it scraped along the fine edge of her conscience, grating her soul in the process.

The Albino Republic was a lot larger than any surface-dweller knew, big enough that ka'Shino should've easily gone unnoticed. She could've spent her days mapping out the near surface tunnels and hunting giant worms for their oil. Instead, the Republic had recruited her for this specific job. Working with explosives was a strength of hers, and using that knowledge to advance humanity was a bonus.

A speakeasy, six feet up on the massive door slid open. Two faceless red eyes checked on her from behind the bars. The eyes tilted back, revealing a day-old shaved chin, under fat lips.

Like a sore throat, the bouncer said, "You're late."

The speakeasy slammed closed, and the gears clicked as the lock was disengaged. The door, too heavy to hang from a

Hard Boiled Cabbage: Big Trouble In Spur Central

wooden building, swung open like a well-greased wallet. She'd been here once before, and the smoke that spilled like fog, made her cough, but not loud enough to be heard over the music inside.

She brushed her hand against the black granite wall as she entered. The security of the underground tunnels was a relief, and while this establishment was better than anything on the surface, it held its own dangers. Strange, how the underground always appeared darker after visiting the surface, but already, the dull ache behind her eyes felt better. Now, of course, the smoke from rolled tobacco would add a new stinging sensation to her sunbaked eyes.

The large room was by far more sinister than most Albino digs, but this wasn't her first time in a place like this. Gin joints populated the upper caves and had few ties to the underground cities despite a few high-ups that frequented them. If it ever did gain wide recognition, it would be due for a raiding. In one corner, practically floating in the smoke, was a circular table where the lowest bet was in bromines.

Another corner of the room held shelves of wooden and metal gears. Juniper ka'Shino never bought from them. The parts couldn't be traced, but you paid a pretty premium for them. She was better off buying from black markets on the surface where gears were cheaper, though as hu'Mar had pointed out, riskier. Ideally, she'd buy the gears for her detonators at any of the legitimate Albino cities since Albinos had a deep and abiding respect for technology. Every invention or innovation submitted to the underground government was met with praise and adoration. Every innovation except for hers. The thanks she received was to be hired for a dirty job.

Albinos had learned how to make explosive materials almost a hundred years ago and were constantly refining that power, power strong enough and dangerous enough to alter mountains. Ka'Shino had trained as a child to use these tools of engineering, but her love of clockworks helped her devise an innovation she called a delayed detonator. It was much more practical than a long, unreliable fuse. If only she'd kept that innovation to herself.

The door behind her closed. The three-and-a-half-foot bouncer, an Albino with sweaty grizzled features, climbed onto a door-mounted stool, engaged the lock, then climbed to the floor. "Come on, tey've been waiting for you."

Ka'Shino followed. He took three short steps for every one of hers, so she had to pace herself. Her skin prickled as she passed gambling tables. She loved her people, but most who occupied these tables, were not her people. Since the upper caves were closer to the surface, intruders to the underworld were more common, and Albinos, Toughs, and others gathered here for some illegal trade. Among the Albinos and Toughs, a few Mops, wolves, and even a pair of hysts (beetle-like animals with hard green shells), occupied the crowd today. The atmosphere might be darker and more mixed, but this was where she'd been hardened and felt free. Finding work usually meant braving the rough crowds that converged in places like this, and while she often disagreed with the sort that gravitated here, she also felt the excitement that came from successfully navigating this class of people.

Ka'Shino tried to avoid eye contact as she passed the various tables. She was here to meet some Republic officials, and the fact that they chose to meet in this den of crime, made her question the nature of this rendezvous. But if these sophisticated Albinos met her in public at the inn where she stayed, they would've drawn suspicion in the Tough town.

At the other end of the room, she passed one more table overflowing with a mob of cats. They paused to watch her walk past. Cats were one thing. Gangster cats were another. The short bouncer coughed to get her attention. Ka'Shino snapped her attention to the door he waited at. The little man knocked, his fists hitting strong enough to break a man's knees. Most likely, this man had fought and probably whipped Toughs that were over three times his size.

They waited for a few seconds, then the door opened.

"Who is it," a voice asked.

"Are you expecting anyone else, because I tought I was te

Hard Boiled Cabbage: Big Trouble In Spur Central

only one working on tis?" Juniper ka'Shino said.

"Come in."

The little bouncer opened the big door a little wider, and ka'Shino entered. Then the door closed behind her, leaving her alone with these men.

Rich mineral water dripped from the ceiling, so ka'Shino had to be careful where she walked. The dark calcified walls, blackened by ages of worm oil lamps, threatened to transfer their sooty past onto her blue cloak. Oil lamps were still a necessity in the wild tunnels, and anywhere on the uneducated surface at night. But thankfully, down here, the natural blue and orange ceiling flows were now illuminated by clean glowing bacteria. If only they could do away with the tobacco smoke, this place might drift toward respectable, but places that encouraged vice, encouraged all sorts of other shady things, and shady was this places bread and butter.

For now, she'd take the dim glowing lights. They felt so much nicer than the sunlight she'd endured the last couple weeks. Of the three men, two were red-eyes she'd never met, and Ernes hu'Toe was the beautiful blue eyed one. All of them were as dark as Albinos could get, and it had nothing to do with actual pigment.

A tall man, lean and full of gristle, rested a knife on the table, atop the cards they'd been playing. "Give me one good reason tat I shouldn't kill you now."

Ka'Shino nearly tripped as she stopped short. "Wha?"

"It's all over te Ministry," Ernes hu'Toe said, his beautiful blue eyes now appeared dangerous. "You were seen leaving Ish hu'Narmin's place, right before he was discovered dead."

"How did you know tat was me?" Ka'Shino took one step back.

"Suspicion, and because you now confirm it," said the shorter red-eye.

The tall red-eye with the knife, ready to attack at the slightest wrong move, added, "Your zeal compromises our mission. I understand tat killing a prophet might keep te Beadledom from learning our plans, but tat isn't your problem to worry about."

"But, I—"

"Hu'Narmin was already past his prime," hu'Toe cut her off. "He presented no risk. You're a foolish girl. Why had I ever tought I could trust you to someting as important as tis?"

"No, I was just—"

"Enough." The short red-eye seemed very contemplative with those swirling ribbons of smoke coiling and expanding around his face. His low voice amplified the tension, carving a deep hole of seriousness like a giant tunnel worm, plowing through an underground field of peat. "We're running out of time."

Hu'Toe allowed his smile to return though it held short of that wolfish charm he'd displayed the first time they'd met. He waved the smoke from his face, clearly annoyed. Smoking was common above ground. Down here, most people knew better. When actual fire was obsolete, anyone still poisoning their lungs with smoke became a second-class citizen. This didn't seem to bother the heavy, deep-toned man sitting next to him. He might be low class, but not socially.

The other red-eyed man, tall and sinewy, said with a high melodic voice, "Te prophets have spoken. Mount Exclusion will open te Great Clutch soon."

Yeah, the prophets said that, but what were these guys holding back from everyone? From me? "If I do tis ting, a lot of people might get hurt," ka'Shino said.

"Ah ka'Shino," hu'Toe said, calm as a snake. "Hurt is a relative concept. Everyone deals wit hurt in teir lives. Just tink of our early history. When we first arrived to tis realm, all of our past progress as a species was obliterated. We were savages. Humans need technology!"

"Humans need history," tall and sinewy added.

Hu'Toe nodded. "If te Toughs get teir way, which tey are very likely to do, ten we will all shift to te next world, and all of our progress here will have been pointless. We can't bring our knowledge wit us. Hurt, pain, untinkable living standards would plague us for anoter tousand years to come."

Hard Boiled Cabbage: Big Trouble In Spur Central

Tall and sinewy stood and walked toward ka'Shino.

She stepped back again even though he left his knife on the table. He towered over her. Then he reached into her cloak and pulled out her pocket clock.

Ka'Shino had to restrain herself from snatching it back. These men, cloaked in layers of danger and secrecy, were already upset with her. The Beadledom could at least be admired for lacking government officials, like these, who kept secrets from the public. The Beadledom was completely open about both their good and bad deeds. For them, anything contradictory was an open invitation for a fight. Why wouldn't a Tough welcome such a challenge? The Albino Republic though, along with other kingdoms around this world, all had their secrets, sometimes shady government agencies who acted in the people's best interest, but not in the most ethical ways. They valued power, deception, and fear. Patriotic as ka'Shino was, she hated being treated like a pawn.

Tall and sinewy twisted the back off the timepiece and lay the gearworks on the table. They clicked and turned for all to see. He'd better not break that, or she might give them a demonstration of how good she really was with explosives.

"Te Ministry is daft," he said. "Look in here and tell me, which of tese gears is te most important?"

Ka'Shino didn't bother inspecting the inside, she knew it all by memory. She ought to, she built it. Plus, she already knew where he was going with this. It was cliche. "No gear is more important tan anoter. Tey're all important. Take one out and te whole clock stops working."

"So, what does it matter if we keep hopping from one gear to anoter. Te goal of life shouldn't be to end up on te hands of te clock. Tat is an end. Tat is where you end up learning te hard way tat tere is no furter progression." Tall and sinewy was right of course.

Ka'Shino didn't need to be lectured. They were upset to be sure. Unjustly so. But they still needed her skills, or else they would've killed her already if she'd truly compromised them. She could still come out of this with her life and a good deal of prestige, but by stopping humans from ascending, would the suffering she caused be worth it?

The long scar on his tall sinewy face was almost as animated as his lips. "True ascension is learning to elevate yourself where you are. Tis world is no better tan any oter. If we are truly to advance as a species, it will be trough understanding tis principle and preserving our history—"

"And our technology," hu'Toe added as he paced closer.

"Yes, and our technology."

The quiet man chimed in. His voice low and grave, like a tomb, caused eddies through the smoke that lingered around his face. "Te prophets see in many directions and always at great cost." He inhaled another deep drag from his cigar. "Some see us shifting. Some see us staying. If we shift, tey go blind to any more of te future. If we stay, tey predict unimaginable marvels. Medicine to cure all ills. Machines to make life better, civilization to grant stability. Advancement is not found in starting over. It's found by building upon knowledge and wisdom."

Hu'Toe put a gentle, uncompromising hand on ka'Shino's shoulder. "Tis is our chance. If we do tis, we will show te world a better way. Tey will listen. Tey too, will learn. Tere might be pain in te short term, but in te long term, we will turn pain into a minor inconvenience rater tan a tragedy."

He was right, of course. They all were. It didn't make playing with bombs around an active volcano sound any more palatable, especially since so many people lived at the base of it. But they had promised to hire their top geologists to help her place the bombs.

"Do you know how much time we have left?" she asked.

" Monts, weeks, could even be days. Te prophets are unusually unclear about tis. Tey can see so much, but details surrounding te actual Tomb of Ascension escape tem somehow. It doesn't matter. We just do te job ahead of us."

Hu'Toe and the tall, sinewy one walked to the edge of the room, hefting a large package.

"Tis is it, ten." Ka'Shino reached out.

Smoker snatched her wrist from his chair with quick,

cold reflexes. The tip of his rolled tobacco glowed a deep red for several seconds. He pulled it from his lips and extinguished it. "We must be careful around tese tings. One stray spark and we'd all be waiting for te gears of life to spin us back into mortality."

Ka'Shino rolled her eyes. Men. "Did you get me what I asked for?"

Hu'Toe untied the bundle. It was identical to the last batch. "Tis should be enough to finish te first explosion. We'll have more ready soon enough." He placed a folded map on top of the stack.

She sighed. Just smoke pellets, again. "And te oter ting?"

Hu'Toe slid a small jewelry-sized box to her. She pocketed it, then examined the map. It was the type only an Albino knew how to read. It showed a bird's eye view of everything, but instead of artistic drawings of mountains and valleys, all elevation changes were marked in contour lines that depicted every ten feet of change. The steeper parts showed the lines closer together while the flat elevations had widely spaced lines. Red lines intersected all of those to show the contours of the underground passage, but it made the map look even busier.

Albinos prized precision. Surface-dwellers were content as long as their homes functioned as shelter and their knives were always sharp. Albinos, miners forced to live underground, became expert engineers and scientists. Their main exports were knowledge, tools, and ore. To a Tough, this map was nothing more than a crude artistic drawing of a large knotty tree ring.

"So I'm only seeing one drop point on here," she said as she read the swirling lines. "I tought tere were going to be four separate drop points."

"Tere will. But a map will only get you so close," hu'Toe said. "I, along wit a couple oter geologists, will assist you in placing te oters. Wit each explosion, shifting will occur. Tey will need to modify each placement for optimal efficiency. Also, if anyone can help avoid collateral damage, it would be tem."

Ka'Shino re-wrapped the bundle and swung it onto her back. The black pellets clicked around as its weight shifted her. She grunted. The thing was big, bulky, and weighed half as much as she did. It would be all too easy to drop the explosives down a fissure in the ground and disappear into the wild lonely tunnels that she'd grown to love. But these men were right. Shifting would be more harmful to their species than staying and building upon the knowledge they already had. It was a worthy cause, and if she was completely honest with herself, she loved working with explosives and timers. That didn't mean she had to like the specific people who'd hired her, though Ernes hu'Toe did have a certain charm to him.

Ka'Shino strained, trying not to stagger to the door as the three men followed. "All right boys, when will you have my last package ready?"

"Write down where you're staying. I'll bring everyting else you'll need tomorrow. Have everyting ready to go," hu'Toe said. "If for some chance, the Ministry gets too close to you, we'll plan on meeting you back here instead."

"Who are tese oter geologists you speak of?" Ka'Shino leaned over a table, giving her shoulders a rest. She wrote her address down, then stood upright too quickly. After windmilling her arms, ineffectively, she fell backward, and like a hyst turned over on its shell, she couldn't get to her feet without help.

"Careful," hu'Toe warned.

"I got it," she said, leaning farther forward this time. "It's a good ting you didn't get me what I asked for. If tat was te case, we'd just be a memory. Oh wait." She let her irritation show. "If tat were te case, my pack wouldn't have been so heavy, and I'd never have fallen in te first place."

"I wasn't afraid of te explosives detonating from your fall," hu'Toe defended, probably lying. "Word is spreading above ground tat an Albino killed one of teir prophets. Folks will be more suspicious of us tan usual."

Ka'Shino's stomach felt ill. She should've never visited hu'Narmin. "Yeah," was all she could say.

"But as long as you're on the subject of explosives, you know we can't risk anyting stronger tan tese pellets being discovered on te surface,' hu'Toe stated.

She knew. Surface-dwellers didn't even know about explosives yet. If they were discovered, better that the surface-dwellers found the lowest tech version than the really powerful stuff.

"Oh, yeah, it's te Newbly's," hu'Toe said.

"What?"

"Newbly, Rouche hu'Newbly and Sasha ka'Newbly. Te geologists tat we're meeting on te mountain," hu'Toe said.

"Oh, yeah." She had never heard those names before, but hopefully they were a better sort to work with than hu'Toe's other partners.

Adjusting her balance, she weaved around the smoky tables of the larger room where glowing tobacco rolls burned, flaring orange as if their little embers begged to blow up her pack. The piano player was singing and playing a new song about someone's gal with tempting blue eyes. Was it her imagination, or was the gang of cats staring at her again?

At the end of the tables, the little kneecap buster opened the hulking door like a vault. She stepped into the fresh cave air.

All that sound snuffed out when the heavy door latched shut as if the den never existed. She leaned against the smooth cave wall, relieved to be out of that place. She hadn't realized how much her eyes and lungs burned from the smoke until they didn't anymore. Her pack was heavy, but it gave her a rush of purpose. She could deal with this, forget her guilt and simply work. She wasn't merely justifying her actions. In the long run, this was the best option. Even if people did die, they'd be reborn, made better by her people. She could do this. She had to do this. This would be her one great deed.

In that dark, echoing maze of underground tunnels, she felt peace, for now.

Chapter 9

The TomFather

A shadow from a nearby land bridge shifted, forcing the warm rays of the morning sun to lighten the inner side of Dick hu'Mar's eyelids. He jumped as he awoke. He didn't remember falling asleep. He leaned up, rubbed his face, and blinked the world into focus. The sun wasn't as bright as he'd thought. It rimmed the horizon with a soft depressing glow. In another half hour, baked goods and scents of morning sausage, sausage for other people, not him, would fill the humid air.

It was a quiet place. The Beadledom forbade all ship travel within this last natural canal. Even though the Beadledom tried to limit travel in the natural moat that ringed the entirety of Mount Exclusion, it was impossible to keep all life out. Vinegar was already here and awake, enjoying a fish breakfast that he'd caught from those very waters.

"I'm guessing you didn't catch two of those, did you?" Hu'Mar's back was stiff and sore from sleeping on the cobble walks.

Vinegar glanced up, scaly flesh stretched from his mouth to the rest of the carcass. "Why would I catch two?"

Hu'Mar's stomach growled. "No reason. Where'd you run

off to last night?"

He dug into his leather bag, grabbed his bread, and broke some cheese from the small wheel he'd saved. He'd have to ration the thing. Meals weren't always a sure thing, even during the best of times. Something in his gut, probably the hunger, suggested that the best of times would allude him for a while longer. He could never catch a real break, at least not the right kind of break.

He labored to his feet, grunting as he stretched. Spur Central loomed to one side in all its rotten glory. One of the canals connected to the forbidden moat, was busy as usual. Unlike the moat itself, this canal was a commercial district, the end of the line, but crowded all the same. Folks from all over sailed there, docking, and hocking their wares to the folks of Spur Central. Already, the morning had awoken with footsteps on nearby boats, voices of Pissers shouting for their crews to wake up.

Very few people were on the streets this early. He wished he could sleep in too, but, lucky him, he'd burned down his apartment. The common street bums and travelers made this place a little risky for camping, but he didn't mind their company. As far as he was concerned, he fit right in with them. Most of them, however, had no problem sleeping in.

The people that were awake this early, had cloaks of various colors with hoods over their heads. Albinos.

One Albino with a large backpack hiked across the artificial bridge that spanned the commercial channel. It was sad what some of these poor souls were forced to endure. From the slouched angle of this one's body, the pack must've been almost as heavy as he or she was. He tried to make out this one's approaching face. With Albinos, it wasn't always easy to tell if they were a man or a woman unless they were right next to you. Many of them wore those thick smoky goggles, and when they removed their hoods, you could see a bald woman and a long-haired man just as often as a bald man and a long-haired woman. Though even the long-haired ones usually kept it bundled in a bun.

This one turned down a busy industrial spoke and disappeared before hu'Mar had a good chance to really see any details. Chances were he wouldn't have recognized the person anyway, but every Albino in the city was now a curiosity to him. Somewhere, drifting through these streets, was the one who'd visited him yesterday and who might be responsible for a few killings. The subtext of their brief conversation had alluded to choices that might hurt some people, possibly even the whole city. Hu'Mar's stomach growled again. He had to focus. Find that Pin of Poison.

The relic wasn't his only priority since he also had to find his next meal. Those two goals could be related if he worked fast enough. "Come on Vinegar. We've got work to do."

Vinegar ignored hu'Mar and kept ripping at the fish. Hu'Mar waited, but as soon as the cat finished his meal, it plopped onto his side. "Please don't do this to me again. Not today."

"What do we know?" Hu'Mar paced around Vinegar.

"That I hate you?" Vinegar offered.

"Jodeign ka'Nairie comes by, not offering much information at all, says she's lost a relic, one that pairs well with a ring she already owns. All she really gives us is a short list of people who knew she had the relic: Duke, Jef hu'Rino, and Maizy ka'Dillie. Then there were the former owners of that relic, as per ka'Feebal's ledger, of which were Ish hu'Narmin, who's dead, then Maizy hu'Dillie, or could that be ka'Nairie's ka'Dillie? Man or woman, the name's too similar to be coincidence. Then there's—"

"You're poisoning my mind with this chatter, Dick hu'Droning," Vinegar said.

"Ka'Nairie is keeping something from us. Why would she fail to mention ka'Feebal?" He stuffed his hands in his pockets. "I hate it when a client withholds information. We'll have to study her a little more. She might not think that her secrets are relevant, but in my experience, one's shady dealings often lead to the shady disaster they hire me to solve."

"Maybe she's afraid of ka'Feebal. I am," Vinegar suggested. "You really should screen your clients better before you say yes to their cases."

"I don't know who this Duke animal is, or Maizy hu-ka'Dillie, but Jef hu'Rino sounds very familiar." Where had he heard that name before?

"Your scary girlfriend could be at fault too." Vinegar groaned, rolling onto his back as if in agony at the exercise.

Hu'Mar rubbed the stubble on his chin. He immediately thought of ka'Nairie, but Vinegar was referring to ka'Feebal, the dealer. And how could ka'Nairie know of her possible double dealings? Could ka'Nairie be afraid of her like Vinegar suggested? She seemed little more than a drunken has-been relics dealer. But since relics rarely changed hands as often as that Pin of Poison had, ka'Feebal had to be a suspect.

"Before we track down Duke or hu'Rino, we need to visit ka'Feebal again." His stomach turned at the memory of her fermented kiss. Even now, he could taste the fumes from her breath, and it helped him forget all about wanting breakfast. "Maybe even find Maizy hu-ka'Dillie."

"How about you go there, and I'll check the alley grounds for this one they call Duke," Vinegar suggested.

Vinegar would search diligently even though right now, the cat was poised for a morning nap. As soon as hu'Mar got far enough away, Vinegar would adopt hu'Mar's ambition and would go stir crazy if he didn't track the name down. On the flip side, hu'Mar would grow lazy and probably fall asleep in ka'Feebal's lap.

He shuddered again. "You're coming with me."

"I wish I never met you as a kitten."

"You say that all the time. Suck it up. We can't undo the past. Let's just get this over with for today." At some point, he'd need to look into this murder angle. It might have nothing to do with his Albino shadow, but being hunted by the Ministry was almost as bad as going hungry and homeless. One mystery at a time. Pay the bills first, then clear his name.

Vinegar rolled onto his feet as if he had no legs to get in the way of his fat barrel roll. It could have been the fur, but he looked a lot rounder than any mouser. "What is thy bidding, oh, bonded one?"

"Let's go visit ka'Feebal before she gets her morning buzz," hu'Mar said. "You can check the alley grounds on our way there, see if anyone knows this Duke or has heard any dirt on ka'Nairie."

Vinegar yawned. In that yawn, hu'Mar could see the cat's displeasure in the plan.

Hu'Mar stretched sore muscles as they meandered through the heart of the city. He often took a stroll on long nights when he had to think, but lately Vinegar had been taking more of those evening walks instead. The spokes of the city often blended together, but he had a rough idea of where he was, most of the time. If he ever got lost, all spokes led to the center. He led the way to one of the smelliest spokes that bordered the edge of the commercial district. It was on the way to ka'Feebal's place, and it stunk of cat.

"Here's your chance, Vinegar. See what you can find."

"This would be a lot easier without you," Vinegar complained.

"Fine. I'll hang back. I'd hate to compromise your style."

Vinegar shrugged his shoulders, much like a human would roll their eyes, and cautiously stepped into the cluttered alley. A human would've had to crawl over the fallen stacks of pallets that filled the alley. They were as tall as a man and propped at odd angles by overfilled garbage baskets that hadn't been emptied in years. This wasn't a place that humans would want to spend any time in, especially if they valued their health. The musk of cats marking their territory filled the place, and the dark shadows that shrouded every nook, cranny, or other sort of hiding place, solidified a heavy sense of foreboding. Even Vinegar appeared nervous.

Hu'Mar backed off a little, letting their bond thin as much as possible to help imbue Vinegar with some of hu'Mar's courage and ambition.

He wasn't far enough away to fully transmit all of his subconscious mannerisms to the cat, but some would make it through. He wanted to be close enough to eavesdrop on any conversation, but he was far enough away, that he could hopefully go unnoticed by the alleyway residents.

Plus, hu'Mar couldn't get so far away that Vinegar's lazy attitude fully transferred over. Then he really would struggle paying attention to the conversation. As always, hu'Mar prayed to the Gears above that nobody killed Vinegar while they were separated since the shock of a fully severed bond would leave him trying to lick his own anus.

Thinking of licking bums made ka'Feebal come to mind again. That first kiss, a cross between wet chalk, the spicy tongue-numbing slab berries, and sickly-sweet alcohol, would forever be imprinted on his mind. By the Gears above and below, hopefully he wouldn't have to kiss her again to get inside.

Vinegar broke into singing, "Hey kitty, kitty, kitty."

Hu'Mar cringed. Vinegar should probably be more respectful. Even humans were wary of the TomFather. But hu'Mar wouldn't have been intimidated by the mobster, and that left Vinegar's caution too lacking.

Reflective eyes on a flat yellow face popped into view. "Vinegar, is that you?"

Hu'Mar recognized Skippy, the TomFather. He wasn't alone either. Shadows with little glowing eyes popped out of corners and cans. Had Skippy collected more minions since last time?

"It can't be him," another cat mewed as it jumped lightly onto a rotten crate. "He's got no tail."

"Yeah, you're right," a third cat agreed, her voice sounded too nasally and confident at the same time. "This one's a lot uglier too. Scat cat, this is our dig."

"Listen, Skippy," Vinegar said, "I'm on the prowl, and hu'Mar back there, is looking for some info."

The cats lifted their heads in unison. Hu'Mar paced as if he wasn't paying them any attention. Sometimes Vinegar went too far, the obstinate cat. The whole idea for hanging back here was to eavesdrop without being noticed.

"He wants to know if you've heard of some loser named Duke," Vinegar continued. "I don't know much about him, other than the fact that he's tight with our favorite up and coming female politician, Jodeign ka'Nipulator."

"Why don't you have your master ask her himself?" The other cats snickered. "Is it because your Dick hu'Coward has a thing for this lady? I heard humans liked to use pets to pick up gals, I just didn't realize that they were having the pet do the actual picking up. If I were you, I'd ditch the human, and forget the consequences."

"Can it, Calico," Skippy said. "We all know Vinegar is spineless. No need to rub it in."

"And tailless now too it would seem." Calico rolled on her back in mirth, then off the crate and gracefully landed on her feet. A perfect landing that would really make Vinegar jealous.

Vinegar sat, careful not to cause his stubby tail anymore pain. The gang of cats weren't often nice to him, but today they seemed extra ruthless. Calico, who was actually a slender black with a few white patches, circled Vinegar while Skippy sat casually on a garbage can and groomed his perfectly manicured orange and yellow fur.

"Why do you let that Dick hu'Man boss you around?" Skippy asked. "You're the cat. We're the dominant species of this world."

"It's Dick hu'Mar," Vinegar defended, surprising even hu'Mar.

"Dick hu'Cares?" Calico sniffed.

"Listen," Vinegar said, "you going to help me or not?"

"Tell us your errand, Pigeon," Calico said.

Vinegar hissed.

Calm down, hu'Mar willed.

"This Duke fellow is one of only a couple individuals who knew that ka'Nairie had a certain relic in her possession."

"Past tense," Skippy observed. "So she no longer has this relic."

"You know her type. She's the sort to rub up against you if she thinks it'll get her ahead, but all it really gets is trouble. Kind of like you, Calico."

Calico hissed back. This could get ugly. "I'm not the one

who—"

Skippy cut Calico off with a low growl, meant more for Calico than Vinegar. Still, both cats swung their heads around and looked straight at hu'Mar for half a breath.

Hu'Mar pretended to mind his own business.

Then they returned to their own conversation. "You just described a quarter of the human female population. Isn't Dick hu'Ever a light-skinned human? I thought they didn't mingle with different colors, so what's he doing helping this gal?"

"No," Vinegar said. "The darks and the lights get along fine. They even breed sometimes. It's the orange Pissers and the pale Bules that they have a hard time with."

"Humans," Calico swore.

"I don't know a Duke," Skippy yawned. "Do you have any other reason for gracing us with your presence this day? Especially with your human in tow?"

"No," Vinegar watched Calico carefully as the black cat circled him. He was obviously familiar with her, and the last thing hu'Mar needed was to break up a cat fight right now. Maybe it would've been better if hu'Mar hadn't been here for this. These cats were too guarded and hostile with him near.

"In that case, it's time to scat—cat." Skippy turned to leave.

Normally, Vinegar would let the two slide away. Maybe it was hu'Mar's instincts kicking in. Regardless, hu'Mar backed up a little more, just in case it helped solidify Vinegar's resolve.

He couldn't hear the cats anymore, and their subtle body language was almost impossible to read. But without Skippy in the picture, Vinegar had something more to do here, and hu'Mar let him be.

Vinegar jumped onto the garbage can where Skippy had sat. Words were exchanged. Then Vinegar leapt off the can and, like normal, landed hard on his head. Or more accurately, he landed soft on his head, but hard on Calico.

Vinegar walked a thin line there, but hu'Mar was too far away now to know what had caused Vinegar to attack. Vinegar twisted back onto his feet. Calico was a thin waste of energy. Vinegar could snap her neck in a heartbeat, but sometimes it was the thin wiry ones you had to watch out for.

Vinegar advanced on Calico, and Calico lunged at him but only got a mouthful of fur.

Vinegar rolled over, slashed out his claws and . . . nothing. Just a slap to the face. That was the paw that Vinegar had lost a few claws from.

Calico and a few of the remaining cats, mostly kittens, laughed. No doubt they were giving Vinegar a hard time for letting a human declaw him.

Vinegar was still in a strike position, and he'd only lost two claws. He showed Calico how sharp his others were.

This time, Calico fell backward, reeling from the pain and shock, her tail fluffed up to twice its size, all her humor gone.

Now hu'Mar, along with the entire neighborhood could hear the "Reaaaaaaaoow!" And the fight was on.

Calico fought like a feral lioness.

Vinegar fought like a human. His missing claws gave him a disadvantage, but his headbutting caught Calico off guard. In the end, a cat was never meant to fight like a human. Calico was hurt more, only because Vinegar's hair was like an extra suit of armor, but he was getting worn out.

Hu'Mar was tempted to break up the fight, but held off, either because his distance had given him Vinegar's lazy mindset or because if hu'Mar broke up the fight Vinegar could never hold his head high around any of the mobster cats in the city ever again. So he watched and hoped for the best.

Then Calico got a few good slashes in and managed to pin Vinegar. Hu'Mar couldn't stand by anymore and let this alley cat kill his palsy partner. He advanced a little, but not before Calico bared her sharp yellow teeth.

Hu'Mar couldn't reach Vinegar in time.

Calico sunk her teeth into Vinegar's neck. It was meant to puncture. It did, too, just not Vinegar.

Calico screamed and flung herself back.

Hu'Mar stopped, then laughed. Vinegar was acting tender where a small patch of fur had ripped free from his neck.

Calico rolled like a tiger fish that had just been hooked

Hard Boiled Cabbage: Big Trouble In Spur Central

as she tried to dislodge the thorny cocklebur from her mouth. Vinegar had a few of them hidden deep in his fur. Those things were too sharp and painful to clean out on his own, and hu'Mar had long since given up trying to help remove them since a little poke from the variety around here usually caused an uncomfortable burning sensation.

Vinegar sauntered around a garbage can. There were cats everywhere, and he was clearly talking with one of them. They chatted for a minute, and, all the while, Calico cried in the background, trying to dislodge the prickly seed.

When Vinegar finished, he strutted past Calico and toward hu'Mar. Calico, cocklebur still in her mouth, growled for an attack. With all the adult cats gone, the only ones left to fight were a dozen or so of kitten minions. Most of these Vinegar could easily best if they came one at a time, but unfortunately, they all attacked at the same time. Vinegar slashed, rolled, and bit. They were all too used to fighting birds and mice, so they tried toying with him.

Hu'Mar was about to intervene for real this time, but Vinegar shot him a look that said, "Give me a minute." So he respected Vinegar's wishes and held back.

The kittens shortly overpowered him, pinning him down with multiple tiny teeth, bared.

Through the cloud of kitties, Skippy returned. "What's all this about?"

Hu'Mar snuck closer.

"Calico is obviously jealous of me. You know how she can be," Vinegar said.

Calico finally got the cocklebur out of her mouth. She hissed bloody spit, then jumped onto a crate behind Skippy.

"Vinegar," the TomFather's expressions seemed to say, "I like you. You got the brains of a beetle, but the heart of a lion. Don't worry about Calico. She won't cause you any more problems, right Calico?"

Calico drooped her head slightly, and growled her disappointment.

Skippy started walking away again, then paused. "By

the way, I'd suggest you try to keep your human away from Jodeign ka'Nairie. Getting too close to her can be dangerous, if you know what I mean."

"You know I can't help that. I made the mistake of becoming a palsy to a minister-wannabe."

Skippy flicked his tail.

Vinegar flinched. "If you learn anything about this Duke fellow, you let me know."

"Not if you're dead," Skippy warned.

The bloodthirsty kittens looked wantonly to Skippy for permission to sink their drooling fangs into Vinegar's hide.

"I'm stuck to a human," Vinegar reminded. "You think I fear death? It might be a relief!"

Hu'Mar finally understood what Vinegar was up to. He was using a trick hu'Mar had often employed. Make the man you're interrogating, feel as though they'd won, then see what falls from their mouth. Humans had a different type of instinct, an instinct that Vinegar was privy to now, but that Skippy could never have anticipated. Skippy knew ka'Nairie. He might even know something useful, something he had to hide.

Cats had their own set of instincts too. The real benefit of being a palsy was that it gave each partner a fresh new perspective, so Vinegar could use a human trick to interrogate a crime lord of the cat variety.

"Maybe Calico was right. Perhaps I should kill you now," Skippy said. "You can be born again, free from this human bond."

"Would you really? I think that'd be a great idea," Vinegar lied, or at least hu'Mar assumed it was a lie. "Skippy, you have no idea how horrible it is being stuck to this human. It's probably worse than having Calico as your number one, though being pals with ka'Nairie could be just as bad."

"Watch your tongue," Skippy said. "How dense can you be?"

"Pretty dense," Vinegar admitted. "I'm just saying, I'd be careful about the humans you're seen hanging around with. They tend to affect your reputation."

Hard Boiled Cabbage: Big Trouble In Spur Central

Hu'Mar knew this was meant as a dig against himself.

"You're treading dangerous ground now," Skippy warned. "Getting too close to ka'Nairie can be as dangerous for you too."

"She doesn't sound scary to me. Only like she has you in her purse. Meow, pussy cat," Vinegar meowed with exaggerated mockery.

Skippy's face remained still, but his tail gave another small twitch, a tattle tail.

Another small cat leaned closer to Vinegar's fur with sharp teeth leaking a bit of saliva. Vinegar ignored it as he pressed Skippy.

"The only thing I don't understand, street savvy as you are, is what could she offer you that you can't already get?"

Skippy's tail twitched again. "I think I'm done with this game."

"Yes, let's see. You've got money enough to keep a gang of alley cats devoted. You've got food enough to get fat on. You command fear and respect. But I don't see humans bowing down before you. Neither do I see other animals paying their respects other than Calico, but is she really the cat you want to trust as your number one?"

The tail twitched again.

"I can talk with ka'Nairie you know, or at least, I can understand her. I'm pretty good at writing too, so communicating with her shouldn't be a problem. Does she have a cute kitty that you're trying to make purr? You help me, and I'll help you."

Skippy sighed. "You're a clever cat. I could do with a cat like you in my gang."

"But you won't."

"No. I won't. Sorry, but if you're lucky, you'll get born again nearby and can join my gang as a fresh recruit. Let's hope that you keep some of that cleverness."

"At least satisfy my last curiosity? Who's this Duke fellow?

"Duke, ha, what could you possibly want with a groomer?" Skippy turned and walked away.

Calico and a couple other cats followed behind him, but just as Skippy was out of sight, Calico turned to the dog-pile of kitties and said, "Finish him." Then she too disappeared.

The cat with the drool lunged first, mouth agape.

Vinegar curled up and slammed his forehead into the cat's maw, then he tumbled to the side, knocking off another kitty. With all claws bared, Vinegar slashed and swiped, freeing himself in a moment and bowled through two stunned cats.

They were younger, so they recovered quickly and caught up faster.

Vinegar paused. "Learned this one from a skunk."

The kitties got closer, and Vinegar sprayed them all. Hot stinging urine shot into their eyes.

Three of them ran away crying. Two remained and advanced. Vinegar turned to face them. He yawned, big enough to show them his own set of teeth and that he wasn't scared.

They paused, then slowly backed up.

"You better learn to respect me." Vinegar stretched then strolled toward them.

At last, they turned and ran off. He didn't even have to kill any of them. This was good. He only had nine lives after all. It was better not to kill those kitties and run up his tally on such a simple errand. Hu'Mar didn't believe in such things, but Vinegar held true to the superstition that killing nine cats in a single incarnation, even in self-defense, would bring very bad luck.

Hu'Mar left the edge of the alley and headed down one of the city spokes to ka'Feebal's place. Vinegar was slow to follow, but he'd catch up eventually.

The further hu'Mar distanced himself from Vinegar, the more he wanted to rub against each lamppost he passed even though it was pointless. He didn't have scent glands in his head like cats did. If he wasn't wearing a shirt, he could rub his armpits on things, but that might feel unnatural.

So while hu'Mar could talk himself out of acting like a cat, most of the time, his subconscious instincts were at war, fighting for dominance. But, as long as his cat instincts were currently winning the battle, he might as well use them.

The upcoming hub that was connected to this spoke had a decorative pool in the center. It was often used as a prison for water creatures that invaded Spur Central. Spies of the aquatic variety were usually incarcerated here until someone ate them. Hu'Mar's stomach growled, and he decided to try his hand at them.

He knelt and stared into the water as he let instinct do the work. With lightning speed his hand splashed into the water, like Vinegar had done on multiple occasions. Instead of catching the passing fish, a frog slapped onto the cobble bench instead.

Where had that come from?

The frog glared at him, croaked, then jumped back into the water.

Forget it. The bond was weakening again since Vinegar was catching up. He'd try again at lunch.

"Good work back there," he said without turning.

"That was more fun than you know," Vinegar said. "Don't make me do it again."

"What kind of animal do you suppose grooms a human?" hu'Mar asked, thinking about Duke.

"Beats me," Vinegar said. "I wouldn't consider ever licking any human's hair. Can you imagine the hairballs! I feel like gagging, just thinking about it."

Hu'Mar shook his head. He'd have to visit a crier after ka'Feebal to find this Duke, but at least there couldn't be too many groomers named Duke in Spur Central.

If he were lucky, ka'Feebal would have something better than bread and cheese at her place, but likely, her cupboards were still empty, which brought another thing to mind. If he was going to get into her house, he'd need a little incentive for her.

He counted his salt again, seeing if he had enough. He hated spending his money on liquor, but that was the only sure way to get her talking. So much for petty cash.

Chapter 10

No Job For Sissies

Juniper ka'Shino rested against a wooden building, and the wall bowed against her weight. This whole town felt ready to collapse under its own neglect. She fidgeted under her pack, bruises already forming from the straps that dug into her shoulders. She closed her eyes and took a deep breath of morning air. The rotten egg smell of sulfur was almost overshadowed by the more pleasant scent of cook smoke, pastries, and chickens. Not as satisfying as the aroma of the damp isolated caves, but far better than the sewer tunnels she'd recently emerged from.

Before ka'Shino's time, a very forward-thinking committee of Toughs, which later evolved into the Beadledom, decided they didn't like filling their streets with their own waste like many of the monarch lands did, so they'd hired Albino engineers to tunnel sewer lines beneath their city to empty into Lake Tallow, the giant moat around Mount Exclusion. But most Toughs had forgotten the service the Albinos had done, and no Tough remembered the back doors and access grates to lesser alleys that the Albinos had built into the sewer systems. Bad luck for them when someone like her was smuggling in hundreds of pounds of explosives.

Hard Boiled Cabbage: Big Trouble In Spur Central

Shrouded by the morning's long shadows, she climbed out onto the road near Mount Exclusion's moat. It had been a ten-minute journey from the underground gin joint to the sewers, then another ten to the surface, but it felt like twice that. She heaved her pack up to lighten the tension on her shoulders. It didn't work. Luckily her inn wasn't too far away. This would be one job she'd be happy to be done with. Already it felt like her pack drew too many unwelcomed and questioning glances, like that man and his cat.

Wait. That cat didn't have a tail.

Had Dick hu'Mar recognized her? He hadn't been the worst surface-dweller she'd met, but one visit with him had reminded her why she was doing all this. Hu'Toe and his companions were right. The world needed her people. They needed their technology. Most of all, they needed their ambition to improve mankind as a whole.

Five minutes later, she stood before the doors. She sniffed deeply to figure out if the sewer smell lingered on her body.

She couldn't tell. Either she still smelled, or the stink was stuck in her nose. Why should she even care? Her shoulders ached, and she yearned to plop down onto her bed.

The innkeeper had actually named this place The Dumpy Din. It was a three-story building that bordered a canal that led from Lake Tallow to Grandmammie Lake, a much larger ring of water that lay a couple of days away. The sailors who traded along these canals were often called Pissers, because every group of people apparently needed a nickname, and on account of their orange skin, the fact that they were always on the water, their crude natures, and maybe because of the carefree way that they were always seen peeing over the sides of their boats, the name stuck.

There were some Mops too, vagrant traders, of various colors given their name for the common household items they traded, like mops. Needless to say, the inns along the canal didn't usually discriminate as heavily against foreigners as the inner-city establishments. Of course, nobody liked a Bule, but if you let an orange-faced Pisser in, you might as well let a Bule in.

Hostile eyes followed her through the dining room as she plodded to the stairs. Was she being paranoid, or did she hear people mentioning Crazy Ish and Bule? She was sure she heard Bule, but did they suspect her?

One man broke her concentration. "Ya got a load thar, sweetie." He was a drunk Pisser. It wasn't hard to tell when a Pisser was drunk. Sometimes their faces turned a darker shade of orange, but usually, if they were breathing, they were drunk. "How 'bout'a hand?"

"No tanks—yipe!" She jumped.

The Pisser let go of her butt. He was grinning—actually laughing and slapping his mates.

Who cared if anyone here suspected her of murder? She lowered her pack and fixed a playful scowl on her face. She didn't feel mirthful, but spending so much time in the upper crust had given her a spine, and she wasn't about to let this sailor off the hook. "Is tis where you're sleeping while in town? or are you just sitting around to get drunk and puke up what passes for food around here?"

"Ya offarin' me a bed, sweetheart?"

She lifted her goggles onto her forehead and fixed him with her red eyes. She didn't know why they unnerved surface men so much, but they did. Demon eyes or witch eyes, they called them.

He couldn't pull his attention from them. She grabbed his mug of ale from the table and took a Tough-sized swig, downing the last of his drink. She held it out, and the Innkeeper refilled it while she grabbed the Pisser's shoulder with her free hand. She puckered her lip, very slow and seductive, as she closed the space between them.

"Whoa's" and "Oooh's" bubbled from around the room. The Pisser just dropped his jaw, surprised that a Bule was playing his game. His dropped jaw snapped shut, and the edges of his mouth slowly turned up at the corners.

Ka'Shino smiled and brought the overflowing mug back around. She waited until his smile was hopelessly optimistic, then she poured the entire mug down his shirt and onto his lap.

Hard Boiled Cabbage: Big Trouble In Spur Central

His smile morphed into twisted rage, and she smashed the mug hard into his face and shoved his shoulder. He fell back in his chair.

The impact left a resounding crack as he hit the ground hard, blood oozing from his broken nose and several small lacerations where the mug had shattered. Cheers and laughter erupted around the room. She pulled her pack back to her shoulder. Adrenaline made the bag feel lighter than before.

She walked up the stairs and to her room. Music soon drowned all other noises from the room. Patience was a good thing, but sometimes, you had to let others know where they stood with you, especially in Tough towns, and doubly so with Piss-ants like that.

Once in her room, ka'Shino locked the door, dropped the pack on the bed, and threw her cloak to the floor. She didn't want to be disturbed. She missed the caves even more. She couldn't explain it, but they breathed, sweat, and spoke to her like no other place had. The smooth walls, the dripping ceilings, the ever-present threat of the unknown, and especially the loneliness. She loved the time to herself after having spent her whole life in the great city of Tuberlow, the underground capitol of the Albinos.

She checked her pocket clock, more for comfort than to know the time. Someday, she envisioned all clocks would be standardized. They'd be divided evenly by a series of numbers, like the big clock at Tuberlow University, the Albino school of higher learning that she'd attended for a year and hoped to return to. But for now all clocks, personal or communal, were labeled according to the relevant tasks of the owner or community. Hers had initials for her normal agenda. B for breakfast because you needed energy for your day. S for study because learning was important. L for lunch because you could forget it while studying. W for work because money didn't just come to you. D for dinner for obvious reasons. W for worry because no woman's day was complete without it. S for snack to drown the worry. And Z for sleep so she could do it all over again.

She snapped the clock shut because despite what it read,

it was time she got to work. At least that Pisser had given her exactly what she needed to stay motivated. She felt good and strong, but her energy might not last since she usually went to bed around this time. If these geologists were really as sharp as hu'Toe had said, maybe nobody would have to die from the explosions.

Below the straw mattress, she retrieved the modified meat grinder from her personal belongings, to prepare her explosive pellets. They weren't bad, but she needed a little more bang from them, and years of experimentation had taught her that she needed to crush the pellets down. So her grinder was full of black explosive dust instead of meat grease.

Her time in Tuberlow had taught her many things, explosives being one such discipline. It was there she'd learned clockwork. It was there her father worked so hard to get ahead but never saved enough salt to season the table with. Her mom wasn't much better. She was Miss Proper and Perfect. Do it right, be good, keep your head down and put your back into your work and everything will work itself out. This was no way to stand out in a competitive world, and ka'Shino wanted to live better.

At the time, escaping into the wild tunnels for two years seemed the perfect method of breaking the cycle of their ignominy. So far, this was proving true. Those tunnels had facilitated her first encounter with Ernes hu'Toe. Like herself, he too had signed on, joining a group to hunt what was left of the ten-foot-thick tunnel worms for their oil.

Once the meat grinder's clamp was secured onto her table, with a bucket below, ka'Shino opened her pack and fed the explosive pellets into the hopper. With each crank of the handle, she turned the gears, grinding and crushing the saline-sized pellets into smaller chips and powder. Her hands were surprisingly steadier than her nerves. Her body worked with practiced confidence while her mind labored with the complications of guilt.

It was fortuitous that surface-dwellers hadn't discovered explosives yet, or it would only be a matter of time before some bigoted Toughs or jealous monarchs decided to collapse the Albino cities.

Hard Boiled Cabbage: Big Trouble In Spur Central

The hypocrisy of it all made her pause. Albinos were afraid of surface-dwellers using explosives against them, and here, she was about to destroy a holy volcanic mountain which might flood a major surface city with lava. At least the Albino Republic was taking precautions to destroy only the Tomb of Ascension. Show her a Tough that would be as considerate if their goal threatened an Albino city.

She wouldn't be here now if her path hadn't taken her into the hunting group four months ago. At the time, she needed the cash, and hunting the giant cave-forming worms, a remnant of a long-ago ascended species, was a very profitable venture. It wasn't without serious risk though, which was one reason it paid so well. It was dangerous, with many hunters failing to return home at all, but when each worm could produce nearly fifty barrels of oil, the bold were richly rewarded.

The group had been a mix of mostly Albinos and a few legitimately crazy surface-dwellers. But Ernes hu'Toe hadn't been like the other worm hunters. He'd been hunting people, people with skills, guts, and a good measure of attitude that bordered on the rebellious. What better place to find such a person than among a group of loners who fought one of the largest most dangerous sentient creatures above and below the earth?

She cranked the grinder again, and black dust puffed from the open ends of the grinder. One small spark and this whole inn would go up in a glorious fireball. Not too different from ka'Shino's own misgivings about her duty. Sometimes she wished she hadn't met hu'Toe. When she had demonstrated her precision with explosives to kill their first worm, he'd pulled her aside and offered her more money than ten worms would've brought in. And her job was important. Her people needed her. The human race needed her. Her time hunting worms had proven that even surface-dwellers were good at heart, even if they'd been trained with ugly biases. That was one of the reasons she had to destroy the Tomb of Ascension. People had to learn to appreciate each other's differences. How could they ever fulfill their true potential if they totally erased their entire civilization by ascending? She packed the ground granules as tight as she could into hardened-pulp tubes. The better they were compacted, the stronger their bang would be.

Ernes hu'Toe had better be right about this. If anyone got hurt because of her…

Chapter 11

The Way to His Woman's Heart

A wasp landed on Dick hu'Mar's hand, and its stinger dug at his callused palm. He trapped the yellow and black nuisance between pinched fingers.

"Wrong move." He squeezed, and it popped like a kernel of sweet corn, the wet pulpy middle spraying out the end, leaving only the dry outer husk.

The door opened a crack, just enough for a sliver of light to stripe the pale face behind it. Either Renu ka'Feebal had a hangover, was leery of visitors, or didn't want to let the swarm of wasps inside. It was likely a combination of all three. He had to get inside. Ka'Feebal was the axle this greasy gear spun around. So much of his case hinged on understanding this relic and how all these people, dead and alive, were connected.

"Ka'Feebal, I don't know if you remember me, but—"

The door slammed shut. He smiled. Okay, she did remember.

He gently rapped against her door again.

From inside, he heard a bolt slide, making him wonder if she was locking him out. Then the thin chain chinked against itself as it fell and banged against the solid wood. Then the door opened wider, and hu'Mar walked in.

"Shut the door behind you, you big ape." Her voice sounded lovely, like gravel against eggshells.

"Do you know why I'm here?"

ka'Feebal sunk into her padded wicker couch and tried to get comfortable. Hu'Mar sat across from her. How to proceed? Maybe he should ask questions first, then bribe her second. Back in Nebylon, he might have tried a soft approach, but soft as ka'Feebal looked, she wasn't the sort to approach gently. A little false flattery might work. She'd see through it in an instant, but who didn't like to play that game every now and then? Especially since this raunchy woman was unlikely to have many suiters that would flirt, of their own free will and choice, with her. But if he could catch her in a good humor...

"This one," she held up a necklace full of relics and tapped a bone that had been carved into the shape of a teacup, "it keeps hangovers away, but it gives you extra gas. I don't have a pair for it, but since I don't get company very often, I don't worry."

"Everybody passes wind." Hu'Mar choked as the implications of her statement were punctuated by a silent follow up. Holding his breath, he leaned closer to examine the necklace. He doubted very much that the choker was missing many matches. Never had he seen so many relics in one place at one time. He could only guess what attributes were at her disposal. "I admire a woman who isn't overly self-conscious about herself."

"What do you know about admiration, Dick hu'Mar? Yeah, I know who you are. You're that grimy fortune teller who preys off stupid people who should know better."

"It pays the rent."

"Ha," she snorted. "What good is rent without a good supply of booze?" She picked up an empty glass, swirled it as if there was some imaginary liquid in there, then tipped it upside down with a frown before replacing it on the short wicker table.

"I noticed that you make your own slab arrack. I thought that liquor was only good for tanning leather, so times must be a little hard for you too?" He wasn't sure if they were, but if ka'Feebal felt like they were, then that might be a motive for stealing relics from the likes of ka'Nairie.

"Ba! I like the hard stuff. Puts hair on your chest." Ka'Feebal smiled, puffing out her substantially soggy and sweat-soaked bosom, fully knowing that she'd placed a real nasty image into hu'Mar's mind.

With a slow exhale, hu'Mar tried to clear his mind. She did like this game. Two could play at it though, and he had an ace up his sleeve.

"You know something, ka'Feebal, I like you." He really did too, as long as he overlooked her flab, manners, and smell. "Most men can't appreciate someone of your—girth. I think they must be intimidated."

"Ah, shucks." She laughed like a donkey. "You slick romantic you. Where've you been my whole life?"

"Lonely and unfulfilled, at least till now."

"Well, you talk a good talk, sweetie, but I'm not sure that you're all that good of a fortune teller." She folded her arms and reclined in the cushion of her back flesh.

"How do you mean?"

"You ain't no Tough. I can see that. Neither am I, to be honest. And outside of Tough country, it's more fitting for a fool to come courting with a gift. You didn't bring me a present, did you?" She wiggled her matted eyebrows up, mocking and encouraging at the same time.

Hu'Mar pulled a small gourd from his pocket. He had the strangest urge to place the dried squash in his armpit, so his clammy sweat would mark the bottle as his own. He avoided the urge. That was a very cat thing to do, so Vinegar was straying further away outside. That wasn't what hu'Mar needed. Great Gears forbid, next he'd be rubbing his head against ka'Feebal, again, which could really lead to dangerous places.

Ka'Feebal laughed. "I knew I liked you from the minute I saw you." She leaned forward, her hand shooting out to snatch the liquor.

"Ah-uh-uh," hu'Mar said, withdrawing the gourd. "I need your help first." He didn't want her to get plastered before he got some answers

Hard Boiled Cabbage: Big Trouble In Spur Central

Ka'Feebal licked her lips like a shriveled codfish in the desert. Her hand shook as she pushed herself back into her chair. "You sure know how to torture a brittle old woman, Dick hu'Mar."

"You're about as brittle as a lava flow," hu'Mar suggested, but left out his skepticism on her age.

Her eyelids narrowed slightly, like a seductive toad. "Even lava needs a little heat to sustain it."

"Perhaps, but when it cools, it forms crystals. I'd much rather spend my time with a nice olivine than a sulfuric river of death."

Ka'Feebal farted again. The smell was different and somehow worse than the normal rotten egg smell of the volcanic air. It seemed more potent and aged like she'd recently drunk some old-bad-booze. Even she crinkled her nose. "Aren't you the smoothest talker ever? I bet the young ladies just line up for a chance to see you, then shove a blade into your gut."

"But not you, ka'Feebal." Hu'Mar dangled the gourd in front of her. "You'd take sour kraut over boiled cabbage any day, wouldn't you?"

"You flatter me." She crossed her arms. The skin didn't sag or flap as one might expect on an old lady, but then again, there was more under her skin than just bone and time—literally and figuratively. "Get to the point."

"I'm interested in buying a relic."

"I don't sell that sort of thing anymore. Now can I have that drink?"

She was a sloppy drunk, but from her ledgers, she was also a meticulous woman. He suspected that she was playing hard to get out of caution.

He wasn't about to give up yet. "Renu ka'Feebal, you haven't heard me out."

"I'm about to herd you out if you don't unstop that cork." If she stared much longer at his gourd, she might start drooling.

"Either you're a really good actress, or you set everything up to have a great alibi," hu'Mar said. "I know your racket. I've seen your books. You've sold a lot of relics over the years, sometimes more than once. Evidently, you still have some relics.

"Your point?"

Why was she dodging him? Time for a little encouragement. Hu'Mar stood, chest out, arms spread to appear as big and imposing as possible. He could be intimidating when he had a mind for it. As he paced around his chair, he gauged ka'Feebal's attention on him before he lifted his gourd, unplugged it, took a whiff. He almost coughed. That made her lick her lips all the more eagerly. This stuff was the sort to knock a big man like him out cold after less than half a gourd. Her eyes were practically bulging with desire. She could smell it too. She was an addict, and if she couldn't get a swig, it would be akin to torture.

So he plugged it again. "People are dying and I need to find out why."

Desperation lingered in her trembling lip as she leaned forward. "I don't care for the Beadledom, and I don't talk to ministers."

Minister? Is that what she still thought? "It's my lucky day. I could care less about those club-wielding preachers and their precious Beadledom."

With some effort, ka'Feebal pried herself from her chair. She leaned in too close, and those wizened eyes stared hard into hu'Mar's. A sharp blade poked his gut. Where had that come from? He pretended not to notice the dagger that threatened to skewer him, and, really, he shouldn't have been surprised. This was Tough country after all.

"You smell like a minister to me," she accused.

"And you smell like an old pickled egg," hu'Mar said, straining nonchalance even though every muscle was tense to the point of aching.

Ka'Feebal grinned. "What did I tell you about flattering me? I know you're no minister and I know that nobody would miss you if you disappeared. And yes, I do remember you snooping through my books yesterday. I wasn't completely out, you know. So why you playing their game?"

"Old habits, new clients, and a couple of ministers who might arrest me on false pretenses. Let's talk about Jodeign ka'Nairie?"

"Never heard of her," ka'Feebal said. Suspicion gave way to reluctance, and her dagger disappeared into a sheath that was tucked into the folds of her nightgown. What else was she hiding in there? She stooped to retrieve two used cups on the floor. There was a dried crust from old drink lining the bottom. Her muumuu was at least a couple days old on her, but she decided it was cleaner than the glasses because she spit in the glasses, then wiped them out with the front hem of her nightgown.

On second thought, hu'Mar didn't want to know what else she was hiding in her muumuu. He looked away in case the lifted fabric revealed the sort of thing that shudders were made out of.

Ka'Feebal slapped the cups onto the coffee table with a loud clunk, then slapped her posterior into her wicker couch again with a large creak from the furniture and a groan from her pursed lips.

Hu'Mar sighed. He walked around the short table, uncorked the gourd and poured just a little bit into the bottom of each cup. He half expected ka'Feebal to lunge for the shot, but she continued to stare at him. He understood. When it came to other people's alcohol, you couldn't be too careful. People got poisoned that way. He picked up his glass, tried not to think of how many times it had been cleaned with spit- and pee-stained dresses, then gulped the burning liquid while suppressing a dry cough.

"Ha!" ka'Feebal shouted, then grabbed her glass and downed it in one gulp as if it were nothing more than water.

She'd been primed, but how tolerant was she to alcohol? Hu'Mar's eyes were still watering. He usually only bought the cheap booze. If plain water wouldn't make a man sick, he'd never drink even the weak stuff. He hated losing his wits, since in his line of work, wits were ninety percent of the game. With any luck, her guard would be down now that the liquor was on the table.

"Dark-skinned, twice as tall as me, and lips that kiss a hundred butts an hour?"

"Sorry?" Hu'Mar coughed.

"Jodeign ka'Nairie!" ka'Feebal said, eyeing her empty glass.

"Right, yes. What can you tell me about her and the relics she bought from you."

Ka'Feebal said nothing.

Hu'Mar sighed. Fine. He refilled her glass, but still just a swallow.

"Listen hu'Mar, honey, this cup is a lot bigger than that."

"But I'm having such a good chat," hu'Mar complained. "I'd hate to spoil that so quickly."

Ka'Feebal inhaled a long audible breath.

Hu'Mar tightened his grip on the gourd in case she lunged for it.

She didn't. Instead, she resigned herself to hu'Mar's slow drip. "That dame is trouble. Stay away from her if you know what's good for you."

Good, she was willing to play by his rules. Hu'Mar relaxed his grip on the gourd. "Is that why you stole her relic back?"

"I never stole anything back from anybody." She slammed her cup back down.

Hu'Mar was about to refill her glass when she snatched the gourd from his hand. "Ah, bolt me down," he sighed.

She took a long powerful swig, enough to knock a horse to the ground. She smacked her lips. "Not bad."

"Your ledger tells a different story. A lot of people have owned that relic in a short period of time. You sold her that Pin of Poison, but you also sold it to Ish hu'Narmin before that. There was also a Maizy hu'Dillie on your list, an Albino, I suspect." Hu'Mar waited a moment for any reaction. Nothing. "Did you know Ish hu'Narmin's dead? Drowned last night? Rumor has it an Albino was involved."

"His goldfish?" ka'Feebal asked, more concerned about the fish than hu'Narmin.

"Dead too."

"That's a shame," she said. "I liked that fish. He hated tea just about as much as me."

Hard Boiled Cabbage: Big Trouble In Spur Central

"There was one other guy who died last night. A palsy who got a little chummy with ka'Nairie's horse. Some Albino hit him too, possibly poisoning him. He might've learned something he shouldn't have." That assumption was a stretch. His death could be completely unrelated, but in hu'Mar's experience, coincidences like this were usually connected somehow.

"Listen hon," her raspy voice was softening from the wine. "You got nothin' on me. Like I said, I'm out of the business."

"If you're not involved in this, then tell me, why you sold ka'Nairie a relic recently, and who'd be interested in that same relic now? Surely someone wanting such a valuable artifact would come to you first."

"Pushy." Ka'Feebal stood, leaving the gourd on the table. "I've got berries to pick. Either help me or leave."

He had to keep her talking, so he followed her outside. Not many people grew slab berries on purpose. Hu'Mar tucked his collar tight against his neck. The last thing he needed was a wasp crawling through his clothes, but if ka'Feebal thought that picking slab berries would scare him away, he'd prove otherwise.

Ka'Feebal lifted her dress again, plucking tender berries and placing them in the fabric at the risk of offending the whole neighborhood. Plenty of wasps landed on hu'Mar, but avoided ka'Feebal. Like him, they too were probably averting their eyes from her lifted skirt.

Here goes nothing. He reached into the hedge that surrounded her home and pulled the reddish black berries from their vines. The darkest fell easily into his hands. Within seconds, he too was swarmed by wasps.

"So why has that Pin of Poison had so many owners in the last couple of decades? I thought most relics rarely changed owners."

His focus narrowed, and he tried not to worry. Wasps could smell fear, couldn't they? One had tried to sting him earlier, but it couldn't penetrate his callused hands. Now they were all over him, threatening to sting every last tender spot on his exposed body.

He wanted to shake them all off, swat them away. But

then they'd really get angry. If ka'Feebal could do this without getting stung, then maybe he could too. When ka'Feebal didn't answer his question, he slowly turned to face her.

Where'd she go?

She'd ditched him. She'd led him here, got him covered in wasps, and left.

Hu'Mar gritted his teeth and dropped his handful of berries. That was when the pain began.

***

Splash. Lake Tallow was so cold that hu'Mar's breaths came in ragged gasps and his muscles stiffened. He doubted that he could shout for help even if he saw someone to shout at. How could a body of water that rested at the base of a volcano be so cold!

Most people didn't swim in Lake Tallow. If the frigid temperatures weren't enough, the sea creatures were more than happy to eat a human. Plus, all the sewers from the city emptied into this ring of water. It wasn't called Lake Tallow for its clear sparkling purity.

Unfortunately, even in the bitter cold, the wasps' venomous stingers and biting mandibles jabbed under his clothes. Kicking with both legs and paddling with one arm, hu'Mar barely kept his head above the milky water's surface while pinching at his shirt and pants.

The cold water did little to numb the pain, so finding more wasps was not a challenge. He bobbed and drifted along the moat for several minutes before all the wasps were either washed away or squished. It was then that he realized that his bond to Vinegar wasn't as weak as it had been at ka'Feebal's. He paddled in a circle till he spotted the cat slowly meandering on the cobbled shore about ten feet above him.

Vinegar sat down and licked his paws. Then when hu'Mar drifted past, Vinegar slumped as if he were being inconvenienced by having to keep up with hu'Mar. So he got up, stretched, then slowly walked along till he was slightly ahead, and planted himself back on the pavers.

Hard Boiled Cabbage: Big Trouble In Spur Central

"Good effort, um-uh… keep it up. Let's see, kick those legs," Vinegar called down between yawns.

"What are you talking ab-b-bout?" hu'Mar said through blue shivering lips.

"I thought I'd give you some words of encouragement," Vinegar said. "It's not near as easy as you might think, but all things considered, I think I gave it a valiant effort. By the way, watch out for the… never mind."

Hu'Mar passed through floating foam that smelled of raw sewage mixed with grease. Great. He was like a net, drifting in the largest, dirtiest chamber pot in the world. He swam to the edge of the moat, drifting past the tall paved walls lining the shore until he found one low enough to reach.

Hu'Mar grabbed onto a low cobble that jutted out, and with considerable effort, hoisted himself up. But his pant leg caught on something sharp, and it ripped a hole, less than a hand width above his knee. Just his luck. No apartment and no change of clothes. This day had better not get any worse.

Finally he collapsed on the pavers and lay there for a few minutes soaking up the heat.

"Look at all these people with their chariots and horse slaves," Vinegar said. "Pathetic. Everyone in such a hurry and for no good reason. By the way, I'm glad you didn't get eaten." Vinegar looked at him. "Yikes, what happened to your skin? You look worse than a teenage human with acne covered chicken pox."

Hu'Mar pulled off his shirt and shook out several wasp husks before ringing the water from it.

"I've always known that you lacked a little in the common-sense market," Vinegar said, staring in disgust, "but taking a bath in Lake Tallow, yeesh. That thing is teaming with pollution and even most fish avoid it there, unless they're making a run for the Clutch."

Hu'Mar slapped his leg where a lone surviving wasp crawled. "I'm pretty sure that's why it keeps getting polluted—to deter them. Besides, you'd probably go for a swim too, if it meant surviving."

"Pardon me, Dick hu'Swollen," Vinegar whined.

"Oh great, I lost my cheese and bread." Hu'Mar plopped onto his back. "Is it possible for you to do anything useful?"

"Is it possible that you didn't totally destroy all our money?" Vinegar countered.

Hu'Mar pulled out his oiled leather pouch. He loosened the drawstring and poured out the salty water. All the chips had dissolved. The bromine was now the size of a saline, and the salines were probably only worth about four of their normal six chips each. "That's deflation for you."

"More like stupidity," Vinegar said.

Hu'Mar pulled his sticky damp shirt back on. It was uncomfortable, but it would dry soon enough. "We'll get through this like we always do."

"You mean, we'll sink lower and lower until we're less than worthless?" Vinegar asked.

"Why do cats have to be so pessimistic?"

"Pessimistic? Really, Dick hu'Majesty? Who risked his position and power by poking his nose into the prince's private life, thereby getting us exiled from Nebylon? Who's following a murder case that makes every minister in the city suspicious of him? Who lost our apartment? And finally, who lost half our money by swimming in the dirtiest body of water in this realm? I bet you didn't even learn anything useful at ka'Feebal's place."

"Hey," hu'Mar said, "I didn't openly expose hu'Regal's royal son. Come on, let's take a look at some of the other names on ka'Nairie's enemy list."

"How about this," Vinegar suggested. "You become a prophet, wash away all the memories of your failures, gain notoriety and wealth, and I'll manage your estate when you're bonkers. You've already lost your mind, might as well make it official."

Hu'Mar ignored Vinegar. Puddles pooled in his step as he walked away from the cat.

"You're going to get yourself killed, then I'll end up like that stupid minister dog," Vinegar meowed, "or ka'Nairie's pathetic excuse for a horse, Beauford. Ich".

"Thanks for caring." Hu'Mar balled his fist. He had the

skills to figure this out, even if his luck was currently in short supply. Vinegar's constant doubting was making this difficult. It was hard enough towing the line with his own insecurities.

"The things I do for you," Vinegar mumbled. "And for what?"

"Duke."

"Huh?" Vinegar looked at Dick hu'Mar.

"Our next visit. He's the next one on Jodeign ka'Nairie's list."

"Skippy knows just about every non-human in Spur Central, and he didn't seem to know any Duke." Vinegar shook his head, then licked his palm to comb his facial hair back into place. "Let's forget all about this before this case turns into a career. Why don't you go back and spend some more time with ka'Feebal?"

"She's not going to give me anything. I might try again later, but we might as well follow up on these other names. Maybe it'll give me more to talk about when I see her again."

Chapter 12

One Slick Armpit

It would have been nice if there were some sort of address book that listed everybody in the city. Only the Beadledom had such a book for tax purposes, and it was probably only half accurate. The best way to find this Duke or Maizy hu-ka'Dillie, would be to inquire among the city criers.

Dick hu'Mar hated criers. They were gossips and traded dirt for dirt. It was their business to be up in everyone else's business.

"Everything denotes that there's a Greater Gear!" A minister called from on top of a soap box.

Hu'Mar plucked at his damp clothing, unsticking it from his lumpy wasp-stung skin. The pain was mostly gone, but the itching was waxing to near unbearable proportions. He tried not to scratch as he passed between the minister and a man across the street who yelled back at the minister, "If you can't see another world, then it don't exist! Trapping a human soul in that Great Clutch will only destroy us all! I say it creates a plague that wipes out a species' ability to reproduce!" Even in Spur Central, there's always that one guy who wants to argue against the obvious.

Hard Boiled Cabbage: Big Trouble In Spur Central

Hu'Mar ignored the debate. The ministers couldn't legally hurt an atheist, but he wouldn't be surprised if they tried to pin some crime on him later. He walked between the debaters, ignoring both sides. Both were fools in his opinion. They could argue all day long and nothing would ever change between them. He had better things to do with his life, like finding that Pin of Poison. He needed a good payday, and if that payday came from someone as influential as ka'Nairie, well, that could only be good for his reputation and his business. Also, if she acquired that seat on the Beadledom, she'd have considerable sway over the ministers. She could order them to drop their case against him. Yeah, this job needed doing, and the fact that he enjoyed the challenge of it, was simply a bonus.

Further down the street, he ducked under a blue cloth shade canopy, this one with small tables that overlooked this particular hub. Criers were good at delivering news and advertisements, but the really good ones earned their salt in their side services. Most people used the service as a means of finding other people and businesses. It was probably through a crier that ka'Nairie had found hu'Mar.

A thin foreign woman, probably of Mop stock, seated hu'Mar where he could enjoy the shade but still watch all the foot traffic passing by the tea-house's stage. Goss hu'Hip owned this particular stage with all its orbiting tables and its accompanying tea service. He was an independent crier, but well connected and sharp as a needle. Commuting foot traffic often diverted to pass his place at the hours he normally shouted the news.

Hu'Mar understood some of hu'Hip's tricks, like how every table at this roadside tea shop was spaced a little too close to the others, making private conversation impossible. Most of his patrons didn't realize they were fodder for his reports. Others knew very well but were more than happy to plant their latest bits of gossip in hopes that they'd make the news. By late afternoon or evening, he'd deliver his news on the other side of town on someone else's stage, much like the current crier was doing on his stage right now. He also had a few apprentices who'd either help listen in on tables or who'd visit all the normal sources like police stations and businesses, then report back to him. But Goss hu'Hip was the main crier. He could overhear a snippet of gossip and, within a day, have dug out a story of scandal or intrigue. His work wasn't so different from hu'Mar's, except that he was a lot more public about it.

"What'll it be for you, hu'Mar?" Goss hu'Hip asked, appearing from behind him, like a large wild cat that had been hiding, waiting to pounce.

"How about a pick-me-upper."

"Ah, a rough start to your day," hu'Hip confirmed. He snapped his fingers that could be, and probably were, used for grinding bones into powder. His line of work attracted few personal enemies but lots of generic ones. For some reason, most people didn't like their private lives sold on the free market.

A timid serving girl ducked behind a curtain that extended to the ground, and hid the kitchen from view. Hu'Mar could hear clay pots clacking together as she prepared their tea.

Goss hu'Hip's strong hand slapped hu'Mar on the back. "Good to see you again. You don't come by often enough."

"Haven't had many field jobs lately," hu'Mar said, knowing that he had to be careful around hu'Hip. "Most of my clients want me to read the stars and tell them what they've already decided for themselves."

"You and I are a lot alike," hu'Hip laughed. "You tell them what they believe, and I tell others what they believe."

The girl set two cups in front of them. Hu'Mar's smelled like spiced apples. He took a cautious sip.

It burned his tongue, and he set it down. "Too hot. You plan to keep me talking for a while?"

"Tricks of the trade." Hu'Hip smiled innocently. "Never could put anything past you, could I?"

"I don't have a lot of time to spend here." Hu'Mar rubbed his tongue on the roof of his mouth. He'd burned his taste buds, but since he didn't have much money to spend on food, it might not matter anyway.

Hu'Hip frowned. "Not even to catch up with a good

friend?"

"I'm looking for some people. There's a Maizy hu-ka'Dillie and something called Duke. Ever hear of them?"

"Listen hu'Mar." Hu'Hip leaned in. "I don't know what you're up to, but can I give you a little free advice? Take a vacation. Word has it that some ministers are looking for you in connection to a double murder."

"It doesn't take long for word to get to you, does it?" Hu'Mar pressed his hands down his wet pant legs, hoping he didn't look too alarmed as water pooled near his feet. "I didn't even know they'd officially turned me into a suspect yet."

"Well," hu'Hip said, unclasping his hands in an open-armed gesture of innocence, "you know what they say about rumor."

"You know me. I didn't do it."

"I know you didn't. But they did place you at the scene with a witness and a half-eaten fish covered in furry vomit." Hu'Hip shot Vinegar an accusing stink-eye. "Word has it that you might have a connection with a Bule who was also implicated."

Hu'Mar followed hu'Hip's stare.

Vinegar was licking his paw. The cat paused, looked at both men, then continued grooming himself.

"What's going on here, hu'Mar?"

"I've got a client, I won't say who, that's lost a relic. This relic has benefits, but unless you want to become poisonous, it's not very friendly to keep around."

"Please don't tell me this client has pasty white skin and wears a cloak." Hu'Hip lifted his head, focusing back on hu'Mar.

"I don't know any Albinos," hu'Mar lied.

"What a relief," hu'Hip said flatly, sounding the complete opposite of relieved, "cause word also has it that you met with a certain character who matches that same description, shortly before people started dying."

Great. If hu'Hip knew about his visit with that Albino, then his sources probably dug it up from the Ministry, which meant they were connecting hu'Mar to the two deaths along with a suspect Albino girl. Not like he hadn't seen this coming, but the confirmation still stung. Could his visitor yesterday really have been the same Albino behind this all?

"I get a lot of folks in and out of my office. I don't take every case they put to me."

"They say the stableboy was poisoned, but that Crazy Ish was drowned. So how did the fish die?" Hu'hip tapped his chin with his index finger.

"I think," hu'Mar said carefully, "that if Banner hu'Tanner and his mutt were to look a little more carefully, they'd find that poison was present at both locations."

"I don't think the Ministry made that connection yet," hu'Hip suggested, "but if they do, that would only hurt your case further. Word has it that they found one of your blow darts. For a man who uses poisoned darts to kill, especially around Spur Central, well, it wouldn't look good."

Hu'Mar lifted his tea and let his inner arm tap his vest. Yes, his blowgun was there with his darts. Maybe he lost one, but how would they know? His apartment was nothing but a heap of ashes. Maybe one of his neighbors mentioned it. Likely, if they suspected him of starting the fire, they'd be vindictive. The tea still burned, but this time he could swallow it without blistering his throat. "All the more reason for me to find whoever has that relic. Given the Ministry's style, they'll think they already have enough to convict me."

"But what if you turn yourself in? If what you say is true, then this person is likely to poison someone else. You'd be in custody, and the ministers would have to admit that someone else was involved."

"You're a smart guy, hu'Hip, but you know as well as I do…" Hu'Mar sipped his drink, winced, then poured the rest of it on the ground, or rather by accident, on Vinegar.

Vinegar jumped and meowed like someone had smashed his non-existent tail.

Though unintended, hu'Mar used Vinegar's sudden pain to emphasize his point. "Ministers tend to be rash and rather unsympathetic." He said, glaring at hu'Hip, sparing no upward glances at his partner.

Hu'Hip's stared at Vinegar, who now hung upside-down by his claws on the fabric canopy. "Point taken."

"They'd execute me before anyone else got a chance to get poisoned. Besides, if there really is an Albino poisoning people, then I'd be an accomplice and one less criminal to worry about while they track down the real killer. Banner hu'Tanner, he might never even connect further poisonings to these cases. He doesn't strike me as being clever in the right sort of way. As for his partner, Bacon, I get the feeling he just wants a chance to gnaw on my leg. Turning myself in would be suicide."

Who could this Albino be? He had advised the Albino who'd visited him to see hu'Narmin, but she didn't seem like the type to murder someone. Yet there weren't many of her kind in the city. What if she was somehow connected to Jodeign ka'Nairie's missing relic? A Pin of Poison could have killed Ish hu'Narmin's fish and that stableboy. It was possible, but his gut told him that she wasn't a murderer, at least, not on purpose. She was in some sort of trouble, but he couldn't see a connection between her and ka'Nairie.

Hu'Mar stood and pulled Vinegar off the cloth ceiling, the cat's claws popping threads in the canopy. "Sorry about that, I didn't see you there."

The timid waitress refilled hu'Mar's teacup. Hot steam and apple spice wafted to his nose. He had to be careful! If he stayed long enough for this to cool, hu'Hip might learn too much and ruin his investigation.

Vinegar still shook. He glared at hu'Mar, his tangled hackles full of accusation and hot tea.

"Gotta say, I'm impressed. Never seen you jump that high before." He dropped the cat on the floor as he dropped back into his chair.

Vinegar batted at hu'Mar's leg, just above his shoe, but he kept his claws in. Likely, he didn't want to get claws tangled in hu'Mar's wet wool socks. He'd already lost a tail and two claws in the last twenty-four hours. Maybe he was learning his lesson.

Hu'Mar's salt was still damp, but luckily it was holding

its shape. He took out the diminished saline and cracked it on the table. He put half back in his leather pouch, leaving just two chips worth for Goss hu'Hip. He pulled the string on his pouch, then thought better of it. He opened it to let it finish drying out.

"I don't know any Duke, but you might try visiting Dussel hu'Nuff over by Sprocket Alley." Hu'Hip blew on his own cup of tea. "He runs a hair trimming salon for rich folk. I get the feeling that this Duke character you're looking for might not be an animal. Hu'Nuff's got his own little network of interesting characters. Aside from cutting hair, you could say that he deals with information too, but whereas I tell the truth as I see it, he tells the truth as he's paid to see it. Get my drift?"

"Sure, what about Maizy ka'Dillie? Might go by hu'Dillie." Hu'Mar silently counted how much salt he'd need to get by for the next couple of days.

"Never heard of her or him."

Hu'Mar sat up straight, this was a big clue in and of itself. Goss hu'Hip knew almost everyone. Even if he didn't know them, he'd at least heard of them. That meant Maizy hu-ka'Dillie must be new in town. What if hu-ka'Dillie was the Albino? It might be a stretch, but Maizy did sound like a name more popular underground.

"Thanks, hu'Hip," hu'Mar said. He paused, "Since you don't know this ka'Dillie, maybe you could tell me something about Jef hu'Rino instead?"

Hu'Hip poked at the wet salt chips on the table.

Hu'Mar couldn't afford to toss another piece of salt on the table, so instead he tossed out an ear-to-ear grin and folded his arms in anticipation. Technically, hu'Hip didn't owe him anything. If there wasn't a good answer to a query, the query had still been asked, and payment was owed. There was, however, the matter of pride. Hu'Hip might be sore for not knowing a person in the city or even any relevant info, so maybe…

With a shake of his head, hu'Hip exhaled audibly. "I thought you said you didn't know that you were officially under investigation? To think I believed your reaction. I must be slipping."

Hard Boiled Cabbage: Big Trouble In Spur Central

Hu'Mar had no idea what hu'Hip was talking about, but he wasn't about to admit it. "Well, anything you can help me with?"

"With Minister hu'Rino heading up the investigation on you, you better be careful. He's been in town less than a year, but he's a sharp one. Don't know what he did before."

"Right." Hu'Mar scratched at a wasp sting on his chin.

"He rose pretty quick," hu'Hip added. "He's now a cog leader for the Central Ministry."

"Sharp man indeed," hu'Mar noted. "Must know how to play the politics pretty well." The Central Ministry was the largest district of ministers in Spur Central. There were six in total with the other five forming sections in a ring around the Central division. For anyone to rise to Cog Leader, let alone in the Central Ministry, they'd have to be sharp.

"You could say that," hu'Hip said. "Do you really not pay attention to the Beadledom?"

"What about it?" hu'Mar asked.

"Hu'Rino's campaigning for the empty seat in the Beadledom."

Everything clicked. He really should pay more attention to politics, especially since his client was a politician running for that same seat. He gave himself a mental kick in the butt for being so ignorant.

"Come on, Vinegar." Hu'Mar scooted away from the table.

"Don't you want to finish your tea?" Hu'Hip called to his back.

Hu'Mar only tipped his hat and kept walking.

Vinegar trailed behind hu'Mar as they wove their way to the center spokes of Spur Central.

Fifteen minutes later, Vinegar was complaining, again. He didn't like walking so much, but they were three blocks from the central hub of Spur Central. The salon was near here somewhere. Hu'Mar walked in a ring, staying about three blocks from the hub the whole time.

All the while, hu'Mar ignored Vinegar's rants. For some reason, Goss hu'Hip not knowing Maizy hu-ka'Dillie felt more important than if the crier had known her. Then there was Jef hu'Rino. Anyone to rise so quickly through the Ministry, then compete directly for a seat on the Beadledom, was a person to watch out for.

So far, everyone could be ka'Nairie's enemies with motive to steal her relic. Could a minister be capable of cold murder though? Lots of killers committed crimes, thinking they were doing something righteous.

Ka'Feebal seemed capable of anything. She was a greedy drunk who had clearly dealt with most of these people.

So now, he had to visit with this Dussel hu'Nuff, who apparently might know Duke. Soon, he hoped he would have enough pieces to see how the puzzle fit together.

As he walked, hu'Mar asked a few people if they'd heard of hu'Nuff's place. Most ignored him or gave a casual nod in the general direction he was going, before returning to whatever was more important than a damp man who reeked of Lake Tallow.

Ten minutes later, he smelled the familiar flammable concoctions that he'd usually associated with Thelma ka'Skrut's hair jelly. Hu'Mar let his nose lead him to the salon. Tucked snug between two other buildings, if not for the smell, he might have missed it entirely. Before he went in, he realized that, for the last ten minutes, Vinegar had actually quit complaining. Either he'd forgiven hu'Mar or he was distracted.

"Ok, spit it out." Hu'Mar finally asked before entering the salon.

"Watch yourself here," Vinegar said, his head twitched from side to side. "We're on Skippy's Turf again. He won't be happy to see you so soon. He might even send some real muscle after you this time since he doesn't like the idea of you digging on ka'Nairie."

"Skippy, the TomFather?" Hu'Mar laughed. "Never mind, I'm not afraid of no cat. Come on." He pushed the door open.

The brightly colored saloon door should have warned him that something about this place was a little off. Most salons had white and red striped doors. This one had every color of the rainbow. Another oddity were the hair stylists. One of them twinkle-toed up to him and slapped him on the shoulder with perfectly manicured hands.

"Wel-come tew Dussel ka'Nuff's hair sa-lon, haw can I help yew," the man said in an exaggerated nasal accent that also reminded him of Thelma ka'Skrut. Did all hair people have to talk like that?

"Don't you mean, Dussel *hu*'Nuff?" Dick hu'Mar asked.

"If yew insist," the hairdresser said with a smile that suggested something hu'Mar couldn't quite understand. What kind of animal had this guy palsied?

The hairdresser shifted in his high heels and pouted his lips. Wait, high heels?

Each of the hairdressers in this shop had an odd sort of bounce in their step. All their clients were women. Definitely not your typical barbershop. Even the hairdressers didn't have any hats. Which was very uncommon for men around here. Instead they had perfectly manicured hair. They must be foreigners, only he'd never seen foreigners like these before.

"I need to speak with Dussel hu'Nuff himself. You aren't him by chance, are you?"

"Aew no, he's nat here right naw. Come on in and wait a while though. He's sure to be back soon." The man took hu'Mar's hat as he tsked. "By the way, I'll be your hairdresser today. My name is Bruuuce."

"Bruce hu'what?" hu'Mar asked uncomfortably as he watched where his hat was placed.

"Just Bruuuce is fine."

Canvasing the room, hu'Mar saw rows and rows of shelving filled with various gourds, each brightly colored and labeled in fancy calligraphy. Some things were familiar, like the razors and sheers, though the ones they had here were quite a bit daintier than the ones he was used to.

He rubbed the stubble on his face. There were a few bee stings behind his bristled shadow, but not many. The wasps had mostly targeted easier skin. "I could use a shave, what do you charge?"

"Far yew hunk, I'd do it pro-bono." The barber placed both

of his hands on the bottom of his ribcage as if to pop out his flat skinny chest. Was he trying to look tough? It wasn't working.

"Pro-what?" Hu'Mar didn't like how he said this either.

"First time's always free." Bruce pushed hu'Mar into a chair, then stuck a large metal pin through hu'Mar's pant leg, expertly avoiding any flesh. Every barber had a place. This wasn't the first time one had used hu'Mar's own pant leg as a temporary pin cushion.

"Free, uh, okay." Lucky that. He didn't have much money to spare anyway. Maybe while he was here, he could learn a few things from these guys. "Just be careful around the bee stings."

"Ah, don't yew worry. Some say I have the gentlest fingers in Spur Central." Bruce touched his shoulder. "Let's take that smelly wet shirt off yew to dry."

"Okay," hu'Mar said. This fellow was either very considerate, or he didn't want the damp shirt soaking the barber chair.

Bruce lifted the shirt off hu'Mar before he could do so himself. He was quick, efficient, but those soft hands brushed against his sides, like no man's hands ever should. Calm down. Bruce didn't mean anything by it. He's only trying to be helpful.

So he relaxed as Bruce swayed to a rack, hung up hu'Mar's shirt, then whipped down a perfectly laundered white sheet, which he draped around hu'Mar's neck. With one hand holding the sheet in place, Bruce plucked the pin from hu'Mar's pants and used it to hold the cloth in place. What an odd man. He seriously wanted to be called nothing more than Bruce?

Hu'Mar cleared his throat. "You don't by chance know a guy who just calls himself Duke, do you?"

"I wish!" Bruce laughed, but it was forced. He did know Duke. "Now relax." The man sharpened a straight-back on a leather strap.

Hu'Mar leaned back in the chair and closed his eyes. If Bruce was just Bruce, and not Bruce hu'something, then Duke might also be a human.

He could see why Goss hu'Hip didn't like this place. It had nothing to do with the service, which was excellent. Bruce jabbered on while he lathered hu'Mar's face with those gentle hands, nothing at all like the callused fingers of his normal barber. It went against everything that Tough culture stood for, but, it wasn't all that unpleasant. Depending on their prices, he might not mind coming back in the future.

If the shave felt smooth, the one-sided conversation felt like grease on butter, minus the weird whiny way the man talked and pranced about. All the info he passed on was political. The man was a well-rehearsed, walking, talking, hair-trimming advertisement for Jodeign ka'Nairie. If one were to take this guy's word for it, ka'Nairie was the obvious shoo-in for the next available seat in the Beadledom council. Either this shop was paid to advertise ka'Nairie's candidacy, or—"So what does ka'Nairie have on Dussel hu'Nuff?"

"What-ever are yew talking about?" Bruce pulled the big pin that held the white sheet around hu'Mar's neck. The pin temporarily went back into hu'Mar's pant while the sheet went over Bruce's shoulder, and Bruce lifted hu'Mar's arm up high.

"Despite all the praise, I've heard that there's a little bad blood between him and your favorite candidate."

"Nou, that's silly. Ka'Nairie's rivals probably planted that in your head. Politics can be sooo annoying." Bruce half laughed. It was the sort of laugh that left an awkward lingering silence, like when you hit your funny bone. Then Bruce flopped a glob of shaving foam under hu'Mar's exposed armpit.

Dick hu'Mar pulled away, then froze as the straight back razor touched the sensitive skin. He stared hard at Bruce, not daring to blink, confused and speechless. "Wha-wha?"

In an instant it was done. Bruce wiped hu'Mar's armpit clean with a rag. Not a single hair left. Not a single nick either. Bruce skirted to hu'Mar's other side and tried to lift that arm as well.

Hu'Mar resisted. "What are you doing?"

"Giving yew a shave? What else 'do yew think I'm doing, yew hairy man, you?"

"What is this? Next you'll be shaving my chest!"

"Oh nooo. Just yewr loins. The hairy chest stays. It's sooo thick, it'd be a shame to lose that finger-combing goodness."

Hu'Mar was on his feet faster than Bruce could say "goodness" a second time. He grabbed his wet shirt from the nearby hook. "I'm good for now. Thanks for the shave. I'll ... um." Hu'Mar staggered, then remembered the pin in his pants. He plucked it out and tossed it onto the chair. "Can you let Dussel hu'Nuff know that Dick hu'Mar came asking for him?"

"Sure thing. Where can'ee find yew?"

Hu'Mar tried to think and inch his way closer to the door at the same time. He needed to chat with hu'Nuff, but these foreigners made him feel terribly uncomfortable. He'd done a lot of dirty things to get information in the past, but for the first time in his life, he felt very much out of his comfort zone.

"Uh-mmm, how about I just..." He was going to say, wait over here, but these men were giving him weird vibes. He could have the man meet him by the bridge, but hu'Mar didn't want to wait around in one place for very long. He breathed out. "I'll be back later. Thanks again for the, um, shave."

"It was all my pleaaasure." Bruce said with one hand on the side of his ribs as he bit a thumbnail.

Hu'Mar shuddered, then left. Maybe he should visit Banner hu'Tanner and explain everything. If hu'Nuff was anything like the other men in this salon, then a conversation with him could be as disarming. It had been a long time since hu'Mar had been at such a loss. He'd dealt with Toughs, Bules, Pissers, and all sorts of sleazebags. This was different. He didn't know what to think of these guys.

Maybe they were involved in something shady. Unbonded palsies could mess with a man's mind, but he'd never known of any animal that could make a man act like that. So maybe it had something to do with unbalanced relics. It was a stretch, but he didn't have any better explanation.

"What are you looking at?" hu'Mar accused.

"Nothing," Vinegar said. "You smell interesting though."

He did have to admit, he smelled pretty good. If only the shaved armpit didn't set him so off balance. It felt slick, like his sweat or skin oils were lubricating his armpit. Was this how a cat felt if they lost their whiskers? Maybe he should've let Bruuuuce

Hard Boiled Cabbage: Big Trouble In Spur Central

even out his other armpit before he ran out.

"Have you been sitting out here the whole time?"

"No," Vinegar said. "I was laying down for a little while."

"So you didn't even poke your nose around? I thought cats were supposed to be curious?"

"Kittens are curious. Cats are content. Besides, like I said, this is Skippy's turf, and he tried to have a few kids kill me last time I was here. He'll send a bit more muscle next time."

"He didn't try to kill you, even I could see that." Hu'Mar pulled his damp shirt over his head. It resisted and made every wasp sting ache, but the sun was shining on him here. Maybe he could dry off and grab something to eat at the place across the street. "You know that Skippy was only messing with you, giving his minions a little practice at fighting. If he wanted you dead, he wouldn't have sent a bunch of kittens to do the job. Besides, why should you care? You're the mighty Vinegar? If I didn't know better, I'd even say that Skippy admires you."

"You're right. I am pretty awesome. It's about time you admit it."

"Admit what?" hu'Mar laughed.

"Stupid human." Vinegar lifted his back end high in the air as if to say, *talk to my rear, because the front doesn't want to hear.* "By the way, where we going now?"

"We got nowhere to go. Let's stay here a while and keep an eye on the salon." He wasn't sure if he'd recognize hu'Nuff, but if he was anything like those other spindly men in the shop, it would be a cinch picking him out of the crowd on the street.

Chapter 13

Little Things, Dangerous Things

Juniper ka'Shino shivered, then rolled a fuse. She used the same granules from her bomb to make the hemp igniter. These were tricky things. When the flame touched this powder, it would eat it in a hurry. Normally, she'd need thousands of meters of fuse if she wanted to be safely away from the blast. Then there'd still be the risk of discovery.

Since discovery was the exact opposite of what the job called for, hu'Toe had needed someone a bit more innovative than their regular explosive excavators. They needed someone like ka'Shino, someone that had set out on their own, and let the harsh world mold their innovation, rather than letting monotonous research dictate all their innovation.

Ka'Shino might know her explosives, but what ka'Shino had become really good at was little machines. Her pocket clock was just one example of her talent. Smart as the residents were in Tuberlow, to this point, nobody had thought to combine a clock with a bomb. Her skills, plus the idea of using explosives to hunt great worms, had merged so naturally. Because of this, she could safely trigger her bombs, all with a mere finger-length of fuse.

Hard Boiled Cabbage: Big Trouble In Spur Central

After finishing another series of explosive packets, making sure that the fuse fit snug in the tiny hole at the middle of this cluster, she tucked it inside a second bag that was half as tall as she was. It rested next to the first backpack bomb from a week ago, when her conscience still leaned heavily towards the self-righteous side of the scales. That was when her decision to run away from her parents boring home and make a name for herself felt as though it was finally working out. The scales were now tipping towards the other end of the pride spectrum, the side that posed the question: Am I a terrible person?

Like the other pack, this new cluster of explosives weighed a lot, but by grinding and pressing the powder into these dense tubes, it allowed her to fit the same amount of explosives that previously filled the whole bag into two-thirds of her backpack, while also making them explode more powerfully. The whole sack would get a little heavier since she'd need to camouflage the contents in case she was searched. She really did not look forward to hiking Mount Exclusion with such a heavy load. Such burdens were meant for Albinos who were too stupid to live in Tuberlow—unlike herself who was too, adventurous—yes, too adventurous to follow in her parents' tedious routines. But, these packs wouldn't do any good down here, and she had nobody else to trust to help her heft them to the mountain, so the considerable weight of it would have to be borne entirely on her shoulders.

Until then, there was only one thing remaining before she was finished with this bomb. Grinding explosives into powder, then packing them up tight like a sausage that could do more than spice one's tongue was good and simple work, but for her, she liked this other part. Working with gears to make practical machines was far more rewarding. So, what better way to calm those nerves than to make a detonator.

Tears of exhaustion blurred her vision. Wipe as she might, they kept coming, darkening her hands and arms in wet streaks of explosive dust. Finally, she grabbed the cloak from the floor and buried her face in it. The idea was to use the cloak to wipe her clean, possibly absorb the exhausted tears leaking from her eyes, and thus clear her vision. Instead, the cloak took into its mind to pretend it was a pillow, and for a moment, her mind drifted back home, where the beds were comfortable, and the meals were dependable. Missing home was a given, though rarely admitted. It didn't help matters to long for the place and people left behind. In time, they'd be back in her life. Back there, Juniper ka'Shino had always been a girl. When finally coming home, she'd return as a woman, an adult who'd learned the ways of the world and had experiences that transformed her into the sort of person deserving of respect. After almost nodding off again, she tossed the cloak to the ground again, determined to finish her work.

She cleaned and dusted her room, careful not to leave any trace amount of explosive dust anywhere. Then, forcing herself to keep moving, rather than sleep, she went to a shelf and pulled down a small wooden box, a bag full of random parts, and her tools, all clinking together and placed them on her bed.

Three hours later, her newly made device was ready for testing. She inserted a key and wound the timer up. It could give her anywhere from a few minutes to a two-day delay. This time, she gave it a few minutes worth of winding.

When the gears ticked to the end, a second wind-up spring caused a metal gear to spin quickly against a chunk of flint. A steady stream of sparks shot down for about twenty seconds. As soon as it ended, a blackened burn marked where the fuse ought to be placed.

Ten minutes later, she had mounted the timer, and was ready to place the bomb. Ready that is, except for the obvious fact that her mind and body were sleep deprived, and really ought to be seen to. There was also a slightly unpleasant odor starting to make itself known. It seemed that a bath should be in order also. But that would have to wait.

Examining her personal pocket clock again, it told her that it was late, or more appropriately since she was above ground, it was early-ish. She'd gotten home right around dawn this morning, and now the morning was almost over. Albinos marked time differently. Underground, the sun didn't dictate the start and end of your day. Instead, the days were divided into shifts. Factories ran at all hours, dividing the workload between three different shifts. Morning, afternoon, and evening were foreign concepts that only applied to those few who ventured to the surface.

Even ka'Shino's clock would've been unreadable to a surface-dwellers. Now that she was up here though, she had to adjust to the time. Night was better for going out in, since the daylight was too harsh for her complexion. With any luck, she'd get this over with before noon.

She sighed, knowing that rest would be best, but despite how badly it was needed, she'd hit her second wind. These long, uneven days couldn't be healthy.

It was hard to believe that she was actually doing this. Her parents probably considered her rebellious. Off to discover her place in the world. They probably hoped that falling in with a few worm hunters for a year or two would teach her how good home had been. If they could only see her now, a patriot hired by the secret science committee of the Albino Republic. Yeah right. They probably imagined her shivering cold in some tunnel with a slacker boyfriend, wishing she were back at home. That however, was incredibly unlikely. Worm hunters were great if you liked greasy men who valued a purse full of salt and a skin nearly empty of liquor more than they valued, well, anything else, let alone a meaningful relationship. Aside from the smell of never bathing, they were a lot like Pissers, but without boats and tans.

Little did her parents know. This job, with its high pay and promised recommendations from Ernes hu'Toe, practically guaranteed acceptance into any of the underground research institutes of her choice.

But what if someone did get hurt?

People died all the time hunting worms. They knew the risks. Just like worm hunters, people here would understand the risk of living this close to the Great Clutch. Or was she just trying to justify herself? After all, there were kids here.

It would be fine. Hu'Toe had promised that the geologists

would take care to keep the volcano from fully erupting and destroying everyone around it. So why did her stomach still feel like eating itself with guilt? Nerves. It had to be nerves. Maybe exhaustion played into it also. Everything would work out fine. Sleep would clear her head and make everything good again. Too bad there was no time for that.

With a grunt, she lifted her very first pack onto the edge of the bed, balancing it on its unsteady bottom. This was to be the first half to her two-part bomb that needed to explode together. Hu'Toe had given her a map for this first placement. Both parts needed to be there before the end of today, and since the packs were both as heavy as she was, it would be easier to deliver the first half this morning. She could then come back, sleep for a few hours, then deliver the second half once her body had a chance to recuperate.

The next set of bombs would be easier. The packs would still be as heavy, but where this first blast needed a double dose, the follow up bombs needed only a single backpack's worth of explosives per location.

Sitting in front of her pack made it easier to loop the straps around her shoulders and tie a leather strap around her waist to carry some of the weight there. Once everything was cinched tight, she closed her eyes, breathed deeply, and braced herself. With gritted teeth, and breath held tight, she and stood, slowly, but surely. Time to deposit her load.

Chapter 14

No Dainty Punches Here

The redhead returned with their food. Hu'Mar's ground cow was square, inside a round bun. That didn't look natural at all.

"That was quick," he commented as he crushed some salt and gave the girl some chips.

She collected the money and spun around, her pigtails slapping her freckled face. "That's because we never freeze any of our meat," she said, then she was gone, off to serve someone else.

"Why would meat ever be frozen?" Vinegar asked as he jumped onto the table and gently rested his rear next to his meal. "More importantly, how could it be done?" He sniffed his sandwich, then pawed the pastry, throwing the bready part to the floor, mumbling something about how the workers here at Dave's Orphans didn't know how to get an order right.

"Way to waste food," hu'Mar scolded. "That bread would've come in handy tonight when we run out of salt to buy dinner."

"It's still there, Dick hu'Dainty," Vinegar said before sinking his teeth into the chicken breast that hu'Mar requested for him. He shook his head and tore a chunk off.

Hard Boiled Cabbage: Big Trouble In Spur Central

Hu'Mar bit into his sandwich and focused on the case. It was better than dwelling on his nearly depleted salt. At least he was almost dry now. They'd spent a little time sunning themselves before stepping into Dave's Orphans for a bite. Dumb name for a food joint, but the food was decent, cheap, and they were still in sight of the salon.

"Hello, Dick hu'Daydreamer, where are you?" Vinegar meowed.

"Ish hu'Narmin, Jef hu'Rino, Maizy hu-ka'Dillie, Dussel hu'Nuff, Duke—"

"What are you going on about now?" Vinegar interrupted.

"—Renu ka'Feebal, any one of them, maybe even all of them have something to do with this stupid relic. They were either previous owners, or they knew that ka'Nairie had it, thus they must be suspect."

"How do you know any of them owned it?" Vinegar asked as he gnawed on one side of his mouth, white sauce smearing his cheek.

"A couple of them were in ka'Feebal's Ledger." Hu'Mar took a small bite of his sandwich, hoping to stretch and savor it as long as he could. Not knowing where his next meal would come from, he wanted to appreciate the one he had right now.

"Since when can a dumb ape like you read?" Vinegar's half chewed chicken fell from his mouth. He inspected it once, then returned to gnawing on it.

"I can read!" hu'Mar snapped. "Just not very quickly."

"Let me guess, you're going to force me to follow you around till you've met each one of them?" Vinegar pressed his head into the table, then rolled onto his back, rattling the table. It could've been a playful gesture, but Vinegar was frustrated.

"Tired of your meal already?" hu'Mar asked.

"It's not bad, for old bird, but that smell! Dick hu'Disgusting, you need a bath. Your stench is ruining my appetite."

"I just had a bath, if you hadn't noticed," hu'Mar replied.

"With soap?" Vinegar asked. "Whatever stink those barbers lathered on you, it's competing with your sweat and Lake Tallow, and it's losing." Vinegar sniffed the leftovers of his chicken, then sniffed in the direction of the salon. "I hate you. You know that, right?" Vinegar said.

"You and the whole rest of the world. In fact, the only person who seems to like me is that barber I just visited." He had to get over those guys. Hu'Mar would eventually need to talk to this Duke guy. Maybe he should let him shave his other armpit, it would give him a chance to talk. Besides, the hairy imbalance was extremely distracting.

"You don't get it, hu'Mar," Vinegar complained.

"I know, but I'm close," hu'Mar agreed. "There's a connection. I just can't see it clearly yet. Finish your chicken. We can't afford to waste food."

"Listen to me, Dick hu'Hairbrained!" Vinegar rolled back to his feet. "How can you possibly have an appetite at a time like this?"

Hu'Mar sat back in his chair. Vinegar was actually shaking with anger.

"I've followed you around for three years now," Vinegar started. "We've had close calls and lean times before, but this case isn't one of those problems you can solve in a day or two. There's probably a simple explanation for the missing relic, but you've turned this into a full-blown conspiracy. Not only that, but it's going to get you killed. Don't believe me, take a look at yourself."

Hu'Mar glanced down at his polished metal plate. Next to a discarded wilty tomato, was his own reflection. His freshly shaved face was bordered by red itchy bumps from ka'Feebal's pet wasps.

"Sure, the stakes are high, Vinegar, but that's what makes it fun."

"That ka'Nairie gal didn't get ahead by playing fair, you know," Vinegar said. "She's a manipulator, and she'll play you as much as she plays the people she's politicking for. In the end, even if you solve her case, you'll end up with nothing. Just like always. You're a gullible mutt. You're good, I'll grant you that, but every time you fall, I'm stuck with the scattered pieces that you can't seem to pull back together. Frankly, I'm tired of it, and

Hard Boiled Cabbage: Big Trouble In Spur Central

I don't know how much more I can take."

"Thanks," hu'Mar said, half admitting to himself that Vinegar had a point, but what right did Vinegar have in pulling him down like that? "You always have the nicest things to say. Didn't we just have a conversation yesterday about how nobody cares to hear from a talking cat?"

"I'm not a talking cat, not to humans at least. This is just internal dialog, and you're little more than a nosy human."

"Being nosy is how I earn my salt," hu'Mar said. "And if I'm not mistaken, those internal thoughts of yours were pointed pretty directly at me."

Vinegar twitched a whisker, then turned his back toward hu'Mar and lapped at the water in his tin mug.

"That's right. Ignore me. It'll give me a chance to think anyway." One peek at the salon reminded him of the question he'd been asking before his food arrived. Why would Bruuuuce deny knowing Duke? Vinegar paused, his nose in the air, water dripped from the hair on his chin. Hu'Mar followed the direction of the chin drip and noticed a man, a very big man, who spotted them, and like his size didn't matter at all, he immediately pivoted and changed direction to come over.

"Are human noses really so weak that they need to add so many extra pheromones to get noticed?" Vinegar asked.

The man approached, nearly gliding, like no seven-and-a-half-foot bison should.

"You Dick hu'Mar?" he asked as he held his open palm out. His voice was cold and threatening, like the depths of a winter lake, wondering if you were worth the trouble of drowning on purpose or on accident. The smells of the salon that clung to his body were the first thing to hit hu'Mar square in the nose, they were strong, and he hoped that was all that hit him in the nose, though he suspected that might be wishful thinking.

"Nope," hu'Mar replied. "My name is Vinegar hu'Veil." It was his way of telling Vinegar to be on guard. If he lifted something from this guy's pocket, which he'd usually do, Vinegar was to hide it from them in case hu'Mar couldn't keep the distraction going long enough.

Vinegar grabbed his chicken and jumped from the table. Hu'Mar displayed his most charming smirk. It was times like this that really got his blood pumping. It was kind of fun. Maybe he did have some Tough relatives in his ancestry somewhere.

The newcomer slapped hu'Mar across the face. "Nice to meet you, Vinegar hu'Veil." This guy was definitely a Tough, maybe more so than a lot of people although everything about him was contradictory. Despite being a big strong man, his face was baby smooth, which could only be described as beautiful and wrong at the same time. His hair was very feminine, long, silky dark, and pinned up perfectly with a jeweled dagger. The only thing truly manly about him were those thick sausage arms, packed with gravel and muscle. His brown wool pants were as tight around his legs as the skin around his biceps, even though they looked like they'd fit loosely around an elephant's leg. Hu'Mar was the sort that could crush lesser men between his fingers, but hu'Mar was a pesky little bug compared to this guy.

Since it was only appropriate, and he didn't want to display any weakness or poor manners in front of this almost dainty bone-crusher, hu'Mar slapped him as hard as he could. That hand would have knocked over a horse, but this slap seemed to hurt hu'Mar's hand more than this guy's face. He barely even registered the hit.

"Nice to meet you too. You didn't tell me your name."

"Dussel hu'Nuff, and I don't like liars, Dick hu'Mar," he replied, deep, low, and slow.

"Sure you like liars," hu'Mar countered. "Else your shop wouldn't be spreading propaganda for hire and you wouldn't have asked my name if you already knew who I was. Why don't you take a seat?" Hu'Mar placed a hand on hu'Nuff's back.

Hu'Nuff swatted the arm away but not before hu'Mar flipped the man's purse to Vinegar.

"You been ask'n questions about me in my shop." He folded his arms. Each bicep was as big as hu'Mar's considerably large head.

"True," hu'Mar said. "I heard you had some beef with Jodeign ka'Nairie, but after visiting your barbers, I think I'm

Hard Boiled Cabbage: Big Trouble In Spur Central

mistaken. She seems to have you all tucked into that crowded bed of hers."

Hu'Nuff grabbed hu'Mar by the throat and lifted him off the floor. "Your lip flaps a little too careless for a small guy."

Hu'Mar grabbed the man's arms and squeaked, "Nobody's ever—called me—small before. I imagine—there aren't—a lot—of big guys—in your—world."

Hu'Nuff slammed hu'Mar down, hard enough to plant his feet below the floor if it had been made of anything less solid than paving stones. Vinegar jumped back, then inspected hu'Mar's feet. Maybe he too was curious to see if hu'Mar's ankles were still above ground. Then hu'Mar flopped a brown billfold next to Vinegar. Vinegar pawed it back, then sat on the leather pouch.

Normally, hu'Mar was careful about the things he lifted from people's pockets. He usually used them for information, then tried to return them. It was clear this time, that returning anything would be more dangerous than its retrieval. Plus, if hu'Mar's suspicions were right, he'd earn whatever hu'Nuff left behind. I hope you enjoy my interrogation, hu'Mar thought to Vinegar.

Vinegar understood well enough what hu'Mar's expression meant, so he replied, "You bet I will." Then he ripped another bite from his chicken and chewed, his eyes wide with eager anticipation.

There are two ways that a human can interrogate another human, as far as hu'Mar had learned. Well, maybe three, but it was so hard to conduct a civil conversation and just ask civil questions around here. When dealing with Toughs, the first way was to beat the information out of them.

The second option, which hu'Mar had performed on occasion, was more—covert. He was actually pretty good at it too, though not usually by choice. It involved letting the Tough beat you to a bloody pulp. The guy being interrogated didn't know he was being had, all he thought was that he had the upper hand, or fist as it may be. People can be really loose with their tongue when they think you'll be too concussed to remember anything they let slip. Hu'Mar almost wished that Vinegar would do something to help turn this into the first sort of interrogation, but Vinegar was playing audience right now. He'd be foolish to expect any help.

"So why do you hate ka'Nairie so much?" hu'Mar asked. "I can't imagine that one little girly can be that big of a problem for a strong masculine guy like you?"

The fist that landed on hu'Mar's nose didn't seem like it should have that sort of power for such a benign insult as that. The blow was probably softened by the thick layer of muscle that wrapped around hu'Nuff's finger bones… probably. Good thing too, otherwise hu'Mar's head might have snapped completely off. Also, to hu'Mar's advantage, his flat nose had already been broken many times before. If his nose had been any more pointed, it might have sunk into his skull like a nail.

Through the fuzzy swirling lights, hu'Mar had visions, real or imagined, of Vinegar chewing chicken and itchy armpits. He tried to get the cat's attention. If every punch was as bad as that, this would be a short interview. He could use some help. But Vinegar ignored any gestures for help.

"At my salon, we support ka'Nairie. You'll not hear us bad mouthing that woman."

"Let me guess," hu'Mar said as he struggled to regain his balance. "You and her had a thing, then she caught you stealing her high heels?"

Hu'Nuff's crimson face contorted as if hu'Mar had hit a nerve. His lips pursed tight, and his veins rose from his skin in much the same way a willow tree raises its roots from the ground. This man could maybe look a little deadlier, but not much. At least he hadn't drawn the dagger from his hair, though, he probably didn't ever have to.

Hu'Nuff charged.

Hu'Mar finished pulling on a pair of metal knuckle smashers that he kept in his back pocket. As hu'Nuff came in range, he let his fist connect. The blow that followed would have laid out a cow. It didn't even hurt hu'Nuff.

Something about the subsequent punches suggested that

hu'Nuff was revenging for more than hu'Mar's sake. This guy had a high degree of pent-up rage. Even that did little to sway Vinegar to action. In the brief glimpses hu'Mar caught of the cat, it yawned and stretched itself out, half bored, half amused.

"What's a tuff guy like'you, want witha relic like ka'Nairie's anywaze?" hu'Mar slurred.

"I've known ka'Nairie a long time. She don't got no relics," hu'Nuff said.

"Tha'z right, cuz you stolem. Dussel hu'Nuff, or should I call you, Duke?" Hu'Mar was one good punch away from passing out.

Hu'Nuff must've known because he kicked hu'Mar between the legs instead.

"Now tha'wazn't nice," hu'Mar gasped.

"I ain't stole nothin, cause I ain't no thief. I don't need that stupid ring of hers, and that Pin is nothing but trouble. Now you ready to show some respect?"

"Juss one more queztun, who'do'ya think yaou are, standin up fir that Jodin kha'Nuri?"

"Mister, you get dumber with each blow. If I'd known you's with the Beadledom in the first place—" He didn't finish. Instead, he let his foot do the talking.

Hu'Mar rolled and flew around, all at hu'Nuff's bidding. After a while, he rested in a sloppy fetal position. Two Vinegars floated into view, circling near his face. They said something to the effect that hu'Mar "looked like a bag of month-old tomatoes," and that "no amount of money was worth that kind of abuse," though he might "be willing to pay to see it again."

"Listen, bub," a deep distant voice said before its hand lifted hu'Mar from the ground. "You tell Jef hu'Rino that I ain't playing his game. I ain't afraid of him, and if he thinks he can bully me into helping him, I'll show him a thing or two. I don't care who he is."

"Ugggghh," was all hu'Mar could say in response.

The hand let go, and hu'Mar slumped back to the floor.

"That was odd," Vinegar commented. "Usually you're more pithy than that."

Hu'Nuff, satisfied, left in the direction of his salon.

Vinegar retrieved the man's billfold and grabbed the small purse he'd hidden earlier and dragged it to hu'Mar's crumpled body. "I'd say that went well. Come on, let's go. I hear whistles blowing. I'm guessing you don't want to be here when the ministers arrive."

"Unggghh."

"Um, you do know that hu'Nuff is gone now, right? You don't have to keep playing hurt." Vinegar stood two feet on hu'Mar's side, and those paws felt like anvils.

"Confounded, Dick hu'Dis-sheveled. Your eyes have crossed." Vinegar removed his paws from hu'Mar's chest though the pain remained. "Well," Vinegar added, "I warned you that this case would be the death of you, didn't I?"

The whistles got louder.

Vinegar leapt onto the table for a better look. "Oh, great. It's Bacon and his pet human. I'll catch you later, Dick hu'Busted."

Chapter 15

Dog Breath

Pain, combined with a bucket of stale water, pulled him out of the comfortable darkness and onto a prickly straw covered slab of something hard. "Oouugghh." It had been at least three months since he'd hurt this much. "That water smells like urine."

"Nope, that's justs you," hu'Tanner said. "So how about yous level up and tells me what's going on."

"Tell ush," Bacon corrected his partner.

Fog floated in big obscuring masses across hu'Mar's brain. He shook his head, but that only increased the pain. All he could remember after getting beaten to a pulp was being back at Dave's Orphans when Bacon sniffed his crotch and said something to the effect that "someone had beat us to him." Hu'Tanner might have told him hu'Mar that he was under arrest, but he might have filled in that part on his own.

Where was Vinegar? All hu'Mar wanted to do was curl up in a ball and hide. Was that because he hurt, or because Vinegar was too far away?

"Another lovely day in Spur Central." He had to think. He groped around for anything to hold onto when his feet touched the cold rough flaked metal of the vertical bars. Dang, he was in jail. He had little time left before they decided to execute him. He had to think quick. "You ministers should really do something about the crime rate around here."

"Come on, hu'Mar, yous in big enough trouble as it is. You gots three murders pinned on yous, plus arson."

"Three?" Hu'Mar blinked long and hard. He figured they'd want to pin the arson on him, but three murders? Who was the third? He tried to sit up, but the wall he wanted to lean against was anchored in the traditional upright position, completely opposite of hu'Mar's prone position, and the physical exertion was beyond his strength. Instead, he rolled his head, letting his cheek rest against that wall's soothing cold stone.

"That's right, funny man, three murders."

"I don't feel very funny right now." He had to fight to keep his eyes open.

"Yeah, maybes not right this minute. Yous bruised, pretty bad too. Probably gots a few cracked ribs, but you'll pull out of it soon enough."

"Who's the third one?"

"Third what? Oh yeah. So you got the stableboy, Ish hu'Narmin, and his goldfish."

"You're going to get me on a goldfish?" hu'Mar asked.

"Well, we thought of pinning it on your cat, but while he was probably involved, you were suspect number one."

"It's a goldfish!"

"Yeah, a goldfish that was a palsy to the murder victim," hu'Tanner argued. "That makes him a possible witness. I could care less how many fish you kill, but if that fish could've testified, it's considered murder."

Hu'Mar blinked in reverse, opening his eyes only briefly for each time they were closed. Another pail of water splashed against his face. The sun was shining directly through a side window, not where he thought it should've been. He rolled his limp head, searching for hu'Tanner.

There was no Banner hu'Tanner, at least not that he could see, though seeing was a relative term right now. Bacon was gone too. He must have passed out again, but in their place was someone else.

A stool scraped across the floor as a tall athletic man leaned down. Hu'Mar had to squint his one working eye to see him properly. Mid-thirties, bald, with a handsome square jaw. He was dressed in a sharp brown leather vest over a cream cotton shirt, all above dark brown wool slacks. He looked more like a politician than a minister.

Hu'Mar wasn't one for jumping to conclusions, but he had a hunch.

"I have a few questions for you," the slick minister said. "It's in your best interest to answer them carefully."

"Only if I get a question of my own for each of yours, Jef hu'Rino."

Hu'Rino lifted his eyebrows. "Have we met?"

"Never," hu'Mar answered. Lucky guess, to be sure, but hu'Mar made a career out of lucky guesses. "Now it's my turn."

"Hey, wait—"

"What's your angle on Jodeign ka'Nairie?" hu'Mar asked.

"What do you know about her?" hu'Rino asked.

"That's not how this works. You want questions answered—I get questions answered. Why you after ka'Nairie?"

"She's a political rival. We want the same seat in the Beadledom council."

"I figured that much already," Dick hu'Mar said. "Since you're a minister and a politician, I'll put this to you frankly, so you don't get it jumbled. She's got lots of friends. Some are loyal, some are compelled. Take Dussel hu'Nuff, also goes by Duke. She employs him and his shop for advertising. She's made friends with some pretty useful gangsters, like Skippy the Tom-Father. I don't know how Ish hu'Narmin fits into all this or the stableboy's role, but I do know that you're one of her possible enemies. You knew about a certain relic that she had. Since yesterday, I've met all these people, come out the worst for it, and now, I finally get to meet you."

Unfortunately, he had an idea where this conversation would likely lead, and as bad of shape as he was in now, hu'Rino wasn't here to improve his health much.

Hard Boiled Cabbage: Big Trouble In Spur Central

"Are you saying that I'm part of some conspiracy that ka'Nairie has planned?" hu'Rino asked.

"Hold on, I just answered your second question. I told you what I know about ka'Nairie, now it's my turn again. What do you know about her relic, the so-called Pin of Poison?"

Hu'Rino's lip twitched, just for a moment. "You must have gotten hit real hard. I don't know what you're talking about."

"I can tell when someone's lying," hu'Mar said. "In answer to your third question, there's no conspiracy, but there are connections, and since you were my next person to interview, this works out well enough. Did you steal the Pin of Poison from Jodeign ka'Nairie?"

"Hey, I'm the one interrogating you!" Hu'Rino stood, little pinpricks of sweat glistening on his forehead.

"Then ask the right questions!" hu'Mar said. "Or in the very least, listen. Did you steal a relic from Jodeign ka'Nairie?"

"Of course not!" hu'Rino yelled. "I've never touched a relic in my life. Why does this even matter anyway?"

"Now that," Dick hu'Mar said, "is the right kind of question."

Hu'Rino knelt down and lifted hu'Mar by the front of his shirt. "You better level with me, mister. My patience is running very low.

Hu'Mar winced with pain, but he was feeling more collected now than before. Either his head was clearing, or Vinegar was nearing. "The Beadledom is full of atypical Toughs. Sure, they could all best most anybody in a fight, but the ones that make it into the Beadledom ranks have another advantage. They're conniving. Just my observation, but she's going to win the seat."

"Com'on, hu'Mar," the minister said. "You know what happens to murderers."

"Aside from a little proximity on my part, you got nothing that ties me to those murders."

"Don't be stupid, hu'Mar. You know as well as I, men've been executed for less."

"Sure, but that don't mean I should be killed." He studied hu'Rino. This guy was smart enough to know that executing hu'Mar was wrong, but he might still turn hu'Mar over to a lesser minister if he didn't get some cooperation. It couldn't be helped. The law around here allowed for too much circumstantial evidence.

Everyone was innocent until suspected involvement. Then they were arrested for questioning and if you told the Ministry exactly what they want to hear, they'd occasionally let you off the hook. Granted, they'd still leave the rope around your neck. It was kind of a sport, seeing that they don't break your neck with the drop. They just wanted to test how tough you really were by letting the crowds bet on how long you could keep from suffocating.

If, however, the Ministry didn't like your answers, then they interrogate you before letting you fight for your life against a much superior opponent, like yesterday's execution, or by sticking you in a public crow's cage. You'd be trapped in a hanging cage for all who pass to see with only your own excrement and urine as sustenance. It would take days or weeks to die. The price of people's bets on your life tended to run higher the longer you lasted.

"All righty, hu'Rino, you know who I am and what I do for my salt. It's like this, I took a case, and she was very convincing."

"A case?" hu'Rino asked. "So ka'Nairie hired you? How'd she pull you from your fortune telling scam?"

"She offered me something I couldn't refuse," hu'Mar admitted. "Money."

"Yous no minister," another voice broke in. "She should'a come to us." It was Banner hu'Tanner. When had he shown up?

Hu'Rino snapped his fingers, and hu'Tanner backed into a shadow again. It was easy to see who was who's superior.

Returning his attention to hu'Mar, hu'Rino said, "He's right. We don't look favorably at freelancers doing our jobs for us. Why would ka'Nairie come to you instead of us if she had a stolen relic?"

"I don't know. Maybe because one of the people on her short list of suspects was a high-ranked minister and political rival?"

Though his mind was still cloudy, hu'Mar was very aware of iron-tight fingers, clamping around his jaw.

"Are you accusing me of theft?"

"Nawt awt awl," hu'Mar replied through pinched cheeks. At least, he wasn't yet.

Hu'Rino let go.

"I'm working the same case you guys are, but from a different angle. Hu'Tanner, you mentioned that the stableboy was killed by poison? This missing relic can cause a person to leak poison, either by sweat, saliva, or any bodily liquid. I suspect that if we find whoever stole ka'Nairie's relic, we'd find the murderer. Remember too, there's one other person involved here, and I'd be surprised to see you connect me with them. Tell me, have you even looked for that Albino?"

"You knows Bules," hu'Tanner chimed in again, disgust laced his voice. "Even if they's enemies, they wouldn't gives another away to us. Plus, all we's gots to work with is an indistinct description from an unstable cleaning lady, but maybe we's can gets a better lead on that Bule from yous."

"I didn't see her," hu'Mar huffed.

"Yous sure about that? What about the Bule who visited yous, right before ka'Nairie cames to see you?"

"Great grease above," hu'Mar swore. "Yes, some Bule visited me, she thought I could tell the future, like I was some sort of prophet. I sent her away. I'd never seen her before and haven't seen her since."

This wasn't good. Their case against him was pretty solid, for a minister's standards. From talking to hu'Hip, he knew to expect this, but it still irked him. It had to be either Thelma ka'Skrut or Rain hu'Grushy that leaked the meeting to these guys. They were the only two who knew about it, and it felt like a betrayal.

"Tell us everything you know," hu'Rino demanded.

"No." Maybe that wasn't the best way to answer the men who held his life on a short leash, but he was getting annoyed. "We don't even know if that was the same Bule. You're grasping at straw. How many people in this city do you think have seen or talked to a Bule in the last couple days. I bet it's a lot more than would care to admit it, especially if you accuse all fo them of murder too."

Hu'Rino grabbed hu'Mar by the shirt again. "Listen bub, you're in a tight spot. All we have is your word against a poisoned dart gun found in your vest, a poisoned stableboy, a dead guy, and his fish, with a witness placing you at the scene of the crime. If you want us to let you go, then you'd better tell us everything."

"There's not many here that like me," hu'Mar said. "But everyone who knows me, can at least vouch for my ethics. I've told you more than I've cared to already. I've got a client, and I'm working for her. Without her permission, I can't divulge any more information about my case."

"You're investigating a crime. That's our job."

"For all I know, her relic was merely lost, and I'm not investigating a crime. The only thing that should involve you is who's doing all the killing. It might be completely unrelated."

Hu'Rino slammed hu'Mar back. His head hit the stone wall hard.

His cloudy mind remained conscious, barely. "Thhank'ou mister, but'I'ave had eh-nough tta drink tadayyyy."

Distant voices floated around the world, barely even there. "I told yous he was banged up bad. Now look at'im. Yous won't gets anything out of 'im like this. Bacon, can yous stay here and let me know when he comes back around?"

A dog barked. Something metal slammed shut.

He couldn't stop the ringing in his head. The pounding thump of each heartbeat sent painful shock waves through his head, and hu'Mar wished he could pass out and let sleep numb him.

A cat meowed some distance away, maybe from the barred windowsill. Vinegar wouldn't come into the cell, not with Bacon on guard, but he meowed again. Hu'Mar's fuzzy mind could only interpret the intent behind Vinegar's whine, and he repeated, word for word, the translation:

Hard Boiled Cabbage: Big Trouble In Spur Central

"Hey, Dick hu'Clumsy, snap out of it." Hu'Mar felt drunk. He wasn't even sure his mumbled words were coherent or if they actually left his mouth.

"Hey, dumb-nut, you've been beat worse than this," Vinegar said. "Get up!"

"Hey dum-ut, oo've'in beat wors'n'is. Get up," hu'Mar repeated in his mind and maybe even aloud again in a futile attempt to make sense of the words. For whatever reason, he couldn't process the meaning. They were just random words, and he kept repeating, like he was stuck in a looping dream.

"Roaw-roaw-rwoawww. Strupid cat." That would be Bacon, but hu'Mar didn't repeat the dog's words. Understanding the accent was too laborious for hu'Mar's battered brain to comprehend right now.

"Easy there poochy," Vinegar said.

"Eezi deer poochy," hu'Mar repeated.

Even though Bacon was no cat palsy, Bacon and Vinegar struck up a conversation using hu'Mar as Vinegar's translator.

"Such a smart dog. I was afraid you wouldn't figure it out." Vinegar paced along the jail's windowsill.

Hu'Mar squinted, trying to observe Bacon. For a brief moment, Bacon's tongue dropped from his mouth, and his tail wagged. Then the tail froze. Had the dog actually believed that Vinegar was complimenting him? Then hu'Mar couldn't keep his eyes open anymore. He let them drift back to darkness. Only the sounds of the conversation and his own semi-conscious interpretation of Vinegar's words entered his head, like he was listening to a dream.

"You'ra real ugly furbawl for'a cat."

"At least I don't smell like garbage every time I get wet."

"No, yew jush smell rike a cat. Mush worse."

"Enough with the small talk. We're on the same side here. You and Dick hu'Pulp are chasing down two ends of the same stick."

"I rike shticks."

"Of course, you do—augghhhh. Listen, I'll make this simple for you. Let hu'Mar go. I still need him. He didn't kill anyone, but he can probably find whoever did. He's pretty worthless in most respects, but solving mysteries is an area he excels at."

"Whry yew def-end-erng heem?"

"Listen, Pork Chops, do you want to find the killer or just hang another annoying human?"

"I rike humans."

Vinegar suppressed a roweling growl. Hu'Mar responded in kind with a moan of his own. Then the cat coughed several times, hacking up a hairball.

"Yew cats ar dis-ghust-hing. Pee-hing on wawls, coughing up yewr own fur." He snuffed to accent his point. Then there was a chomping sound, like Bacon had just eaten Vinegar's discarded hairball.

"Dogs pee on everything too, plus they eat poop and vomit."

"Dawgs jush mark thar tear-ar-tory. Cat peeh makes ah place un-in-haub-iht-hable. Alsho, whith pooh, don't dog it till yew try it. Beshides, yew do it toooohh."

"I most certainly do not!"

"Evry time yew eat ah mouse, yew eat hish pooh, peeh, and shtomach shtuff."

"That is different," Vinegar argued. "Clearly we don't see eye to eye, or in your case butt-hole to nose-hole, no offense."

"None tak-hen."

"Here's the skinny, I don't care much about Dick hu'Deadbeat. You can string him up on a rope or in a crow's cage for all I care. Sure, I'll have to find a new human to bond, unless I want to go mad like you. All I'm saying is, like him or not, he'll find the real killer. Talk to your minister buddies and cut us some slack. You can always string him up later if you don't like who he brings in."

"Why do yew care?" Bacon asked.

"I don't. I'm just telling you like it is. See you around, Ham Sandwich."

The voices ended, and hu'Mar's head fuzzed even more, till the throbbing slowly drummed him to sleep.

Some time later, hu'Mar sat up and rubbed his temples.

Hard Boiled Cabbage: Big Trouble In Spur Central

His head throbbed, his body trembled, and he had painful itchy bumps all over. It took him a moment to remember where he was. As his vision cleared, a furry face came into view not more than two feet away from him, and he smelled Bacon. Nothing like hot steamy dog breath to welcome one back to consciousness.

Right. He was in jail. He started to stretch, but a sharp pain in his ribs changed his mind. Instead, he settled on rubbing his eyes.

When he squinted through swollen eyelids again, two brown eyes blinked back, then a long tongue flopped out and panted more hot air into his face. It smelled faintly of hairball. That reminded him, Vinegar—where was Vinegar? How long had he slept? Ka'Nairie, he needed to visit with her. This case was grinding out of control. There was plenty she hadn't told him. Why were clients always so scant with their trust? He had to get out of here.

"Are you thinking normawl again?"

Hu'Mar reconsidered his situation. He was trying to piece together a mystery for five salines per day, thinking he could stand upright and work on this case again, all while talking to a dog who spoke human. "No, I can't be thinking straight," he said.

"No hu-man does," Bacon replied. "But if you're good'nuf to know dat, you're good'nuff to me."

"I feel sober now. You can let me out, officer. I promise I won't drink ever again." Why had he ever taken this job in the first place? Obviously, ka'Nairie had black market relics that could get her in trouble, and a political rival in the Ministry who'd be all to happy to frustrate her campaign. The case was more trouble than it was worth.

A slimy tongue sponged up his face. Hu'Mar snapped back into reality.

"I said, I'awl help you out."

"Wait, you're going to let me go?"

"Nooo. You're goin'tew eshcape. After dat, you're on your own. Find da real killer before we find you again."

"But why—"

Bacon barked loudly, then gave a pained yipe, followed by whimpering.

A good 'ole-boy guard, too young and wiry to be trusted with a real beat, came running from outside and saw Bacon on the ground. The dog's legs twitched in mock pain.

"What's going on!" The guard unlocked the cell and pulled out his club. He charged in and took a swing at hu'Mar.

Hu'Mar charged back, fist already cocked. The guard's head snapped back from the inertia, just as the club came down on hu'Mar's head. Both men went down. Hu'Mar, apparently more used to hard knocks, recovered first.

The guard stirred, and hu'Mar wrapped his fingers around the dropped club and gave the young man a gentle tap on the skull. Just enough to put a cheesy grin on the boy's face for the next hour.

"Good ruck," Bacon said.

"Thanks, pooch. I owe you one."

Since no more guards were around because it was dinner time, hu'Mar took an extra moment and rummaged through a cabinet. He retrieved his gear-studded boxing knuckles, his blowgun, and all his poisoned darts. It would be stupid to leave them.

Bacon had chosen a good time to help him leave. He was still surprised that the dog had let him go. In the back of his mind, he remembered a dream where Vinegar had tried convincing Bacon to let him go. Had that been more than a dream? Whatever the reason, he was glad to be out of the small jail. With any luck, and with Bacon's help, his escape would go unnoticed for at least the rest of this evening. If only the world would stop spinning so much. He ran, half leaning, toward the densest part of the city.

After ten minutes of running, his head hurt too much to continue. He stopped in an alleyway and waited for his body to calm down. He curled up, nursing his bruises. He licked the wasp stings on the back of his arm, and some of the dark bristly hair stuck to his tongue before he realized what he was doing. He gagged and coughed, then scraped the hair from his mouth.

Hard Boiled Cabbage: Big Trouble In Spur Central

Stupid cat! Where was Vinegar?

Outside the alley, people walked by. Men headed home from work while other men strolled to bars to fight other men for fun. Women danced into bars to watch those men fight, the single women maybe aiming to start a fight or two of their own. The married ones were probably there to avoid their husbands at home. Kids ran around because their parents were too busy avoiding each other to pay them any attention. With the exception of a hooded Bule, nobody else came into his alley.

Even that Albino didn't stay long. She had a large pack that seemed heavier than anything hu'Mar would've wanted to carry, and she brushed by without giving him a chance to see her shrouded face. All he caught was a wafting of something familiar, but unknown. Almost like charred coal, but with a hint of sulfur. Aimlessly, he climbed to his feet and stepped forward to follow. The brown cloak was the same one that girl had worn to his place before he'd met Jodeign ka'Nairie yesterday, and that smell was like her black combustible pellets. Could she be the same Albino? Was she also the murderer? She flashed him a passing glance back, barely long enough for him to distinguish any facial features. She could have been the one he'd met, but she hurried out of the alley before he could examine her any better.

Did she recognize him? Was that why she'd flashed him a second look? Her pace was quicker than his. Maybe she was avoiding him. When he caught up, he arrived at the end of the alley only to see her disappear around a corner. In a moment, he stood at that corner, searching through the crowd of other passerbys, hoping to catch another glimpse of her. Unfortunately, brown was a very common color, but was that her cloak over there?

He ran to another corner, but she was gone. He suddenly felt all alone again. With each heartbeat pounding through his skull, he mulled deeper over his predicament.

Why should he even care about the case? He didn't owe ka'Nairie a thing. True, she had paid for two days in advance, but for the trouble he'd gotten after only one day, the extra day's wage should be considered hazard pay.

Then, like a sunrise on a rainy day, his mood shifted slightly. He'd already agreed to the case, and he couldn't have predicted people would die. He should tell Jodeign ka'Nairie what had happened. She could call him off, and he could run back to Nebylon, even though King Jerry hu'Regal had a price on his head. Maybe they'd forgotten everything, and he could set up shop there again.

There was another shift, but smoother, like a gear coming full circle.

Confidence rushed back. Not just confidence, but determination. No, he was a dead man in Nebylon. At least here, he could survive, and he could be just as tough as any Tough around. Maybe his life was scattered now. But he was Dick hu'Mar, and he had agreed to the job. This was what he did.

"Vinegar! he yelled. "Where have you been? I had to talk myself out of thinking like a lazy cat again."

Vinegar popped his head around the corner of the alleyway. "Yeah? How do you think I felt? One minute I was enjoying a nice nap in the evening sun by the jailhouse, and the next minute, I feel this annoying determination and loyalty to find you. By the way, nice alley. Is this where we're staying tonight? Looks cozy."

"We're not staying." Hu'Mar limped over.

"Please tell me we're moving on then. I'm sure we could go back to—"

"We're not giving up on this case either."

Vinegar plopped to his side. "Just you watch, one of these days, I'm going to use that ambition I get when separated from you to force myself into something I know I'll thank myself for later, like leaving and not looking back."

"I don't see that happening," hu'Mar said. "You like being lazy and playing games with your mice too much. I swear, that's all you do. Play games, eat, and sleep."

"It's a lot better than working hard, still starving, then getting all your bones broken by hair stylists and ministers."

"You don't get it." Hu'Mar shook his head. He had to stop though because his neck was too bruised. The less he moved, the better.

"Come on, we're going to pay a visit to ka'Nairie. I need to get some questions answered." He was about to leave when a glitter of something on the street caught his eye. Leaning over, he picked up the necklace. He'd seen it before. Not just one like it, but this very one, last night. That seemed like so long ago.

Chapter 16

Not Easy Being An Outlaw

Juniper ka'Shino rubbed her eyes as she crossed the street. They stung and were undoubtedly red, at least the parts were that should have been white. Despite that, and the heavy pack digging into her shoulders, her legs labored unceasingly to move her swiftly through the streets.

Absent-mindedly, her hand found and rubbed the gear within a gear that hung from her necklace, a nervous habit. Her attention was on the man following her. There were people on the street besides herself and him, but most were practiced at ignoring any Albino. With a glance back at her pursuer, her toe caught on an uneven cobblestone. With arms flaying, she stumbled, trying not to fall. Aside from accidentally ripping the necklace free, the maneuver did nothing. Her face smashed into the rough cobbles as her pack pinned her to the ground. She groaned slightly. Was this it? Not even one bomb delivered, and that man was closing in.

Ten minutes earlier, she'd woken to shouting in the streets. With a grumble, she'd shuffled to pull the shutters in, when a half-hearted inspection revealed the cause of the commotion below.

Hard Boiled Cabbage: Big Trouble In Spur Central

If she hadn't been awake before, she was quite alert by then. Six ministers fanned through the streets, knocking on doors, shouting for the occupants to open up. One of the doors belonged to an Albino she'd seen in passing and, the ministers dragged the residents out.

Ka'Shino backed away from the window. Were they after her? Had they tracked her to here? Ernes hu'Toe had been right, she'd been sloppy.

A knock pounded against her door. She jumped and almost screamed. They were here! She couldn't be captured. She still had work to do. She tied a rope around her backpack and lugged it to the window. She'd have to risk going out the second-floor window. It wasn't far down, but could she do it without the other ministers seeing?

Her door rattled again. She willed the minister away, hoping they'd assume the room was empty. A quick survey of the street showed that no ministers were looking, so she lowered the pack to the ground.

Was it over then under, or under then over? Ka'Shino wasn't all that good with knots, but she gambled with over then under and tied the rope to the bed frame. She placed one hand on the window frame to climb out when the door clicked open. She fell with surprise back into the room.

"Why didn't you open te door? I have te last delivery of smoke pellets for your project," a pale faced man said as he re-sheathed the knife he'd used to pry her door open. He lumbered in and heaved a huge bag of pellets next to her bed.

Shaking, she stood. Her heart beat feverishly fast as sweat tickled her scalp and dripped from her hair to her ears. "I'm sorry, I tought you were a minister."

She dug out her pocket clock. It read half past dinner.

"Why would you tink I was a minister?" her guest asked.

She pointed out the window. Below, two ministers slapped around the Albinos they'd dragged out of the apartment, and two more ducked around the corner toward the Inn's entrance.

"I tink it's time to leave," ka'Shino suggested.

"I tink you're right," he said. "Good luck, don't get captured." He dashed down the hall.

She locked the door and peeked out the window to make sure he made it out. Shouts rang out between the ministers, and there he was, running with two ministers hot on his heels. The two who'd been harassing the other Albinos across the alley, joined the pursuit. She sighed with relief. He'd led them away from her. If they really were looking for her, then he'd be beaten, but spared. He wasn't a girl, so he could not possibly be the one they were searching for.

Now, what to do about her bombs. She leaned out the window where she'd lowered the pack, and luckily nobody was near it. She tugged at the rope, but it was too heavy to lift more than a few feet above the ground. There was the option of going down and retrieving it, but that might not be the safest thing right now.

She crossed the room to the door. Her fingers touched the handle when somebody banged on the door again. She tripped and fell onto her bed. The straw stuffing rustled. This time, it couldn't be anyone friendly.

"This is hu'Din." The innkeeper. "I've got some ministers here who'd like to speak with you."

How many ministers were prowling around here? Considering how they'd spoken to the two Albinos outside the alley . . . no thank you. Quietly, she tiptoed back to the window, draped her cloak over her shoulders, and pulled on the new heavy pack of pellets. If only he would've waited to drop those off, this would be so much easier. With one unsure tug of the rope, she trusted her weight to the rope, then climbed out the window as the innkeeper gave another hard knock.

"You in there?" he asked again.

The sound of metal on metal clinked. He was sticking a key in the door. She slid out the window and down the rope. A little over three quarters of the way down, the knot gave out, and the rope went limp in her hands. In the short second between holding to a rope and hitting the ground, her only thought was for the knot. It should have been under, then over. Her feet hit first, jolting her backwards as she crumpled to her pack, then her butt.

Already on her butt, she pulled free from the new pack, then sidled over to one of the refined bombs and looped those straps around her back. With a good tug on the buckles, the pack cinched up tight to her back. Her packs weren't exactly out in the open, this alley had long been neglected by anyone with a sense of pride about their cleanliness. Nobody back in Tuberlow would have ever let the streets around their homes or businesses get so cluttered with old useless garbage like this. Still, she pushed them further out of site, the canvass cloth blended perfectly with the rotted crates and bags of items someone once thought worth saving, but now nobody would find value in. The other explosives would have to stay here till she returned.

With some effort and a bit of rocking, she stood again. By now, the ministers would be in her room. If they took the time to search it thoroughly, they might come to the window. There was no time to waste, she hiked toward the street, passing a ragged man who licked his arm like a cat might. A double take revealed him to be that fake fortune teller, Dick hu'Mar. Was he with the ministers?

With a tug on her cloak to make sure her face was concealed, she quickened her pace. Had he noticed her? He'd sure changed since their first meeting. Everything about him appeared battered as if he'd rolled down a cliff and landed on a bed of cacti. The footsteps behind her suggested that he was following her.

A flat out run would be very suspicious, and getting stopped by a skeptical Tough became increasingly risky, but she walked as fast as her legs would move, hoping that to onlookers, she appeared to be nothing more than a lowly Albino, late for work. The footsteps stopped behind her—that or her heart was pounding to loudly for her to hear properly. Risking a short peek over her shoulders, hu'Mar had stopped and was staring straight at her. She whipped back around to keep moving and quickened her pace. That was when her foot had caught that protruding cobblestone and she'd fallen.

All that in ten minutes. What a gear-grinding way to

wake up. Her hands hurt, her face was bruised. She couldn't get caught. Get up!

Rolling to her side, then her knees, she forced herself up. Everything ached.

The dusky light was still enough to irritate her sensitive eyes, and in the heat of the moment, she'd forgotten her fogged goggles. With one hand up to shield her eyes. She used the other to push through the doorway of a nearby shop.

Hu'Mar barreled out of the alley a few seconds later. He searched down both crowded streets, and his gazed focused well beyond her. Still, she pressed herself tighter into the doorway. When his cat followed casually behind, it stopped and made eye contact with her. It was going to tell him. Her mind raced. Then, without so much as a second glance, the cat ignored her while hu'Mar berated it for being too far away. This might have been the only reason the cat didn't rat her out, but whatever the reason, the cat kept her secret.

Hu'Mar bent over picked something off the ground. Ka'Shino placed her hand to her neck. Her necklace! It had been her mother's. Betrayal, anger, guilt or some combination of the three burned inside of her. She'd lost her mother's necklace, the same one that helped focus her ambitions. With teeth clenched, more upset with herself than with hu'Mar for taking it, she eased back into the street, wary of everybody. Hu'Mar had taken off in the wrong direction.

She checked her pocket clock again. Being above ground, she'd relabeled it to meet a Tough's timeline, so her schedule was all messed up. According to her clock, it was now time to start worrying, even if her body told her that it was time for breakfast. She could do both, though she might just get angry instead. She hadn't slept much, and soon she'd need to skip her studies to deliver the second half of her bomb to Mount Exclusion before the sun set. Otherwise, she'd need to bring a light and that might look suspicious to any insomniac Toughs with an eye on their salvation.

Soon the guard post loomed at this end of the land bridge that led from Spur Central over Lake Tallow to Mount Exclusion. It was a natural rock formation, an arch that Lake Tallow had carved out at the cranking of the gears, some million or so years ago.

To ensure that no non-humans crossed over, the Beadledom posted ministers on both ends. The one stopping her today had a weasel-long face with a polished cudgel that almost ached to be used. Juniper ka'Shino steeled herself.

His partner leaned against the wooden bell shack. In case of attack, they could ring for reinforcements. Those big brass bells would remain silent tonight, but his beady eyes and pudgy grin suggested that he looked forward to a little bell ringing of a different sort.

"Hey there, Buley. What business does a pasty like you got on the big rock? Or did you just come to say hi to me?"

Weasel One and Porky Two laughed as if this was some inside joke.

Ka'Shino bowed submissively, not wanting to cause a scene. "Please sir. I'm just delivering—" she considered what these two would never care to search, let alone steal from her, "—soap."

As expected, weasel boy sneered. "Hear that? We got ourselves a tidy Bule." He backhanded her. She could've kept her balance, but she let herself fall to her back, rolling uncomfortably. Better to make them feel strong. Resisting would only attract more attention.

Let them laugh. Her face stung, but she repressed a smile. These two Toughs had their fun. She crawled back to her knees, then inched past them on all fours. One of them kicked her in the butt. It would bruise, but if that was the worst they cared to dish out, then so be it. She labored to stand under the weight of her pack, then hiked the length of the bridge.

On the other end, two more guards greeted her. "What's your business, Bule?" These two looked less menacing and more bored. Not a good sign.

They were going to search her. It was evident in the way they approached her. Unlike the last two, these guys weren't bullies. They just didn't trust Bules. Smart fellows.

"I've been asked to update te maps of te tunnels around here. Wit te shifting about to happen, te Beadledom wants every possible in-way to te Great Clutch to be protected." Her lie was better this time. Crawling on your hands and knees gave you time to think of things you should've said.

"So they hire a gopher. Let me look in your pack."

"Of course." She dropped it to the ground. This would have been easier tomorrow morning because the morning shift were used to her. Unfortunately, deadlines waited for no one, and now she'd have to get both guard shifts used to her coming and going.

The Tall man, shaped like an upside-down triangle undid her pack. "What's this stuff?" He pulled out blackened cheese cloth. "Why you looking so nervous?"

"Nervous? I'm not nervous," she said. The sweat on her brow was from the exertion of carrying such a heavy pack. The prickle in her spine was from her nerves, but they couldn't see that.

Hopefully she'd packed well enough that they wouldn't see what was taking so much room in her pack. If they did, would they know enough to be concerned? What would she say?

He opened the cheese cloth. His grimace turned into a smile. He jabbed his partner. "Move along, Bule."

"But my—"

"I said move along. You probably stole this anyway."

Ka'Shino lowered her head and walked on as fast as her burden allowed. Only when out of sight did she smile with satisfaction. "Men."

There was one sure way to get a man to look the other way. She'd half expected someone to search her pack, so she'd placed something on top that not even a respectable minister could resist, at least none dealing with a lowly Bule.

Raisins were rare here. Chocolate was even scarcer, and chocolate-covered raisins were a treat that only the wealthy could afford. A bored guard, who really had no fear of a weak Bule, would see the opportunity for what it was. They didn't really care about searching her. And the candy was the perfect opportunity for them to confiscate something and send her on her way without having to spend any more time searching her.

She walked another five minutes, then stopped to rest. The crags of the volcanic hillside branched in multiple directions, hiding each other by large cliffs and jagged fissure canyons. Everything was steep, and despite the unique, razor-sharp terrain, if one wasn't careful, they could easily get lost or hurt up here. Her shoulders were killing her. She was close. Where was it? With a heave, she pushed off her perch and walked another two minutes, then found her footprint from this morning.

Following in those earlier prints, it reminded her of how very little sleep she'd gotten. Every new stride she took now, fell short of the morning's print. As soon as this job was finished, she'd sleep for a week. Not only did this mountain conceal innumerable side trails, but most of those trails led to all sorts of cave systems. Of course, the main trail led to the famous cave that held the Great Clutch. Some of these smaller caves could also lead to there, but many didn't. Some went deep underground and to the moat, where a daring amphibian could conceivably sneak up. Others led to lava pits or gas pockets that meant certain death.

She dug in her cloak and pulled a round rock free. It was semi-translucent, but other than that, it didn't appear to be anything special, at least not out here. But once she entered the small cave at the end of this trail, and her eyes adjusted to the darkness, the rock glowed with the same bio luminescence that had lit the underground speakeasy where hu'Toe and his cronies had given her the explosives. As much as it curdled her blood, that place was now the only safe place to return to.

The glowing rock cast less light than an oil lamp but was adequate for her needs. Besides, an open flame with her load would've been dangerous. She walked carefully, ducking here, twisting there, her eyes adjusting even more the deeper she traveled.

This particular side shoot dove deeper toward the volcanic core before it became impassable. There was some water at the end of this cave, but it didn't connect to anything that she was aware of. In fact, it was so boiling hot and acidic that it could melt any creature's skin or shell off. Some caves were completely submerged and big enough to give credibility to the tales of boat-sized water beasts finding their way into the Clutch room. Ka'Shino had never actually seen that room before, but many stories said that land met water and air there. Any species that lived on this realm could compete for the tomb.

Traveling these side caves could be dangerous. This close to the shifting, other species might very well have sent advanced scouts to map the mountain. Ministers were also stationed closer to the Clutch room, and there was a big difference between the ministers on Mount Exclusion and the ones in Spur Central.

The ministers in the city were by nature more domesticated, but the Clutch Guards were real brutes. They weren't your typical meat heads. They were tall, muscular, and clever. To be on the Clutch Guard was the highest promotion any minister could aspire to. Everyone bowed to these men and women.

If there was any minister that ka'Shino couldn't afford to run into, it would've been a Clutch Guard. With at least two relics each, their skill and cunning weren't the only things to fear. Even the Albino elites, with all their technology, were wary of the ministers stationed at Mount Exclusion.

But she hadn't encountered any of these Guards earlier, not in her cave. This cave provided no access to the Great Clutch, nor was it a route other animals would take to access the mountain. She hiked underground for a mile. It was getting hot, and ka'Shino had to stop and rest several times.

Most people would not have risked this cave. It was too close to the lava flows.

The heat and the sulfuric air would threaten to kill most creatures, but she had a borrowed relic for this very purpose. It kept the heat from fatiguing her and the sulfuric air from collecting acid in her lungs. It didn't make her muscles any stronger or the atmosphere any more comfortable, but it did have the nasty side-effect of turning her blood, sweat, and saliva venomous.

She felt the front of her cloak for where the needle-shaped relic threaded through a thin necklace against her chest. Her

Hard Boiled Cabbage: Big Trouble In Spur Central

parents really were the best, and she did love them, but their way of life was not for her. There were big things happening in the world, and she wanted to be a part of that excitement, but as much as she hated losing her mother's necklace, at least it hadn't been this relic.

At last, she found the pile of explosives from this morning. The relief of dropping her pack almost brought tears to her eyes. Undoing the top, before anything else, she pulled out another cheesecloth bundle, one the ministers hadn't confiscated. Melted chocolate gooped into a pile of deliciously coated raisins. She peeled them off the cheese cloth with her teeth. Melted chocolate was still chocolate.

Next out of the pack were the explosives. This load effectively doubled the size of the bomb in this chamber.

She sorted through the packed tubes and recovered her timer. In appearance, it resembled her own pocket clock, but the face of the clock had different labels: Get Out, Act Casual, Ignore Guilt, Boom.

Of course, there had been no reason write those labels on the timer, since nobody in their right mind would stick around to watch the clock pass all those times, but ka'Shino was the methodical type. Now it was time to hook everything up.

She jammed the compacted black powder tubes into the fault line of this cave section. By the time she finished, there wasn't even any room left in the onyx-colored crack to fit her hand through.

Next, she fastened powder-infused hemp ropes to her wooden clock. To this, she added one of her explosive bundles. She pulled out her own pocket clock to note the time, then cranked the key on the timer to the spot labeled "Get Out."

Ka'Shino took a deep breath of the noxious air. Coughed as it burned her lungs. Her nose and eyes watered. The relic was doing its job, but the toxic air here still hurt. With the wooden clock ticking down, she jogged for the exit.

By the time she exited the caves, she couldn't stop coughing, wheezing, and stumbling. No Tough would inspect that cave, not unless they too had something that would allow them to brave such a forbidding environment. Of course, the Clutch Guards would be granted some relics like the one she'd borrowed, so it might be possible, if they had the right ones.

According to the timer in the cave, ka'Shino knew that it was time to "Act Casual." She took a little abuse from the guards as she returned over the bridge. The first group hardly noticed her, but the bullies at the other end pushed her around and asked where her pack was.

"I fell down and lost it over a crevasse. I have to find more supplies and come back anoter time."

"Tough luck being a weak clumsy Bule!"

They could laugh all they wanted. She'd get the last laugh, though it would probably sound more like sobbing. While it was out of the question to stay at her inn, she walked, half stumbled, back there anyway. Her work was far from finished, but all of her remaining explosives were stashed in the alley there. It would be no fun hauling it all back down to that wretched speakeasy, but no minister would look for her there. Along the way, she passed a fairly clean neighborhood, or that is to say, fewer men loitered about. Idle men were always dirty. They were either drunk, wanting to be drunk, looking for a fight, or coming out of a fight.

This spoke, still crowded like most inner-city spokes were filled with children. A little girl, about five years old, played in a yard with a little boy, maybe seven years old. She had him pinned to the ground and was pushing weeds into his nose.

Ka'Shino's chest tightened. She checked at her pocket clock again. Yep, it was about time to "Ignore Guilt." The kids' mom called them in for the night, and the children made up excuses and stalled.

As ka'Shino passed by, hoping she'd done the right thing, she had to remind herself that hu'Toe had promised minimal casualties. The bomb wouldn't hurt anyone. It was only meant to weaken the mountain. There were still three more bombs to place. With any luck, the Great Clutch would be destroyed, but the people of Spur Central would be otherwise unaffected.

It would all turn out well. It had to.

Hard Boiled Cabbage: Big Trouble In Spur Central

They'll be fine, she reassured herself. So why did she feel sick to her stomach over it?

Chapter 17
Politics As Usual

Jodeign ka'Nairie was easy to find. Visible from several streets away, big bonfire-sized torches lit the venue and chased away the darkness of the early evening. It was a political debate, located in Spur's public amphitheater near the inner spokes of the city. Where better to find an upcoming political socialite?

Like much of the stonework in Spur Central, amphitheaters like this existed long before humans arrived on this world. Those early architects had been clever. The circular theaters allowed one's voice to transmit sound to every part of the pit. It was a marvel to experience. Unfortunately, crowds couldn't navigate the corridors and stairs without being cramped, so hu'Mar had to pick Vinegar up to keep him from getting trampled.

"You know, those pasty Albinos built this amphitheater, don't you?" Vinegar pointed out, happy to brag about his knowledge.

"I bet they didn't design it," hu'Mar said, for no other reason than he felt like arguing with the cat.

"True, they copied it, like any human now cares," Vinegar said, not rising to the occasion. "Too bad humans put so little effort into reading. There's plenty they could learn from the past."

Hard Boiled Cabbage: Big Trouble In Spur Central

Hu'Mar found his place, just in time to see the beginning. Like always, these debates were well attended, so there was standing room only, for pretty much everyone.

Despite the great acoustics, little of the debate was ever heard by anybody because of the commotion caused by the bookies and spectators own talking. Mostly they shouted insults, encouragements, and in the case of Jodeign ka'Nairie—cat calls. Although if they knew any cats, they might look for a different term to describe their lusty fervor. Then there was the gambling.

Gambling was the real reason everyone came. This was the top form of entertainment. A king or similar leader of neighboring nations might only have twenty percent approval ratings, but here, the ratings were always high. Instead of campaign signs and vague platitudes, Tough candidates distributed trading cards of themselves. Hu'Mar never cared for such things, and he couldn't understand the point of carrying a numbered miniature portrait of any politician.

Sure, these events might start with a word or two from the candidates about how they'd run the government. After all, the people needed to know that their candidates were skilled at throwing insults, and not just punches. Unlike other cities, where politicians would engage in stoic, but otherwise empty debates, here things got interesting.

On the side of the performance pit, ka'Nairie's horse, Beauford, stamped with delight. The five-gallon fedora was a dead giveaway. He liked the debate as much as any human spectator, and why shouldn't he? He was an unbonded human palsy.

Ka'Nairie shouted something to one of today's rivals, which hu'Mar was sad to see, did not include Jef hu'Rino.

Over hu'Mar's shoulder, somebody yelled, "Ten salines on hu'Ruffin!"

Another guy shouted, "Two bromines on our lady ka'Nairie!"

Several bookies squeezed through the crowds, taking bets and handing out tickets. They sent complicated hand signals to the debate's moderator, who in fact was nothing more than an oddsmaker. He or she would then run the numbers and update the tote or betting board.

Once the crowd of punters had tickets, the oddsmaker lifted his hands. The spectators hushed, and the debaters could be heard despite the hundreds or thousands of whispered conversations.

In that silky seductive voice, ka'Nairie began, "The Great Clutch will lift the seal off the Tomb of Ascension any time now. We need strong leadership in the Beadledom to ensure that Spur Central can defeat the coming armies. I will lead us to victory!"

She had two opponents today. One was Joe hu'Ruffin, the other hu'Mar hadn't heard of before, but the tote board listed his name as Donelyn hu'Groom. He had one-to-three odds and was the first contestant to counter. "Sexy legs and poisoned lipstick might stop a man cold, but we won't be warring against humans. We'll be fighting wolves, hysts, whales, sharks, and all sorts of dangerous animals that could care less about how tight your leather bra is!"

The crowd roared its delight. Whatever else hu'Ruffin had to say was lost before everyone quieted down again.

It was nearly time for the part everyone had been waiting for. The tote board adjusted its odds, and ka'Nairie was first to draw a knife and stab it into the debate desk. "Then it's a duel! We'll see if you're as tough as you think you are!"

Hu'Ruffin slammed his own dagger into the table, accepting the challenge. Hu'Groom lost some points on the tote board for being last to accept the challenge. It was a sign of weakness to duel the tired winner of the first fight.

"I don't need to watch this," Vinegar said, leaping out of hu'Mar's arms and curling up near his feet. "Don't get too excited. If you step on me, I'll claw your eyes out while you sleep."

"You wouldn't," hu'Mar grumbled.

"Just saying," Vinegar defended. "You gave me fair warning about my tail, so I'm giving you fair warning about your eyes."

Since ka'Nairie was the challenger, hu'Ruffin chose the weapon. They didn't call him Big Joe hu'Ruffin for nothing. He picked a massive metal war hammer, taller than any man. He hefted his and swung it, watching to see whether ka'Nairie collapsed under the weight of hers.

Ka'Nairie plucked an even bigger war hammer from the rack and spun it above her head like a glittering baton. The noise of the crowd could make the base of a fifty-story waterfall sound like a yawn.

Ka'Nairie and hu'Ruffin danced around each other, their hammers spinning and twisting like children's toys, even though each hammer had a heavy metal head the size of, well, a head.

Unlike a sword, war hammers weren't meant to clash together. Instead, they could be swung past the reach of an enemy, crushing skulls and armor before the enemy could get close enough to attack. They were so heavy, that even a skilled swordsman would find it next to impossible to parry.

But, however strong you were, once you committed to an attack, the momentum of your hammer was set. So two hammers against each other turned into a game of strategy and deception. A feigned attack here, a ready block there. Hu'Mar already knew who would win this duel. Hu'Ruffin thought that a big unwieldy weapon would play to his strength better. But this wasn't about strength. Just dropping one of those hammers on someone could kill.

The two twirled around the arena, swinging at each other. Whenever they got too close to the stands, the standing spectators would compact into each other. A wild swing could take out a whole swath of onlookers.

Hu'Mar would probably be able to lift one of those weapons, but just watching them spin the war hammers around was enough to make his arms and back ache. Big Joe hu'Ruffin was about as hairless as anybody hu'Mar had ever seen. Nothing on his arms, chest, or even head. What he had, were large bulging muscles with biceps as big as Beauford's butt. Jodeign ka'Nairie shouldn't have been able to lift her hammer, let alone swing it with such ease.

Not only could she lift it so carelessly, but this weapon played to ka'Nairie's strengths. She was a manipulator and a strategist. Hu'Mar couldn't decide what he liked more, watching hu'Ruffin sweat with worry or ka'Nairie sweat with fluid, confident motion.

The two danced around each other multiple times. Then ka'Nairie let go with one hand and let the hammer twirl in a long, swooping motion that carried it behind her legs, over her back, ready to come down on her opponent as it finished its long arc. It was almost like ka'Nairie was treating hu'Ruffin as big nail that needed pounding into the ground. Clearly this would have been a mistake.

Hu'Ruffin saw his opportunity and stepped in close, so that the head of her hammer would overshoot him. He lifted his handle to block the oncoming shaft, a move that would likely hurt his wrists, but cause the unbalanced momentum of her hammer to rip itself from Jodeign ka'Nairie's grasp. He braced for the heavy hit and positioned his legs so that he'd be properly balanced for a counter swing once she lost control of her weapon. Under normal conditions, he would be in a prime position to strike back and win.

Before the hammer had time to complete its arc over ka'Nairie's head, she let go of the hammer all together, its momentum carried it straight up, into the air. She jumped in close and punched hu'Ruffin hard in the neck.

He stumbled back, just far enough for her hammer to complete its airborne somersault and landed squarely on his shoulder.

With what had to be a broken collar bone, hu'Ruffin dropped his hammer. In an uneven twist, it landed heavy on his foot. He hopped back, holding his neck with one hand, his foot with the other. Then he fell down, backward. Hu'Mar was surprised that he hadn't crumpled outright when the hammer first hit, but this was Tough country.

Ka'Nairie scooped up her hammer, stepped over to him, and dangled the weighty chunk of death about a foot above his face.

His eyes went wide. He tried to talk, but his crushed throat was still fighting him. He slapped the ground several

Hard Boiled Cabbage: Big Trouble In Spur Central

times.

A horn blew. The match was over. Ka'Nairie dropped the hammer, not on hu'Ruffin's head. The crowd shouted for blood, but she wouldn't give it to them. Not this round. She'd won.

Tickets were waved in the air. Some were happy. Some were poor. The tote board was updated to reflect new odds for the next duel. Jodeign ka'Nairie had ten minutes to rest while everyone placed their revised bets. The crowd hummed with excitement, counting their money. Only hu'Mar kept his eyes on Ka'Nairie, which is why he was the only one to notice how she ever so slyly, reached below her exposed knee, pulled a little item out from inside her calf-high boot and placed it in a pocket attached to the top of that same boot. It had to be Her Ring of Strength. Like most relics, it would need contact with skin to work, it didn't matter that it wasn't her finger. Hu'Mar had already suspected she'd been using that during her fight.

Donelyn hu'Groom was next. Since he was the second duelist, supposedly fighting a more tired opponent, Jodeign ka'Nairie got to choose the weapon. Despite this and ka'Nairie's easy show of grace in the last fight, a lot of people were still betting on hu'Groom. Hu'Mar couldn't blame them. From the conversations drifting past him, he gathered that hu'Groom had proven himself in the past to be a slick, smart, even dirty fighter, the sort who rarely got in over his head.

On top of that, ka'Nairie's head and shoulders drooped noticeably with fatigue. It could've been a ploy, but she did look more tired, verging on sick. He hadn't seen that in her earlier. Undoubtedly, she was using her one good relic to give her an advantage, but without its pair, she'd quickly be at a disadvantage.

He watched closely, remembering what he'd learned about her relics. The ring of strength's problem was that it built up the toxins in her blood, slowly poisoning her, hence the obvious fatigue now. Without the Pin of Poison to convert that toxicity into something her body could handle, she might not make it through this next round.

The crowd shouted for their weapons of choice.

"Swords!"

"Chains!"

"Rocks!"

"Panties!"

Jodeign ka'Nairie ignored everyone's suggestions. She chose horses.

Hu'Mar had seen several duels in his life, but never one using horses as a weapon. Hu'Groom straightened his back in confusion also. It was a smart move on ka'Nairie's part. If she was as tired as hu'Mar expected, then a well-trained warhorse could do the fighting for her.

She whistled for Beauford.

Her strong, too-human horse galloped over on his back two hooves. His front two hooves pawed at the air like a boxer. Only when he dropped to all fours next to her, did she climb onto his back.

Hu'Groom puffed his chest out, like a man pretending not to appear worried. Hu'Mar guessed that most people even believed him. While he could've easily beaten Big Joe hu'Ruffin, ka'Nairie was throwing him outside his comfort zone. He called someone over to him, likely his campaign manager. If he backed down now, then his popularity would drop so fast that he'd never have a chance of winning the election. If he stayed and lost, then he'd be too weak. The manager left, returning moments later with a mean black warhorse.

The man whispered into hu'Groom's ear. Hu'Mar could barely make out hu'Groom's smile. Something had changed, and it couldn't be good for Jodeign ka'Nairie. She sat atop Beauford, who twitched uncomfortably when she rubbed her strong muscular leg against his side. Was he nervous? One quick glance at hu'Groom's warhorse would do that.

"You know, it's hard to sleep with all this noise," Vinegar complained. "How's your girlfriend doing?"

"I thought you didn't care?" hu'Mar said without lifting his eyes off her.

Almost miraculously, ka'Nairie wiped away most of her fatigue. She radiated confidence and eagerness. Maybe she had feigned fatigue for show.

Hard Boiled Cabbage: Big Trouble In Spur Central

"I don't care about her, but I think it would be nice to get paid," Vinegar mewed with a little more interest than hu'Mar would've expected.

"I can't imagine she's got much energy left by now." Hu'Mar pressed a knuckle to his chin.

Since ka'Nairie didn't move her ring back to a place her skin might touch it, he suspected that she wasn't willing to risk using it anymore.

Arms of spectators, all clutching salt or tickets, reached across hu'Mar. It was almost impossible to see through the excited crowd to ka'Nairie. How could a horse be used as a weapon? Then he noticed that hu'Groom's horse was outfitted with armor.

Donelyn hu'Groom mounted his black steed. The beast was saddled with hooked spikes, and even the horse's helmet held a long wooden spike. All he needed to do was get close enough to snag Jodeign ka'Nairie, and she'd be ripped from her mount.

Five minutes passed, then a new scorecard was placed for all to see. Apparently, the addition of horses gave the bookies something else to allow betting on, and of course, that meant they'd make more money. An announcer yelled out the horse's history.

"On the left, donned with battle armor, Milton, current property of Boss hu'Diem, captain of the 2nd Tough Roaming Regiment. This horse was victorious in all six uprisings and all four of the minor cross species skirmishes during the last two years, proven deadly with over three hundred kills to his name alone, and given the honorary status of horse trainer to three dozen and ten other horses."

Cheers applauded the warrior, deafeningly loud, as only a culture of warriors could fully appreciate.

"On the right, Beauford, an unbonded palsy, who to the best of our knowledge has never fought in any war and who fancies foreign-made fedoras."

Beauford bowed. The crowd laughed and jeered.

Ten minutes later, the bookies all raised their arms high, and the crowd settled to their seats. The stadium went silent as the oddsmaker called attention to the next duel. The odds were now nineteen to one, in hu'Groom's favor, at least for the humans. Beauford had even worse odds, with Milton pulverizing him, fifty-five to one. There were other names on the scoreboard, each from previous or upcoming debates, but who, for entertainment purposes, were scheduled to debate on different days. Among them, ka'Nairie still maintained the popularity vote, but losing this debate, if it didn't kill her, could seriously drop her down the rankings. Still, she waited on top of Beauford and by all casual observation, seemed one-hundred percent unperturbed. With no armor, just her standard leather outfit, which matched Beauford's naked tan hide, how could they possibly hope to defeat hu'Groom's armored warhorse?

Hu'Mar alternated watching the audience and the fight, searching every face. If any one of the suspected relic thieves were here, they were hiding too well within the throng of spectators. They weren't his real reason for being here anyway. He needed to snag ka'Nairie when she was done. He'd been through a lot in the last two days, and she'd held out on him.

The only hint that Beauford was nervous, was how his muscles twitched. At least, that's how it looked from hu'Mar's vantage. If he could notice the twitches from here, that likely meant they were full on nervous flinches down there. Ka'Nairie patted Beauford on the neck and whispered something in his ear. Then she gave him a gentle kick, and Beauford slowly circled his opponent, eye's wide and wild, ready to go berserk at any moment.

Hu'Groom's challenging stare nearly matched Beauford's as he mirrored ka'Nairie's circling horse, maybe twenty paces away. Snot sprayed in a defiant mist from Milton's large nostrils

Jodeign ka'Nairie was first to break the circle. She charged, head bent low to Beauford's neck, more like a racer than a duelist. Hu'Groom reacted a second later, sitting tall like a general leading his troops, he charged in to meet her. Both riders held on as their horses reared and swung hooves dangerously close to each other.

The black horse, wild and savage in appearance, danced,

reared, and fought like nothing hu'Groom was prepared for. Hu'Mar hoped that the guy would fall off, and if not for Milton's quick judgement in posture, he would've too. But the horse was looking out for his rider as much as he was attacking Beauford.

Beauford held back, swinging his hooves like a human boxer and dancing around to confuse the opponent. Jodeign ka'Nairie clung effortlessly to the back of Beauford's reared body as if they'd practiced this hundreds of times.

There was no doubt in hu'Mar's mind. Though a great warrior, Milton was not familiar with this sort of fighting. Nor was hu'Groom familiar with the commands to fully utilize the horse's abilities. Despite the frightening visage that the warhorse portrayed, Beauford might actually have the upper hoof.

This didn't stop hu'Groom. He whipped Milton around and gave him another command. The horse bucked, swinging his hind legs back in bone-shattering kicks. Maybe hu'Groom did know a few tricks after all. To his credit, he kept his balance. Since he'd commanded the horse's movements, he could anticipate them and brace himself.

Beauford was cowed, temporarily, after a kick nicked him in the neck. But since Beauford thought and acted more like a human than any horse, ka'Nairie gave him his reins. As skilled as Milton might be, he was still trained to fight with commands. As such, he struggled to think for himself with hu'Groom on his back. If he'd been smarter, he would've realized that hu'Groom didn't know how best to use him, then he could've relied on his own experience. Unfortunately, horses were too stupid to realize that most of them were little more than trained slaves, and in this case, he was at the mercy of an inexperienced task master.

This battle would end soon, and since the whole purpose for hu'Mar's visit was to talk with ka'Nairie, he had to wonder how she might exit the stadium. Triumphantly through the main gates with the people? No. If she won, she'd leave from the arena gates, meant solely for performers. The other possibility was that she'd lose and limp her way out those same gates. Hopefully, she didn't die. He felt a twinge of guilt that his first concern was failing to get paid. Either way, his best bet was to gain access to the arena gates.

"Who's winning?" Vinegar asked.

Beauford charged the black horse, but right as Donelyn commanded Milton to kick its hind legs again, Beauford halted.

The kick went high, and Beauford ducked under and turned sideways. Milton's legs landed awkwardly across Beauford's back, just between his neck and Jodeign ka'Nairie. While the warhorse struggled to keep its balance, surprised at being turned into a wheelbarrow, Jodeign ka'Nairie pulled out a dagger and sliced one of its leg tendons. It severed as snappy as a thin tight cord touched by a razor blade.

Milton lurched forward, nearly throwing hu'Groom. Its one hind leg was useless, but it still remained upright.

Cheers and boos pelted the stadium. It wasn't over yet. The black stallion was trained to compensate for wounds during combat. He charged on three legs, running like an off-balanced spinning top, ready to topple.

Beauford sidestepped to dodge, but Milton leaned, almost falling into Beauford. Its hooked saddle snagged ka'Nairie's boot and ripped her from her mount.

She fell out of the boot and landed hard on the ground, her head hitting the hardest. Hu'Mar leaned forward. This wasn't looking good. The unsteady stallion had become unpredictable, and with ka'Nairie dazed and barely mobile, her odds were quickly evaporating.

"Get up," hu'Mar pleaded. Of course, he had been paid for two days in advance, but it would take several more days to clear his muddied name. He expected her to pay for that as well. Plus, he didn't want to see such a beautiful Tough specimen destroyed. She was conniving, dangerous, even manipulative, the perfect candidate to be in the government.

Hu'Groom eased back around and commanded his horse to stomp her to mush. The horse was all too pleased to obey. Its front legs lifted.

Hu'Mar didn't want to watch, but looking away was impossible. Partly it was morbid curiosity and concern that kept his eyes on her. He couldn't believe that someone as beautiful as her could ever be hurt. Mostly it was because he'd bet his last saline on her, and if she lost, then she'd be responsible for taking everything, including that, away from him.

Suddenly Vinegar climbed hu'Mar's torso, his claws dug into his shirt and skin.

"What the—" Hu'Mar grabbed the cat, if only to keep those claws out of his skin. "I thought you didn't care."

Vinegar ignored him and stretched his neck, tense and intent on ka'Nairie's fate.

Milton's hoof was a fist-length away from her chest when Beauford bucked and kicked the black horse square in the neck. Milton's hooves came down, barely rubbing against Jodeign ka'Nairie's vest.

She moaned and tried to roll away. The black horse must have known that he'd be put down for his injury, because he was madder than any horse hu'Mar had ever seen. It also probably felt betrayed by a brother horse. After all, Beauford had attacked him without his rider.

Milton bucked and kicked and kicked and drooled.

Hu'Groom held on for dear life, his knee snagging on his own horse's spikes. Even if he wanted to bail off, he was stuck for the duration of the ride.

Beauford caught a couple of Milton's kicks, one knocking him to the ground. Milton arched around in a limping gallop, then lowered his spiked helmet and charged the fallen Beauford. He'd skewer Beauford, then return for ka'Nairie.

Despite its limp, it moved fast, passing so close to Jodeign ka'Nairie, it almost stepped on her. She raised her hand in protest, but Milton passed without slowing. Then it toppled and rolled.

Legs flayed about, kicking as it crushed and stabbed its rider with its own spikes.

The crowd hushed, not believing what they'd seen. As ka'Nairie climbed to her knees, she revealed a dagger in one hand. The crowd erupted. The sound practically vibrated the stadium, as if every stone was shaking under the cacophony. That was gutsy. Hu'Mar chuckled. She hadn't raised her hand to protest the charge. She'd raised it and sliced another tendon on the black horse's passing front leg. A three-legged horse was bound to be on the butcher's block tomorrow, but a two-legged horse couldn't even stand.

She slowly walked over to Milton. It settled down, long enough for her to plunge her dagger into its throat. It took a minute for the horse to bleed out. Its rider was dead before it was, killed by his own spikes.

Ka'Nairie listed from side to side, probably ready to faint. But she climbed back onto Beauford, who was also a little dazed. The two only needed a moment to compose themselves. But in that moment, she sat tall, and he galloped without any sign of fatigue. If hu'Mar hadn't been watching himself, he would never have guessed that they'd both nearly died. With how they exuded confidence and pomp, waving and strutting, one might think they'd planned the whole show. For all hu'Mar knew, maybe they had. This would be great for her reputation and election. The majority of the spectators were another story. As ka'Nairie and Beauford trotted around the stadium, disappointed spectators threw their tickets at them while excited winners rushed to the box to pick up their winnings.

Vinegar relaxed in his arms. "I wasn't even worried."

"Right." Hu'Mar tried hard not to let his own elation show, but it was difficult to keep from grinning. He had winnings to collect for himself, a bonus, on top of what he still hoped to get paid. At least now he wouldn't starve while he finished the case. He'd turned one saline into three bromines and a saline. Not bad for risking the last of your salt, which was feeling more like a lifestyle now, than a gambling strategy.

Hu'Mar quickly collected his salt while ka'Nairie finished prancing around the arena, never leaving her horse. She perched atop it like a monument for everyone to admire, and they did. Politics the world over had this one thing in common, showmanship. That's why the talking portion of the debates only took up a minor part of the actual debate. Everybody cared about the talking points, but they all voted based on perceived strength, power, looks, and style. She was an entertainer, and so what if

Hard Boiled Cabbage: Big Trouble In Spur Central

Tough culture took the political arena to this extreme. They were an extreme sort of people. This didn't make their system any less genuine. If anything, it was more authentic, since it refused to hide any pretense about the nature of politics. Even those who'd lost money on her, reverenced her. If every political debate went this well, she'd be a Beadledom shoo-in.

Too bad Jef hu'Rino wasn't one of the contestants. That was one minister hu'Mar would've been happy to have off his back. Then again, hu'Rino was clever. If he ever debated ka'Nairie, he could use his knowledge of her relic against her. Using a relic to win these debates would be a definite strike against any candidate if exposed. He still might. Though to her credit, she probably didn't need the relic to win. It merely made the fights easier.

Hu'Mar wriggled and pushed his way through the crowd. He fell over once, and found it easier to crawl between the muscular hips and legs that supported an unmoving bulk of Toughs in one of the groups blocking his way. It would've been easier to continue like that all the way to the exit, but hu'Mar had his pride. As soon as he could, he stood again, and began shoving his way out. The problem with being a big guy, was that he couldn't squeeze between tight places very well, especially when those tight places were men and women even stronger than himself, all with no tolerance for being shoved in any direction. Just trying to move a stubborn Tough might invite a fight. He had no time for that. For one, he didn't want to lose consciousness again. Two, ka'Nairie wouldn't stick around here forever. And he had to talk with her.

Chapter 18

Lot of Pain For Blessed Little Gains

"Don't tell me you're in love," Vinegar said, weaving between the thick muscular legs of the departing spectators.

Hu'Mar ignored him, pushing his way through throngs of arrogant Toughs, careful not to encourage any of them into violence. That was a hard line to walk. On one hand, you had to be tough. On the other hand, you couldn't be too tough. Too many people around here would take that as a challenge.

"Come on, Dick hu'Hopeless. I saw how you were staring at her."

"I had money riding on her." Hu'Mar edged away from the common gate and crawled over a waist-high wall. The ground on the other side lay farther below, and even when he hung from the edge of the wall by his fingertips, his feet still dangled above the access corridor that led to the arena. With one long exhale, he braced himself to fall the rest of the way to the earth when Vinegar jumped onto his shoulders.

His fingers slipped, and he landed hard on his feet before crumpling to the dirt. It didn't hurt, but his blood steamed at Vinegar for catching him off guard. The only people here were the stage crews, none paying hu'Mar any attention as they hauled away the platform used during the initial verbal portion of the debate.

A few paces away, the corridor turned into a tunnel that accessed the arena from below the stadium seats. Hu'Mar snuck inside and waited. It was about twenty long paces deep, and since Vinegar was acting indifferent to hu'Mar's caution, the cat casually walked in through the middle of the arched opening. Hu'Mar glared from within the shadows. The cat missed the meaning. If he still had a tail, it would've waved majestically. "You might want to move," hu'Mar warned.

Vinegar lifted his nose higher into the air, commanding more authority. Nobody paid him any attention though, which probably was the reason he was always so grumpy.

"Why are you pressed up against the wall like that?" Vinegar asked. "That's a horrible attempt if you're seriously trying to hide."

Without warning, massive hooves, as big as the cat's head, pounded from behind as if trying to punch holes through Vinegar. Each horse hoof assaulted the dirt like several war hammers, spraying dust into his face, disorienting him with the deafening thunder of their speed. Hu'Mar would laugh as soon as they passed and Vinegar was safe, but for now, he held his breath with tense amusement.

Vinegar dodged, ran, fell, scrambled back up, and froze as the two horses entered the arena. Finally hu'Mar was able to release his laughter as he focused on the light at the end of the tunnel. Ka'Nairie should be along any minute, and he needed to get things straight with her. As he waited, Vinegar bumped into his leg, happy to hang out near the wall now. He was dazed and couldn't stop himself from shaking, but he survived.

"Aren't you even a little concerned that I almost turned into horse-hoof jam?" Vinegar asked.

Hu'Mar let his smirk land unceremoniously on Vinegar.

The cat bristled, anger replaced his anxiety. "Don't look so pleased with yourself. Remember, ka'Nairie could care less about you. If you had a heart, she'd break it, and you'd be all the better for it."

Vinegar danced against the opposite wall where a ray of sunlight still slivered into the tunnel. "This is taking forever," Vinegar complained.

Thirty seconds of waiting, and the cat was already impatient. Could hu'Mar possibly suffer any more if he did lose Vinegar?

"You humans are pathetic. Seriously, how long does one human need to gawk at another. Ka'Nairie doesn't even have any fur on those smooth black legs and arms. You'd never see me chasing a hairless feline. I've seen one of those once before: they're creepy. It's a wonder humans breed, given how ugly you all are."

At last, Vinegar ran out of insults. He was about to nap when the clip clop of hooves came near. He flinched, alert this time. Hu'Mar couldn't stop himself from chuckling again. It was the same two horses from earlier. They had ropes behind them and were dragging the dead black horse out of the arena. Behind them, two people dragged hu'Groom's corpse from the stadium.

A short time later, ka'Nairie emerged with Beauford as her only companion. She saw Vinegar first, sniffed in disgust, then searched around until her eyes met hu'Mar's. A thin smile curled across ka'Nairie's face, the kind that said, I should have known I'd see you again soon. She stayed in her saddle. "If it isn't my fortune teller. How's the search going?"

"I think there's more to this case than you're telling me," hu'Mar said, stepping out of the darkest of the shadows.

"What? Don't you like a good challenge?" ka'Nairie asked.

"A challenge is one thing. A setup is another thing completely."

"Are you accusing me of something?" Ka'Nairie's smile vanished.

Hu'Mar grabbed her boot and yanked her off Beauford.

She gasped as hu'Mar swung her around and pinned her against the wall, one hand to her throat, the other free to defend himself if she tried anything. She didn't look like she'd do anything. She actually looked like she was ready to collapse.

Hu'Mar had seen her take on two challengers, nearly fall

from exhaustion, and then regain her strength like it had never let her down. He should be more careful messing with her, but things didn't add up. Now that she was off the horse again, she was as limp as a drunken snake.

"That's no way to treat a lady," she cooed, struggling to maintain her composure.

"What do you know about Crazy Ish?"

Recognition flashed in her eyes. "I don't know who you're talking about."

"How about Renu ka'Feebal?"

"Listen meat-head," ka'Nairie said, all her sensual pretense gone. "You don't like the case, fine. I'll find another hound for my relic."

"You mean, you'll find another fall guy to keep men like Minister Jef hu'Rino off your case?"

Beauford sat on his rump behind hu'Mar, a little too close for comfort, but he did little more than listen to the conversation.

Ka'Nairie studied hu'Mar, then smiled. "You're clever, I'll give you that, but that wasn't my intention." Her hands dropped from hu'Mar's wrists. One came up with a small leather purse. Her leather outfit seemed far too skin-tight to hide such things, not that he was looking, at least, not very much. At least it wasn't a dagger.

"Is it more money you need? Here, take it," she said.

Difficult as it was, hu'Mar used his free hand to push the bag aside. "You're not buying me off like that. I took a job, and I'll see it through. You pay me when I'm done. What I need right now are answers."

While hu'Mar's free hand pushed her purse away, Jodeign ka'Nairie's other hand came up with, of course, a dagger. The blade dimpled hu'Mar's skin, right around his navel.

"Listen big boy, I can't tell you anything you don't already know. I just need you to find what I've lost. You don't need to dig up my whole life story."

Hu'Mar tightened his grip on her neck. "You can't tell me, or you won't tell me?"

She pressed the dagger harder against his belly and gave him one of her classic smiles, seductive and menacing. Gears-a-grinding, this woman knew how to make a man's knees tremble. They were at a standoff. He could snap her neck, and she could run him through, though neither had any desire for that.

Instead, they leaned in and kissed each other. It was a hard, mean kiss that could have choked either one of them, though he was pretty sure she sucked harder than he did. She bit and drew blood as he pulled back. She smiled as she licked her upper lip.

He tucked his lip in and sucked the wound, then turned his head and spit.

She pulled her knife back. He loosened his grip on her neck. Then Beauford punched Dick hu'Mar in the back of the head with his hoof.

The last thing hu'Mar saw or heard for a while was Vinegar, rolling on the ground, laughing at him as only a cat could, hissing and choking on his own mirth.

In his dreams, ka'Nairie's kiss lingered. He was vaguely aware that this couldn't be reality, but he didn't care. Here, he could fly, holding close the strongest, most attractive woman he'd ever met. If this case could bring him closer to her, he'd solve it. Even the torture he'd endured to this point had been worth it, if only for that violent kiss. Maybe he should challenge her to a fight someday. She might be worth the risk. She might also kill him. He would have to time it right so that she was weak enough for him to win. He'd also need to ensure that she wasn't using that ring of strength if such an opportunity every arose.

The dream turned fuzzy, and his hold on ka'Nairie slipped into fog. There was something else, a clue, something important, almost out of reach, but if he stretched his mind, he might grab hold of it. He was so close to making sense of—something. Then, even that faded to dreamlessness.

Chapter 19

Broomsticks and Beefcakes

"Ungh," hu'Mar moaned as he blinked away the fuzz. It wasn't working, so he reached out and pushed Vinegar aside. That helped. He felt his skull. Tender. He sat up, pressing his hands to the side of his head. A blacksmith's anvil would've felt lighter than the headache resting on him.

Amidst the ringing, his mind slowly trickled back to him. He remembered Bacon, and how the dog had stuck its neck out for him. He remembered ka'Nairie's debate. He remembered her kiss and slid his hand down from his temple and touched the spot she'd bitten. It was swollen. He licked it, and the taste of his blood made his stomach jitter. She was still keeping secrets from him. It was frustrating, and yet he smiled.

"Not many humans or animals of any sort could shrug off a punch like that," Vinegar yawned. "Let alone—smile from it. You must have a head full of bone and no brain to walk away from such a blow."

There were plenty of Toughs here who could handle it much better than he, but he hurt too much to argue. He struggled to his feet. Vinegar was staring at the red hazy moon. The street crews would be lighting the oil lamps and raking out the uneven spots in the road.

"How long have I been out?" hu'Mar asked.

"Not nearly long enough, but the stadium is cleared out. What's your next grand failure?" Vinegar asked as he followed.

"Failure?" Hu'Mar rubbed his lip again. He could feel his pulse in it, beating for Jodeign ka'Nairie.

Vinegar understood in a way that only a palsy could. "Humans," he snorted.

Then it happened: the hair on the back of hu'Mar's neck tingled. He had the strangest sensation that he was being watched, and Vinegar was suddenly on edge too. Somehow, he knew that the short hairs of Vinegar's hackles were struggling to stand on end underneath his tangled mop of fur. His left whiskers twitched, and slowly, Vinegar turned his head sideways. His right whiskers flinched.

Three triggers in a row. That was bad. Vinegar could be infuriating sometimes, but the cat had uncanny and accurate instincts. With all his hair attuned, Vinegar focused on what was ahead. All hu'Mar could see, were some tall wooden buildings, ugly things, but nothing out of the ordinary. Yet Vinegar's attention was focused not on the buildings but on something in the distance. Hu'Mar's throat tightened. Mount Exclusion. Was the Clutch finally lifting?

Cats could instinctively sense these sorts of things. According to Vinegar most mammals had the ability as well, but usually none so good as cats. For instance, a dog's whiskers weren't as sharp, on account of all the slobber that splashed on them. Vinegar broke his distant stare and locked eyes with hu'Mar.

"Are you going to tell me what it is?" hu'Mar asked.

"You're worse than dogs," Vinegar said, not rudely, but worried. "You know, you humans could do this. Your brains are big enough. Even your women have way more whiskers than we do, so you should be better than any other animal at this sort of thing."

Hu'Mar had received this lecture a hundred times before. Vinegar didn't bother finishing it this time, but according to

Vinegar, humans couldn't sense the cosmic warning signs because they either shaved, plucked, or groomed all their whiskers to the point that they'd become completely desensitized and useless. Humans' hackles were usually intact, but whenever those caught the cosmic vibrations, humans automatically assumed that they were being watched. Funny the things you could learn from bonding a cat.

"Reaow-reaow-reaow." The deep warning rolled through Vinegar's throat, almost involuntarily, pulling hu'Mar from his thoughts.

Then other animals from around the city joined. A chorus of dogs barking over there; birds took flight back there; rats darting this way or that, looking for a safer place. The humans, for their part, shouted and threw boots at all the noisy animals. Hu'Mar had to admit, if not for Vinegar, he'd probably be exactly like all these other people. What could they hope to accomplish by throwing their boots at some alleyway dogs? The dogs would simply run off with their boots, and they'd be left barefooted.

"What do you suppose it is?" hu'Mar asked, one hand massaging his temple, the other holding his stomach. He really respected the cat, sometimes, but there was no way he'd let on. "If it's anything short of the Clutch lifting, I don't care to hear it."

"It's not my fault you want to crack your skull on this case," Vinegar said.

"I never said I wanted to. I just said I have no choice. Maybe it somehow escaped your notice, but the Ministry wants to lock me up in a crow's cage."

"Listen, Dick hu'Prick! Can't you hear that?"

"Why don't you tell me? All I hear is a long D flat from an invisible violin inside my head."

"Do I need to step away for a minute?" Vinegar asked.

Hu'Mar said nothing.

Vinegar understood.

Together they left the arena, waited for a chariot to pass, its driver wrestling against his horse that sensed danger too. They crossed the street and paused by a large wooden apartment complex that abutted the walking path. They both waited, but for what?

Hu'Mar's mind drifted. It was hard to concentrate with an enormous headache in the shape of a horse hoof, trotting around your skull. He leaned against a wooden wall for support. From the other side of the wall, somebody smacked the boards. "Hey, you stinking bum, go spread your body odor on someone else's apartment."

Hu'Mar leaned away, swayed, wanting little more than to curl up right there and fall asleep. He didn't even have the energy to argue with the tenant, like he might otherwise do. Besides, the last thing he needed right now was a fight.

"Well?" he asked Vinegar again.

Vinegar weaved between Dick hu'Mar's legs as they walked on. "I don't know. Probably nothing."

"Nothing indeed." Hu'Mar knew better. These cosmic warnings were never of good fortune. Vinegar was down-playing it. Hu'Mar hadn't seen or heard this many animals on alert since that nasty storm three years ago in Nebylon, the one with the twisting pillars of wind and hail.

"Nothing we need worry about, I'm sure of that," Vinegar defended. "Why, are you scared? Dick hu'Daisy?"

Hu'Mar tottered, braced himself against a building, then vomited. There wasn't much to come out, just stinky stomach juices, but he felt a little better afterword.

He wiped his fat dripping lip. "All right, you rambling geezer. You have an idea what this alarm is about, so just spit it out."

"I said—" A muffled thunder emanated from the mountain. Vinegar froze, lifted a paw as if he'd stepped on something.

Supposedly, Vinegar's paws were more sensitive than hu'Mar's calloused—everything, but then he felt something too, almost as if the thunder came from below him. Was his stomach rumbling with nausea again?

The ground shook hard, and hu'Mar almost lost his balance. "Gearquake!"

Wooden buildings squealed as they swayed on their foundations. Pottery that wasn't ground level, crashed. Rocky fences tumbled to the ground. Then, as quickly as it had started, it stopped.

People rushed from their homes. Shouts of "Gearquake!" "The Tomb is open!" and "How many times have I told you to empty that stinking thunder mug!"

The thought of a splashing thunder mug gave hu'Mar a chill. He was glad he didn't have to deal with that one. Undoubtedly, countless numbers of those chamber pots were now shattered, leaving nasty messes.

Every man, woman, and child had raced out of their homes, weapons and armor at the ready. If Mount Exclusion really had opened the Great Clutch, then the war for ascension would finally be here. This was the time they'd prepared for their whole lives.

"See, no big deal. Just a little ground movement" Vinegar stood tall again.

Hu'Mar's stomach still quivered from the shaking ground. It had lasted only a moment, but he felt the same as if he'd been on a Pisser's boat for a whole day. He bit his lip, but the sting from ka'Nairie's bite quickly caused him to release it.

He stared into the distance, thinking. "Crazy Ish."

"What?"

"Ish hu'Narmin," hu'Mar repeated. "We have to go back to his place."

"But the Ministry?"

"The Ministry will have its hands full here. They'll be itching as bad as everyone else to know if the Clutch has opened."

"I think we should—"

Hu'Mar picked up the cat, tucked him close with one arm, protecting him from anyone who might bump into them, while making sure that he didn't drop the cat. Then like a kid running with a crystal ball, he charged toward Crazy Ish's place, though his endurance slowed to a quick jog after he'd passed a couple cogs. Between panting breaths, he whispered, "No. This is something else."

Dust and bugs drifted from rooftops, all the itchiest debris found its way down hu'Mar's sweaty back as he hurried through the city. He needed to get to Crazy Ish's place as quick

Hard Boiled Cabbage: Big Trouble In Spur Central

as possible. The ramshackle buildings, three and four stories of old weathered wood looked like they'd topple with each sway. The quicker he got to hu'Narmin's place, the less likely he'd get crushed.

As soon as he passed the tallest building that Spur Central had to offer, he slowed. There were no more ground shakes, hopefully. He tried to catch his breath.

"Dick hu'Hurry, what's this all about?" Vinegar asked, limp and resigned.

Hu'Mar dropped the cat. "Back at hu'Narmin's place, that old coot."

"The one who was as senile as Crazy Ish?"

"She mentioned something about everything crashing down. Even called me by name."

"Big deal. What's in a name?"

Hu'Mar sneered at Vinegar who was trying to keep up. "She didn't know who I was! She just assumed it was me because Crazy Ish predicted that I'd be in the middle of something terrible."

"Well, he was right," Vinegar huffed. "And she was nuts."

"No. There's something else. I just didn't see it at the time."

The lamps on this side of the city weren't lit, but hu'Mar's eyes had mostly adjusted to the moonlit streets when he arrived at hu'Narmin's nearly empty house. There were no ministers, and almost every Tough had congregated near Mount Exclusion to see if the Great Clutch within the Tomb of Ascension had opened. Almost everyone didn't include the old cleaning lady, Yolick ka'Kilden. Hu'Mar heard her rummaging through the house and found the dim light of her oil lamp in the window before he saw her cross it.

He'd half expected to see her here. Without any ministers to impede her, she'd be free to loot and profit from the prophet's notes. There had to be some perks to being a housekeeper to an old senile man that could see the future.

Hu'Mar slowly filled his lungs with a couple of deep calming breaths. If she was still as much a loon now as she was last he met her, he'd need his mind as clear and prepared as possible. He hated dealing with wackos, but sometimes the job necessitated it.

With a penetrating squeal, the front door creaked open, and hu'Mar entered the house. It smelled of old tea and urine. Vinegar entered only a few steps before spinning around.

Hu'Mar grabbed for his tail, only to remember that it was no longer there. A minor inconvenience. "Vinegar, don't you dare. You know I need you in here."

"After the way ka'Nairie treated you, you're still playing the part of her lap pooch?"

"Listen, you know you can read better than me. Hu'Narmin used to keep a journal of his foretellings. That crone was quoting from them, so they must be around here somewhere."

"I thought that was his fish's job?" Vinegar said.

"No, his fish remembered everyday mundane things," hu'Mar said as he looked under teapots, in cupboards, and in bookshelves. "His prophecies were usually recorded though. Where are they?"

Vinegar tiptoed into the middle of the room while hu'Mar studied the walls, desks, and drawers from where he stood. The pale, whitewashed walls almost hid Yolick ka'Kilden's pale face. With her wiry ashen hair, she stood erect in the kitchen doorway, her wrinkle-free, skin-tight dress perfectly accentuated her featureless figure and matched her pale gray hair. She was, for all intents and purposes, the very definition of drab and gray, if drab and gray had just escaped a boarding school for crazy old women. If not for those folded arms and squinting eyes, she might pass as a usable broom.

Her wooden shoes, the kind that went out of fashion fifty years ago, clicked against the hard-packed earthen floor as she stepped into the main room.

"Who are you and what do you want?" Her eyes widened as if it would help her focus better. It must have worked because she saw through his bee-stung, goose-egged bruises. "You! Murderer!"

"Easy, lady, I just came to ask a few questions."

Hard Boiled Cabbage: Big Trouble In Spur Central

"You're not stepping one foot inside of my house, you big brute!"

"Since when was this your house?" Hu'Mar shoved past her and entered the kitchen.

"Just give him a slap on the face," Vinegar said though they both knew she couldn't understand him. "Just a small one would be the spring that stops his clock."

Hu'Mar glared at Vinegar. His stomach still felt queasy, and his body was nearing total exhaustion. The last thing he needed was a distraction.

Vinegar rubbed against Yolick ka'Kilden's leg. "Wow, that is without a doubt the most uncomfortable leg I've ever wiped my scent glands across. They feel like wooden balusters with hairy splinters."

"Listen, I don't want to be around you any more than you probably want to be around you, but you've got something I need," hu'Mar said, ignoring the cat's commentary.

Ka'Kilden put a hand to her chest, which could have easily doubled as her back if her head was pointed the other way. "How dare you!" Ka'Kilden snapped. "And tell your stupid dog to stop rubbing against my leg."

Vinegar paused. "Dog?"

Hu'Mar suppressed a laugh. Take that, Vinegar.

"Fine," Vinegar said as he strolled to a cushion on the floor and curled onto it. "I'll let you two flirt as much as you like. I'll stay out of the way."

"Hu'Narmin's prophesies," hu'Mar insisted, "where are they?"

Ka'Kilden's eyes momentarily drifted to Vinegar, then to the bookshelf behind him before she snapped them back to hu'Mar. They were hard as rocks and twice as crazy.

"Forget about it." Hu'Mar shoved her aside and powered toward the bookshelf that held all of hu'Narmin's journals.

Ka'Kilden leapt onto his back, like a lizard, tugging and hissing. It was hard, but hu'Mar tried to ignore her as if she were a twit of a kid who was easier to put up with than to fight. He pulled one book after another, slowly read the titles, then threw them onto the couch. Finally, ka'Kilden dug her fingers into his face, and hu'Mar threw her onto the pile of books as well. Each book was labeled with a date. Most had already passed some time ago. Most of the foretellings were from hu'Narmin's prime, but a few were written after his days of service as a Beadledom prophet. The one book that covered this time period was not here.

He searched around while Vinegar was still cozied on his floor cushion. True to his word, he was remaining useless, amusing himself by gently flipping through a thinly bound leaflet.

Across the room, sat a woman's carry bag, full and blocky. Of course. That was why ka'Kilden was here after all. Hu'Mar crossed the room in three large steps.

Ka'Kilden gasped. "You have no right—"

Hu'Mar hefted the large bag onto the end table beside the couch and pulled books from it, reading the titles in succession. "Goodie ka'Gladie's Book For Good Housewives, One Hundred And One Uses For Salt, How To Win A Man In Ten Recipes Or Less..."

Hu'Mar picked up one book, clearly a manuscript, that looked like a work in progress, possibly hu-Narmin's last, unfinished journal. His fingers shook as he slowly turned it in his hand.

Ka'Kilden screamed like a war hawk and lunged for it. Hu'Mar was too quick. He spun around, and she landed hard on the floor. Yep, this must be it. He read the title. "Broomsticks and Beefcakes." His shoulders slumped

Ka'Kilden gasped.

So this old shrew was writing a romance novel, how creepy. He opened it to annoy her more. He couldn't read well, but apparently, he didn't need to. His eyes popped wide, and his blood nearly turned to sludge. If he had anything left in his stomach, he would've purged it right there.

She sprung up like a wolf trap to stop him, which might have normally surprised him, but compared to the illustrations inside, nothing she could've done would've shocked him more.

She ripped the manuscript from his fingers, and he gladly threw both her and her book onto the couch. He'd seen a lot of things in his life, but those images were enough to cause nightmares.

Ka'Kilden cradled her book, her face a deep sea of red. It was nice to see another color, other than pale-gray, on her. "I will kindly ask you one last time to leave," she said weakly as if his seeing the book had sapped her strength.

"Hey, Dick hu'Beefcake," Vinegar yawned over the tea-stained book he was reading on the floor. "Why don't you simply tell Yolick ka'Broomstick what you're looking for?"

Smart. "You quoted a foretelling with my name in it. I need to see the book that it came from," hu'Mar tried.

"See, that wasn't so hard, was it?" Vinegar lifted his head from the pages to shoot hu'Mar a patronizing sniff.

"Wait, what are you reading?" hu'Mar asked.

"Nothing."

Ka'Kilden gasped again.

"Really?" hu'Mar said. "What's that open book in front of you doing then? Reading itself to you?"

"Oh, this. No. I already finished it. It's just some silly book of fairy tales and ramblings by Crazy Ish."

Hu'Mar raced over and snatched the book up. Vinegar barely scampered out of the way.

Then he opened it. "This is just scribbles. Can you read this?"

"Didn't I just tell you?" Vinegar replied.

Ka'Kilden jumped onto him again, screeching and clawing. Hu'Mar felt like he was fighting a grapevine with claws. She was more vicious this time.

Vinegar sat on his butt, eyes glued to the scene.

"A little help here?" hu'Mar suggested.

"I make it a point never to involve myself in fights with animals that are larger than me," Vinegar said.

After fingernails dug several bloody grooves into hu'Mar's face, he managed to wrap both hands around her short ashen hair. Her scream rattled the expensive glass cups that she was likely here to steal.

With hair in hand, hu'Mar ripped her off his back like she was a leech, then whipped her across the room. She landed, and the impact apparently knocked the wind out of her as she gasped great thin lungfuls of air.

Hu'Mar picked up the book. "Come on Vinegar, we've got what we came for."

"That's not yours," ka'Kilden gasped, trying to pull herself back up.

"Nope, but it's not yours either," hu'Mar reminded. There were foretellings in here that involved him, right now, and there was also a high probability that hu'Narmin foresaw his own death. If hu'Mar were a prophet, he would've done so. That could be the break he was needing, especially since he was running out of time and money. "Keep your mouth shut," hu'Mar said as he tugged at the front door, dodging Vinegar, who raced out from between his legs, "and maybe I'll drop it back off when I'm done with it." He then slammed the door, leaving ka'Kilden to the rest of her pillaging.

Chapter 20

Bad Poetry, Disturbing Prophesy

The streets were unusually crowded. The city workers scrambled to fire up all the remaining streetlights that they'd neglected in their excitement. While some people were headed home, many more had decided to make an event out of the false alarm. The gearquake had not opened the Great Clutch, but you didn't get a whole city full of Toughs out in armor and glory, just to send them home an hour later. This had been exciting and hinted at the final battle they'd spent their lives dreaming of. So, they made an impromptu holiday out of the occasion. Chariot races in the street threatened crossers, and courtship fights broke out in nearly every hub hu'Mar passed.

To help heighten the commotion of the party, local ale houses brought their merchandise to the streets. Otherwise level-headed men and women were now working hard to become staggering buffoons as quickly as possible.

In the middle of several main streets, large sums of salt were placed on jousting matches. Little kids with wooden swords played war in the smaller spokes. Foreign musicians and storytellers drew crowds at every cog. Everyone had a brief taste of glory even if the tomb hadn't really been opened. Somewhere deep inside, they all knew that if it had, they would've seized it before any other species, so it was a successful, if not anti-climactic test run.

The real cherry on top of the moment was that the whole disturbance would be a beacon, summoning every other walk of life to the area. Many would come to fight for the Great Clutch, while others would want a good show. The Tough's would get what they'd prepared for since the moment they first punched their mothers for a toy withheld. They would get their war.

Every Tough was excited. Many said they could smell the Eternal Gears shifting, whatever that smelled like, but while everyone else was excited about the prospect of war, hu'Mar was only anxious about opening that book.

"If I were a prophet," hu'Mar told Vinegar, "I'd have foretold my own death." Assuming hu'Narmin also foretold his own death, that very prophesy would show hu'Mar the man's killer and hopefully tie the murderer to ka'Nairie's relic. "Come on Vinegar, we need to find a quiet place to read."

"Why? You can barely even read print, let alone cursive. And if you're expecting me to read to you, know that I've had my fill of it for the day, and it's getting late."

Hu'Mar headed straight for the water district where the Pissers docked their boats and cheap inns could be found aplenty. There was crime around there for sure, but hopefully the Ministry was sufficiently distracted. If they found him, they would arrest him, and even Bacon wouldn't be able to help him then. He approached one inn called the Dumpy Din. It didn't look too bad.

He stepped inside. The place was surprisingly crowded and rowdy. The smell of grittles caused his empty stomach to heave since he still felt sick from his run in with ka'Nairie and her horse. A musician played a squeezebox in the corner, and guests sang and danced, their voices more on key than the squeezebox despite their inebriation. Booze, served from an older gruff, probably the innkeeper himself, sloshed and foamed onto every table as mugs were emptied. There were few women, mostly mops, and most of them had the attention of the Pissers. For whatever reason, Pissers didn't usually bring their women on their boats, and they were the majority of this place's business tonight.

The only thing that surprised hu'Mar was the number of people actually indoors, but it made sense. They could fight if they had to, but since the streets were overflowing with Toughs, it was a good night to avoid possible confrontations.

Hu'Mar searched for a place to rest, but there was standing room only in the main room. So he picked out a young man at a barstool who couldn't be much older than nineteen. He was rocking, like he was still on one of his boats, staring at his half full mug. Hu'Mar wrapped an arm around the boy to steady him, then grabbed the mug. The boy quickly stole the mug back.

"You sure you can handle that, boy?" hu'Mar encouraged.

The orange-skinned youth, half green and pale from drink, stared at hu'Mar with glazed eyes, then downed the remainder of the mug in a couple gulps, slamming the mug onto where he thought the bar was. The mug thudded on the floor instead, but didn't break. He smirked.

Hu'Mar smiled back, then let go of his shoulders. The boy's eyes rolled back almost as quickly as his body did. Before hu'Mar could've said good night, the boy was snoring on the floor, and hu'Mar sat on the empty stool, placing Vinegar on the counter.

The old gruff serving drinks from behind the bar found hu'Mar. "What'll it be tonight?" he asked.

"Got a room?" Hu'Mar didn't want to spend another night outside. Besides, he stunk really bad. A good cleaning would do him good.

"Depends, you got money?" he asked, wiping his hands on his dirty apron.

"Not much. What's your going rate?" Hu'Mar grabbed his salt pouch and gave it a small shake, letting the innkeeper know that he at least had some money.

"You're in luck. I'm full, but one of my long-term guests got chased off by a few ministers earlier. If you don't mind sleeping in an uncleaned room, I'll give it to you for four chips a night. I doubt she'll be coming back tonight."

"Are the ministers still keeping an eye on her room?" hu'Mar asked.

"Nah. But she ditched out a window. Spooked her something mighty. Just don't touch anything of hers you find in there. I'll want to pack it up for her in case she comes back tomorrow." He rubbed the double-length stubble on his cheek. "She was a good gal. Hope she's not in too much trouble. You know how ministers can be. It's the room with the donkey's tail on the door, still unlocked. Can I bring you anything more?"

"No thanks." Hu'Mar was hungry, but ever since waking up from Beauford's kick, he'd felt sick to his stomach.

"Alright." The innkeeper crossed behind the counter, set down some empty mugs, and retrieved an oil lamp. "Grittles in the morning, only two chips. Sleep good, traveler." He handed hu'Mar the lamp.

"Thanks." Hu'Mar collected Vinegar, and together they found the room. He lit the hand-held lamp on a hall sconce before entering.

The blankets were slightly crumpled, and a small open trunk in the corner held some off-white garments with a pair of goggles resting on top. Albino garb.

Hu'Mar sniffed. Aside from himself, the room smelled exactly like that black pellet that had burned down his apartment. Carefully, he placed the lamp on the small desk in the room. Then he dropped Vinegar on the bed and rifled through the clothing and searched the room. In a corner, he found a bit of black dust. It had to be the same stuff. He sprinkled the dust over the lamp flame, and it flared and fizzed. Same stuff all right. If this lamp fell over, this could be the second building that hu'Mar had accidentally burned down because of the black stuff. Caution was necessary.

The Albino he'd seen earlier had been in an alley near here. He kicked himself for losing her before. Maybe she'd come back for the rest of her stuff, and he could question her. He could only hope. Normally, hu'Mar might have lit another lamp to take with him to clean up, but given the heightened possibility of combustion in this room, taking the same lamp to the washroom made more sense this time, and skipping a bath was out of the question. Nobody, not even himself would be able to concentrate on hu' Narmin's book with the stench he was making.

The washroom was down the hall on this same level. It held two metal tubs, soapy and warm from the small coals under each. One tub was occupied, some traveler, not a Pisser, soaking and enjoying every minute of it. Hu'Mar stripped and stepped into his tub. It was hot but felt good. He didn't waste any time by relaxing, choosing instead an abrasive wool rag with plenty of soap, scrubbing good and hard till his skin hurt. When he no longer smelled like yesterday's regurgitated meat, he dripped his way back to the room, wearing a towel, so that he could hang his dirty clothes on the door for cleaning. Unlike his burnt down apartment, where ka' Muunel did his laundry for free, he'd have to pay to get it clean here. As soon as he was back in his room, he kicked Vinegar. Just enough to wake the cat up. "Come on, we've got hu'Narmin's book to read before sleeping."

Vinegar complained. The animal was good at that. Sometimes hu'Mar wondered how animals could even think properly. If it weren't for palsies, you'd guess that they lived on stinks and instincts alone.

"I need your help. I can't make heads or tails of this chicken scratch."

"It's called cursive, you big bloke." Vinegar could be so disrespectful. But most cats hu'Mar had talked to were like that, and maybe all lower animals were. And to think that some people actually treated their palsies like equals, even part of the family. That was sacrilegious and borderline insane.

"Listen cat, I've got better things to do than learn to read. That stuff is better suited for animals that prefer to sleep and dream away their whole lives."

"You don't sound like you want my help very much." For a dumb cat, Vinegar was smart enough to back out of kicking range as he said this.

Hu'Mar wasn't about to beg, so maybe he could trick him.

Hard Boiled Cabbage: Big Trouble In Spur Central

"Okay, then just tell me what you read. If you're so smart, you should be able to remember."

"Nothing more than nursery rhymes and nonsense. You wouldn't like it."

"Humor me."

"Oh, that's right, dumb stuff is kind of your thing."

"Come on, we both know you're going to tell me. Let's get moving already. I've had a long day, and I'm really tired, and I don't feel good."

"You're tired?" Vinegar said. "I have to take five steps just to keep up with one of yours!"

"Yeah, but you haven't been knocked around like I have."

"That's just the concussions speaking." Vinegar stretched. It was his version of rolling his eyes. "Just so you know, Ish hu'Narmin had a wayward way with words, at least whenever he was prophesying. But even though his mind was deteriorating with every foretelling, he still managed to rhyme everything. I'm guessing hu'Narmin might've been a great prophet in his prime, but he was, without a doubt, the worst poet I've ever read.

From, "good morning, Tough boring, your wife will murder you," to "the price of corn, in the next morn, will double your daily salt," hu'Narmin kept a journal of every foretelling he'd ever written. Some were of his days working for the Beadledom, and some were just for well-paying visitors.

The book wasn't terribly long because for every memory he foretold, he lost a memory from his own past. Unlike being palsy to animals, being a prophet meant you weren't channeling a specific species of animal, but you were channeling the Great Gear itself. The only problem was that you were unable to bond the Great Gear, so your mind took on certain characteristics of it—existing in time but being without time. It was like trying to read the teeth of the Great Gear while standing on the teeth of the gear. You spun it faster to read the next tooth, but the tooth you were on would spin away from you.

"Wait, wait. Read that one again."

Vinegar stared at hu'Mar, then licked his paw and flipped a page back to reread a prophesy from a few years ago, just after hu'Narmin left the service of the Beadledom.

> Through darkened paths comes Dick hu'Mar,
> Who's chasing the wrong thing;
> Men's fate he holds both near and far,
> And death's true destiny.
> One man—one Bule,
> hu'Mar—ka'Shino,
> And me no more a tool,
> You and me they'll kill—tis their destiny.
> We'll war in vain;
> The ground will crack and tremble.
> No blood run cold will offer gain;
> We're but slaves to destiny.
> Death will come in splendid glory,
> For when the world will shake,
> The Tomb in lava's crematory,
> Will change our destiny.
> There's more to this than I can see,
> For when the gears will grind;
> The victim of conspiracy,
> There is no destiny.

"That makes no sense," Vinegar said.

"But it's what I was looking for," hu'Mar said. His skin prickled, and he shivered, the warm night doing nothing to curb the nervous chill. "Hu'Narmin solves at least two pieces of a puzzle for me." They might be unrelated, but he doubted it. He could care less about the whole ascension agenda. That was a Ministry problem, not his.

Hu'Mar clenched his teeth together. He lived for this sort of thing, even if it felt scary, piecing together puzzles that nobody else had even bothered asking questions about. While the prophesy didn't all make sense yet, it was a challenge, and Yolick ka'Kilden had been right. Somehow, hu'Mar was at the center of it all. But he hadn't killed hu'Narmin, so why say as much?

"Okay," Vinegar said, "I'll bite. I can read what humans say and write, but only a human mind can possibly understand human insanity, and this is poetry, which is even worse."

"Look at the pieces," hu'Mar explained. "We have a case that involves a beautiful but dangerous, scheming politician, Jodeign ka'Nairie. She can play the crowds and has leverage with some local street gangs and groups of odd people.

"We also received a visit from a nervous minority, that Albino who treated your tail. She was all worried about the future. Then we found a man who can really read the future, and he's dead with a witness placing an Albino at the scene. Last night, our apartment burned down, and we camped under a bridge because she carried some black stuff that looked like dirty salt that burned faster and stronger than any charcoal I've ever seen. From the dust in the corners of this room, she must have had a lot of it too. Then there's that quake from Mount Exclusion.

"Don't forget your little conspiracy," Vinegar snickered. "Hu'Narmin prophesied that this is all your fault. I think I believe him."

"Conspiracy? Me and an Albino?" Hu'Mar shook his head.

"Maybe its your destructive personality," Vinegar offered. "You persistently hurt yourself, so why not everyone else around you? You're good at finding fault in others, but what if you turned that focus inward?"

"Be practical. Philosophy isn't your strong suit." Hu'Mar plopped onto his back. The straw bedding, combined with his still cranky stomach, made him want to close his eyes and curl into a ball despite Vinegar still being near. "The Albino girl, this ka'Shino, the prophesy suggests that I have something to do with her. If I'm not responsible for the quakes, then she might not be either.

Vinegar leaped onto the bed at hu'Mar's feet and began plucking at the sheet with his claws. "Don't forget Maizy ka'Dillie. It could be an alias for your pale friend. If this Bule knew about ka'Nairie's Pin of Poison, then she might have stolen it.

To place those concussive pellets in one of Mt. Exclusions side tunnels, she might need something like that Pin to keep the gases from killing her."

Hu'Mar sprang upright. "No, that's not it. How could I be so stupid? Ka'Nairie's no victim. She's a schemer." He stood and paced the small room. "Let's say you're half right, and that Maizy ka'Dillie is an alias for this Albino. Yes, she would need a Pin of Poison to navigate the caves of Mount Exclusion. But why would she cause the mountain to tremble, especially if she was worried about the dangerous repercussions? She must've been hired to do it. Why else would a prominent Tough like ka'Nairie bring a Bule into her confidence, if not to hire her? Ka'Nairie is scheming to disturb the Tomb of Ascension so that she can get the Great Clutch to open early… with death in splendid glory…"

"Then why hire you?" Vinegar clawed at the bedding, popping more threads, as if they offered some sort of cathartic relief.

"She needs an alibi if things go wrong." Hu'Mar sat on the bed and placed a hand over his gut. It still felt like he'd eaten something bad. Even after his recent bath, a fevered drop of sweat prickled his forehead. This was probably the reason why ka'Nairie was withholding vital info from him. "She needs proof, if her plan fails, showing she never had access to those caves because someone else had stolen the relic that would have allowed her access. She's covering her contingencies."

"But why?" Vinegar asked.

"To be a hero." Hu'Mar fell to his back again, causing Vinegar to bounce on the bed. He was sure about this, mostly. "She's a Tough. She craves power. She's brilliant, so it totally fits. Everyone else to her is a pawn. The only other question is, why there was a Maizy hu'Dillie on ka'Feebal's ledger? Could it be that his name was written incorrectly, and as ka'Nairie stated, the name is really ka'Dillie, possibly an alias for this prophesied ka'Shino? She could have either been a co-owner of the relic, or she owned the relic at one point, then transferred it to ka'Nairie, or in the very least, told her about it. Then again, maybe ka'Feebal stole it back from ka'Nairie and resold it to this hu'Dillie."

Hard Boiled Cabbage: Big Trouble In Spur Central

"Nah." Vinegar lay next to hu'Mar, his thread ripping finished. "I think this is still your fault. The prophecy also says you're chasing the wrong thing. Mark my words, you'll see."

Hu'Mar pushed Vinegar off the bed. The cat landed on his head but kept on purring, the short fall doing nothing to remove his smug little attitude.

He'd been chasing the wrong thing before, but now he was on the right path. It had to be ka'Nairie. She'd paid them but had given them too little to go on as she finished her plan. All she had to do was place a human in the Tomb to become a hero and gain the highest seat in the Beadledom. She'd have power until she and every human died and moved to the next gear.

"Oh well." Vinegar jumped back on the bed. "I guess if you're right, humans will be gone in a century or so, and cats will take their rightful place as the dominant species of this world."

"I don't know." Hu'Mar curled onto his side. "I think your species will miss having humans around. Your type have never been good at building any of the comforts you enjoy."

Vinegar popped a single thread near hu'Mar's feet but otherwise ignored him.

"I am worried about that Albino though, this ka'Shino. If she has the Pin of Poison, she's being set up as a fall girl. My guess is that she accidentally killed hu'Narmin's fish by poisoning. Then hu'Narmin, already senile, would have adopted all the fish's traits, and so he would've felt dry out of land and drowned himself. If my guess is correct, the Ministry will harass every Bule in Spur until they find one that goes by the name of ka'Shino."

"It's the same girl that visited us earlier, isn't it?" Vinegar said, then closed his eyes to sleep. "It's too bad, really. She could tell that you were a dolt. I liked her."

Hu'Mar padded his jacket. His poisoned darts were still there. His stomach was getting a little better, but now he had a hard time keeping his eyes shut. Part from his revelation, part from the fact that he'd slept earlier today, even if it had been from a few too many hard knocks on the head, which were still throbbing.

He pulled out one of his darts and examined it. It was a weapon mostly unfamiliar to Toughs, as they preferred blunt bashing weapons and heavy slashing steel. Darts were too subtle and thereby considered dishonorable, in the same way that a kid's toy was not meant for adults. This was a blind spot for sure, especially when those darts were poisoned. But since hu'Mar was no Tough, he felt no shame in using it.

With the slender dart concealed in his vest next to the blowgun and other darts, hu'Mar eased off the bed, careful not to wake Vinegar. "Time to get busy," he whispered under his breath, clenching his fist. It hurt. With all these bruises he should be resting, but Albinos preferred the night, so if he was to find ka'Shino, he had to be out when it was the best time to find her.

Chapter 21
To Be A Killer

Juniper ka'Shino paced her new rock-walled room. It was small, it dripped, and she barely took three steps before she had to turn around and walk the other way. Still, it was her own room, and the barkeeper hadn't disturbed her since her arrival. Of course, she'd paid him extra not to.

Outside of her little sanctuary, men, women, and animals of all sorts were gambling, drinking, and conspiring. She loved the underground but hated joints like this one. There wasn't a soul here that hadn't likely murdered multiple people. She, herself, hadn't killed anyone directly, but in the ever-aching pit of her guilty stomach, she felt she'd done as much or worse than anyone here.

The old worn floorboards that bridged the slick, damp cave stone beneath, creaked under her feet as she paced. Ernes hu'Toe was two hours late.

There was a knock at her door. She flinched. It was a silly reaction. No ministers would come down here. There was always the risk of running afoul of thieves and murderers here, but this knock was expected and overdue. She threw on her cloak. One of the two shoulder bags full of explosives tipped.

Hard Boiled Cabbage: Big Trouble In Spur Central

The third bag was still at the inn, or rather, tucked into an alley behind the inn. She'd only had enough time to haul these two packs over and refine the last of the pellets, which in itself was a lot. So as long as the ministers were on their little Bule hunt, even a place like this was safer.

She righted the explosives on her bed, then opened the door. A fog of cigar smoke spilled from the greater room beyond. Butterflies flew like panicked crows within her belly, This wasn't hu'Toe. Reflexively, she reached for her dagger from within in her cloak. Whatever his intentions were, he was a stranger, a typical low life, and the sooner he was dealt with, the better.

After briefly checking out her chest, his reptilian gaze snaked past her into the room. "Hey, lonely lady." His too flat nose aimed around her, checking out the room. Half his lip lifted in a dirty smile, and he stepped one foot into the doorway, his snickering lips exhaled a mix of tooth decay and rum. "Think you could—"

Ka'Shino had the hilt of her dagger first in her fist, then in his temple. He crumpled to the ground. He was lucky he got the butt end of her knife and not the sharp end, but he'd wake with a nasty headache and a big lump.

"Tsk, tsk, tsk."

Now that was a voice she'd heard here before. Hu'Toe emerged from the shadows and smoky haze of the gin joint. The pale, never-flickering bioluminescence on the cave cast Ernes hu'Toe in an eerie turquoise glow. It made his rare blue eyes seem like they were the only living part of him and the rest of him, a pale corpse. Did her skin look as lifeless in this underground atmosphere? She'd overlooked these traits when she was younger, but having spent a little time among red-, brown-, and orange-skinned humans, she could see how her people might be viewed as demonic. Still, she couldn't help but think to herself that hu'Toe was a heartthrob. Tall, lean, perfect posture, and more confident than any man she'd ever met.

"You're late," she said, trying not to waver like a giddy schoolgirl. Why did he have to make her feel so light-headed?

"I was waiting till te crowds dispersed from te bridge.

Your last bomb sure drew some attention." He stepped closer, not even looking down as he stepped over the crumpled bum at her doorstep.

She took a step backward into her room. It suddenly felt a lot smaller and hotter in here.

He inspected her shoulder bags, then nudged the man at her doorstep. "Tose look like heavy bags. Why did you have to take out my helper?"

"But he—"

"He was a pig," hu'Toe said. "At least you're cautious. Don't know how we're going to carry all tree of tem now. Where is te tird one, anyhow?"

"Didn't have time to bring it over." Ka'Shino hadn't felt guilty until now. Something about hu'Toe's perfect posture and easy manner made her want to please him. "It's still at the inn, I mean, hidden in the alley behind it."

Hu'Toe's composure didn't slip one bit. "We'll have to go back tere later for it."

"Can we even cross te bridge tonight wit all te commotion?" ka'Shino asked. Under any other circumstance, she might've enjoyed a long hike with hu'Toe. However, crossing to Mount Exclusion with even one full pack of explosives would be sweaty and grueling. After already wearing herself out from carrying them here, she wouldn't make a great impression. Oh, well. Not like she really stood a chance with him, right? She wasn't really even that interested, really.

"Crossing will be easy," hu'Toe answered with confidence. "Tose tat are still out are all too drunk to be a problem. Te guards are halfway trough a long shift and are finally relaxing for te night." He heaved one of the large packs onto his back. Then with a grunt, he lifted the second one and helped ka'Shino strap it over her back. "Besides, I tink tey will have teir hands full tonight."

Hands full? With what? As soon as he let go, the bag nearly crushed her. Like before, she was consigned to a long, spine-compressing hike to and up the mountain. Before leaving the room, she retrieved the small jewelry box that hu'Toe had given her on their previous meeting here. From it, she pulled out the thin bone she'd used last time. It had a string threaded through it, to wear as a necklace, but for now, she tucked it into her cloak pocket. It was a dangerous thing to carry, but long hikes through Mount Exclusion would be made much easier with it than without it. This was the very reason she'd requested it.

Together, they exited the small room, into the larger common area of the speakeasy. The bar and tables were more crowded than usual, and the tenders had their own burdens to heft as they struggled to lift drink prices fast enough to keep pace with the draining demand on their kegs.

Ka'Shino smiled as the dwarfed bouncer pulled the massive door open for her to leave. He didn't bother to grace her with any response. Chains rattled and bounced against his miniature sweat-stained vest. He was in every way the opposite of the honest innkeeper she'd come to respect, before being driven back here.

She liked most people, even if most people didn't like her. Every hard face here reminded her of their opposite from the Dumpy Din inn. Both groups were despicable in their own ways, but they were different. At the inn were drunken Toughs, who after a few drinks, turned into pleasant, even vulnerable babies. Here, a few drinks might more likely end in a murder.

The Pissers, used to the rocking of their ships, only stopped swaying when they had a drink or two in them. Oddly enough, this caused them to fall more often than when they still had the rocks. They were a rowdy bunch, but occasionally brought news faster than the traveling musicians, if it was interesting enough. Mostly, they could laugh the loudest and dance holes in the floorboards and, occasionally, get a mug of beer poured down their laps.

The traveling musicians weren't merely artists who entertained for a room and meal, they often brought news and stories from abroad, stories that hadn't reached the ears of the criers, though the criers were always keen to skim a story or two from them whenever a new one came to town. These storytellers and singers lived in poverty but were proud of their art. They could turn an empty inn into a bustling destination hotspot and set a mood meant to manipulate your thoughts and emotions. Ka'Shino loved listening to these performers.

The waitresses were almost pretty, always poor, and ever eager to make a lonely old man feel that someone cared, especially if the man was generous enough to tip before service.

She liked the transient atmosphere of the inn, but her favorite had been the innkeeper, the glue to the whole atmosphere. Day after day, night after night, he polished glasses, mopped up vomit, cleaned rooms, found time to talk to just about every visitor as if they mattered, never forgetting a name or face, and of course, he did it all with a smile.

His joy was in his business, and he could care less how pale your skin was, as long as he collected his money with an eye toward his eventual grand retirement, a retirement he'd never find because he'd never know how to leave the inn. It was as much a part of him as his own blood and sweat. Maybe someday, she'd start an inn like that.

Ka'Shino's back bent even further as she hiked on, following hu'Toe through underground tunnels, sewers, and eventually the streets of Spur Central. Thoughts of the inn faded. She no longer imagined what stories would be told by the musicians, or what dirty jokes the Pissers might be slapping each other over. It would be a party at the inn, but for ka'Shino, each step brought her one step closer to Mount Exclusion, exhaustion, and guilt.

Chapter 22
Midnight Stroll

With Vinegar asleep, hu'Mar walked down the single creaky stairway into the main gathering room of the inn. It was lively. Men singing, dancing, playing some type of card game known only to Pissers. The commotion made his headache throb. Maybe in another life he could enjoy such times, but that was not the card he'd been dealt.

Vinegar usually wouldn't approve of his sneaking out. The cat liked to be warned if his bond weakened, but as of late, even Vinegar had been sneaking out without warning hu'Mar. It had been hard these last several months, he'd grant Vinegar that much, and sometimes, you had to get out and stretch. Still, everything hu'Mar did seemed to make Vinegar crankier. Hopefully if the cat woke tonight, he'd assume that hu'Mar's absence was merely hu'Mar visiting the privy. Hu'Mar did stop by the stink room on his way out. He was glad for the darkness of night. His kidneys felt bruised, and he didn't want to see if his pee was any other color than yellow.

With his vest cinched tight, and his mind too active to sleep, hu'Mar stepped out into the starless night. On restless nights like this, he usually only had to walk a block away before the bond wore him down and Vinegar's apathy helped him feel ready for sleep. However, tonight, as he exited the building, the weakened bond only served to thin his grasp on the case. He kept walking, letting his legs carry him aimlessly through the old city. If he could only find ka'Shino, then all the pieces would fall into place, or so he imagined. Knowing this was an unlikely outcome for this midnight stroll, he allowed his mind to drift where it might. It was hu'Narmin's prophesy that had him all shaken up. Everything was connected, he was sure of it, despite whatever Vinegar thought.

With each deep inhale of sulfuric air, his bruised muscles and cracked ribs ached. Hu'Mar's stomach was feeling better now. What was all this suffering worth? That was Vinegar's mindset creeping in, but on a deeper level, he felt it inside himself too. It was depressing to think that he was nothing more to ka'Nairie than a pawn, an alibi. Nobody seemed to care about the work he did. It only brought him trouble, yet it was all he knew how to do. His life was one runaway carriage wreck after another.

He rubbed his eyes. Whether it was very late, or very early, the city-wide party had finished or moved indoors. The only people still out this late would be looking for trouble, but they didn't bother him. The city bothered him. The time for the Shifting was close. Hu'Mar could almost taste the blood of war that figuratively danced across their lips. It tasted a lot like the blood that leaked onto his tongue from his own split lip, except that it felt more pointless.

When he'd first moved here, the old stone structures, above and beneath the ground added to the mystery and oldness of the place. He thought that maybe he'd gain a deeper appreciation for the Great Clutch by living here. But from the ancient stonework to the neglected and rotting wood-paneled buildings, Spur Central gave him a feeling that if humans didn't ascend soon, then this city would fall under its own weight. Since he no longer cared about ascension, at least, not as much as he cared about money and recognition, all the city represented to him was a festering boil, its crime and injustice oozed and hurt.

Sometimes, humans could be so far-sighted that they neglected the here and now.

Hu'Mar placed a hand on his vest. The blowgun reassured him, and he kept walking. After another couple of blocks, he was rubbing against every street pole and building corner he passed. Normally, he would've stopped himself, but every time he thought about of exercising restraint, the job forced its way back into his mind. So, rather than fighting right now, he gave in to it all, allowing his cat instincts to run their course, and the case to skirt the edges of his conscious mind, experiencing it from a different perspective.

After another block, he hummed, low and throaty, like an ugly version of a purring cat. His mood had improved. Then without any clear reason why, he stopped mid-step. Vinegar's instincts took over, and he dropped into a shadow. Men were coming. Not Toughs, but outsiders, perhaps ten people, at least two Bules. Hu'Mar even saw a Morp, one of the stragglers from a previously ascended race. Morps were nearly human in stature, and hairless. Their skin grew in long thin strands, like it had been grafted over several dozen mops. However, most of this group was made up of normal, albeit small, people. Not one man among them could've weighed more than two hundred pounds. There were a few women too. Not very nice ones from the look of them.

He spotted two more groups with roughly the same mix. Two Bules, another string-faced Morp, and a handful of others, not a single Tough among them. One group split away, and the other two passed hu'Mar's hiding spot. The group that split off, then separated into smaller teams of two.

They all fastened on red masks. Just as he'd suspected, these were the atheists. Of course, they'd come out on a night like this.

Every city hu'Mar had ever visited had a group of atheists. Since they thought that whichever species attained the Great Clutch would die forever, rather than ascend, they naturally fought to prevent their own race from gaining the Great Clutch. This often meant open protests, debates, and in this

Hard Boiled Cabbage: Big Trouble In Spur Central

case—terrorist attacks.

Atheists were not usually from Tough stock. Toughs were bred and born for gaining the Great Clutch, so atheists knew better than to attack a Tough in a head-on battle. But if an opportunity opened for atheists to cripple them while they were drunk or sleeping, you could bet on them showing up.

On a nearby wall, one of them used a stencil to paint the international symbol of the atheist movement: a red gear broken in half. While one person tagged the stone buildings with the broken gear, their partner torched the wooden buildings around it, hu'Mar knew that a long night for the ministers was about to get a lot longer.

"Don't get involved," hu'Mar told himself. This wasn't his fight. He could care less about the Great Clutch or these people's agenda.

They set fire to a bakery, then a smithy.

Whistles and shouts came from the distance. The two arsonists closest to him jumped and scurried to finish before anyone found them. The man with the torch ran to another building, an apartment. From somewhere deep inside, he heard a baby scream.

"Just great." Hu'Mar stepped out of his shadow and lifted his blowgun.

The man with the torch leaned over to start the building ablaze when the dart stuck in his throat. He swatted at it as if it were a nothing more than a blood beetle, then fell over dead.

Hu'Mar strolled over, casual as a cat, and kicked dirt on the fire until it went out. He kneeled, plucked the dart from the man's neck, then loaded it back into his blow tube. The poison was baked on and would outlast a dozen blows. Footsteps approached as he stood. It would be the man's partner.

Raising the blow tube, he paused, then changed tactics. He could still aim, but a little exercise felt more in order this time. Depositing the tube in one pocket, hu'Mar gripped his brass gear knuckles from another. Each connected gear had a hollow spot, just big enough to fit each of his fingers. The teeth of the gears pointed out, concentrating any blow to the apexes.

His first instinct was to play with his attacker, like a cat playing with a mouse, prolonging the inevitable. He might have done it too, but the assailant approached too quickly for hu'Mar's tiring mind to think properly.

With a flinching spin, fist now out of his pocket, the metal gears that guarded his meaty fist cracked that ridiculous red face mask and smashed the man's forehead. The man staggered back, skull dented, never to stand again.

Hu'Mar walked away. His headache had finally dissipated to a minor discomfort, and that annoying stomachache was a distant memory. Getting involved in protecting this city wasn't his idea of a good time, at least not when doing so anonymously, and for free. Tonight however, busting a couple jerks had been the very thing he needed to settle his mind. Ka'Shino was nowhere to be seen, but that had been expected. It was time to head back to the inn. Sleep finally felt long overdue.

The inner city would be bustling with atheists and ministers who were busy busting said atheists. Better not to cut straight back the way he came. Instead, he took the scenic route, along the edge of Lake Tallow. The calm moat stunk worse now since he'd taken a bath and washed the moat's scum from his body. At the same bridge that he'd slept by the night before, a few remaining guards edged away from their posts. Not far enough to abandon them directly. While they tried to get a better look at what was happening in the city, two Bules with heavy loads crossed the bridge, unnoticed. Ka'Shino, plus one? It had to be. She was up to something dangerous, not only for her, but for everyone here in the city.

Indecision danced across his mind. The cat side of him said, move on, while his own promptings insisted on investigating. In the end, he had to know. "Ka'Shino!"

It was barely noticeable, but the Albino in the back faltered for half a step. It could've just been that heavy pack on her back, but he doubted it.

One of the guards swung to meet hu'Mar's shout. They should've looked the other way, but the two sneaking Albinos weren't the ones shouting random names.

Hard Boiled Cabbage: Big Trouble In Spur Central

"Hey," the guard yelled as he jogged over. "What's your business here?"

"Just out for a stroll." Hu'Mar decided against tattling on the two crossing the bridge. "Thought I'd knock around a few atheists while I was at it."

He needed to talk with ka'Shino, but since she was already in danger from the ministers, he'd catch up with her later.

"So that's what this is all about." The guard turned his gaze back to the city. Orange glowing lights flickered through hazy patches of smoke.

"I'm guessing there's about three dozen of them wreaking havoc around the city. Probably in retreat now. They don't usually stick around for any real fighting."

"Cowards," the guard sneered.

"Can I ask a question?" hu'Mar said. "Any reason you'd have a few Bules on the Mount?"

"Disgusting, aren't they? I don't know why we even hire them. If you ask me, they can't be trusted. It's them red eyes of theirs. Why you ask?"

"No reason. I just wondered why I always seem to see them crossing over."

"If it were up to me, they wouldn't. They're harmless enough, I guess, and somebody's got to clean the high guard's privies, or something like that."

Hu'Mar focused on Mount Exclusion. Cleaning supplies for a privy wouldn't have required heavy packs like what they'd been carrying. He couldn't see the Albinos anymore, but there was no way they'd crossed the land bridge already. The thing would've taken a couple minutes to traverse with those heavy packs. But they'd passed over the crest and were hidden by the back-hillside of it.

The guard focused on the city. The atheists couldn't be seen from here though.

"Well, I'll go see if I can find any stragglers," hu'Mar excused himself.

"Kill a couple for me," the guard said. The man was probably itching for a fight. Likely, he'd joined the bridge guard hoping for a lot of fights. Problem was, nobody ever came to the bridge looking for trouble when the Great Clutch was still sealed. Now he was stuck guarding a land bridge while the lowly ministers had all the fun.

The only people he should have been concerned about were the invisible ones that had snuck past him, but everyone had their blind spots. For these guards, their ignorance of the non-combative Albino's was a clear weakness.

Chapter 23
What Game Am I Playing?

Juniper ka'Shino almost tripped under her load. "Focus," she whispered to herself. For a second she thought she'd heard somebody call out her name. Obviously, that was ridiculous. Nobody but Ernes hu'Toe knew who she was. She lifted her neck to get a better view of him. Hu'Toe didn't even strain under his pack, and his was heavier.

When she'd hiked up here to deposit the two halves of her first bomb, she'd been alone and able to take several breaks. Hu'Toe lacked any such visible fatigue. This whole plan was his from the very beginning, and the progress of it fueled his energy. Fully psyched up, he looked ready to climb the steep trails with no more strain than a daily stroll to the market. She'd like to see how well he'd hike it if it was his third time in one day!

Hopefully, he'd help carry the last bomb up also and not just tell her where to put it. She wasn't sure if she could carry another one up here on her own.

"Te trick is, placing te bombs in te right spot," hu'Toe explained. "Mount Exclusion is like a clock spring made of balsa wood and filled wit lava. It's a wonder it hasn't torn itself apart ages ago. I've been surveying tis mountain for years, and te placement of each bomb is critical. Wit one at each pressure point, te whole mountain will weaken enough for our purposes."

"What if it doesn't act te way you expect?" ka'Shino asked. "What if people get hurt?"

"Tere's a moat around te mountain. What's te worst tat could happen?"

She wasn't sure. Lava flows were uncommon, except around here, but when you spend your whole life underground, you quickly learn what can be found underground, or you die. Lava was one of the more scary things. Hot and unforgiving. It flowed thick under Mount Exclusion and in some caves higher up. When underground, it wasn't likely to kill you, because the gases it produced would get you before you ever saw the bright orange flows. But like all Albino leaders and politicians, hu'Toe was smart, and since his specialty was geology, he ought to know best.

They approached the end of the land bridge. She'd crossed it before, not without a little harassment. Hu'Toe had crossed it hundreds, if not thousands, of times, yet that didn't stop one of the guards from spitting on him as he walked by. Laughter from the guards caused her chest to tighten. She hated crossing paths with these people. They were telling some stupid joke about Bules. They might be rude, but they also assumed that after having made it past the first two guards without any problem, the two lowly Bules had already been cleared. Without an alarm, there was no reason to stop them.

After all, it wasn't like they were acting sneaky or suspicious. Sure, they might have used some distraction to get past the first set of guards unnoticed, but it hadn't been hard to distract them, and now they were simply hiking along, like they belonged there. And though ka'Shino hadn't set the Atheists to their destructive tasks for this purpose, she suspected that hu'Toe might have arranged the night's discord.

There were good people around though. For some reason, she thought about Dick hu'Mar. He'd still called her a Bule, but he also helped her. If not for him, she might've caught even more attention from the Beadledom when buying parts for her timers.

But because of that same advice, he might have also doomed himself and all of Spur Central—some fortune teller. The irony.

Yes, he had been decent to a lowly Albino like her. Not many people were. Though, being an Albino did come with some advantages. Very few humans, Toughs or otherwise, would've been permitted to cross this bridge, especially at this hour. If however, you were a pathetic Bule, you did what your betters told you to do.

Why strain a mule's back when you could break a Bule's? Bules were almost invisible. Bules never complained, never argued. Best of all, they worked at night. They could work jobs that nobody else wanted and be gone before anyone showed up to see them during the daytime.

After they'd crossed and were far enough away from the guards, ka'Shino's left knee buckled. She stumbled forward, almost face-planting into the jagged rock. The whole mountain was nothing but jagged rock. The only plants that clung to this unforgiving landscape were droopy bushes, that more resembled dangling ropes with leaves than anything else. Her right knee hit the ground hard, keeping her from smashing her face, though this might arguably hurt worse. She gasped, about to call out, but her voice failed. The knee protested any attempt to right herself. A few hard breaths later and hu'Toe was there, holding out a hand.

"I need to rest." The words came out labored as she gripped his wrist. Every ounce of her strength was devoted to righting herself and not falling again.

Hu'Toe said nothing, but he did help her limp to a few boulders. There, he helped her sit, then with a grunt, eased himself down.

Only when they'd both unstrapped their packs did ka'Shino notice his sweaty forehead and shirt where the shoulder straps had strained. This had been a lot harder for him than she thought.

"Sorry, tey're pretty heavy."

He wiped his face with trembling hands. "All I want to know, is what did you use for stitching on tese packs? No wool tread could hold tis weight witout popping."

"You carry it well," ka'Shino commented.

"I was terrified of dropping it. If I fall hard, would tis pack go off?"

"I doubt it, but you might break my timer." She smiled, her bruised knee already feeling better.

"I'm sure you of all people could fix it if tat happened," he said.

She was suddenly, acutely aware of the unattractive, possibly smelly, sweat matting her own shirt to her skin. It had been a whole labored day since she'd last bathed. "Tese ones are made from wooden gears. Tey'll break easy, but even wooden ones are hard to come by when, well, you know."

"Toughs tink tey're so much better tan us," hu'Toe agreed. "Plus, I don't get why tey revere te gear as too sacred to really put tem to tere full potential. Te whole cosmos is patterned after te tings, doesn't tat mean tat we should be using tose patterns to better our lives?"

"Careful. Now you're blaspheming," ka'Shino teased, and the lack of a huge pack on her shoulders made her feel light in body and spirit. She wasn't flirting. This wasn't the time. And even if she was, it was just the exhaustion manifesting itself, nothing more. They were about to set off a bunch of bombs on what was arguably the most sacred ground in this whole realm. Her sobering worry surfaced again. She wished she could turn that stupid reflex off. But what if hu'Toe was wrong and people did get hurt from their activities?

As if reading her mind and not wanting her to dwell on it, hu'Toe stretched. "Let's keep going. Te rendezvous point is just anoter ten minutes from here."

"Rendezvous? Wit who?" ka'Shino asked.

"Sorry, did I forget to mention? I cannot wait around for te second bomb to go off. Te Newbly's will be helping you place te tird bomb."

Ah, the geologists mentioned at the speakeasy. Had it been wishful thinking on her part that hu'Toe would stay with her the whole time? "Why not just place bōt at te same time?"

"Because," hu'Toe said, "we expect te second bomb to change te dynamic of te mountain's structure. Te tird bomb cannot be placed yet, just in case te cavern tat it goes in gets expanded. Placement is critical. It must be inserted at te very end of te cavern to be effective. Te Newbly's are aware of tis and will know where to take you."

"Let's not keep tem waiting," ka'Shino said. She wanted to rest longer, but that would cause her to cramp up. Better to remain tired than pained. She rocked back and forth twice, using the pack's weight to push her off the rock.

Hu'Toe, having given up looking macho, grunted and strained against his straps as he lifted himself off a lower rock. After hiking what felt like ten minutes or so, ka'Shino considered questioning hu'Toe's rendezvous point. Then they rounded a corner, and nearly bumped into a man and woman who were quietly waiting for them.

Ka'Shino gasped and almost fell backward.

Hu'Toe caught her shoulder strap. "I'd like to introduce te Newbly's. Tis is Rouche hu'Newbly." He gestured to the fat brown-haired man.

Rouche hu'Newbly was short and looked as though he could roll all the way down the mountain if he tripped. He wasn't a Tough, but neither was he an Albino. He had to be a scholar from one of the neighboring kingdoms. Ka'Shino had been told to expect them, but she'd assumed they would be Albino.

"Pleased to meet you," hu'Newbly said, sticking out his pudgy hand. His voice was high and whiny. From his red face, ka'Shino guessed that he didn't talk to very many people.

As hu'Toe carefully took off his pack, hu'Newbly rested one hand on his belly and gestured back with the other. "This is my wife, she's—"

"Hello dear, I'm Sasha ka'Newbly."

Ka'Newbly was definitely Albino. She was tall and muscular with long, thick hair, white as pure desert salt, and had a deep voice that both comforted and controlled any situation. Even her eyes had that coveted blue tint that was so rare among Albinos. Though ka'Newbly's beauty and presence would've normally intimidated her, the woman's manner was so sincere, it put ka'Shino immediately at ease.

"Sasha ka'Newbly, it's nice to meet you," ka'Shino said.

She wanted to ask ka'Newbly about her husband. Marrying outside one's pigment was never seen in the Albino community—but hu'Toe interrupted, "We've only got a few hours before it's light again. Tese guards'll get suspicious if we're not off te mountain witin a couple of hours. Plus, I'd like you to show us all how to set your timer, just in case you all get separated somehow. You can never be too careful."

Ka'Shino sat down, glad to shrug off her pack again, and pulled out a timer. The demonstration took only a moment. It wasn't complicated. Then hu'Toe wished them good luck and raced back down the mountain.

"Tat man is always so busy," ka'Newbly said. "I swear, he must tink he's running te whole resistance by himself."

"Resistance?" ka'Shino asked. "I tought Ernes hu'Toe was just a government geologist, maybe recruiter or organizer for tis one mission."

"No dear, we're te lowly geologists. Hu'Toe is te top geologist of te High Council. Tis whole ting and more is his idea. Sure, we know a few tings too, we aren't completely stupid after all—"

"Don't sell yourself short, dear," Rouche hu'Newbly said. "You and I are great geologists."

"Tank you dear, but te trüt is, we haven't been studying tis very much. Tat man is in charge of making sure tis all goes off according to te High Council's directive, and we're just here because he needed some geologists wit a little know-how to place te bombs. We're still placing tem roughly where he's calculated tey need to go."

Ka'Shino hesitated for a minute, then summoned the courage to ask what had been nagging her. "Tis ting we're doing, is tere any chance it might, you know, hurt anybody?"

"I worry about tat too," ka'Newbly said. "But hu'Toe is adamant tat it will all work out well. He assures us tat any lava discharge will stop at te moat. Enough of tis tough. We've got work to do."

Ka'Shino wanted to shy away from her pack. Her shoulders were bruised, and she wondered whether she would really be able to stand again if it were strapped back on. She had little choice though. Rouche hu'Newbly was too short and the wrong shape to be carrying anything heavier than his belly, and Sasha ka'Newbly, strong as she looked, would never be able to carry both packs. Only a Tough with a hankering to show off could do that.

She sighed and bent back down. When this was all over, a few days of rest would be in order, if she could, that is. Perhaps it all depended on whether glory or guilt won the rights for dictating the narrative of her future. She was pretty sure she couldn't experience both at the same time.

Chapter 24
The Bells of War

Dick hu'Mar woke to a weight on his chest and pointy little teeth, biting his nose. He rolled to the side, dumping Vinegar off him. Getting comfortable again was unlikely, thank you very much Vinegar, so he sat up and rubbed his face till his blurred vision remembered how to focus. Vinegar stood directly in front of him, demanding.

"Feed me," the cat mewed.

He brushed the cat aside. "Go feed yourself." He didn't have food for himself, let alone a cat. "Bring back a couple extra rats, and I'll eat with you."

"Not a chance," Vinegar said. "Last time, you only ate the meaty parts. Rats are too much trouble to catch for an ingrate who wastes ninety percent of the food. I'll grab a mouse or bird for myself, thank you very much. You can fend for yourself."

Hu'Mar got up, walked to the room's little desk, sat down, then placed his head on the desktop. He blinked, and as soon as he re-opened his eyes, the morning seemed lighter. Vinegar was somewhere close also, chomping on a mouse's body. "That was fast."

Vinegar looked up, confusion and kidneys dangled from

his face. He bent back over his meal.

Hu'Mar stood, his chair tipped over as he stretched and bumbled across the room. There was no water basin to wash his face, so he'd have to use the inn's common washroom. Vinegar followed him out. The washroom was wet with drips from several other customers who'd waken up and washed before him. The basins themselves had a milky clarity to them and needed replacing soon. Hu'Mar dug his hands down deep, hoping to draw some of the clearer water from below. He splashed it on his face, massaging the sleep from his eyes.

Vinegar stared, a tail dangling from his lips. "You're disgusting," he said. "I wouldn't even dare drink that water, and you're splashing it on your face?" He slurped up the tail.

"This coming from someone who just ate a dead rodent?"

"Would you prefer it be alive?"

A noise from outside caught hu'Mar's attention. "What now?"

He went to washroom's window. The fires from last night were all out.

Then the city bells, placed at the land bridge to cross to Mount Exclusion, rang out once, echoing throughout the whole city like a ghost. Tense silence followed. Those bells were reserved for one purpose only. Not a sound followed for several seconds. Not a human or animal so much as stepped on a creaky floorboard. The whole city held its breath. Then the bells clanged again, steady and unstopping this time.

War.

Hu'Mar left the window. The sounds of men and women strapping on armor filled the streets. Pissers tumble out of the inn, eager to get back to their ships before any real fighting broke out. Kids ran from apartment to apartment, dragging weapons behind them, like the visible foam of excitement, hinting that everything was about to spill over in a huge mess upon the streets.

Hu'Mar walked slowly downstairs as the remaining guests rushed by him and Vinegar. The innkeeper had a line of three customers waiting to check out. Hu'Mar fell in the queue. Once his tab was squared away, he pushed through the doors and met the day. The background noise of the town had now fully shifted from its normal invisible hum to an invisible clinking. A few minutes later, armed individuals and families, weapons in one hand and picnic baskets in the other, came pouring out of their homes. For generations, they'd been preparing for this. It was a family event. Go off to fight a war at the city gates, try to keep the ants off your lunch, then go back home with the family at the end of the day. If you were lucky, you'd kill more enemies than your friends and win yourself a few salines from whatever bet you made with them.

"Hu'Mar?" A familiar squeal reached his ears. "Dick hu'Mar!" Thelma ka'Skrut had just exited another inn across the street. She ran over, working those tiger tights for all they were worth. "It's war! Isn't that great?"

The ministers and his neighbors might blame him for burning down his apartment, but ka'Skrut was eternally oblivious.

"Nice hair."

She pouted her lips and cocked her head in a pleased flirtatious sort of way. Her strawberry blond hair was woven to sheathe at least five different crystal-encrusted daggers. Her special hair jellies kept it helmet hard. He pitied the tooth that tried to puncture that scalp.

Ka'Skrut bumped his hip with hers, a playful invitation that said, "anytime you want to fight me, I'm yours for the beating," and not for the first time, hu'Mar wondered how many large cats had been slain to make all her pants. As tight as they were, probably just one. She cat-walked around him, each leg crossing in front of the other, as if trying to summon the seductive and playful gait of the animal whose skin she wore. If there was any shred of self-awareness to how ridiculous she really looked, her mind refused to admit it. Skinny legs and a big bubble butt were the least of her problems. How could anyone think that imitating a cat would make them attractive? Maybe you had to live with a cat to understand. If ka'Skrut had paid any real attention to him in the whole four months they'd been neighbors, she would've known that cats were more of a turn-off.

"Ready to fight alongside this?" She asked, twirling a large whip, like a tail.

He had no doubt that she was good with that thing, he'd heard her practice with it on a number of occasions. A good whip-fighter could decapitate a smaller animal with a flick. Larger species could be caught off guard, yanked in close, then finished off with a dagger.

Hu'Mar followed ka'Skrut down the walk a few steps, focusing on the whip and not her face. This was as close to an invitation for a date as anything, and he needed a way out. In the streets the bustle of activity was ramping up, and in a way, it distracted from ka'Skrut's advance. Because fighting was a family activity, even infants were strapped to their parents' backs, like another set of blades. Those kids were literally cutting their teeth on the hilts of their mothers' swords. Hu'Mar wouldn't be surprised if the mothers occasionally unsheathed their babies and swung them at an enemy like a sword or maybe a club. For all he knew, the babies would be as effective, being of Tough stock and all.

"Hey, hunk-a-licious, you coming?" Ka'Skrut asked as hu'Mar fell behind.

"I left my battle hammer in my room. I'll catch up."

She popped a disproportional amount of hip out and grinned. "I'll be looking for you out there." She blew a kiss with too much lip and not enough shame, then butt-pumped down the street toward the outskirts of town, following the crowd as if they all had a sixth sense for where the battle would take place.

"Not a word," he pointed at Vinegar, who's purr sounded remarkably like a snicker. Hu'Mar might have vomited if he had anything in his stomach. There was so much wrong with that lady.

Since he didn't own a battle hammer or a desire to fight whatever skirmish everyone was rushing to, he decided to visit ka'Feebal. Careful not to let ka'Skrut see him leave in the opposite direction, hu'Mar surveyed the streets. Armor-clad boots pounded the ground, making him glad that he was among the larger species in the city, unlike Vinegar.

Plenty of chariots raced madly one way, with a large girl scout marching band plowing through in the other direction. It was enough to make him reconsider leaving the inn, but he had his case to worry about, and if he was to piece everything together, he needed to see ka'Feebal. She didn't strike him as one to rush off to battle, but he'd have to get there before her hangover left and she filled up on booze again for the day. He needed answers only she could give. Did she tell anyone about ka'Nairie's Pin of Poison? How potent was the poison made from the Pin's use? Was there a way to counteract the poisonous effects of the relic? And did ka'Feebal know about ka'Nairie's plans to force open the Great Clutch? Did she know ka'Shino and Maizy ka'Dillie, hu'Dillie or whoever? Hu'Mar could care less about the Clutch and its consequences, but if ka'Shino was in danger, then he felt like he should help her. He might even get some answers.

Outside of ka'Feebal's, Vinegar rolled onto his back, his chest raised and lowered fast in exhaustion. "Mind if I stay outside for this?" he asked.

"I could really use your help here," hu'Mar said, half watching Vinegar, half inspecting the buzzing slab bushes. His stings from the prior day were now itchy, and he really didn't want to relive that experience.

"You do your thing, Dick hu'Mighty. I'll do mine." Vinegar rolled away, emphasizing that the conversation was over.

Cats always had a way of committing, whole-heartedly to anything and nothing at the same time. It was an art that only a cat could appreciate.

Hu'Mar didn't bother knocking, he pushed the door open and entered ka'Feebal's place. She'd played him for a sucker twice already. He was done with formalities.

As predicted, ka'Feebal lay sprawled on her wicker sofa. Without bothering to check if she was really asleep, hu'Mar strode to her only other room, the kitchen. The place was even dirtier than her main room. It was filled with empty bottles, skins, and bowls that had once served or brewed her booze. If a kitchen could get drunk, it would look and smell like this one.

He grabbed an empty bowl and placed it under a water pump. The lever was overdue for oil but still worked well enough. Not daring to trust his lips to any of her dishes, he puckered his lips under the pump after filling the bowl and sucked in a quick drink before the water died, in case he had to do a lot of talking. Then, careful not to spill his bowl, he walked to the main room where ka'Feebal snored.

Hu'Mar doubted that she was really asleep. If he ever tried sleeping in her contorted shape, all those unnatural angles would've left him cramped for a week. With both hands, he lifted the large bowl above her head, then turned it over. Cold groundwater hit her with a splash, causing her to hit the floor with a sploosh followed immediately by a, "Wa-yaghhh!"

Hu'Mar slowly set the bowl aside while she woke up or pretended to wake up. "Good morning, sunshine," he said as she clawed herself up, using him as a cane. "Did you miss me?"

She let out a breath of rancid air.

Hu'Mar suppressed a cough. "Did I say sunshine? How about moonshine?"

Her face contorted, doubling her flabby face wrinkles, especially around those angry eyes. Impressive.

"Who'aw'y'n'whuda'ya'thingin?" Her voice sounded like gravel grinding in a pot of mud. She slumped down into her wet chair.

"Hmmm." Hu'Mar picked up the bowl and went back to the pump.

When he got back, ka'Feebal's eyes were closed though she was sitting up. He was about to throw this one on her face too but then thought better of it. He dumped it down her back.

Her spine sucked into her stomach, and her sweaty chest protruded like lumpy clay. At least her eyes were open. Her mouth too, but no muttering of incoherent words came out. This time they were all very coherent and could peel the bark off a slab berry bush.

Luckily, hu'Mar was made of stronger stuff, and the language washed over him. "I'm so glad I caught you here awake.

I was a little worried that I'd come too early, and you'd still be sleeping."

Ka'Feebal's eyes rested for a moment on the wooden chain clock on her wall, probably Albino-made. The hand pointed between "slab arrack" and "whiskey." She moaned, leaned forward, and hu'Mar pulled the remnants of last night's cup away from her.

"No drink for you yet."

"But it's already mid-morning," she complained.

"We got some things to talk about first."

"I don't talk to anyone on an empty stomach."

"You don't talk to anyone on a full stomach either. At least, when you're not pickling your intestines, you're still conscious."

"Consciousness is the last thing I need." She slapped both sides of her face and dragged her hands down her cheeks, stretching them till her hands clasped her wet nightgown. She grabbed it and peeled its wet fabric out, examining it, maybe trying to remember if it was wet from her sweat or the water hu'Mar had dumped on her.

Hu'Mar turned away, until he heard the gown slap back against her skin. He'd rarely met anyone more in need of a bath than her. But her hygiene was the least of his concerns. "Give me what I want, and you can poison yourself for all I care."

"Hain't no drink that can kill me. I've tried 'em all." She grabbed her head and squinted.

Hu'Mar picked up the bowl again.

"No-no!" She said, wincing at her own volume, then said more softly. "How many times do I have to get rid of you before you'll stay gone?"

"Only two ways to get rid of me. One is to kill me, the other is to tell me what I want to know." He had his suspicions, and if she could give him anything to support those assumptions, then he'd feel a lot better about going to ka'Nairie with his accusation. He brushed a clear spot on the coffee table in front of ka'Feebal and sat.

"Give me a minute to clear my head, and I'll give you that first one."

Hard Boiled Cabbage: Big Trouble In Spur Central

"Listen, ka'Feebal," hu'Mar said softly as he leaned in close. He guessed that ka'Shino currently had the Pin of Poison, but he couldn't go accusing ka'Nairie of planning something blasphemous like tampering with the great Clutch without proof. "I just need a few answers. I'm not with the Ministry, and I'm not here to make trouble."

"Trouble, ha! I need to pee."

Hu'Mar followed her out the back door to the privy.

"Whaddya going to do? Watch me pee?

"Honestly, you smell like you already did that. I'm not about to let you give me the slip again." If this case didn't crack soon, he'd have to take Vinegar's advice and run, and he was tired of running.

"Ungggh," she said as she slammed the wooden door to the craphouse.

Hu'Mar leaned against her house, careful not to upset the humming wasps that surrounded the place. Her feet lifted out of sight from below the door to squat on the raised seat within. In his mind, he practiced his interrogation. Who did you tell about ka'Nairie's Pin of Poison? How do I protect myself when I find them? And how much do you know about ka'Nairie's plans? He could hear her mumbling a lot of incoherent gibberish as she took care of her business.

After a couple minutes, she still hadn't come out. He walked around the tiny shack to make sure there wasn't a loose panel to escape from. He was about to knock, then said, "Screw it." He yanked the door open, tearing the little wire latch inside.

Ka'Feebal had a bottle of something strong pressed to her lips. Her eyes lit up, and she tried to guzzle the last of it before hu'Mar tore the bottle away from her.

"You're the drunkest sow I've ever met."

"I just needed something to clear the demons."

"Come on, we got things to discuss."

Back inside, and with half a bottle pickling her gut, she actually perked up and looked lucid enough to talk.

"Who are you again, and wadda ya want? And what's everyone running around outside for?"

"You know who I am, and I need to know about relics, namely those sold to Jodeign ka'Nairie. There's a minor problem with their ownership. As for the rest of the world, the Clutch is about to open. Atheists and animals of all sorts are congregating at the city's borders. War's about to break out."

"Aye, I need a drink. Can I get you something?"

"Let's talk first, then you can get plastered."

Ka'Feebal slumped into her sleeping chair. "Honey, I'm out of the business. There's not much I can tell you. My memory is shot, and I haven't seen a relic in years."

If he hadn't already read some of her more recent transactions, he might be willing to believe her. A winebibber like her could get away with a lot. Hu'Mar was no dummy—not this time around. She couldn't be trusted any more than a non-biting blood beetle. She was also dangerous in more ways than one. He could sense it. Maybe it was her ability to ditch him every time they tried to talk, or maybe it was the bone necklace that hung limp inside her shirt, just barely tucked where few sober men would dare look.

Of course, he couldn't prove that the necklace was a relic, but not many people wore bone jewelry. Not many people were like ka'Feebal either, and had she called him honey? What a lonely life she must live, if she was willing to call him honey. Maybe a different approach, one that had gotten him in the door the first time they met.

Hu'Mar slumped next to her on the couch and wrapped his arm around her soft damp shoulder. "Listen cute-cakes, I don't care about your past life or whatever dirt has stained your soul. I'm a simple man, with simple needs. Right now, what I need is a friend to help me understand relics.

Her eyebrows furrowed. She studied him, leaning back slightly. Slowly her bafflement was replaced by good humor. She smiled, revealing a full set of teeth. They were barely even yellowed.

Hu'Mar blinked once, surprised at her dental hygiene. Within that eye blink, he found a knife poking into his side. Her hands were strong and steady, not the shaky sort that he'd

Hard Boiled Cabbage: Big Trouble In Spur Central

have expected from a drunk.

Ka'Feebal's smile faded. "You're not like most ministers. You got guts, I'll give you that." She squeezed his bicep with her free hand. "Ooh-yeah. You got good tone too. Maybe I should've let you get a little warmer with me before I decided to gut you."

Carefully, hu'Mar lowered his hand, but the pressure against his belly increased, threatening to skewer his side.

"Ah-aah," ka'Feebal teased. "What do I gotta do to keep you away? I got nothin' for ya. I don't wanna kill you, but I'm running out of better ideas.

A small clickity clash drew ka'Feebal's eyes away, and she gasped.

The distraction was enough. Hu'Mar plucked the blade before she rebounded. Thank you, Vinegar.

Vinegar sat next to a canvas bag, decorative fragments of bone spilled across the floor.

Arm still around ka'Feebal, her blade now in his hand also, hu'Mar leaned in close. His soft whisper was meant to tickle and annoy. "You know, those look a lot like relics to me."

"I found them in a crawl space below her house," Vinegar said, licking his paw with smug accomplishment. "There were other things down there too, partial skeletons from some really old animals."

Ka'Feebal cringed and pulled away. Hu'Mar drew her near with the stolen dagger positioned at her belly. His embrace went from mock affection to undeniably threatening.

"You clearly know how to show a lady a good time," she complained.

"I don't see any ladies here," hu'Mar said. "If there were, I'd do my best to be a complete gentleman. Now let's talk relics, specifically the Pin of Poison."

"You know, besting a woman in a fight around here ain't easy. I've never been bested, till now." She batted her eyes at hu'Mar. He understood her implication. Now it was him who needed a drink. "What do you want to know about that Pin?" ka'Feebal asked, her tone switching to serious.

"It's missing. I've been hired by its owner to find it."

"No, you haven't," she said, "because I'm the owner."

"Listen, ka'Feebal, I'm only guessing here, but I saw your books. The Pin of Poison shows up far too often as sold and resold. Let me take a stab at your racket. You sell an artifact to a willing buyer, then within months, you've resold it to another party. I'm going to guess that you've stolen back the Pin of Poison and sold it to an interested party, say an Albino? So what is it?"

"I knew I couldn't trust her." Ka'Feebal spit on her floor. "Political brat!"

"S'cuse me?" That wasn't the answer he'd expected.

Ka'Feebal met his eyes. "That's my relic, and I never sold it to anyone. I rented it out."

Hu'Mar let go of her, surprised. "Rented?"

"I told you I stopped selling those things long ago. I meant it too. I only sold what was necessary to compensate for the cost of acquiring those bones in the first place. Once I did that, I kept the rest, living off the rentals they fetch. Still not legal, but I was honest about that part. Besides, its not like I care what the Beadledom thinks is legal or not. Question is, how do I help you find my Pin of Poison?"

"Just like that, you're cooperating now?" Maybe this would be easier after all, but it changed his assumptions, leaving him with . . . what? He wasn't sure yet.

"It's my property. If Jodeign ka'Nairie doesn't find that thing soon, she'll pay dearly. I'm sure you don't want that either, 'cause you won't be collecting your pay when I finish with her." She fingered the bony fragments of the necklace under her shirt.

Hu'Mar estimated that there were at least ten relics on that single chain, and what they could endow ka'Feebal with was anyone's guess. Considering how skilled ka'Nairie was at all forms of confrontation, ka'Feebal was either completely clueless or a lot more dangerous than he'd ever imagined.

That little dagger to his belly had been little more than teasing on her part. Some sense of humor. If his suspicions were right, she could do a lot more damage to him without it. He handed the knife back to her.

Hard Boiled Cabbage: Big Trouble In Spur Central

She grabbed it and casually tossed it onto a cluttered table. Vinegar jumped, but the blade plunked tip down, missing every empty wineskin, and stood vertical in the wood table, like she'd unconsciously avoided puncturing the vessels that would hold her booze later on. It was little tells like this that hu'Mar thrived on. Could she possibly know how much she was giving away?

"I need to know everything the Pin of Poison can do and why anyone would want to steal it."

"All right handsome, you got it. For her sake, I hope you find it." She sat back. "The Pin of Poison comes from a jynx, more specifically its ribs." Ka'Feebal paused.

Hu'Mar didn't have to count far back. The jynx inhabited this world about three shiftings back. That was the same shifting that had brought humans into this realm.

"Do I have to explain everything?" ka'Feebal asked?

"Assume that I know the basics, like everyone else," hu'Mar said, which was true.

"In that case, you don't know nothin," ka'Feebal laughed. "Okay, its like this, not every dead and ascended animal can create a relic, only the corpse of the one that got trapped in the Great Clutch will work. As you may or may not have heard, the jynx was a venomous, four-flippered sea creature."

"I saw that creature under her house," Vinegar commented, "What was left of it."

Ka'Feebal ignored Vinegar since she obviously couldn't understand cat. "The Pin, when properly carved, has the ability to drain, or rather, convert toxins in the body. Anything that would normally hurt you or make you tired, is rendered ineffective."

"Ineffective to you, the holder of the relic, but enough to kill anyone you come in contact with, it would seem," hu'Mar added.

Ka'Feebal chuckled. "They all have some nasty side effect. Spit, boogers, blood, piss, and sweat, you name it. But it depends on how long you've been using it. If sparingly, you won't have developed many toxins, and you'll only make others sick. Lean too heavy on it, and sure, you're deadly."

Ka'Feebal surveyed the bag that Vinegar had brought in. Hu'Mar almost missed it, but a double take of the various shades of bone mixed with the proud twinkle in her eyes, suggested that she might be very rich. "How many different Clutch bodies have you managed to collect?"

Ka'Feebal's face tightened. The twinkle left. "What makes you think I have anything more than what you see?"

Hu'Mar shifted his attention to Vinegar. "She's got about three partial bodies, and another bag of mixed bones from who knows what." There were few redeeming traits to having a cat as a partner. Despite all their feigned indifference, they were good at snooping.

Apparently, ka'Feebal was a rich woman indeed. Kingdoms would go to war for part of a single tomb-preserved body. How she'd come in possession of three partials plus, was a mystery in itself.

"Never mind. Its not important," hu'Mar said. Ka'Feebal was actually talking, so he couldn't spoil this. Perhaps she wasn't a mere bone collector, and instead with those strong, steady hands and her skill with that knife, she might, in fact, be the artisan who'd carved the Pin of Poison and all the others in that bag. How many different kinds of relics could be carved from one corpse?

Ka'Feebal smacked her lips, clearly sizing up hu'Mar.

Hu'Mar tried not to get distracted. "The Pin of Poison sounds handy, especially if you plan on overexerting yourself or expect assassination by poison."

His mind kept coming back to the debate, if it could be called that. By the way ka'Nairie had recovered from her first fight, he might suspect that she still had her Pin of Poison. Something wasn't adding up.

"Or handy if you plan on being the assassin," ka'Feebal added.

Hu'Mar rubbed the new whiskers on his face. It reminded him of that close shave he'd had at Dussel hu'Nuff's salon. Unconsciously, he lowered his shaved arm. "So ka'Nairie's ring, do you own that one too?"

"No," ka'Feebal huffed. "That one's been handed down to her through generations. It's a strength Ring from the spinal bone of a Morp two shiftings ago. It also happens to be her collateral if she loses my relic."

"That explains how she was so strong during her last political debate," hu'Mar said. "Seems like a good advantage for a busy political head."

"Don't forget the side effects," ka'Feebal said. "The ring doesn't give strength freely. You might be as strong as a river, but that river only has so much water. Excessive fatigue is the ring's downside. Eventually you need to rest. Unfortunately, it doesn't know when to stop channeling your strength. It will keep your mind and body strong, long past the point of exhaustion. The wearer's body will continue to be strong while the body builds up more and more toxins until they've accumulated to the point where your own blood poisons you to death."

"Which brings us back to your Pin of Poison and why she would want to rent that from you."

"The Pin of Poison would keep her from poisoning herself with her ring," ka'Feebal confirmed. "She'll feel less fatigued while it makes her own bodily fluids all the more toxic to others, but as long as she's aware, she can manage it. Who knows, if she wants to assassinate someone, she might be able to use that to her advantage."

"During ka'Nairie's debate yesterday, she appeared to recover super-fast from the fatigue her ring caused. How could she do that if she didn't actually have the Pin with her?"

"Either she used her ring again and risked poisoning herself," ka'Feebal said. "Or, she still has the Pin, and she's playing you for some reason."

Hu'Mar considered this, scratching his whiskers again. "Yeah, maybe I was wrong. She still might have it after all." His concentration was broken when Vinegar laughed.

"What's wrong with your cat?" ka'Feebal asked. "If it's coughing up a hairball, I'm kicking you both out."

"Spit it out, Vinegar. What's so funny?"

"A palsy," ka'Feebal rolled her eyes. "Of course, you'd be

one of those."

Vinegar tried to stop his fit of laughter, ending it with a sneeze. "You really think she could be playing you? You're head over heels in love with her, blinded by your emotions. You're nothing to her, like you're nothing to everyone else! You're not even worth her time to play with."

"I'm trying to make sense of this here," hu'Mar sighed. "How do I know for sure that ka'Nairie doesn't actually have the Pin still?"

"I think I'd know if she did," Vinegar said. "Because I'd be an unbonded palsy right now."

"Come again," hu'Mar asked.

"She kissed you when she first met you, the same day that Crazy Ish and the stableboy were poisoned. She kissed you again after her debate. If she had used the Pin, you'd be dead now."

"Hmmm." Vinegar had a point. But he also felt terrible all day yesterday after ka'Nairie had kissed him. Could that have been a coincidence, or was it just the concussion from Beauford's kick? If she'd been poisonous then, wouldn't he be dead now, or could he have survived? She'd been a pretty strong kisser, and if she hadn't used the Pin for very long, maybe she wasn't at full toxicity?

That wasn't right either. "She wouldn't have kissed me yesterday if she'd been using the Pin of Poison, would she?" he said softly, almost to himself, hoping she valued his life more than that.

Ka'Feebal collected the relics that Vinegar had scattered across the floor and wasn't paying much attention, but Vinegar heard.

"Either she kissed you because she'd gone so long avoiding fluidic contact with other humans and she was desperate," Vinegar said, "or she was still hoping that she had enough poison left in her system to kill you. Since nobody would be desperate enough to kiss you—" Vinegar paused, watched ka'Feebal for a second, then added, "well, nobody except for maybe her, if she was really, really, really drunk—"

"She wasn't trying to kill me," hu'Mar countered as ka'Fee-

Hard Boiled Cabbage: Big Trouble In Spur Central

bal picked up the last of her relics and wrapped them gently in the canvas sack. "Vinegar, you said you saw more bones below the house?" He had an idea. It was crazy, but it was the only thing that made sense. "Ka'Feebal, darling, how many of these Pins did you carve?"

She cinched the canvas bag and stared him in the face. A stone would sooner budge, but hu'Mar had been reading stones his whole life. It was all making muddy sense. Ka'Nairie's visit, the poisoned stableboy and senile prophet, the victory at the stadium, the Albino who was concerned about the future of the city, the prophesy, even the atheists in the street last night, and Dussel hu'Nuff, the unusual salon owner. And the last piece of the puzzle, ka'Feebal, had just fallen into place

"Vinegar, I've figured it out. Vinegar—"

The cat was staring into space. Hu'Mar had seen that expression recently. Vinegar's eyebrow whiskers twitched. The cat turned slowly around, and all the whiskers on his face visibly spasmed.

Hu'Mar closed his eyes and tried to feel his own senses, but all he could feel was ka'Feebal's eyes on him. Or was that his own primal senses warning him, like Vinegar had taught?

"What in holy clockwork are you doing?" ka'Feebal huffed.

Ok, it was just her staring at him. He opened his eyes and followed Vinegar's gaze. Which way was this house oriented? Ah, yes. Vinegar was pointed directly toward Mount Exclusion, like last time.

Vinegar growled a low rumbling, "Roawwww-raow-roawwww," barely aware of hu'Mar's and ka'Feebal's attention.

"What's wrong with your furry rag?" ka'Feebal asked.

Vinegar snapped out of his trance, apparently realizing that he was making a scene. He tried to look casual, sitting and licking his paw, but he couldn't shake the shakes. "It's going to happen again."

"Better if we're not under a roof when it happens," hu'Mar said right before something boomed in the distance.

"Better not be under a roof for what?" ka'Feebal demanded.

"Whiskerless humans," Vinegar complained as he hurried to the door.

Hu'Mar didn't have time to explain. Ka'Feebal's upright dagger started rattling, then fell over. It danced on its side across her wooden table until it clanked and clattered onto the floor. Little balls of dirt vibrated and skittered around the earthen floor as hu'Mar grabbed ka'Feebal's wrist and dragged her to the door.

Outside, in the open, Vinegar crouched, afraid to trust his feet on the shifting ground. "Hard dirt should never move like this," he complained.

Closer booms sounded as hu'Mar charged out of the door, nearly tripping on Vinegar. Ka'Feebal wasn't as careful. She spilled to the ground, sloshing over Vinegar, like a skin of liquor.

Behind them, hu'Mar heard the sound of old ripping wood as ka'Feebal's roof converted into a floor, sandwiching a lot of ka'Feebal's liquor between the hardpack earth and the newly placed floorboards.

As quickly as it had begun, it was over, and hu'Mar lifted ka'Feebal's leg to let the cat crawl out from under her. "You okay, Vinegar?"

"I'm going to have nightmares after that," Vinegar said, his eyes still wide.

"Good," hu'Mar stated. "Let's go. We've got to find that Albino."

"No." Vinegar planted his butt on the ground. A small after-tremor bounced him up once, but he sat again. "No, Dick hu'Doesn'tknowwhentoquit, I'm done chasing you around."

"But Vinegar, I think I've solved it. I just need to find this Albino girl." Then, rolling ka'Feebal over, he asked, "Ka'Shino, you know how to find her, don't you?"

"If I did, why should I tell you?" ka'Feebal asked, her attention more on her wrecked house than on hu'Mar.

"She's in trouble. If these gearquakes don't get her, the ministers will. How can I find her?"

"Hu'Dillie," ka'Feebal said, resigned. "He's an uppity up Bule official. I don't know this ka'Shino, but if she's connected to my Pins, then she'd have to know hu'Dillie."

"Where do I find him?" hu Mar asked.

"He said all messages go to the Drunken Dwarf." She thought for a minute, still dazed. "It's an underground—"

"Yeah, yeah, I've heard of it." He'd been to the speakeasy once or twice. "Thanks, and sorry about your house." Hu'Mar squeezed ka'Feebal's hand. He actually felt sorry for her. She might have been pickled, but she wasn't completely sour. "Come on, Vinegar, lets go."

Vinegar did nothing.

Hu'Mar clenched his jaw, long enough to cool his frustration a little. "Fine. You want to feel human for a while, you got it. While you're at it, find Beauford for me. He'll probably be near ka'Nairie. I'll catch up as soon as I can." Hu'Mar stalked away. He only hoped it wasn't too late to help ka'Shino.

Chapter 25
Too Late

Juniper ka'Shino screamed with the strain. Blood rushed to her head, which was now slightly below the rest of her body, on account of her body being dragged down the slope. Her shoulder felt ready to disconnect as several sharp rocks dug into her prostrate ribcage. Panic laced the edge of her mind as each painful rock failed to slow her gradual slide. The hot gaping hole in front of her waited, patiently like a sinister nightmare—first, an eternal anticipation of death, soon to be followed by a life ending fall.

Deep orange and black magma from Mount Exclusion swirled at the edge of her vision. The heat alone made it nearly impossible to see clearly. Still, ka'Shino clung tight to Sasha ka'Newbly's hair. Only a miracle could save the geologist, as the rest of her body dangled helplessly over the fissure.

The Newbly's had successfully helped ka'Shino place the second and third bombs. The second had exploded on schedule, and the third would blow soon. None of them had expected the mountain to keep rocking this long after the blast. They were on their way down the mountain to Spur Central to collect the fourth and final bomb when it happened. If only hu'Toe

Hard Boiled Cabbage: Big Trouble In Spur Central

were still here!

When the fissure opened and swallowed Rouche hu'Newbly, ka'Shino couldn't do anything for him. He'd been swallowed by the magma before anyone had time to react, but ka'Shino, in the fractured second it took to realize what happened, had managed a dive to catch his wife, even if it was only by the hair of her scalp.

Ka'Newbly waved and kicked, too panicked to realize that this was not helping.

"Grab something!" ka'Shino yelled to the geologist through gritted teeth. Her fingers burned, both from strain and the heat below. If that woman didn't come to her senses soon, her muscles would cook into useless hunks of meat, unable to move ever again. The most disconcerting sensation for ka'Shino, was when she felt the roots of ka'Newbly's hair giving way, like feathers being plucked out of a boiled chicken.

Ka'Shino reached with her other hand, but she slid on the slanted earth and had to keep herself from falling as well.

After several joint-popping seconds, ka'Newbly grabbed the lip of the fissure with one hand, then the other. Her blue eyes contrasted sharply with her flushed-red face.

Ka'Shino's lungs burned as she gasped what felt like her first breath of arid air since diving for her companion. With ka'Newbly somewhat more secure, ka'Shino reached into a pocket with one hand, the other still holding her companion's hair, and she retrieved her Pin of Poison. She had to hurry for both their sakes. Ka'Shino needed its protection from the fumes to help ka'Newbly up, and ka'Newbly needed it to help herself climb out of the toxic pit before the fumes poisoned her.

Another tremor shook the ground, and ka'Newbly's fingers slipped.

Ka'Shino dropped the Pin on the ground and tightened her grip on the lady's hair. The hair snapped straight. Then there was that odd sensation of plucking a chicken again, only this time, the weight of ka'Newbly's body only lasted a few seconds before the only weight tugging against her strained fingers, was that of ka'Newbly's hair.

Ka'Shino leaned over and watched the nearly bald Albino tumble and plummet a hundred feet. Her scream was muted by the rumble of rock and hiss of vents. She plunged with a graceless red splash into the lava below. It looked less like falling into water and more like falling into red and black gravy. There was no further splashing, no flailing about. Not a single finger broke the surface of the bright magma flow. Like Rouche hu'Newbly, she was simply gone.

Ka'Shino rolled away from the open furnace, coughing. No more tremors rocked the ground. She tried to open her stiff fingers. They felt like rusty hinges. Realizing that she still held most of ka'Newbly's hair in her aching fist, she sat up and manually pried each finger open, working them until they could move on their own again. With another series of honking coughs, she retrieved the Pin and let it subdue the noxious gases inhaled during her struggle.

Ernes hu'Toe must have known the dangers, so he'd sent them and then took off in the first chance he had. Her blood boiled, partly from the heat, but mostly out of anger.

The impact of the second explosion had exposed the placement for the third bomb, just as the third would soon reveal the placement for the fourth bomb. With each detonation, the whole volcanic mountain was destabilizing. Some caverns collapsed while new ones were expanded. Fissures and vents spread across the whole side of the mountain. Placing that fourth and final bomb would be treacherous, possibly even suicidal.

Ka'Shino climbed atop a large boulder that gave her a clear view of the mountain slope, including Spur Central. Her breath caught. All around the borders of the city, war had begun.

Tens of thousands of wolves and dogs, more than ka'Shino had ever seen in one place, were charging into the waiting Toughs.

On another front, a storm cloud of hawks fought both the humans and the dogs.

Farther out still, dust clouds billowed from multiple directions. Armies of animals and humans alike were marching on Spur Central, either to fight or lend aid.

A little closer, an orange steaming glow snaked into the moat. If the lava was penetrating the moat already, then the next explosion might turn Spur Central into part of the volcanic landscape despite what hu'Toe had told her.

From up here, she could also see into the moat. Marine life, thrashed and fought each other, making the unprotected portions of Lake Tallow appear as if they were boiling, while more fish and other water bound creatures joined the fray from connecting waterways. She'd seen fighting fish in a crystal bowl once before. Some didn't even have any visible teeth, and they could still strip an opponent of their flesh in minutes. Whatever was happening below the surface there, she was glad it was mostly hidden.

Her pale face burned in the morning light, and she pulled her cloak over her head to shade her skin. This was ridiculous. If the warring didn't cause enough damage, then the ever-reaching arms of lava would. Both made her sick.

Maybe it didn't matter if the lava did kill the lot of them. If Mount Exclusion got destroyed, then maybe this senseless violence would stop repeating itself every thousand years. She tried to focus on this thought. It made sense, but it felt wrong.

Knowing that all who died would be born back into the world did little to assuage her guilt. Every death meant severed relationships. Most species would never remember their past lives.

Who was she? Definitely not a killer.

Her gut turned, twisting her whole body after it. She took a short sharp breath, left her large empty pack, and raced back to the third bomb. There was still time to stop this. All she had to do was disarm it, then refuse to place the fourth and final bomb.

She reached the mouth of the last cave, but ten paces in, found the ceiling had collapsed. The way was blocked, though that didn't stop her from digging at the rocks and boulders till her fingers bled. A wail of a sob forced its way up her throat, it was useless. She could only hope that her detonator was damaged or that one more explosion wouldn't be enough to finish off the mountain.

Head hung low, fatigue nagging at her, she returned to her pack. It was mostly empty, save for the extra padding of clothes loaded on top to look like laundry, in case they were inspected. Whoever they belonged to might like them back, but returning to the inn or speakeasy with them might be dangerous. Still, leaving it here would be worse. Swinging the pack onto her back, nearly empty, the thing should've felt considerably lighter, but it now held a new weight, heavier than any physical load. She slogged carefully down the jagged mountain trails or what was left of them, and her knees wanted to buckle with every footstep, just like they had when hiking up this mountain.

The burden of expended life weighed heavily on her shoulders, but there was some comfort knowing that she would not allow the last bomb to go off. She'd done enough damage. The wars would've come eventually, but what if they kept killing each other, just to have several more years before the Great Clutch even opened its Tomb? There'd be another war with more pain and life destroyed.

Then a hand grabbed the top of her bag, and she fell backward.

"Bule. What are you doing up here? And what's in the bag?"

Juniper ka'Shino looked at a guard. His hand was on the hilt of his sword. Her eyes followed the ornate blade as it widened like a stretched-out teardrop, before coming back to a deadly point.

"I'm, I—" she stuttered.

The guard pushed her over with his foot, her pocket clock fell to the ground a moment before she did. She stared at the clock as the guard swung that razor-edged blade at her head.

She winced. The sound of sliced air rushed past her ears. She didn't feel anything but wasn't sure if she would. Any second her head would roll off her body, and she'd be stuck in the ether until the light of rebirth brought her back to this world.

Instead her shoulders were lightened. The guard had split open her empty pack. She breathed out a sigh of relief, then her eyes turned back to her pocket clock on the ground. The hands of the clock were both pointed towards feeling guilty. Her dark world came rushing back with all the claustrophobic menace that she'd never even felt in the tightest of the dark caves she'd traveled. It was guilt: guilt for being so selfish that she'd feared for her own life when she might have been the cause for so much pain and death to others, though seeing the prescription of guilt on the clock also eased the actual feeling of it, as if this time was meant for that, but soon it would pass, and she'd be on to the next part of her day soon. It didn't make sense, but it somehow felt better.

Planting both knees and hands into the jagged rocky soil, ka'Shino breathed.

There was no remnant of explosives left in her bag. All the guard saw was a dirty sack, with the few articles of clothing she'd stolen from a clothesline earlier this morning. There'd likely be a few men and women going into battle with little more than their undergarments this day, and knowing Toughs, even if she took all their clothes, it wouldn't stop them from rushing into battle wearing nothing but pride. No self-respecting Tough would miss a battle over something as trivial as clothing.

Satisfied that she wasn't up to the trouble she'd been at, the guard kicked her once in the stomach, then jogged to catch up to his companions.

Face burning, stomach aching, nauseous from nerves, she picked up the clothes. A drop or two of blood spotted some of the garments, but that didn't matter. The spots would be a lot less noticeable than the large slashes running through many of the garments.

She had to work at the damaged pack for a few minutes to stuff it all back in, then she hiked the rest of the way to the inn where her last bomb waited, hidden, in the alley. Now, what to do with it?

All around, atheists scurried around the streets like cockroaches, burning homes and businesses while the majority of the population was out fighting.

The inn was nearly empty. The owner alone was pacing

around his establishment. In one hand, he held a short club with a smooth black rock attached to the end. He'd smash any atheist's skull before letting them burn his building down.

Ka'Shino waited until he went in front of his inn before she crept around to the alley behind, her legs clumsy and almost too tired to stand. It had been a long morning, but her anger kept her from thinking about rest.

Why had hu'Toe left her with the Newbly's? She couldn't help but feel betrayed. Was he really so busy that the bombs were such a lower priority to him? Did he know that it would be so dangerous? Certainly, he had to. She almost wished that he'd been the one to fall into the lava. That probably wouldn't have stopped his plans, but ka'Newbly and her husband didn't deserve to die for his scheming. The only thing to do, was to get rid of the last bomb before hu'Toe came searching for it. There'd be some explaining to do, but maybe she could blame it on some overzealous atheists.

She pushed some trash cans aside. Her breath caught.

"Hello, Bule," a hulking Tough woman said through the missing teeth of her wide grin. "You'll never believe the conversation I just had with another one of your kind."

Malice radiated from this 200-pound meat tenderizer, but the threat of death wasn't all that bothered ka'Shino. The fourth bomb was missing.

"His name was Something hu'Toe, had blue eyes, not those creepy red ones you underground witches usually have."

"Where's my stuff?" ka'Shino demanded, her voice shakier than intended.

"Oh, you mean that device you were going to destroy the Great Clutch with?" She tsked. "Yeah, that other Bule told me about it. Said you were an atheist. Dangerous one too. Can't have saboteurs like you running around, can we?"

Ka'Shino could wait to be killed by this Tough, or she could try and surprise her and maybe, with a lot of luck, best her. The lady might have a lot more meat and fighting gristle on her bones, but ka'Shino's brain had to be stronger. If there was any hope to ever find hu'Toe and stop him, she'd better be right about this. She lunged at the antagonizing slab of muscle, throwing all her weight into her shoulders as her momentum pounded into the other woman. It was all a matter of mass and momentum.

She hit—and bounced off.

That had hurt. Blinking the stars from her head, she tried to collect her thoughts before the Tough fought back. The retaliation didn't come yet. Instead, the Tough's laughter filled her ears.

Maybe this beast of a woman would taunt her long enough to come up with a new plan of attack. Then again, no such luck. The Tough, thick as she was, moved with the impossible speed of large clock spring. Before ka'Shino could react, hu'Toe's assassin had her throat in hand.

Ka'Shino struggled to breath, to squirm, punch, kick, anything, but it was hopeless. It was futile to imagine fighting someone with this kind of strength. Her feet were not touching the ground, and with both hands, ka'Shino grabbed the single hand that choked her. The world swirled, and all she could see were the chipped and missing teeth of that smile that was all too happy to squeeze the life from her. It was the smile of a zealot, and ka'Shino was little more than an enemy on the wrong side of the battle lines.

Then that toothless grin slackened. Ka'Shino's feet touched solid ground, the hand around her throat loosened, and she inhaled a painful wheeze of a breath. In a moment, her knees hit the ground and her left hand barely had time to seize her fall as her right hand cradled her own neck.

Whoosh.

She craned her neck up, and a second feathered dart had appeared on the Tough's neck. The Tough swayed, yanked one dart out and inspected it before her eyes rolled back into her head, and she fell over, head crashing into a half rotted wooden barrel.

Not sure if she wanted to see, ka'Shino twisted toward the doorway. It couldn't be! It was that confounded fortune teller, Dick hu'Mar. He pocketed his blowgun into his vest, lifted his hat, then licked his palm and rubbed it through that dark greasy hair, like a cat cleaning itself.

"Glad I found you," his gravelly voice almost sounded like a 300-pound fat cat purring. He replaced his hat on his head. "I figured you must've climbed out this window when you abandoned your place here, so I was hoping to find some clue to track you and hu'Dillie. But you're actually here."

"Hu'Dillie?" Ka'Shino whispered, confused, as she pushed herself from the ground, then with all the rage she'd intended for the Tough, she slapped hu'Mar across the face.

Chapter 26

The End of a Partnership

Hu'Mar had the sudden urge to claw ka'Shino's eyes out. Instead, he forced himself to remain calm. Her next attack was a lot weaker, and hu'Mar caught her wrist. Her knee did connect with his crotch though.

"Of all the thanks I get—" he mumbled as he tossed her back into a wall. "What was that for?"

"Another person dead, and on my conscience!" She curled up, and then the waterworks came flooding out.

Hu'Mar didn't know what to do with crying women. He wanted to place a hand on her shoulder, but something told him that was the wrong move. Instead, he opted for blunt confrontation. "How many more are going to die?"

Ka'Shino sniffed. Wet eyes stared from a flushed angry face. "What do you care? I've never met a Tough who valued life all that much."

"If I were a Tough, I might agree with you. But I ain't a Tough, and I do care. You've been tampering with the Great Clutch, and by the looks of it, the worst of the destruction has yet to happen."

"Why are you here?" ka'Shino asked.

Hard Boiled Cabbage: Big Trouble In Spur Central

"You're in trouble and need help." Hu'Mar leaned against the doorframe.

"I can handle my own problems." Ka'Shino grabbed her few belongings and stuffed them in her shredded pack. She then started for the inn's entrance.

"Yeah, I can see that." Hu'Mar shifted, blocking the alley. "Let me make this a little more clear. You nearly got killed. You've got a bunch of ministers on high alert for a suspicious female Albino, and there's two other Albinos hanging out in the inn's lobby, neither of which appear very friendly, pretending to drink. My guess is they're waiting to see if their Tough assassin killed you."

A second ago, ka'Shino looked ready to push past him, but now she paused right before him. This close up, he realized she was shaking.

Carefully, he took the pack from her goose pimpled arms. "Talk to me. I can help."

She made eye contact with him. He held her there, not willing to blink or appear weirded out by those red eyes.

Finally, she let her head fall. "Let's walk. You over there, I'll take this side."

As they exited on opposite ends of the alley, hu'Mar spied into the lobby over his shoulder. The two Albinos still sat near the window. He studied them for a moment so that if they noticed his attention, maybe they'd overlook ka'Shino slinking against another building as she slipped away from the inn.

Instead of the traditional fabric robe-like cloaks that most people here associated with Albinos, these two wore heavy gray leather trench coats. As before, they each had half a glass of booze, neither of which had been drained one bit since he first saw them.

One of them noticed him and tapped his companion. Why would they care about him? Oh, right. He was still holding ka'Shino's pack. They must've recognized it. Stupid mistakes. Hu'Mar tucked it under his arms and tried to ignore them as he put his back to them and walked. He only risked glancing back once he was out of the alley. The Albinos' table was now empty except for those two half full glasses. "Great, just what I need."

He jogged down the street, each step shooting painful reminders of the abuse his body had taken since meeting ka'Shino for the first time. He slowed as he caught up to ka'Shino. "We got to hide, quick."

Screams and shouts and random animal howls filled the air like clouds drifting overhead as they ran down two alleyways until they reached the canal that ringed Mount Exclusion. Ka'Shino slowed and stopped, her jaw hung loose as she stared at the land bridge. The battle lines were almost to the bridge now, but she pointed across the moat to where two men in cloaks were hiking up a jagged trail.

"What is it?" hu'Mar asked.

"Hu'Toe, with my bomb," she gasped.

"What's a bomb?" Hu'Mar had never heard that word before, and who was this hu'Toe?

Ka'Shino shielded her eyes and examined the sun, which was halfway between noon and dusk. "I'm guessing by the time he gets it placed, and sets my timer, it'll go off right around sunset."

Hu'Mar had all sorts of questions. Aside from the ones about this bomb thing, and hu'Toe, he wanted to know why her own people were after her. What was her connection to ka'Nairie? And obviously, could she shed some light on hu'Narmin's prophesy? But now was not the right time. "Come on, it's not safe here." He shoved ka'Shino, urging her to keep moving.

Then something small punched hu'Mar square in the back. His back spasmed, arching, as he hopped in a circle to face his attacker. He knew it would be the two Albinos. A small part of him said it was better to run. That was the cat in him, but Vinegar must be getting closer because Dick hu'Mar's stubborn determination was growing stronger by the minute, and a little confrontation didn't sound bad either. He might even get some good solid answers for a change.

Unfortunately, once facing them, he was surprised by their distance. How had they hit him that hard from so far away?

Hard Boiled Cabbage: Big Trouble In Spur Central

If they did it once, they could do it again. It was hard to interrogate someone who was standing a good twenty paces away. His pessimism hinted that he was about to get the worst kind of beating—one without any answers.

He tried to weigh his options. Thinking with a palsy close by or far away was easier than when they were bridging the gap. Even when they were far away, at least those unnatural instincts were clear. Now everything was muddled. Grinding his teeth, hu'Mar forced himself to concentrate on thinking as logically as possible. Well, if getting answers was out of the equation, why not finish them off quickly?

In a moment, his concealed dart gun was in his hand. Palming it, so that its shaft was hidden behind his thick arm, he felt ready to confront his pursuers.

The two men stepped onto the cobbled street, side by side, legs apart, each hand tucked into the belly pockets of their dusters. They had something concealed within, maybe blowguns, maybe sling shots. The cobble pavers between them and hu'Mar felt like a barren no-man's land. Battle was raging nearby, but this was a place of tense calm. Tall buildings lined one side of the cobbles, the moat the other.

"Who are you, and what's your business with Juniper ka'Shino?" the one on the left called out.

Juniper, so that was her first name. He'd half expected it to sound more like her alias, or as he was coming to suspect, that of her partner's alias, Maizy. Hu'Mar tightened his grip on his blowgun. He was pretty good with it, but these guys were likely no amateurs with whatever weapon they hid either.

"What's she to you?" he said.

Hu'Mar's only warning was a slight shift in thug one's posture. A ruffle and a hiss came from his cloak, and then hu'Mar was bent over, his gut aching with a punch he never even saw.

"Our business is our own," the second man on the right said. "You're the one who doesn't belong here."

"Jealous, are we?" hu'Mar coughed, whipping his blowgun up.

Another flap of coat, that same air-slicing hiss, this time

from the second thug's cloak. Dick hu'Mar tried to brace for it, but again the punch was too fast to see, let alone block. He dropped his blowgun.

"Are you well?" the first man asked. "You don't look good."

"I ain't looked good since the day I fought my way out of the birth canal. I was ugly and mean then, and I've only gotten worse since. It takes more than a couple of punk Albinos to ruin my day." Vinegar must be close. He felt fully like himself. He spotted the ball of lint and yarn walking closer.

The first man put a hand on his companion's shoulder, keeping him from hitting hu'Mar again. "Most Toughs would've called us Bules. You don't seem like a brainless Tough to me."

"Most Toughs would've killed at least one of you by now just for following them. I can take a sucker punch or two, but I ain't no Tough."

"So what are you?" the Albino asked.

Hu'Mar forced himself to stand while keeping his stomach from retching. He wanted to charge these guys, take away whatever advantage they had, but Vinegar was also trying to tell him something. "For now, let's just say that I'm concerned that a good girl has gotten into some trouble that's a little over her head."

He only gave the Albino half his attention. Maybe arrogant casualness was what the situation warranted, maybe not, but he wanted to see what Vinegar had to say.

"What if I told you that she's in good hands?"

"Your hands?" hu'Mar asked, glancing away from Vinegar. "I get the feeling you have something to do with the trouble she's in."

The second man twisted his head around, noticing hu'Mar's distraction. He focused back on hu'Mar, a devilish grin on his ghostly face. "Hey, that your cat?"

Hu'Mar didn't like the man's tone. "Why would anyone want a dirty furball like that?"

"That's funny," he said. "Because I could swear you and it were palsies. You have that look to you." He pretended to purr and shimmied like a cat rubbing against an invisible pole.

Hard Boiled Cabbage: Big Trouble In Spur Central

Like hu'Mar had done when he rubbed against the door jam on his way out of the inn. "Tell me, mister, what's your rodent telling you?"

The first Albino peeked over his shoulder to see Vinegar. It was now or never. Hu'Mar charged. Unfortunately, he only covered half the distance before an invisible hissing fist pounded into his side. He tottered slightly, trying to ignore the sharp pain. Two more came, one catching him in the temple. A terrible headache blossomed in his skull. The blows were so fine, not like fists, but like the bumpy knobs on the end of brass knuckles.

He fell a few paces away from the two Albinos and endured two more impacts. A small pliable pellet fell to the ground. Another soft pellet bounced off his forehead, increasing the headache. It must have come from a very powerful form of blowgun that needed no lips to blow. Obviously, they weren't trying to kill him, or they would've used something sharper or harder.

The talkative Albino risked coming closer. "Ready to tell me what your pussy cat said to you?"

"What good would a cat be to me? I was only looking at it because I was surprised to see something more hideous than two ugly Bules."

This earned him a swift kick in the back.

"Sorry," hu'Mar said. "Didn't mean to hurt your pride. If I were that cat, I'd run away before you got jealous and tried to kill it."

Vinegar was backing away. Hopefully that meant he'd gotten the message.

The Albino gestured to his partner who was half facing the cat.

Hu'Mar closed his eyes, as the bond weakened quickly. A distant and pain filled "Reow," sounded from a distance. Then there was a splash from the waters of Lake Tallow, and sudden fear gripped hu'Mar. Gone was his arrogant self-confidence, replaced by a feral fear of his captors. With teeth bared, he unclenched his fists, ready to swipe at them, but had to remind himself that he lacked claws for such a defense. His mind was too cloudy to think straight.

The nearest Albino was silent until his companion returned. "Where's the cat?"

Hu'Mar knew the answer before the word left the Albino's mouth. "Dead."

"You should've brought it back alive."

"Sorry, I guess my air sling was too strong for its body. I killed it with a single shot. It made it all the way to the moat, so I kicked it in."

Hu'Mar retightened his hand into a fist, as anger and disappointment burned away the fog in his mind. Vinegar was gone. He was a palsy without a bond. He'd go insane if he didn't find another cat and soon. This was not a distraction he needed right now. His face reddened, deeper than a sunburned Bule as he got to one knee. These killers would bleed for that.

The Albino placed a foot on top of his balled fingers. "Ungh-ah—none of that." He knelt down and pulled out a dagger, placing it under hu'Mar's chin. "We didn't mean to kill your friend. We just wanted to threaten it. I guess I'll just have to threaten you directly. Whoever you are, whatever your game, stay away from ka'Shino, she's nothing to you. Frankly, she's not much to us either, not anymore. She's becoming a liability, and you know how that goes."

"Speaking of loose ends, where'd she go?" asked the cat killer.

"Oh great." The first Albino pulled his hood back and spun around. "Ernes hu'Toe isn't going to like this."

"What should we do with this guy?" the second asked.

"Leave him. He's nothing."

After they were gone, hu'Mar crawled back to his blowgun. He slid to the wall of a building, opposite the moat, and leaned against it. He hurt. Purple welts stung his whole body, and that sucker kick had possibly cracked another rib. On top of that, yesterday's pains still lingered. He didn't know how much more abuse his body could take. He hadn't been smart enough to drop this case earlier when it was still possible, but he was in as deep as he could be now. Either he figured this out, or death would relieve him of it sooner than later. Then he grinned. This beating hadn't been completely in vain. He'd assumed that he'd get nothing out of these two Albinos, but he'd been wrong.

Like ka'Shino, this Albino had let a name slip. Hu'Toe. Plus, there was that short bit of info that Vinegar had passed along before he was sent swimming with the fishes. Poor cat. Despite everything, he really did like the tangled eyesore.

Chapter 27

Partners

Juniper ka'Shino clung to the rock wall that dropped into the moat. From the corner of her eye, she saw hu'Mar's cat go flying into the water. If it was floating, it might pass by her, but would still be out of reach. Besides, she couldn't swim, and it was taking everything she had to keep from falling in herself. The dark shapes that passed beneath her shaking feet were ample reminder that another world lurked below that glossy surface, and it would be more than happy to rip her apart.

After what felt like ages, she strained and lifted her head above the cobbled street. Hu'Mar sat against a building, barely moving. The two Albino thugs that hu'Toe had sent after her were running up little alleyways and back, looking for her.

She let herself dip below view. The rocks of the moat wall, cooled by the water below, felt good against her face. Once her arms began to tremble from the strain of holding her body, and it felt like they might give out, she abandoned her hiding spot, and pulled herself above the street.

Nobody was there, except hu'Mar. With arms that felt like limp soggy pasta, ka'Shino clawed the rest of the way up, then rolled onto her back. To risk staying in the open for too long would be foolish. Who knew if those thugs would return.

Holding her tired arms, she ran to hu'Mar as quietly as her feet would permit. The cobbles of the pavement made little sound under the light treading of her shoes, yet every random pebble that scraped between them, also scraped at her anxiety. Could anyone else hear that?

Hu'Mar was bad off. He'd been beaten within inches of his life, and from the look of it, not all of it had happened today. There was something else though—a resignation. His cat, the one that had splashed into the water—hu'Mar's palsy bond had been severed.

She knelt beside him and placed a hand on the back of his. They were strong hands, the sort a woman might like to depend on. He flinched as if now realizing that he had company. She thought of taking her hand from his, but didn't, as he blinked several times before sitting up straight.

"You all right?" he choked, as if trying to turn the focus back onto her instead of himself.

"Yeah, I think they're gone." She didn't know what to do. Hu'Mar had turned out to be a decent enough guy after all. It hurt to see this strong-willed man reduced like this, especially since he'd lost his cat trying to protect her. "You know, there's lots of cats around. Maybe we could find you another one?"

"You don't have many palsies underground, do you?" hu'Mar grunted as he tried to stand.

She knew that this palsy stuff wasn't as simple as finding a random species and claiming it, but to hu'Mar's point, no. There weren't many species besides human that lived in the Albino cities, and thus, she hadn't been exposed to the practice until she came topside a couple of years ago.

Once up, ka'Shino took hu'Mar's arm.

"Thanks." He let her help hoist him to his feet.

He stood and stretched. Cracks and pops, muted by skin and muscle, creaked a little too audibly. Ka'Shino saw him flinch as something, probably broken ribs, spasmed in his chest, and she had to steady him to keep him from falling over in pain. "Clearly, I'm no Tough," he half laughed, half winced.

Not much of a softy either. For a guy who looked like he'd been put through a meat grinder, yet still wanted to keep going, there was something admirable there.

"You know, I really did like that cat. It was ornery and ugly, like me. You're right though, I will need a new cat soon enough," hu'Mar said. "The younger and hungrier it is, the easier it will be to convince it to share a bond, but that'll have to wait. What's this thing you called a bomb?"

Ka'Shino bit the bottom half of her lip. Clearly, she could trust hu'Mar, even though she barely knew him, but that didn't negate the conditioning she'd learned underground. Nobody was supposed to share any information about bombs with those from the surface. Top-siders dwellers were deemed too bigoted and irresponsible to wield such a power. With a bomb, it was only a matter of time before some fanatic attacked and collapsed an Albino city.

Hu'Mar waited, gently folding one arm across his chest. Those penetrating eyes scraped at her layers of reserve. "Bolt me down, why not?" As if she cared anymore. Maybe he could even help.

Chapter 28

Who's Fooling Who

Dick hu'Mar could hardly believe that a single package, one that could be carried in a backpack, could have enough power to rock an entire mountain. He'd witnessed firsthand what her black powder was capable of in small quantities, but never imagined that the stuff could produce such massive gearquakes.

Shouts, cries, howls, and all sorts of noises combined into an invisible hum. The battle had entered the city. It raged nearby, and it might even be at the land bridge heading to Mount Exclusion. So much for the Toughs' cocky over confidence about holding the hoards outside the city. By now, more species would have joined the fray. On a normal day, hu'Mar might have entertained a mild interest in the whole event. Now that he had the temperament of a cat, he bordered between disinterest and disgust.

So many people and animals striving to smash one of their own in between two heavy stones. Yet, while his developing cat instincts were mounting to replace all his human instincts, a part of him still wanted to save as many of these people and animals that were wrench bent on killing each other.

Leaving ka'Shino to her guilt felt like a good idea, but he

knew that was the cat in him. The human part of him, remembered that if he didn't act, then things would get worse. If only there was enough time to go slum around alleyways and find a stray kitten that he could trick into being a palsy. Unfortunately, time was ticking, quite literally in this case, on two of this Albino's bombs.

Plus, he was actually getting closer to solving ka'Nairie's case also. This really was all tied together. His chest ached, as did the rest of his body, but that didn't slow him down. With what ka'Shino had explained to him, everything was clicking together. His previous theory, half confirmed and half corrected, meant that he needed to act quickly. They jogged to the land bridge.

"How long do we have before the next bomb goes off?" he asked.

Ka'Shino retrieved a clicking devise from her cloak. It was in a square box probably with gears inside. It reminded him of the wooden timepiece in ka'Feebal's place, but much smaller and more complex. The needles pointed to different words, but hu'Mar didn't waste time trying to decipher their meaning.

Ka'Shino however, was more than up to the task. "If we keep up this pace," she interpreted, "we might make it in time to disarm it."

"This pace?" Hu'Mar surveyed Mount Exclusion as they ran along the moat. On flat ground, maybe he could sustain this jog if he wasn't worn completely out already. Running those steep trails though? In this condition? He tried to push it out of his mind. He had to do it, but first, they needed to cross the land bridge. Unfortunately, the thing was nearly clogged with battle.

The elite Clutch Guards had finally been called out. While humans and animals of many varieties raged in a confusing mass of battle just off the gate, the Clutch Guards with their superior strength, training, and of course, relic-enhanced abilities, formed an impenetrable wall. Wolves flew twenty feet or more into the air with a single blow from a Clutch Guard's hammer. Another Guard sliced a 400-pound, armor-clad boar clean in half with one strike.

The water below churned like a boiling cauldron as other

Guards launched spears with the speed of shooting stars, piercing much of the marine life and intervening in the underwater battles that were only visible to the Clutch Guards with their relic-enhanced vision.

"How are we going to get through that?" Ka'Shino slowed, her shoulders slumped.

Hu'Mar squinted, trying to focus on the people, not the overall battle as a whole. She had to be here somewhere. She wouldn't miss this. "There, come on."

Ka'Nairie was atop Beauford, like Vinegar had said, before he was killed. The beautiful and deadly woman was carving a path through enemy lines, up the land bridge, toward the Clutch Guards. She must've had her ring on because her attacks were almost as powerful as the Guards'. Hu'Mar squeezed ka'Shino's hand tight so they wouldn't get separated. Together they raced, each picking up a weapon from some fallen combatant along the way.

Ka'Shino chose a dagger, tore her other hand from hu'Mar's, and found another. He was surprised at how well she used the short blades. For himself, he grabbed a club since his blowgun would be completely ineffective in this fray.

Only by luck did they manage to find themselves in Beauford's wake. They fought and protected the horse's metal-plated rear, backing toward the horse as ka'Nairie pushed through and to the line of Clutch Guards.

The Clutch Guard nearly stopped hu'Mar and ka'Shino, but hu'Mar shouted, still barely making his voice heard, "We're with her!"

The Guard didn't argue. They were too busy to properly interrogate anyone, so they let them pass. Once past the bulk of the fighting, ka'Nairie kicked Beauford in the side, the horse galloped up the mountain trail.

"Wait!" hu'Mar shouted.

Ka'Nairie peered over her shoulder, then did a double take, halting Beauford. Her lip curled, like a plan had finally come together. Hu'Mar could guess that plan. He hated it. This politician would use him or ka'Shino like she had used everyone and everything around her. She was a perfectly beautiful, but poisonous snake, and still, he couldn't help but like her. In a second, she smoothly swung Beauford around, galloped over, and lit off the horse.

She was radiant, in a manic sort of way. Sweat glistened over her exposed skin, her muscles tight from the work of slaughter. Maybe it was all the abuse he'd taken on her behalf, maybe it was the way she sneered at ka'Shino, or maybe his mind was too far out of sorts without Vinegar, but despite her beauty, hu'Mar easily forced all thoughts of romance from his mind. In its place, he found ignorance. It came easier than expected. He didn't really care if he pleased her anymore. He wanted his salt, and he wanted to move on. Somewhere in the back of his mind, he realized that he'd gotten more satisfaction from helping a lowly Albino than he had gotten trying to impress this piece of eye candy.

"You found my Pin." Ka'Nairie drew a long sword. The razor-sharp blade balanced ka'Shino's chin on its edge. "I'm guessing she works for Maizy hu'Dillie?"

Ka'Shino whimpered, afraid to even twitch. Already a thin drop of blood trickled down the steel from a paper-thin cut.

"No, not her!" Hu'Mar threw his hands up to stop ka'Nairie but thought better of it. "She doesn't have your missing relic."

Ka'Nairie spit on the ground. Clearly, she didn't buy it.

Given his earlier suspicions, the final piece of the puzzle clicked into place. Ka'Nairie had said hu'Dillie, not ka'Dillie this time. She'd misspoke on their first meeting, meaning that ka'Feebal's records were correct Maizy was a male Albino, and there was only one other male Albino that had been mentioned in connection with all of this. "Maizy hu'Dillie's real name is Ernes hu'Toe, and he's been manipulating you."

"And I'm such a fool to fall for a Bule's scheme?" She twisted the sword sideways so that ka'Shino's neck was all that stood in the way of its cutting edge. "So spill it, Buley, what did this hu'Toe do with my Pin?

Ka'Shino slowly, discretely, reached into her robe, but

hu'Mar realized what she was doing. Bad idea.

Hu'Mar stepped toward the sword, his own neck forcing ka'Nairie to back the blade away from ka'Shino. "I know where your pin is, and she doesn't."

"Where is it?" Ka'Nairie sheathed her weapon, like she even needed the thing. He noticed the Ring of Strength on her finger. Even if she wasn't wearing that, her hands alone would've been lethal enough to kill them both at any time.

"You met with hu'Toe," hu'Mar thought out loud. "He promised you that he'd get the Great Clutch open early. You jumped on that idea. If you could place a human in the Clutch before anyone else suspected, then you'd be a hero, easily elected to the Beadledom. Shoot, they'd probably place you at the head of it."

"You're stalling." Her words were cold and impatient as her fingers flinched. "Get to the point."

"Hu'Toe asked for your Pin of Poison, the one you rented from ka'Feebal. Either you refused, or when you decided to give it to him, you couldn't find it. Naturally, you suspected anyone who might have known that you had the relic or who knew about your conspiracy to open the Clutch early. At some point, you might've informed hu'Toe about your contract with ka'Feebal. If you don't return the Pin to her, she gets that family heirloom on your finger. She's got an addiction to relics, and I get the feeling that she's not one that even you would dare make angry."

Ka'Nairie rubbed the Ring of Strength with her free hand. "What does this have to do with hu'Toe?"

"Hu'Toe needed that Pin." He paused as ka'Shino tugged on his arm. He staggered to the side as an arrow passed right where he'd stood.

Ka'Nairie caught the shaft with her bare hand, cracked it in two with her thumb as if it was nothing, never taking her attention from hu'Mar.

Hu'Mar cleared his throat. "Right, well, hu'Toe needed that Pin, so he contracted with ka'Feebal to acquire a second Pin of Poison. The problem was that he never intended on opening the Clutch for you. Rather, you financed and, probably, bribed the guards to give him easier access to this mountain. But he plans to destroy the Clutch, not open it."

Ka'Shino's grip tightened on his arm. He was running out of time, but if he could only get ka'Nairie's help, he wouldn't have to worry about the Clutch Guards. Then they'd stand a better chance of finding the bombs and disarming them before the mountain turned into an active volcano.

"See, that's the problem with people like you," ka'Nairie growled. "You don't like Bules, so you don't trust them. Now either you have my Pin, or you don't!"

Hu'Mar let his eyes drift down her leg. Which leg had that rash from two nights ago?

She must have assumed that hu'Mar was dodging the question, letting his eyes rest on her perfectly sculpted legs. "I thought not," she said.

"Wait," hu'Mar said, but it was too late. He lost her undivided attention.

Ka'Nairie grabbed ka'Shino and threw her onto Beauford's back. Hu'Mar lunged to grab ka'Shino's outstretched arm, but ka'Nairie was too strong and fast.

She backhanded hu'Mar, sending him sprawling onto the rocky trail. "Listen, fortune teller, next time I see you, you better have my Pin, or else don't bother."

"Leave ka'Shino. She's nothing to you!" hu'Mar protested, though a gnawing suspicion soured his stomach. Ka'Nairie now wanted ka'Shino, and there could only be one reason why. He had to stop her.

Ka'Shino pulled her two daggers and slashed expertly at ka'Nairie. Ka'Nairie had relic-enhanced strength and a lifetime of training, but this relic didn't make one's skin any tougher. The cards looked to be in ka'Shino's favor.

She slashed with one arm, only to have ka'Nairie parry the blow by hitting ka'Shino's wrists. This was followed by ka'Shino's other hand, blocked again. After half a dozen parries, ka'Nairie caught the Albino's wrists and squeezed until ka'Shino dropped the blades in pain. The daggers clinked on the rocks below about the same time one of ka'Shino's wrists snapped.

Ka'Shino gasped and screamed.

"Ka'Nairie!" hu'Mar shouted, running to catch up.

"Go back to that shack you call a home, hu'Mar. She's going to be a hero even if she's a Bule." Ka'Nairie grabbed Beauford's reins and kicked him onward. "Others would object to having a Bule enter the Great Clutch, but hey, to me, all humans are created equal." She spurred Beauford, and he galloped up the trail.

Hu'Mar pushed himself to his feet and ran after them. He didn't have time for this. He limped as fast as he could after them. Several switchbacks and a side-ache later, he spied the Clutch entrance well ahead of him. The trail led straight to it with a sheer drop-off to his right and a steep slope to his left. There was no way of sneaking up on the two really tough looking Toughs that stood guard. They parted long enough to let ka'Nairie enter, but she had to dismount and leave Beauford outside to do so.

Checking on his blowgun, he made sure that he had at least three darts still. He palmed those in his left hand, leaving the blowgun hidden behind his vest. Normally the darts would kill a man, but since these guards probably sported a few relics each, he doubted that it would do more than stun them. That was good because he didn't want to kill anyone he didn't have to.

It took him several more minutes to cross the face of the mountain.

The guards stood taller as he approached. "Halt! What is your business here?"

"I have a message from the front lines for Jodeign ka'Nairie," hu'Mar huffed. He hoped he had enough lung to shoot his darts. He reached into his vest as if to pull a letter.

"It'll have to wait. She's asked not to be disturbed."

"Trust me," hu'Mar promised, "I need to see her."

Then as fast as he could, he drew his blowgun, planted a dart in the nearest guard's neck, reloaded, and rolled as the second guard leapt a full ten paces in a single bound. His long sword nearly took hu'Mar's head off.

Hard Boiled Cabbage: Big Trouble In Spur Central

Hu'Mar barely finished his roll and shot a dart at the guard's neck. He missed because the guard leapt into the air again, with unreal speed.

Still on the ground, hu'Mar rolled twice before feet pounded next to him. The tip of the sword sliced through the first layer of his vest. Had he rolled even a quarter of a turn more, he'd be impaled, like a beetle being pinned to a board for a bug collection.

Hu'Mar stabbed the last dart into the soft unprotected skin behind the guard's ankle.

For all his acrobatic prowess, the guard flinched and jumped back. He soared and tumbled as if he'd never learned to control the agility his relic granted him. He hit the ground hard and moaned as he slipped into unconsciousness.

The guard's blood barely even showed on the dart's needle, which hu'Mar's managed to hold on to. Hopefully, it still had enough poison on it. Hu'Mar slid it into the back of his blowgun and shot Beauford in the neck.

Beauford whinnied, then staggered dizzy for a second. Hu'Mar didn't have much time. Jumping to his feet, hu'Mar raced to the horse's side. Right where ka'Nairie's leg would rub, he placed his hand, petting the horse's flank. He felt nothing. He tried to image where her rash had been and how that would translate to her leg position on Beauford. Still nothing. He pet the horse's hair down, then from side to side. Finally he ran his hand against the bristly fur and poked his finger. Yes!

Beauford staggered, stamped his feet, and bit hu'Mar's left arm, peeling away a chunk of his shirt and skin. Hu'Mar ignored the pain and pinched the sharp needle that was stuck in the horse's flank. The thing was stuck pretty good, but when Beauford bucked away, the Pin of Poison lost its grip inside the stallion's thick skin.

A single drop of blood trickled down Beauford's side, and hu'Mar inspected the Pin. It looked intact, although several days in a horse's side had turned it from bone-white to dirty brown and gray.

Beauford was no dummy though. He knew all along that

he had the relic. Hu'Mar could only guess at Beauford's reasons for hiding this from ka'Nairie, but he had his suspicions. Whatever Beauford's motivations, the relic had protected the horse from the lethal effects of hu'Mar's dart, and now he was mad.

Hu'Mar dodged from side to side as Beauford rocked back onto his hind legs and kicked like a human boxer. The last thing that hu'Mar needed was a hoofprint in his chest. He patted his vest, hoping against hope that he still had a dart remaining. Nothing. Then he had an idea.

He dodged another kick and dove for the first guard he'd incapacitated. He removed the dart from the sleeping guard and loaded it into his blowgun.

Beauford charged, so hu'Mar jumped away, and Beauford bulled into the guard instead, his hooves stamping at any human flesh he could find.

Hu'Mar winced. The guard now had at least one arm and a leg bent in completely unnatural positions. He felt sorry for the guard. That would be sore in the morning, if the guard ever woke. Hu'Mar doubted that his dart would've killed the relic enhanced guard on its own, but getting stamped by a horse was no light ordeal either.

With his blowgun reloaded, hu'Mar raised it, but not before Beauford spun around and kicked his hind legs. Hu'Mar windmilled backward to avoid getting clobbered, but the hoof connected with his blowgun, sending the weapon flying over the edge of the cliff.

Enough of this. Hu'Mar ran into the entrance of the cave. Beauford wouldn't be far behind, and hu'Mar had no idea how long he needed to run before finding ka'Nairie. Time was against him on multiple fronts, and he'd be lucky to make it through this day alive.

Chapter 29
The Tomb Of Ascension

Ka'Shino steadied her broken wrist against her chest while Jodeign ka'Nairie dragged her along by her other hand. She tried to distract herself from the pain by marveling at this holy site. Often, she imagined what it would look like here. Plenty of paintings existed, each depicting some splendid rainbow of color, brilliance, and artistic stonework, but it was well known that the Beadledom had burned any exact depictions of this place long ago. The last thing they wanted to do was give other species a clear representation of the place.

Unfortunately, this cave looked nothing like the beautiful paintings. In fact, it was pretty boring, worse than the worm-carved tunnels she'd spent so much time in. There wasn't even any glittering crystal to sparkle; only rock, surrounded by more mono-colored rock. Her wrist throbbed and she focused on keeping up with ka'Nairie to lessen the pain of her broken bone.

"I've heard a great deal about you," ka'Nairie said, sounding a little more reasonable than she had outside.

"From who? Hu'Toe?" ka'Shino asked.

"If that's his real name, then yes." Ka'Nairie pulled her into a large open cavern.

Hard Boiled Cabbage: Big Trouble In Spur Central

A cool breeze wafted through with the smell of the moat that surrounded the mountain. The ceiling was three times as tall as a human and wide enough for a whole neighborhood game of throwing, but she guessed that instead of kids tossing crystal balls, small armies were more likely to have exchanged mortal blows in this place.

"When I heard rumors that some Bule had killed Ish hu'Narmin, I thought, why would a Bule be visiting a spent prophet? I asked Maizy hu'errr, I mean, Ernes hu'Toe about this. At first, he had a hard time believing that it could be his girl, but it made sense. To open the Clutch, he needed a tunneling expert who could cause the mountain to shake.

He said that the third tremor you caused, would jumble the Clutch open early. However, those same gearquakes might damage Mount Exclusion and its neighboring residents, not to mention start the war early. Sounds like a recipe for guilt, especially for the faint of heart. Since I've rarely met a Bule whose resolve could match that of a Tough, well, it was obvious to me, that she might get cold feet. Does that sound about right?"

Ka'Shino could barely believe what she was hearing. Hu'Toe had manipulated the most conniving Tough in Spur Central! No wonder he'd gained such easy access to Mount Exclusion. "He threw me under the chariot!" she whispered under her breath. Ka'Shino was so angry that the pain in her wrist faded to the back of her mind. She had to find a way out of this. To her right, was nothing but solid cave wall. To the left, the cavern stretched out, an underground battlefield, waiting to be filled with blood. Where was the actual clutch though? For that matter, where was anything she could use to her advantage. She needed to show this Tough how strong an Albino's resolve could be. Just think! Her eyes darted around the torch-lit cavern for any possible means of escape. There had to be something she could use to her advantage.

Ka'Nairie led her along the right side of the cavern where their path led to the far end of the cavern. There, between the ground and a massive black hole, a towering stone made of obsidian rested on what might be a low boulder or altar or threshold made of onyx. This had to be the Great Clutch.

Across the cavern between a dark stretched long hole and the entrance, two Guards had their backs to her. Although they acknowledged ka'Nairie, their attention was focused the blackness below, but no, not a hole—water. That was the source of the cool, wet air. A deep and slow underground river flowed there, leading up to the Clutch.

If any water animal found this river, it could travel right up to the Clutch, and these two Clutch Guards were the last line of defense against any water species accessing the cavern.

Ka'Shino found no way, no tool, nothing that might give her a chance of escape. Her only hope was reason, and she doubted that a Tough would respond to something like that, but she had to try. "Listen, ka'Nairie, hu'Toe isn't who you think he is, he's an atheist."

"Please," ka'Nairie laughed. "Think I'll believe that? How well do you actually know him?"

"He's not trying to open the Clutch for you," ka'Shino argued. "He's trying to destroy it all together."

Ka'Nairie ignored this and asked, "How long till the next gearquake?"

Ka'Shino pulled her pocket clock out with her good hand and estimated that it would happen any time now. "It's too late to stop it. Please, let me go. I won't be able to stop it anyway."

This much was true, but maybe she could still find out where hu'Toe had hid her fourth and last bomb. Her third would make the mountain unstable, but the fourth, if everything went according to plan, would cause the whole mountain to erupt, destroying—everything! Her stomach lurched. It would, she knew it for sure now. Unable to hold it back, vomit erupted from her lips, stinging as it invaded her nose. If the last bomb went off, nothing would ever ease her conscience. Her knees buckled and she would've slumped to the ground, but even with her acidic stomach juices staining the front of her clothes, ka'Nairie held tight to her broken wrist, the pain keeping her upright, even if barely.

"You don't understand, do you?" ka'Nairie said. "I'm not

trying to keep you from stopping the next gearquake. I'm planning on putting you inside the Clutch when it opens."

Ka'Shino paused, then stumbled when ka'Nairie pulled against her arm. "It won't open!" She knew it wouldn't open, or at least, she hoped it wouldn't. She didn't want to be sacrificed.

"You should consider yourself lucky," ka'Nairie said, her voice leaving no room for argument. "You killed hu'Narmin's fish, which led to hu'Narmin's death, all to keep your deceit quiet. You committed sacrilege by tampering with Mount Exclusion, so any minister who finds you has orders to execute you on the spot. At least this way, you get to die with honor."

"No, it's not like that." Ka'Shino pulled her arm, but the broken bone pulled her back like a sharp unyielding leash. Even without struggle, the pain was quickly becoming unbearable, but in the recesses of her mind, she knew that to stay was death. If she had to tear her hand off to live, then it might be worth it. The only thing preventing her from a full-on struggle, was the guilt. Wrestling with two foes was splitting her efforts, between her mental incrimination and ka'Nairie's strong grip and physical determination, both battles were doomed to failure.

Ka'Nairie drew her sword with her free hand. "You don't have to be alive for me to place you in the Clutch."

Ka'Shino struggled, but it was no use. Maybe she deserved to die. Maybe machines of fate were offering her a mercy here. She closed her eyes and gritted her teeth, but the blade didn't pierce her.

Risking a peek, she saw ka'Nairie's craned neck looking toward the entrance. The hurried footsteps of someone sprinting, followed by the galloping of a horse, echoed toward them. It was hu'Mar, with ka'Nairie's horse close behind.

One of the Clutch Guards at the river yelled.

Chapter 30
Falling

Hu'Mar pumped his legs and arms like his life depended on it, because it did. He could hear, almost feel, Beauford's steamy hot breath as the horse caught up. He'd be trampled to death any second.

Behind him, he heard a large thud, not like pounding hoofbeats, but like something meaty being slammed hard. Beauford whinnied a loud and painful scream.

Hu'Mar slowed to a jog, then a stop. Beauford's five-gallon fedora flew over hu'Mar's head. Crouching, trying to catch his breath, he faced his pursuer. The horse was on the ground, and a relic-enhanced Clutch Guard with a large fishing spear on his back, punched the horse hard enough in the face to knock him unconscious.

"Wow, thanks," was all hu'Mar could think to say.

The Guard unlatched his spear, twirled it once, and aimed it straight at hu'Mar.

Hu'Mar's breath caught. Saved from being trampled to death, only to be impaled. He wasn't sure what was better.

"You can go back to guarding the river," a familiar voice ordered. "I'll handle this,"

Hard Boiled Cabbage: Big Trouble In Spur Central

The Guard squinted with distrust. Ka'Nairie, despite not being officially elected to the Beadledom, had somehow leveraged a measure of authority here. Reluctantly, the guard took up his position again where the river entered the cavern.

Hu'Mar placed hands on aching sides and released the breath he'd been holding. He could feel ka'Nairie's accusing eyes stare daggers at his back. Nothing like a woman's wrath. He smiled. Then pivoted to meet her glare.

His smile vanished as soon as he saw ka'Shino's neck, held by the edge of ka'Nairie' sword.

"I can't say that I never pegged you as a killer, or an honest person," hu'Mar said, "because I always assumed you were both. But I never expected you a coward."

The hairs on his neck prickled. Ka'Nairie spit on the ground, then shoved ka'Shino aside. Then, from her waist, ka'Nairie removed a small dagger. She tossed ka'Shino her sword. It clanked on the ground at ka'Shino's feet, but the Albino refused to pick it up.

"Who's the coward now?" ka'Nairie asked.

"Take off that ring and make it an even fight," hu'Mar challenged as the hairs of his neck began to prickle.

Ka'Nairie bared her teeth in amusement. She pulled her ring off and stuck it in her pocket. "Pick up the sword," she commanded.

Ka'Shino slowly bent down and grabbed it by the handle. This couldn't end well.

"Stop," hu'Mar demanded. "Ka'Nairie, the Clutch isn't going to open. Hu'Toe really is trying to destroy the Clutch once and for all. He's been using you to gain easier access to the mountain. There's two more bombs on this mountain, and if we don't find them, they'll cause this whole thing to erupt."

"A bomb?" ka'Nairie asked. "What's that?"

Hu'Mar sighed, his lip twitching at the same time. It had taken ka'Shino long enough to explain that to him the first time. There was no time to lecture now. "Don't you get it? He's jamming the Great Gears to keep any human from ever ascending again. You're not going to be the Beadledom's hero!"

Ka'Nairie, torn with indecision, clenched her fist tight around her dagger. She leered at hu'Mar, then ka'Shino, then the Clutch in succession.

Hu'Mar couldn't ignore the tingling of his neck and whisker hairs anymore. "We have to get out of here. The third bomb is about to—"

A low reverberating pop sounded from the cave walls. The solid floor no longer felt so steady under his feet. Loud, small pops cracked all around them. They were in the middle of a massive drum, and the whole mountain was beating and shifting. Dust and rock fell from the ceiling.

Large cracks formed in the smoke-stained ceiling. Boulders the size of Beauford fell. The Clutch Guards, ever on duty, nearly caught some of them as they deflected them into the river, damming it from future intruders.

Hu'Mar ran ahead of the crack and its falling debris, then dove into ka'Nairie, knocking her to the side as a heavy stone pummeled the ground where she'd been standing.

Two of the torches fell from the walls and were buried. Dust poured from the fissures like a cloud, putting out the remaining two torches. Darkness fell like a lung-crushing blanket.

"Ka'Shino!" he tried to shout over the noise, but he could barely hear his own voice.

One of the guards cried out. They were strong, but not invincible, and by the way his shout cut short, he must have been buried and killed.

At last, the shaking slowed, then stopped. A few loose rocks fell, but it was over for now. Hu'Mar coughed.

Beside him, ka'Nairie moaned. "Was that what you call a bomb?"

"I can't see a thing," hu'Mar said. The dust was heavier than any fog he'd ever encountered. He coughed again, then ripped the bottom of his shirt and tied it as a filter around his mouth. "Are you okay?"

Ka'Nairie was coughing too. He heard her follow suit, by ripping a length of cloth. He briefly considered her tight leather outfit and where she could've possibly taken a strip of cloth from, then felt a final tug on the back of his shirt. Right, she was taking it from his shirt.

A faint glow illuminated the dust ahead. It was coming toward them.

"Ka'Shino!" hu'Mar's call was muffled.

"What happened?" The pale figure wasn't ka'Shino. The remaining Clutch Guard, gray as a stone statue, sash wrapped around his face, had a single dark spot on his arm where some blood soaked through the layers of dust. He no longer held a spear, but had a torch in one hand, though it struggled to pierce the dusty air.

"The Clutch," ka'Nairie coughed. "We need to check on the Clutch."

He felt along the wall till he found the last remaining torch. He pulled it from its sconce and lit it with the guard's flame, then let the two go. This torch did precious little to penetrate through the choking cloud too. Rather than follow ka'Nairie to the Clutch, he'd searched were he thought ka'Shino had been last. He stepped carefully since now the floor was littered with sharp jagged stones.

He cleared his throat, mucus trying to battle the onslaught of bad air. Even with his improvised filter, staying here much longer would be the death of them all. Lungs weren't meant to live on rock dust, but he had to find ka'Shino. Then a weak cough sounded slightly to his right.

"Ka'Shino."

He found her feet first. A large boulder, too big for him to move, pinned her legs down. More rocks lay all around her. Dark splotches spotted her dusty body. Hu'Mar's knee sunk beside her, the dust parting to form a silty mud from blood. Not good.

Gentle as a cat, he placed a hand on her cheek.

She opened one eye, her other seemed stuck shut. "Hu'Mar—" she choked, too weak to even cough.

"Easy," hu'Mar whispered. "I'll get you out of this."

"Too late," she strained.

"No, no. You'll be fine." Hu'Mar trembled. There was no hope for her.

"No," she managed to cough. Little flecks of blood hit his face, but he ignored them. "Too late to find the last bomb. I don't know where it is."

"Relax, it'll be okay," hu'Mar promised, knowing that his promise was empty.

"It's a good thing," ka'Shino half coughed, half laughed, "that we can't remember our past lives, eh? I'd hate to remember—" She paused, unable or unwilling to finish the thought.

"I'll find the other bomb," hu'Mar promised.

"No," ka'Shino whispered, almost too weak to speak. "Not enough time. You really are a—a good— Don't waste—your life—on a fool's errand."

She grabbed hu'Mar's hand, forced her other eye open and seemed to see straight into hu'Mar's soul. She gripped his hand tighter than he thought she had strength to, smiled once, then her arm fell limp, that sympathetic smile still frozen on her delicate face. Hu'Mar reached into his pocket and retrieved her gear necklace he'd found back in the city. Then, placing it in her palm, he tightened her fingers around it.

Hu'Mar continued to hold her hand until someone else's hand rested on his own shoulder. A glance down revealed dirty feminine fingers, dark brown. He bowed his head once, then stood to face ka'Nairie with the Guard at her side. He hadn't even heard them approach.

"Let me guess, it's not open," hu'Mar spoke softly through clenched teeth.

Ka'Nairie bent next to ka'Shino and picked up her sword. She held it up, revealing that the blade had been shattered in half by a stone. It was then that he realized, she was trembling. "It's—I'm—Oh, what have I done?"

Suddenly, hoofs scraped and scampered. Like a silhouette behind a curtain, the dusty shape of a horse charged toward the Clutch.

Hu'Mar caught ka'Nairie as she fell into his arms. Like her blade, she was broken now too. Whatever strength she once possessed was now drained by failure.

"Come on, lets get out of here," he said.

Hard Boiled Cabbage: Big Trouble In Spur Central

Together they hobbled, feeling their way out. If ka'Nairie's sword was still intact, it would have been dragging behind her limp arm.

"Over here." The Guard pointed.

They followed him to where the cavern narrowed. Red light from the afternoon sun filtered through the smoke and dust as they passed through the narrow cave entrance. The dirty air wasn't all from the cave either. Smoke billowed all around the mountain, like Hu'Mar had never seen before.

Hu'Mar carefully stepped around the two Guards he'd incapacitated earlier. They were still unconscious. At the edge of the cliff, hu'Mar stood between two huge banner flags that symbolized the Clutch Guard. He pulled the ripped cloth from his mouth and inhaled the comparatively fresh sulfuric air as he surveyed Spur Central below. The battle at the land bridge had paused. People and animals were stunned by the Mountain's transformation. Bright smoking rivers of lava snaked from various parts of the mountain. Pockets of the moat were now steaming as dead fish and other sea life floated to the surface. The city itself had been shaken badly. Several buildings had collapsed. Several others were on fire.

Ka'Nairie fell to her knees. "It's a disaster."

Hu'Mar was about to respond when he heard an angry inhuman scream. At first, he couldn't place the sound, but then again, he'd never really heard a horse shriek like that before. At the same moment that recognition dawned on him, Beauford charged from the Tomb, eyes bloodshot, hoofs bleeding, and teeth bared like a ravenous wolf. He plowed, headlong into hu'Mar.

In a fit of contortions that hu'Mar didn't know he could even do, he twisted as he fell and caught the ledge of the cliff. His feet struggled against the drop below, frantically feeling the mountainside for some sort of purchase.

Chapter 31
Hanging On The Edge

Helpless to do anything but watch and strain to keep from falling, hu'Mar saw the Clutch Guard charge the horse again. When one of them charges, there are usually only two good options: die quickly, or die painfully. Beauford ignored this bit of common knowledge, and acting like a mad horse instead of a human for a change, he bucked sideways and kicked hard enough to crack through a hyst shell. With the man's momentum, either the horse's leg should be shattered, or the guard should have a hoof sticking out of his back. Neither happened, at least, if it did, it happened faster than the eye could track. What hu'Mar saw, was the Guard flying backwards, as he crashed into ka'Nairie who'd gotten up to help. Both tumbled in a heap.

Beauford had never seemed average by any standard. Even now that his hat had fallen away, the horse was anything but a subservient domesticant. His nostrils flared and those eyes, not horse eyes, but angry human eyes, promised murder. He bared his huge teeth in a ridiculous, yet frightening grin. His rock-dusted body resembled an evil stone statue come to life. If hu'Mar survived this, Beauford would surely haunt his nightmares. Maybe he ought to let go, deprive Beauford the

Hard Boiled Cabbage: Big Trouble In Spur Central

satisfaction of crushing his fingers.

The last couple of days had hurt. He was financially ruined. His palsy partner was gone. He'd solved ka'Nairie's case but without the payment or any hope of recognition. Even worse, the girl he wanted to protect was dead. He had no friends, and he'd burned his neighbors out of their apartments. If the ministers captured him again, he'd be executed. It would be easier to let go now.

Why should I go on? hu'Mar reflected as the hot wind brushed against his shaking legs, his sweaty feet threatened to slip in his shoe and send him falling down the cliff face to his doom. His life had been one big disappointment after another. He'd powered through his failures, winning just enough to keep on living another day, but could he really continue like that? Did he want to? Even his unending ambition hadn't stopped him from realizing the obvious, that he was, himself, a failure.

But his grip tightened on the rocky ledge as a measure of his former ambition gripped. He didn't want to die. I am Dick hu'Mar, he thought. I love the fight! "Ha!" he laughed, realizing it was true. In fact, he wanted to whoop and shout. He wanted to jump up and box that stupid horse, taking whatever blows the powerful beast returned in stride. He might never get ahead in this life, but he enjoyed battling every minute of it. Maybe there was some Tough blood in him after all. He set his jaw, wishing he had more time. Beauford would erase hu'Mar from this moment, and he didn't want to be erased.

The horse reared his legs, ready to trample hu'Mar's fingers, and hu'Mar tried in vain to shimmy out of the way. Then another tan figure, smaller this time, like a large dog, crashed into Beauford's neck, sending him off balance.

Within moments, several ministers lassoed ropes around Beauford's neck, restraining him. Beauford spun around and fought, backing away from his attackers and dragging them by their ropes. Ka'Nairie was trying to calm everyone down, waving her broken sword like an extension of her arm. Beauford still struggled, edging closer to hu'Mar again, but three determined ministers held fast to their ropes.

For whatever reason, probably disbelief that her faithful steed deserved to be tied, ka'Nairie sliced one of the ropes with her broken stub of a sword. The other two ropes smoked as they slipped through the grip of the ministers gloved hands. A kink in the rope caused them to fully let go.

Beauford lost his balance and fell backward over the cliff, brushing hu'Mar's back as he fell. He whinnied and ka'Nairie screamed in protest.

Hu'Mar refused to look down and watch. His own fingers were losing their grip, and he didn't like the idea of his body splashing into whatever pulp Beauford was about to be.

A dull thud reached his ears from below as hands from above hoisted him up. It was Jef hu'Rino and Banner hu'Tanner. Bacon was to the side, still licking dusty horsehair from his lips.

"Grease me," hu'Rino swore. "Hu'Mar, you keep popping up wherever there's trouble."

"Just doing my civic duty, minister," hu'Mar winced, turning to lie on his back. He hurt. Every wound from every encounter he'd faced these last couple days throbbed. "How did you find me?"

"Re forrowed yoar cats," Bacon said, his head nodding toward the trail.

"My cats?" Suddenly, hu'Mar realized that he hadn't felt like a cat for some time now. When had his sense of humanity strengthened?

He struggled to his knees and followed Bacon's attention. There were a lot of cats there. One of them, a large ugly mop of a cat, came forward.

"Vinegar, I thought you were dead! How long have you been following me?"

Vinegar sat and licked his paw. "What makes you think I was here for you, Dick hu'Vain? You left me to die in that moat after those pasties shot me. Good thing these floating locks of fur are useful for more than mere good looks."

"Right. Then why are you here? And who are they?" hu'Mar asked, realizing the second half of the answer as soon as it left his lips.

Hard Boiled Cabbage: Big Trouble In Spur Central

"I recognize real character when I see it," the Tomfather of Spur Central said as he strolled next to Vinegar. Skippy licked his flat stubby gray face. "I offered Vinegar a chance of a lifetime. Second in command to me. You know, you really should've shown him more respect."

"Respect? Him? I didn't shortchange him in any way," hu'Mar argued.

Skippy eyed Vinegar, as if asking for a translation of what hu'Mar had said.

"Ha," Vinegar snorted instead. "Hu'Mar, since I've known you, you haven't had any respect for even yourself, let alone for anyone else."

Ouch. Hu'Mar wasn't sure how to respond. There was something a little too true in Vinegar's words, and he was glad that ka'Nairie couldn't understand cat. "If you're not here because of me, why are you here?"

Vinegar studied the ministers, then looked to Skippy and his gang, then back at hu'Mar as if picking his words carefully. "As all of humanity should know, we have no ambition to attain the Clutch. At the same time, we wouldn't mind seeing the Humans leave our world. We're here to help. We have a plan to save the Clutch, but we can't do it alone."

All the cats turned to Bacon.

"Rut argh dey rooking at me forrr?" Bacon growled nervously.

Skippy explained, and hu'Mar translated the plan. The Ministry and the single conscious Clutch Guard didn't like it, but couldn't think of a better approach. In a very short time, the last bomb would go off and the Tomb of Ascension would be buried or destroyed. The Ministry needed to call a cease fight. Since wolves made up the majority of the opposing army and were nothing more than Tough versions of dogs, Bacon would act as translator to coordinate a temporary truce.

Vinegar explained, "With the wolves' heightened sense of smell, they can track down hu'Toe's last bomb faster than any human or cat could. If you want to save the Great Clutch, this is the only option."

Stopping a fight mid-battle was going to be a real trick, but it had to be done. Still, something about what Vinegar said seemed off. Hu'Mar couldn't put a finger on it yet, but it bothered him, deep inside. What was he missing?

Chapter 32

Two Dogs with One Stone

It was nice to have the Ministry on his side again, even if that meant literally on his side, helping him hobble down the trail. At least they weren't threatening him anymore.

At the base of Mount Exclusion, they surveyed the land bridge. Battle still raged, but with the aid of the enhanced Clutch Guards, the Toughs had pushed the battle back toward Spur Central again. Hu'Mar had never seen so many wolves in one place. It appeared that the Toughs and wolves were evenly matched. Some of the wolves even had relic-enhanced abilities and proved a match for even the stronger Clutch Guards. An army of Eagles with razor sharp claws circled in companies, diving and shredding easy targets, but archers, placed on the Mount itself, pegged each one that flew over the moat. Other animals still battled outside of Spur Central, even challenging the rear of the wolves, dividing some of their attention from the humans, but so far, the battle was very much the humans verses the wolves, and it was still too early to tell who might win.

"How we going to stop this?" hu'Mar asked hu'Rino.

"I'm still trying to convince myself that it's a good idea to let wolves near Mount Exclusion," hu'Rino grunted. "You do realize that once they've found and disarmed this—so called 'bomb', they'll have taken possession of the Mountain? Then we will have to fight even harder to take it back from them before the Clutch really opens."

"Yeah," hu'Mar agreed. "But think about how fun it'll be."

Hu'Rino studied hu'Mar's face for a second.

"Think of the children," hu'Mar added. "They're all fighting easy, boring battles with war-hogs and other inferior animals. This will be a challenge worth any Tough's salt."

Hu'Rino laughed. "Hu'Mar, I hate to admit it, but you aren't half as bad as you are ugly." He slapped hu'Mar on the back.

Hu'Mar grunted in pain as his ribs shifted. "So what's the plan?"

Ka'Nairie, who'd been silent this whole time, probably nursing her pride and mourning her fallen horse, piped in. "Let me handle this one. Dog—"

"Bacon!" Bacon clarified.

"Dog, you're with me. Meet me over there." She pointed to a huge stone slab that overlooked the battle."

"Here, pooch," the Clutch Guard that had accompanied them down said. He pulled a bone marble from his pocket. "We keep these for emergencies. Stick it in your mouth, but don't swallow."

"Rut is it?" Bacon asked, licking up the marble. "AND WHY—"

He stopped short and jumped. hu'Mar winced and put his hands to his ears. They were now ringing with the incredible volume of Bacon's voice.

"I see what it does," hu'Tanner commented.

"We keep them in case an enemy breaches the Clutch, so we can call for backup," the Guard said.

"RUT HAPPENS IF I SWALLOW IT?" Bacon tried to whisper, but it only reduced his volume to a loud shout. "RUT IS THIS RELIC'S SIDE EFFECT?"

"You didn't swallow it did you?" the Guard asked.

Bacon lowered his head, his floppy ears appeared floppier, and his tail tucked between his legs. He whined. The high pitch shrill made hu'Mar's skull want to shatter. The cats all fell on their backs and rolled, trying to bury their faces in the rocky ground.

The Guard rubbed his temples as the shrill whimper stopped, and explained, "The side effect is hearing damage, obviously. It amplifies all sounds coming from your body, including the back end. Be careful what noises you let escape your body until you poop out the relic."

Bacon nodded as quietly as he could.

"All right, let's do this," ka'Nairie said. She put on her Ring of Strength, climbed onto a boulder and jumped higher than hu'Mar had ever seen a human jump, even higher than some of the Clutch Guards. She landed hard, slapping the stone overlook with the palm of her hand.

The stone boomed, cracked, and sprayed a horizontal cloud of dust in every direction. The battle paused to take stock of this sonic disturbance. Bacon leaped onto the cracked stone next to ka'Nairie and barked in both dog and human for the battle to stop.

Hu'Mar, holding his ears, instructed the dog on what to say.

Bacon first spoke in human, then in dog, not giving much time between for the battle to resume. Humans hollered in protest. Wolves set their ears back, skeptical, but their wagging tails gave away their excitement.

Ka'Nairie wasn't an official member of the Beadledom yet, but her presence, along with Jef hu'Rino and the other Clutch Guard, lent the instructions the legitimacy it needed for the citizens of Spur Central, and even the Clutch Guards, to stand down. Skippy's gang of cats wisely hid from public view.

"The Clutch is not open!" ka'Nairie shouted. "The dog speaks true. Hurry, let the wolves through, or there will be no Clutch to fight over! We'll take this mountain back tomorrow!"

Bacon barked his orders to the wolves, and the fighters of Spur Central reluctantly let the wolves pass. The wolves moved slowly at first, afraid of a trap, but were soon racing up the mountain.

Hard Boiled Cabbage: Big Trouble In Spur Central

"All humans need to fall back!" hu'Mar yelled, and ka'Nairie repeated. She added instructions to help fight on the other fronts.

A few of the Clutch Guards remained behind to keep an eye on the wolves, but most everyone else dispersed, migrating to whichever battle sounded most intriguing to them.

Ka'Nairie jumped down. "What now, fortune teller?"

"Might I make a suggestion," Vinegar sauntered by, while the rest of the cats crossed the bridge. "I'd get as far away from Mount Exclusion as you can."

"But the wolves," hu'Mar protested, then gasped. It came to him. Up higher, he'd been bothered by something Vinegar had said, but now he knew. "You'd already left when I burned down our apartment."

"Lucky me," Vinegar yawned.

"Yet, a few minutes ago, you used the word bomb. You knew what those black pellets were for?" Hu'Mar could barely believe it. He searched for any other possible reason but found none. "You—you—"

"Ha!" Vinegar laughed. The other cats hissed their amusement in unison. "You're right. I recruited Ernes hu'Mole. That ground-lover set his bomb and ran off the mountain as quick as he could. Those wolves don't stand a chance of stopping it."

"Pretty good joke, huh?" Skippy said as he headed the line of cats toward the bridge. "It'll take decades to re-birth all those wolves. We would've rather that they'd attained the Clutch and rid their kind from this world all together, but even the best laid plans of Bules and cat gangs go their way. Come on, Vinegar."

"But Vinegar," hu'Mar pleaded, "You don't want to follow him. What about us?"

"Ha, you don't get it," Skippy snickered. "Even I could have never thought up something this big on my own."

"Hu'Mar?" ka'Nairie asked. "What are these cats saying?"

Hu'Mar ignored her. "You planned this?" he asked Vinegar.

Vinegar looked as smug as ever. "And to think hu'Toe will go down in history as the orchestrator, but of course humans usually get all the credit. Now they can take all the blame. If not for me, he'd still be looking at rocks with a magnifying glass. We need you humans. This was always about keeping you from ascending. You enslave horses and other docile animals for your labors, so why wouldn't we do the same thing, Dick hu'Chattel? Cats have silently guided your kind for centuries. I got a late start, due to our little palsy arrangement, but it also gave me an advantage among my own kind. It's funny," Vinegar started toward Skippy, "when I'm with you, I'm just another pussy, but on those nights I leave you, your traits turn me into something more. Skippy's teaching me how to control them so that I don't lose who I am while still using your better traits to my advantage. Good luck, Dick hu'Lonely. I'll be so much more on my own while you go back to surviving on your boiled cabbage."

"Vinegar," Skippy called impatiently.

Vinegar turned tail and jogged to his new crew, and they disappeared over the bridge.

Hu'Mar felt the uncomfortable sensation that he was being watched.

"Ahem," ka'Nairie cleared her throat. "What was that about?"

Hu'Mar turned, slowly and realized that she and the ministers were all watching him. However, that prickly feeling on his neck was growing stronger. "The wolves are as good as dead. We have to run—NOW!"

Chapter 33

Running Away Or Fighting On

By now, hu'Mar was well aware of the urgency that his instincts were warning him about. He ran, hoping that the others would follow. All he could hear, besides his own beating heart, was Bacon, barking and shouting a warning behind him.

Most likely the dog was trying to warn everyone, including the wolves. He was a good dog, but it was too late. Vinegar had won. The bomb was seconds from going off. The cats had succeeded. Humans would not ascend, and as a bonus, the cats' hated rivals would lose a significant portion of their population today. And here hu'Mar had with nothing to his name and no future.

But for some reason, that didn't bother him so much anymore. He'd treated Vinegar poorly and misjudged a lot of things, but one thing he remembered, stuck in his mind as he and the others ran over the land bridge. While hanging on the cliff, he'd felt so sorry for himself. He'd been so concerned about his reputation and his wealth, or rather lack of, then there were his glaring failures. When he was about ready to let his fingers slip off the cliff, that had been when Vinegar came within range of his palsy connection. He remembered how he felt, and how

Hard Boiled Cabbage: Big Trouble In Spur Central

his resolve to keep going had strengthened. Yeah, he might be poor. People hated his guts. Perhaps the occasional failure would always be around the next corner. The thing is, he could own that. If Vinegar could be more without him, then surely the great Dick hu'Mar could find an advantage to his inner cat that could help him make something of himself, even if he had to nail a reminder to his forehead. Whatever he became, he could and would do it with a smile.

The concussive boom was worse than the earlier gearquakes, more like rocking in a Pisser's shore-boat in a storm. He chanced a glance behind him. Clutch Guards, ministers, and ka'Nairie were all charging toward him. The mighty land bridge behind them collapsed in sections into the moat.

Section after section fell, taking a group of Clutch Guards with it. He focused his attention forward and sprinted as hard and fast as his aching body would carry him. The bridge became springy and nearly toppled as the ground shifted. Each step held the chance that his portion of the bridge would be the next to go splashing down.

First Bacon passed him. Then ka'Nairie with her relic-enhanced strength ran ahead. Banner hu'Tanner and Jef hu'Rino flanked him while the third minister fell through a crack and was swallowed by the collapsing bridge.

At last, the three remaining humans dove onto solid ground as the massive bells from above the guard shack tumbled from its mounts and crashed to the ground, smashing a large chunk of the bridge into the churning waters below. Hu'Mar rolled onto the cobbles. He wanted to scream with pain as his broken ribs grated together, but the sound wouldn't come.

He held his chest as he recovered a measure of composure. At last, hu'Rino stood over him, offering a hand. Hu'Mar refused it, knowing that any help offered would hurt more than anything. Slowly, he knelt, then got to his feet.

"Bind me!" hu'Tanner said, gawking at the destruction. "What a mess."

"It's just begun." Hu'Mar remembered Crazy Ish's prophesy and what ka'Shino had told him. In a way, this had been his fault. If he'd been better to Vinegar, the cat might not have felt a need to destroy the Tomb of Ascension. "That mountain will explode and Spur Central will be destroyed. We're far from safe."

"Come on," hu'Rino ordered. "We've got a station around the corner with a few horses. We'll get you saddled up."

"What about you?" hu'Mar asked.

"There's a lot of people left in and around the city. If what you say is true, we've got an evacuation to conduct."

They hurried around a corner and to the stable next to the Ministry building. "Take your pick." Hu'Rino stuck out his hand.

Hu'Mar grasped it. "Be safe."

"As much as I hate to admit it, hu'Mar, it's been good knowing you. I hope to see you again under better circumstances. Till then, keep your nose clean"

Hu'Mar let go, and hu'Rino, along with hu'Tanner mounted up and rode into the city with Bacon shouting the call to evacuate.

"You going to go with them?" hu'Mar asked ka'Nairie.

She looked tired. Her vibrant brown face now sagged with a shade less color. "I think—"

She didn't have time to finish before another explosion, louder than any they'd heard to this point, shook the stable. The entire city was cast under a dark shadow, making the late afternoon feel like early evening.

"Oh, no," hu'Mar whispered under his breath, too terrified to speak any louder.

Mount Exclusion was erupting.

Chapter 34

Ashes Ashes, They All Fall Down

The next sonic concussion slammed hu'Mar hard onto his back. He stood and nearly fell again as the world spun. His hat was gone, and every hair on his body tingled with the sensitivity that he wouldn't have noticed when Vinegar was around. At least the cat had taught him one good lesson about listening to your instincts before he'd abandoned him. Right now, those senses said that this was far from finished.

Feeling about in the darkness of the stable and pushing through the pain of bruises and broken ribs, hu'Mar stood steady again. He found Jodeign ka'Nairie, who surprisingly fared much worse than he. With some effort, he helped her up, and they stumbled outside the stable. She rested far enough from the wall that if it collapsed, she wouldn't be crushed. Hu'Mar ran in and fetched the first horse he could free. Back outside, they all crouched down together, and hu'Mar leaned against the horse's side, calming it and steadying ka'Nairie at the same time.

The moment passed slowly, but eventually their night vision came into focus. Then it began to snow. Hu'Mar had seen the stuff only once. He held out a palm and let a flake land on it. No, not clean white snow, but gray ash. There were big flakes of it, and tiny particles, the sort that made your lungs burn. Hu'Mar grabbed ka'Nairie's hand and squeezed. It was limp. He wasn't completely confident in her ability to stand on her own yet, so he took a moment to rip some more of his shirt off and tie it around her face to filter out some of the ash. He pulled off his vest, removed the rest of his shirt, then put the vest back on. He tied the sleeves around the horse's bridle and tucked the dangling remnants around the horse's mouth. It wasn't great, but it would have to do.

"Come on, let's go." Hu'Mar helped ka'Nairie onto the horse's back, then jumped up behind her.

The horse sat down, sliding hu'Mar off his back, then stood up again.

"Looks like he doesn't like carrying two," Jodeign ka'Nairie laughed and coughed, nearly falling off herself.

"Take that ring off," hu'Mar said.

Ka'Nairie's face fell. "I forgot I was wearing it. I'm afraid I'll collapse if I take it off."

"The toxins in your blood are already overpowering any strength it might give you. If you don't take if off now, it'll kill you," hu'Mar said, hoping that she still had enough strength to ride.

She slipped it off and tucked it into her pocket. Even that little bit of exertion threatened to topple her from the horses. It danced a little, every bit as nervous as they were. Ka'Nairie slumped visibly but held on. It was good enough. Silence fell all around them. Hu'Mar hadn't noticed its absence until it had returned. He didn't like it. With the horse's leather reins in one hand, he led them through the crumbling city. Every step felt ominous as if the mountain was taking one last breath before it vomited its lifeblood out.

In the eerie silence, hu'Mar's thoughts drifted. The fact that Vinegar would not be coming back, stung. Knowing that since before ka'Shino and ka'Nairie's visit, he'd been playing them all, hurt even worse. Hu'Mar's thoughts and instincts would be off, but the more he thought about it, the more he realized that they had been off for years. He was a good fortune teller back in the day before he'd been run out of his childhood kingdom.

Things were different now though, and it wasn't the fact that he had cat instincts to cope with. He'd lost ka'Shino, allowed the cats to destroy the Great Gears of this world, which was leading to the destruction of his current city of refuge. Despite all of this, hu'Mar would leave Spur Central anyway, but not because he was getting run out. He was ready to leave by choice. Life was precious and wonderful, but around here, life was cheap. Everyone knew that you got reborn after you died, so few people cared about killing. But ka'Shino had valued life above all else. She wanted to live, and she wanted others to live.

Unlike rabbits, humans could not remember their past lives. Dying should be a big deal. Wasting your life should be even worse. Hu'Mar couldn't go on hiding from his past anymore. He had to stop feeling sorry for his mistakes and circumstances, or else he might as well die and let his story reset. For the first time in a long time, he wanted to see what he was capable of accomplishing, regardless of his limitations and irrespective of what others thought about him. It filled him with excitement and energy that no amount of cat instincts could take away. Plus, if Vinegar could learn to control his human instincts, then why couldn't hu'Mar learn to control his cat instincts?

"Too bad I can't bond another cat as long as Vinegar's alive," hu'Mar chuckled softly. "Oh, well."

"What are you going to do about it?" ka'Nairie asked, her voice weak.

Hu'Mar shook his head. "Never mind. We should leave Spur Central now."

"Wait, I'm not leaving my city," she said, trying to grab the reins from hu'Mar, a feeble attempt.

"You want your relic back, don't you?"

"If I don't get it back soon, Renu ka'Feebal will either kill me, take my own relic, or both."

"Then we should get going."

"Are you saying my Pin relic is outside the city limits?"

"It will be soon," hu'Mar hinted as they passed through the bulk of the inner city. What remained was single-level homes, like that of ka'Feebal and other more outlying residents.

Ka'Nairie kept silent, pondering something. After a minute she coughed, then started to speak, but whatever she was about to say got cut short by another thunderous eruption from Mount Exclusion.

They all jumped, then turned to witness the destruction. From here, they could see some of the outlying battle. Of course, by now, all fighting in the city itself had stopped. Everyone watched as impossibly blacker clouds billowed and puffed, its smoke rising in the twilight of dusk.

Hu'Mar felt it on the back of his neck first, then inside his gut, an indescribable discomfort, almost like butterflies in his belly, or more appropriately, like sand dancing on a vibrating drum. The sensation quickly moved to his feet. From there, it moved to the rest of the world.

Rocks clattered in place, and hu'Mar had to crouch just to keep his balance. The two large banners mounted at the entrance to the cavern of the Clutch were lowering. They weren't just falling over, but they were sliding, along with the whole side of the mountain, as if they were melting.

Hu'Mar rubbed the hairs on the back of his neck. Even the stubble of his three-day old mustache quivered. They were still too close to the volcano to be safe. His cat instincts were clear, and he wasn't about to complain.

Ka'Nairie stared, dumbstruck at the mountain. Hu'Mar yanked the reins and made the horse run to keep up. The ground below felt unsteady, like standing on the floor of a large carriage. He sprinted, only checking back a couple of times to make sure that ka'Nairie was still holding on.

"What are you—" She protested but was cut off by a deafening blast that made all conversation mute by comparison.

Hu'Mar pulled the horse to the left as a nearby home crashed down, sending stones tumbling their way. One wrong footstep could send any one of them crashing painfully to the ground. He couldn't tell how long the noise lasted, but the steady pounding of it eased into a loud unrelenting boom, accompanied only by the high-pitched ringing in his own ears.

Dry aged wood from the old houses twisted and splintered, scattering along their path like a giant game of drop sticks. One little spark would set the whole city ablaze. It wasn't a matter of maybe catching fire, but of how quickly before it happened, and how fast it would spread. The threat of it, only spurred him on faster, ignoring every pain in his beat-up body that went along with the pace.

The horse whinnied and he turned back to look into the horse's face. Hu'Mar didn't have to be a horse palsy to tell from the horse's head gesture, that he was being invited to climb onto its back with ka'Nairie. Maybe it finally decided that it could move faster carrying both of them, rather than being led along by the leash of a slower human.

Hu'Mar jumped on behind ka'Nairie as horrifying streams of glowing orange magma continued to burst from the side of Mount Exclusion, like the pulsating artery of a stuck pig with high blood pressure. Boulders and rocks rained from the sky. Hot hissing globs of melted rock splashed all around. The horse ran for all it was worth. It trusted hu'Mar's softest commands as hu'Mar relied on his cat instincts to swerve them from the worst of the debris that fell in crushing heaps from the sky.

Moments ago, he could clearly see the whole of Mount Exclusion, but now, he could barely make out where the flags had once denoted the opening to the cavern of the Clutch. Not only were they gone, but so was the whole side of the mountain where the Clutch should have been. In its place was a rushing storm of smoke and brimstone.

Hu'Mar couldn't help but compare it to a disease. Only this was no simple head cold with lava flowing from its nose. It looked more like the world was vomiting in the most violent manner, thrusting the toxins of generations out its ever-widening mouth.

The formerly advancing armies were now gone as if they never existed. Hu'Mar didn't know if they had all dispersed, been charred into ash, or were buried under rubble. With all this ash, it was getting harder to see anything. On top of that, the raining lava was igniting those fire's he'd been afraid of. The flames and their smoke would soon obscure even the mountain.

He coughed, his lungs barely able to keep up with his needs. Then a boulder crashed directly in front of them. He'd been using his cat instincts to navigate the worst of the raining death, but had allowed himself to get momentarily distracted. The horse whinnied and bucked nearly throwing them as hu'Mar reached over ka'Nairie, stroking the animal's neck. "It's all right," he reassured as best as his voice could croak. "We got this."

Hu'Mar gently kicked the horse's sides and rounded the boulder. More debris fell, and the horse finally took its own initiative to divert around them. Good thing too, because hu'Mar wasn't an experienced rider. He gave the horse its head and let it run as fast as it wanted away from the city, away from the raining rock and ash, away from Mount Exclusion and what remained of Spur Central.

Once out of the city and still spooked, it refused to slow, outpacing every refugee on the road. It was huffing and sweating. Hu'Mar didn't know much about horses, but this was pushing the bounds of any animal's endurance. Usually when a horse was ridden this hard for this long, they tended to fall over dead, or so he'd heard. "Good girl," he soothed, though in truth, there hadn't been any time to check and see if it was a girl or a boy horse.

The only response he got was from ka'Nairie, as she rested her head back onto him. She must be completely exhausted to respond like that. He held her tightly as she relaxed even further. Good thing too, otherwise she would've fallen right off. He wasn't even sure if she was conscious right now.

He tried to calm and slow the horse and pull back on the reins. It wouldn't be good for any of them if it gave itself a heart attack, but it didn't work. So he did the next best thing. He removed the Pin of Poison from his pocket and poked it into the horses rear flank. It didn't even notice, but soon its breathing became steady and its stride evened out. It kept on running through the night and on till dawn.

Finally, hu'Mar placed the Pin back in his own pocket,

making sure that some of it poked through the cloth and rubbed against his skin. He needed the endurance now. His butt was tired and sore from bouncing so long on the beast's back. Without the help from the relic, the horse tired quickly again. Finally, it stopped, and hu'Mar slid off. Ka'Nairie, drowsy as a drunken Pisser, tried to climb off, but hu'Mar had to catch her as she fell. His body shot with pain as she landed in his arms. She was a lot heavier than she looked—that or he was a lot weaker than he thought. Either way, she needed the Pin more than he did.

Stiff and bowlegged, she tried to work some natural movement back into her limbs.

Hu'Mar stretched, hoping that the relic would've eased some of the discomfort from his broken and bruised bones. Unfortunately, the relic-enhanced endurance didn't help with that sort of problem. He was about to give ka'Nairie the pin when he went dizzy. The ground competed against his will, and the ground won the glory of sending him into a painless bliss of unconsciousness.

Chapter 35

Courting ka'Nairie

The sun barely brightened the morning through the clouds of ash and smoke. The ever-present thunder from Mount Exclusion could still be heard in the background of hu'Mar's mind. He rubbed his face, staring beyond the large hilly field of cabbages where he lay at the cloud of destruction. How many people could've survived?

What about Vinegar? He couldn't see any possible way of the cat making it out in time. When next he finds some kittens, he'd try bonding one of them. If he found a cat willing to be a palsy, and the bond worked, it would mean that Vinegar was truly dead. He wasn't sure how he felt about that. The cat had been about as loyal as a cat could be, at least until it completely betrayed him and attacked all humanity. Already he missed Vinegar. Would he ever find a cat quite as ugly?

He sat up. It hurt, but he could bare if for now. Ka'Nairie lay next to him, still sleeping. Her face looked blotchy and sick. He touched her hair and forehead. She was hot, probably had a fever.

She blinked a couple of times before she recognized hu'Mar. Straining, she grabbed him. It took all he had not to hiss from the pain as she pulled herself up next to him. They both gazed over the green hill at the great view of destruction. Her eyes moistened. "I worked so hard, and now it's all gone."

Hu'Mar kept his mouth quiet. It was hard to say anything when holding back his own wails of pain. Instead, he held her and rubbed his head into hers, like a—a cat. He pulled away quickly. But then she nestled into his shoulder. He liked this lady. Yes, she was manipulative and rough, but also vulnerable in a way that made her more human.

Ka'Nairie was the stuff fantasies were made of. She was smart, deceiving, sometimes reckless, and a little more than crazy, exactly what he expected every good woman should be. Part of him knew that it could never work. He went above and beyond the call of duty, risked life, limb, and sanity for her. Why?

Tracing a hand down the back of her tan ash-stained vest, he rubbed against the smooth brown skin of her arms as she held to him for comfort. This is what he had dreamed of. Right now, it would be so easy to try to make a relationship work with her.

When he'd watched the single Toughs' court shipping the other night, all he could think about then was ka'Nairie and how unlikely it was that he could win her heart unless she threw the fight for his love. The way she held to him right now suggested that she might, and even if she didn't, she was weak enough that he'd stand a chance.

He held her for several long deep breaths, enjoying the moment and solidifying his resolve. There are moments that feel too perfect, where time slows down, and everything, including this green cabbage field on a hill, overlooking a deadly volcano, is beautiful. He let out a shaky breath. Well, I've come this far to help her, he thought. Now she needed him more than ever before. He pulled her away from him just enough to look into her eyes. They were wet, wide, and waiting. His stomach did one final summersault before he pulled her in tight, pressing his lips to hers. He kissed her long, and she kissed him hard.

Suddenly, he pulled away. "This can't work. I'll become more like a cat: snuggly one minute, ignoramus the next. I'll be happy as long as I'm fed, fat, and lazy, but as soon as you ask me to fight, I'll complain till you hate me."

She pulled him back and kissed him nearly suffocating him, obviously not interested in excuses.

This time when they let go, he took a step back, allowing both of them to take a deep breath. She put her hand to her chest and gave him a soft smile. Gears above, she might really go for him. His breath came in shallow excited gasps. He knew what he needed to do, but that didn't make it easy, not for him. "Grease me for this," he muttered under his breath as he balled his fist in anticipation, gave her his best, most confident smile, then swung his fist as hard as he could into her kisser.

It was cruel, and it was a sucker punch, but it was necessary. She fell backward, hitting the ground hard. Shock, anger, and amusement took turns playing across her face.

Hu'Mar turned, gritting his teeth. That had been kind of fun. He heard her jump to her feet. She actually growled at him, but he ignored her, walking toward the horse. It stamped nervously as he approached. He'd just reached the horse when blessedly strong hands gripped his shoulder and spun him around.

Jodeign ka'Nairie wasn't angry: she was murderous. According to Tough tradition, he shouldn't have turned his back as if the fight were finished. Hu'Mar could see the print of all four of his knuckles in her face. She pulled the dagger from her beautiful ashy black hair and held it before her.

"Sorry," hu'Mar said. "I'm not a Tough, so I'm not familiar with all the rules of your mating rituals?" It was only a half lie.

He had hit her when she was most vulnerable, something she might have actually welcomed, but by turning his back to her, he'd rudely suggested that the courtship was won and that he had bested her. Toughs fought for love and respect, and while fair had little to do with war, it sure mattered for love, or at least around here it did. That punch though, hadn't been about love or respect. Well, maybe it had, but on a completely different level. He'd taken it too far on purpose.

"Mate?" Jodeign ka'Nairie laughed. "You are so below me. I can't believe you'd even entertain such a fight!"

"You're just sore about being beaten so quickly," hu'Mar

said casually. "We've got a long road ahead of us. Up ahead is the kingdom of Nebylon. You might be on good terms with the king there, but I'm not, so we'll have to ride on and maybe settle down in Jerush or Salone."

"I'm not going anywhere with you," she sneered, advancing closer with that blade. "I'm going back to Spur Central."

She swung the knife at him, and he caught her arm, barely. Despite her weakened condition, she was strong, even without help from any relics. Had she not been so weak, he might not have been able to stop her. Still holding her blade hand, he pulled her to try for one last kiss. It was a long shot, but she needed one last straw to cement her resolve. She dropped her knife and kneed him in the groin before yanking herself away.

Her knife on the ground, hu'Mar let go. That had better be enough because he was done, but still he refused to let his smile waver. "I'm not going back there with you. There's nothing for me in Spur Central, but there will be survivors. Shucks, I'll be surprised if even half of the Beadledom survived. They'll need you more than ever."

She stared at hu'Mar, her angry clenched jaw slowly smiled.

"It's a good thing you didn't give me that beautiful smile before I slugged you," hu'Mar said. "I might have been a perfect gentleman and had a harder time pushing you away."

"To think that my rivals all called me Jodeign ka'Niving," ka'Nairie laughed. "And here I stand, bested by a Bule and manipulated by a lowly fortune teller."

"What're you going to do now that the Clutch has been destroyed?" hu'Mar asked. "Winning the Clutch for the human race has been the whole purpose behind Tough culture."

Ka'Nairie shook her head. "The Beadledom is likely in shambles. I'll probably be able to step into power without so much as an official election. I don't know what to do once there though. Not anymore, at least."

"Don't worry," hu'Mar said. "I'm sure you'll find something. There's always a need for meat heads out there."

"Thanks for saving me from the volcano, and from being

a pathetic Tough," she said.

"Hey, you hired me. I'd never get paid if I let you die."

"And if I had ridden off into the sunset with you?" She threw him a flirtatious sideways smirk, suggestive enough that hu'Mar knew it was impossible, like when they first met at his office three nights ago.

"Yikes," hu'Mar said. "Then I'd for sure never get paid. In fact, if I had any money left at all, I'd rather give all to you now, if it kept you from marrying me. It'd be a lot cheaper in the long run."

"Ha!" She laughed, then held her stomach. "And the relic you promised? I bet it's covered in rubble and ash by now, isn't it? Or did you really even know where it was?"

Hu'Mar frowned. "You feeling okay?"

"I feel like crap. It'll take a few days to recover, but I'll pull through. This is the most I've ever dared use the Ring without the Pin. It's weird though, I haven't worn the ring all morning, and yet I seem to be feeling worse instead of better."

"Well, me poisoning you probably didn't help much either."

Her eyes lit up, lips parted, confused. "You poisoned me?"

"Just a little. No more than when you kissed me after your last political debate," he said. "Over the last couple days, I've been beaten and abused. I shouldn't have had the strength to get you here in the first place."

"Y-you," she stuttered, "you had the Pin of Poison this whole time?"

Hu'Mar shook his head. "Not the whole time." He scratched the back of his neck. "I meant to give it to you last night, but then I kind of fell asleep." He retrieved the Pin from his pocket. It sure had come in handy. He might not have escaped Spur Central without it.

"Who stole it from me?" She snatched the relic from his fingers.

"Nobody," hu'Mar said. "You had it the whole time."

Ka'Nairie folded her arms and waited for an explanation.

"When you kissed me three nights ago, I felt nauseous.

It might have been coincidence, but after you kissed me again, you made me physically sick like I'd been poisoned."

"But I didn't have it," ka'Nairie protested.

"No, but if you recall, you were running seriously low on energy during that debate until you mounted Beauford. That rash on the inside of your leg, where do you think that came from?"

She didn't take her eyes off hu'Mar but bent over and rubbed the rash with her finger. "Go on."

"When I visited your hairdresser, his… flamboyant helpers, used my pants as a pin cushion. Since the Pin of Poison is about the size of a small hair pin, I figured you probably kept it hidden in your hair. When Dussel hu'Nuff, or Duke as his friends call him, was working on your hair, he probably stuck the Pin in your pants without you noticing. My best guess is that you left in a hurry before he remembered the Pin, and you rode off somewhere with Beauford."

"Yeah, that was the first day I was meeting with Maizy, er, I mean Ernes hu'Toe," ka'Nairie confirmed. "But I would've noticed the Pin in my pants at some point?

"You would have," hu'Mar confirmed, "if it hadn't rubbed against Beauford's flank where it stabbed him and stayed."

"But why would he have let it stay there?" ka'Nairie asked. "That doesn't make sense."

"You're not a palsy," hu'Mar said. "But unfortunately, I've palsied a cat, and I can tell you from experience, they have their own motives. Even as a palsy, I didn't see Vinegar's betrayal coming. You think because they're with you or because they serve you, that they'll stick around through anything. It would be easy if they were as stupid as insects, but they're as smart as you or me, and sometimes just as deceptive. Beauford saw a chance for horses to escape their slavery and ascend. So he played loyal to you, hoping that the Pin and your trust might eventually give him the opportunity to take the Clutch for his kind."

"Was that the cat's goal too?" ka'Nairie asked, studying their new horse as if it might be eavesdropping on their conversation.

"Nah," hu'Mar said. "Cats actually like humans, despite what they say. They want us to be the horses of this world. We build modern conveniences, and they lay about enjoying the fruits of our labors."

"What about the poisonings and murders?" ka'Nairie asked.

"Easy," hu'Mar explained. "Beauford and the stableboy were sharing carrots. The stableboy got poisoned from Beauford's saliva. Ish hu'Narmin was killed indirectly by Juniper ka'Shino—"

"The Bule from the Clutch?" ka'Nairie interrupted.

"Yeah, her," he continued. "She had a Pin of her own, but she might have also been contaminated by Beauford's slobber when accosted by him outside my apartment. She accidentally poisoned hu'Narmin's fish, and Crazy Ish, not having enough sense left in his brain, got slammed with fish instincts from losing his palsy, and so he drowned himself, thinking that he needed water to breathe."

Ka'Nairie twisted the bone Pin between her fingers. "So much trouble for this little thing. You know, Renu ka'Feebal came by my place yesterday. That woman is dangerous. I had to sneak out of my house so she wouldn't see me. She really wants my Ring. I thought that maybe it had even been her who stole the Pin back from me, just to pin the loss on me and obtain my family heirloom."

"Yeah," hu'Mar agreed. "I considered that too. There's more to that lady than what she lets people see."

"Think she survived?" Ka'Nairie put an arm around hu'Mar as they stared over the distant ruins of Spur Central.

"I'd almost count on it," hu'Mar said. "She's probably drinking lava right now and getting mad at the mountain for not giving her anything stronger."

Ka'Nairie laughed. Already, the Pin of Poison was helping her since she no longer held her stomach. She gave hu'Mar one last squeeze but held back a poisonous last kiss. "I'll see you around, fortune teller." She jumped onto the horse's back, causing it to lift its head from the field, a half-eaten cabbage in his mouth. Ka'Nairie clicked her tongue and tapped the horse's flank to turn him around.

"Hey!" hu'Mar called as the horse trotted away.

Ka'Nairie reigned it in and twisted in the saddle.

"Fortune tellers don't work for free," he said.

Ka'Nairie smirked. "You didn't give me any fortune."

"That's debatable."

"Listen, hu'Mar, thanks, I mean that. But we've all lost something today. If the Tomb of Ascension weren't bad enough, many of us have lost our lives and our homes. It'll take everything we have to rebuild. Hard times are here. I wish I could repay you, but for now, let's just say I owe you." She kicked the horse and galloped back to the rubble of Spur Central.

Spoken like a true Tough politician. He smiled. He reached inside his own vest pocket and pulled out a leather pouch with the initials J-N. From it, he counted three bromines, ten salines, and several salt chips. He cinched the drawstring on the money bag, tossed it in the air once before slipping it back into his vest pocket.

He smiled and chuckled softly to himself. What kind of fortune teller would he be, if he couldn't predict that she'd refuse to pay? The only fortune tellers that went out of business were the ones who didn't know how to pick a pocket. He purred as only a human could, which sounded more like a grumbly hum as he walked away. He cursed, realizing what he was doing, but continued to purr all the same.

He had a lot of thinking and reflection still to do. Jodeign ka'Nairie's case was solved. So too was the mystery surrounding Juniper ka'Shino. Despite his body, which would take time to heal, he felt better now than he had in a long time. One question still nagged at him: Ish hu'Narmin's prophesy, the one that mentioned him by name.

Some of it made sense. Some didn't. True, he'd been slightly involved with it up until now. After all, his brief association with ka'Shino and ka'Nairie had brought him near the catastrophe that happened on Mount Exclusion, but not enough to justify being specifically named in a prophesy about it.

Maybe indirectly he was responsible, for mistreating Vinegar, driving the cat to seek fellowship with the Tomfather of Spur Central. This whole thing might have been Vinegar's plan to get into Skippy's gang. Skippy obviously liked the idea, and since Vinegar could speak human to communicate with the Albinos, it made the crazy plan possible.

Though hu'Mar hated the thought of it, something told him that this prophesy, this riddle, had yet to fully be realized. Otherwise, Vinegar would have been mentioned, not hu'Mar. He shuddered at the thought. It was time to get moving. If there was anything left in hu'Narmin's words, it would catch up to him eventually. Maybe if he put enough distance between himself and the destruction back there, then he could forget this whole mess. This was one mystery he didn't want to solve.

He'd lost Vinegar, but gained, something—something he couldn't quite put into words, but it was good. He had a little money in his pocket, and for the first time in a long time, he looked forward to whatever the future brought.

Bending over, he picked a large green cabbage, scaring a large manic rabbit from behind another nearby plant. As the rabbit raced down the road, trailing a litany of undiscernible curses behind it, hu'Mar stared into his cabbage long and hard as if it could divine some mysterious future. When it told him nothing, he reared his arm back, ready to test his aim at the retreating hare, but paused, considering the poor-man's food one more time, then tucked the ball under his arm and hiked along the open road.

Chapter 36
Afterward

The crawl space was too confined to risk a candle, so Renu ka'Feebal wriggled out from under her flattened house, pushing the large sack of bones ahead of her. The sun was up, a pinprick of light in a dark as night sky, like a bright star that would never hurt the eyes. Thick ash and smoke had replaced the showering boulders. Mount Exclusion was still pumping lava, but the concussive part of the eruption had ended.

Unlike the less fortunate Toughs around here, she could breathe more easily, thanks to her countless relics, of which she counted often. Everyone else in the city was scrambling about, not sure of what to do. Their precious Clutch was destroyed; all hope of ascension gone. Most likely, knowing the Beadledom, if they even survived, they'd lead the remaining Toughs on a crusade to do who knew what. Frankly, ka'Feebal could care less.

She sorted through her bones, relics, and half-formed relics. Hu'Mar's cat had only found some of her bones. Even that felt like a violation. If there was even one bone missing, every cat around would regret the day Vinegar stole from her. Luckily for them, nothing appeared to be missing. She'd spent her whole life searching for and collecting the remnants of long dead bodies. Every bone in her house had once resided inside the Tomb of Ascension. There was deep power in those bones. With the Tomb destroyed, this city would never come back to life. She bent down and picked up a small pendant, then pulled out a pocket file and beveled an edge. She felt its power increase.

Butterflies filled her stomach. Honing a relic was an art form. Each piece of bone had power, true, but giving it the perfect shape, somehow magnified the power. It might magnify the pitfalls too, but paired with the right relics, the side effects could be managed. It was as if the bone was still living and had a will to be something more than an ivory remnant of a carcass. It wanted to be beautiful, rewarding anyone willing to make it so.

Of course, no relic could ever replace food, no matter how powerful it was. From time to time, she had to loan her relics out. It was a necessary evil to make a little income. The necessity of it ate at her every time. There was no denying that she was an addict. Few people even knew that this hobby could be addicting, but after years of breathing in the dust of relics, to have any of them unaccounted for was torture.

Reluctantly, she grabbed several travel boxes and carefully packed all the relics away. Each relic had a name, a personality. Even if there were duplicates of some, like the Pins of Poison, they had their subtle personalities. Not one of them was missing, except for that second Pin of Poison. She'd collected its twin from Juniper ka'Shino's corpse. After not finding ka'Nairie at home, she'd hiked Mount Exclusion. Whether she passed ka'Nairie on a different path, she didn't know, but when she entered the Tomb of Ascension, she found the dead Albino, along with one of her Pins.

If not for her relics, she would never have made it off the Mountain alive. Even now, despite the stink of the volcano, she smelled of her swim back across Lake Tallow. That body of water was now a memory, all its water and sea critters, now replaced with flowing lava.

Just like with ka'Shino, it didn't matter if ka'Nairie was dead. She'd find that woman or her corpse if necessary and collect that Pin, and hopefully that Ring of Strength too. With a whole half a skeleton left from where the Pin of Poison came from, she could easily make another Pin of Poison, but that Ring of Strength came from a species that ka'Feebal only had nine relics from. It was rare indeed. She wanted it, needed it. Strapping her last box shut, she carried them outside to her waiting donkey truck. Of course, there was no actual donkey, that would have to be her job to pull it. No big deal.

She placed all the boxes on the bottom, a toiletry or two and a single change of clothes above that, then filled the rest of the truck with skins of her slab arrack. With one last look at her shack, it was time to leave it forever. It wasn't like it was home, not really. Home was wherever her relics and skeletons were. Right now, that meant home was a donkey truck.

She grabbed the two poles, where the beast of burden would normally be yoked, and lifted. "Ah, home sweet home."

The only problem with this home, was that it didn't leave a free hand for a wine skin. She'd have to make a drink holder. There was no telling how long she'd be on the road, so a little comfort would be nice. Only one thing left to do before leaving this ash forsaken city: find Jodeign ka'Nairie and take that Ring as payment. No excuses this time.

If her path ever ran across hu'Mar, and if he really did know where the Pin of Poison was, she might hire him to recover that for her too. This day couldn't possibly get much better.

With a joyful whistle, she pulled her cart out of the fenced yard. She was about to work her way toward ka'Nairie's house, when who should come trotting up, but ka'Nairie herself.

Ka'Feebal sagged in unison with her hopes as ka'Nairie stopped and tossed the Pin of Poison to her. The little needle bounced off her chest and landed on the ash, leaving a dimple where it sunk to the earth beneath.

With a sigh of resignation, she rested the cart, then bent over to find the relic. When she stood, all that could be seen was Jodeign ka'Nairie's back and the bouncing butt of her horse as they trotted away.

No Ring of Strength today. Her afternoon had just turned a little more depressing, but at least she had her own relic back.

Hard Boiled Cabbage: Big Trouble In Spur Central

She picked up her cart again and pulled it away from Spur Central where ash still fell in large, beautiful gray flakes. She was in no hurry, had no worries, and no place to go.

Hours down the road, she passed a field of cabbages. All those decorative green domes poking out of the ground, like a community of silent heads, made her hungry for a little company. She'd never wanted, nor needed that in the past, but her mind kept drifting to the one man who'd proven a match for her wits. *Who are you, really, Dick hu'Mar?*

Find more great entertainment from Blue House Publishing and LightMinded arts at www.LightMindedarts.com

Dear Reader,

Please visit my website at www.LightMindedarts.com There you can follow my storytelling journey. I love to write books. I also love all forms of storytelling, from visual to personal. As such, I have started an independent film studio, where I can turn my written words into movies.

While I plan to continue writing, I also plan to express my art in multiple forms. It's not easy being self published and running an independent film studio these days. Artists have struggled for as long as I can remember, and I don't plan on creating for the masses, I plan on creating what I feel is good. This may not always fit mainstream media.

So... If you enjoyed any of my content, I urge you to share it with your friends and family. You, and people like you, are what makes my job possible, and who help ensure that my style of content can continue. Without your support, I'm just another lonely struggling artist.

Thank you for reading.
I wish you and yours the very best.

Sincerely,
Brent Lindstrom

www.ingramcontent.com/pod-product-compliance
Lightning Source LLC
LaVergne TN
LVHW040038080526
838202LV00045B/3395